LEVIATHAN

LEVIATHAN

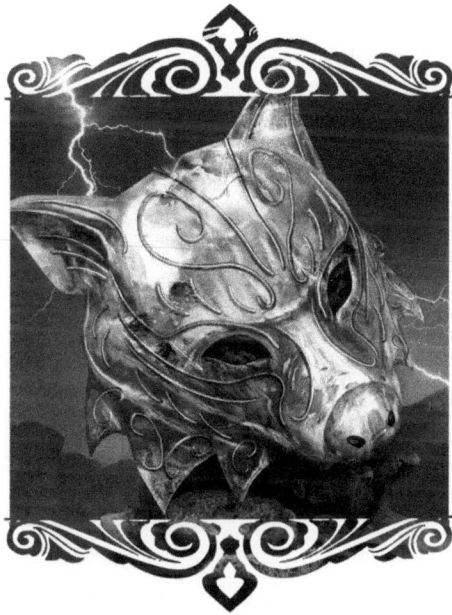

ROBERT McCAMMON

LIVIDIAN
PUBLICATIONS
• 2024 •

Lividian Publications
4900 Carlisle Pike #313
Mechanicsburg, PA 17050

ISBN: 978-1-941971-40-6

Cover Artwork Copyright © 2024
by Vincent Chong
Interior Design by Kate Freeman Design

Lividian Publications Trade Hardcover

To you, the reader.
Thank you for supporting my work and
for your visits to Matthew Corbett's world.

PROLOGUE

"BROTHERS AND SISTERS, WE ARE GATHERED TOGETHER TONIGHT ON A subject of the most somber gravity," said the man who stood at the center of the gray stone floor. Around and above him at a height of nearly fifteen feet was a circular gallery that at present seated thirty-nine persons in individual high-backed chairs. A hundred years ago this place had been a monastery carved from the Italian pine forest near a city of renown, and still held the faint ghostly aroma of spiced incense along with the musty smell of ancient age. The walls were as gray as the floor and torches burned from sockets hammered into the stones. Gray verging upon black was also the heritage of this place, for one of the monks in that long-ago era had mixed toadstools into the mushroom and barley soup, poisoning to death more than half of his twenty-eight brothers, after which he fled into the nearby swampland and was forever swallowed in its darkness. The local farmers knew the story well and kept far clear of the tile-roofed structure. Had the monk been struck with lunacy? Or led into cold-blooded murder by the very Devil? It was enough to know that righteous men should stay away from the place, and when the black coaches were seen conveying their occupants to and from the haunted locale it was also best to bolt the doors, pour a cup of wine, settle before the fire in the company of wife and children and pretend that God was still present in this world.

The man who had addressed his audience wore a formal black suit with a white shirt ruffled at the collar and cuffs, his boots polished to a mirror shine, his dark hair pulled back into a queue and secured with a black ribbon. His face was sharp-nosed and gaunt-cheeked and he spoke his native tongue with the husky gorgia toscana dialect of Tuscany, better known as the "Tuscan Throat".

"Before we proceed to our event," he continued, "we shall first hear from Master Argella concerning the recent business activity in the Lombardy province."

At that introduction, another man stood up from his chair toward the left side of the gallery. He also was formally dressed, had gray hair and a trimmed gray beard. He looked toward the gallery's center, where two figures sat side-by-side in identical high-backed and ornate chairs against a backdrop of two vertically hung banners, each bearing the emblem of a stylized scorpion, one black against red and the other red against black.

"Grandmaster and Grandmistress," the man began in the nearly musical hornpipe effect of the Lombardo dialect. He waited for one of the figures—a male, seated to the other's right—to nod assent. Then he went on, directing his comments to the audience as a whole: "On the twenty-first of April we seized with admirable success a shipment of gunpowder in route to the Hessian General von Gort's supply depot. On the twenty-seventh we attacked a shipment of muskets and bayonets designated for the supply center of the French General Montand, with no less success but unfortunately our intentions were known. Of my crew, I lost four men killed and six wounded. The arms were taken by using explosive bombs created from von Gort's extremely effective powder."

He waited for a small ripple of bemused laughter to subside. "As you understand, we have no stake in the current military situation other than our own benefit, which overshadows all. Therefore our emissaries are in the process of putting up for bid on both sides the remaining stock of powder and the weapons, which we predict will heartily enrich our coffers. I might add that General von Gort had confined the representative we sent and threatened to hang him. In retaliation we took action against his favorite horse and delivered to him a casket containing its vital organ. Since the creature was named Stout Heart, we decided to reveal the quality. I doubt there shall be further problems on that front. Of course…there is the problem *here*." He motioned with a disdainful hand toward a single empty chair in the gallery. "But soon, I understand," he said, "that shall be remedied to the satisfaction of all…especially myself, since I have lost in the action upon General Montand an excellently capable associate who also was adept at carving my smoking pipes. A sad loss indeed." He turned his attention to the two figures who sat before the scorpion banners. "My report is ended," he concluded, with a lowering of the head and a half-bow.

The second figure—feminine, seated on the male's left—lifted a hand and made a motion to wave the man back to his chair, which he instantly obeyed.

The gentleman from Tuscany once again took the center of the floor. "If you please, we will now entertain Master Trazini concerning another matter of interest."

Standing up from his gallery chair at this prompt was a heavyset gent with dark hair cropped close to the scalp, his granite-hard face adorned with a large hooked nose and a chin as square and forbidding as a clenched fist. He wore a dark blue suit with thin white stripes and a white silk waist-coat, a lighter blue cravat knotted about a thick throat. Enrico Trazini of the Veneto province cast his dour gaze around the gallery until he came to the man and woman who sat before the scorpion banners. "Grandmaster and Grandmistress," he began, with the same slight lowering of the head Argella had displayed. His voice was the grating of stone on stone, his dialect also sufficiently different in accent and emphasis from the previous speakers, as the many regions of Italy held dozens of separate patterns of speech though all were based upon the same language. In truth, this nocturnal gathering was the only place where regional warfare and enmity was not in full flag; these participants had sworn their allegiance to a more mercenary command.

Trazini said, "I offer to you a decision on the next step of our investigation. Not to mention our search," he added. "So far it has been unsuccessful."

There was a pause before the male figure spoke. "Details," he said; it was a smooth and quiet voice, nearly only a murmur, but a tone assured of absolute power.

"As you are all aware," Trazini ventured on, "my crew has undertaken a search for the object of our desire. We were successful in learning that the corpse of the sorcerer—let me amend that—*alleged* sorcerer Senna Salastre was found in the possession of yet *another* alleged sorcerer by the name of Nerio Bianchi. This Bianchi charlatan had used so-called potions and elixirs to preserve the corpse, and therein lies my report."

To Trazini's subsequent silence, the female in the gallery spoke with a similar ease of power to the male's: "Continue."

"Yes, Grandmistress. My crew had given Bianchi a period of time in which to—and I dread to say this, but I must—*conjure* up the location of the object we seek. If one believes what Bianchi says, he's been able to communicate with Salastre from the world of the dead." And here Trazini gave a frown that might even send the uneasy spirits of the deceased monks scurrying to their tombs. "I must admit, all this is fanciful to me, as I am a man of logic and reason, and thus—"

"Precisely why you were given this assignment," interrupted the Grandmaster. "Your logic and reason have proven dependable, but now we wish to hear not your logical and reasonable opinion, but rather the re-sults…if any."

"Yes sir, of course." Trazini lowered his head like a schoolboy expecting a whip strike. Then he straightened up, cleared his throat and continued. "Bianchi claims—reports—that by the use of what he terms 'spirit-writing' he has made communion with Salastre. This 'spirit-writing' evidently involves sharing a quill with the dead man's hand. A repugnant practice, to my tastes, but Bianchi claims he has secured one word repeated on four different occasions...that word being 'leviathan'."

The woman spoke up: "And this means what?"

Trazini gave a shrug. "Who can say, except the dead? This is all the information—supposed information—to the question Bianchi was supplied: Where is the mirror crafted by Ciro Valeriani?"

"And also it is supposed," the man said, "that Salastre aided Valeriani in the crafting of this object?"

"It is said so, yes." Trazini's frown deepened. "May I speak freely?" He waited for a response. It was the woman who nodded, and he went on: "Tales of this mirror being a doorway to the underworld must be the ravings of lunatics. I put as much sense into this as I do tavern tales of the *babau,* the *gata carogna* and the *borda*...all infantile fantasies. Yes, I've seen this so-called spirit-writing and the word 'leviathan' scrawled on parchment, but its quality makes a chicken scratch look like the quilling of a da Vinci. And furthermore, I and none of my crew have ever witnessed the actual writing, as Bianchi claims the hand of Salastre will only move for him in the privacy of his hovel." Trazini shook his head, as if in pity for the misguided minds who had set him upon this assignment though he made sure he was looking at the floor when he did so.

He lifted his face once more to the central portion of the gallery. "I have to ask: what purpose is there in pursuing this? It is not a *business* venture, and as we are modern men—and women—it seems to me our time would be better spent in other, more worthwhile endeavors instead of the fantastic notions from fearful peasants."

A silence fell.

The two figures who sat before the scorpion banners seemed to be pondering both the question and the opinion. They were each lean and well-dressed, a dark gray suit with a blue cravat for the male, a violet-hued gown with red trim for the female. The situation of the torches caused their faces to be garbed in shadow, but plainly could be seen their hair and here was a striking peculiarity: the male had a glossy, tight cap of black hair but for a burst of red on the left side of his head, the shape being nearly as if the large claw of a beast had riven the flesh down to the blood. The female wore her mane in long black tresses, and yet on the right side of her head the growth of red hair resembled the spider's art in constructing a web of intricate design. If one viewed closely and dared to examine, it might be found that one skull's design linked to the other, and thus formed both a completeness and complexity of conjunction.

They remained silent until the man said in his quiet voice of understated power: "Master Trazini, your position is noted but I inform you that neither myself nor my sister must explain our motives. It is simply up to you to supply the effort. Our father—and certainly our grandfather—would see you whipped to an inch of your life for such a statement, but as you say... we are modern men and women, and you will need your back to return to the assignment." He looked out upon the gallery. "Does anyone have any idea what this word 'leviathan' might mean?"

"I recall a ship by that name," answered the much-aged Master Calliagna from over on the right. "A warship it was. Oh...pardon, that was many years ago. I recall also that the ship went down in a storm off...Sicily, I believe it was...in...was it 1688?"

"It very well might have been," said the Grandmaster. "I doubt that has anything to do with our current interest. Anyone else?"

There was no further reaction.

The Grandmaster—a man in his early thirties—once more turned his gaze upon Trazini. In the shadowed face the eyes caught red glints of torch-light. "A disappointing report. You will return to Bianchi and impress upon him that if you do not witness the spirit-writing for yourself in the space of one more week, he will be brought here to meet the Grandmistress, whose toys grow cold for lack of use. Now: is that all you have?"

"Well...there's one other thing," said Trazini, his stony voice crushed to pebbles. "My crew has learned that Ciro Valeriani had a son by the name of Brazio. We are currently searching for him, but we believe he's changed his name and is in hiding."

"*What?*"

The sharp word had issued from the woman's lace-collared throat. She leaned forward, her ebony eyes fixed upon the offending figure. "I didn't realize until this moment, Master Trazini, that you are stupid beyond belief."

"Grandmistress, I—"

"*Hush,*" she commanded, and his mouth closed. "You throw figs at the idea of this—shall we say—*special* mirror, yet you're blind to the fact that if Valeriani's son has changed his name and is in hiding...there must be a very good *reason* for his not wishing to be found. What might that reason be? Possibly that he knows where the mirror is? Or possibly he has it *himself?*" She turned her attention to her brother. "I say double and redouble the efforts to find the son. As for Bianchi, one week to witness this spirit-writing and then bring him to me. Agreed?"

"As always," was the smooth reply. Then, to Trazini: "You have your task." As Trazini returned to his chair, the Grandmaster spoke two more words: "Lupo, begin."

From a curve of darkness on the floor below emerged a hulking figure in a long black hooded cloak with scarlet trim. Torchlight revealed that under the hood was the silver face of a wolf…a metal face created by a master artist, the mask decorated with cut grooves and embossed spirals meant to convey the very maw, bones and hair of the fierce, predatory Italian creature it so depicted. Thus was the legend of Romulus and Remus and the glory of Rome brought to this fortress of *Famiglia Dello Scorpione.*

Lupo reached the center of the floor beneath the gallery, gave a bow to the audience above, and then motioned toward his left with a black-gloved hand. Two underlings came from an archway wheeling an iron cart on which was fixed a burning brazier. Also on the cart stood a rack of sharp-edged instruments—axe, hatchet, several knives, a cleaver and a pair of iron tongs—that made jingling musical sounds of the most sinister quality as the cart was pushed to Lupo's side. Coals within the brazier seethed red hot, the curl of smoke rising up to a vent far up at the zenith of the roof. The two underlings—who were in training but had not yet received their approval and initiation as masters to the Family of the Scorpion—retreated to the chamber from which the brazier had come, and returned in another moment wheeling a second cart.

In it was a man chained to a chair, chains about his neck and mid-section and securing his arms to the armrests. He was slender and small-boned, with sand-colored hair grown long about his shoulders. He wore tan breeches and a white shirt that was bloodied from his nose that had been broken in his struggle against the chains. In truth, the cell he'd been locked in and his meager diet for the last few days had sapped most of his will and strength, for as much as he fought he knew there was no escape.

In his mouth was a leather ball gag, the cords knotted around his head.

He was wheeled alongside the brazier and the waiting Lupo, who put the axe, the cleaver and the tongs into the red coals. One of the underlings went to work with a bellows, fanning the burn to a higher sear.

The first man who'd spoken at the beginning of the gathering now emerged from where he'd been waiting. He pointed a finger at the individual confined to the chair of lost hope.

"This," he intoned, "is Antonio Nuncia, lately of Master Di Muzzo's crew. You will note the empty seat where Master Di Muzzo could usually be found, but at the moment he is confined and sentenced to a month's worth of bread and water…the penalty for poor judgement in approving associates." He circled the man in the chair, who sat with sweat glistening on his face, his eyes sunken in dark hollows and his nose still dripping blood. "Antonio Nuncia came to us from the Circus Venezia, where he was equally adept on the trapeze, at physical contortion, and juggling. It was considered that he would be useful as what is termed a 'snake-man', one who gets into places other men cannot…down a chimney for instance, or hiding within a wine barrel delivered to an estate where precious jewels are to be found and taken. In that capacity he served the family and Master Di Muzzo very well indeed. *But*." He lifted a finger for cautionary emphasis. "Our Antonio Nuncia was not content with the realities of his station. Thus lies his unfortunate decision to sell information to the French General Montand regarding our plans to seize the muskets and bayonets. Of course we were successful nonetheless, but as Master Argella has stated we lost several of our own. When our spy among the French reported this affront, we took immediate action and caught this man just as he and his wife and two children were packing a coach to flee with his ill-gained coins…but as you know—and he now knows—no one escapes from the Family of the Scorpion. Gentlemen and ladies, we cannot abide such treachery as exists in the wretch you see before you…it is a bad example for all. And now…it is time for retribution, is it not?"

He was offering the question to the Grandmaster and Grandmistress, though the answer was already verified.

The woman said, "Lupo, bring the first one out."

The wolfman went through the archway on his left, walking quietly on soft-soled boots. He was replaced for the moment by a stout, brown-bearded violinist, who stood near the brazier tuning his instrument.

When Lupo returned, he was holding the hand of an eight-year-old boy.

The child—sandy-haired and small-boned like his father—was dazed and staggering due to the drug recently administered in his cup of apple cider, but otherwise clean in his apparel and unharmed. At the sight of his son, Antonio Nuncia thrashed against the chains and tried to scream around the ball gag, to no avail. If the little boy looked upon his father and had any realization of what was happening, there was no sign of it.

Lupo nodded to the violinist, who began the tune of what might have been a strident Italian military march. As Nuncia continued to wear out his last remaining strength in futile struggle, Lupo released the child's hand and marched in circles around him in time to the music. The little boy blinked, uncertain of where he was or who he was in company with, and perhaps he smiled up at this new playmate in the guise of a wolf in the instant before Lupo brought a hooked blade from beneath his cloak and slashed the child's throat from ear to ear. With the gushing of blood and the boy's head hanging as if from a slender hook, the eyes still staring and the last smile of life fixed upon the mouth, the body crumpled to the gray stones in a forming pool of red.

Nuncia's body contorted against the chains, his face about to burst the vessels that pulsed beneath the flesh, but his natural talents failed him and he fell back like a witless scarecrow.

"Next," said the Grandmaster.

Lupo wiped his blade on one of Nuncia's breeches legs and slid the knife back into its concealed sheath. He went through the alcove as the violinist—his musical program planned beforehand—began a stately tune suitable for the *barriera* dance. When Lupo returned he was guiding with hands on both shoulders a russet-haired little girl ten years of age wearing a yellow floral-print gown.

Nuncia thrashed once more, but was perceptibly weaker. The child stared fixedly at her brother on the stones and all the blood, but also was in a drug-dazed state that fogged both her vision and her mind, thus no one could know if she recognized violent death. Her mouth twitched as if to ask a child's question, but nothing emerged. Lupo grasped one of her hands and twirled her around and around to the violinist's tune, and just as she staggered off-balance from this motion he took her hair and pulled her head back. His other hand did the work with his hooked blade.

She fell alongside her sibling; she contorted once…twice…in a bizarre emulation of her father's ability, and with her knees drawn up to her chin she was still.

The gallery made no sound. The violinist played on, stepping back as the blood began to course between the stones at his boots.

"The wife," said the Grandmistress, who was now leaning forward in her chair. Torchlight caught an arched nose, a square chin, teeth slightly bared between wine-dark lips and perhaps a sparkle of moisture at the temple on the red-marked right.

Beside her, the Grandmaster buffed his fingernails with a small horse-hair brush.

When Lupo brought the woman out—her hands tied before her because she had not been afforded the scorpion's mercy of sense-blinding drugs—she cast her sight upon the two small corpses lying beside her bound husband and the burning brazier and her body stiffened as if her spine had been thrust through with an iron bar. Her scream rounded the gallery, echo upon echo, and in that instant she went mad. In the next second she might have been a ravening wretch from any beggar's slum, and falling to her knees she began to lurch toward her dead children, all the while jibbering and sobbing…then punctuated with another maniacal scream and wild laughter to make the cold spirits of night flee for their souls.

Lupo let her wallow in the blood as if she was swimming there in a lagoon of dreams. When he cut her throat with the hooked blade—his formidable strength such that her head was nearly severed from the neck—it was almost done with regret…that he could not allow this interesting display of mind-crushing madness to continue as a further entertainment to the gallery.

But then it was finished.

Yet…not quite.

The wolfman motioned to the underling who had been continuing to bellow the brazier's fire. His motion was: *More.*

He lifted the axe from the coals; it was not yet ready, but an inspection of the tongs was satisfactory. Not red-hot, but hot enough for the task to come.

Up at the gallery's center, the Grandmistress made a soft noise deep in her throat.

Her brother paused his nail-brushing. "Venus," he said quietly, "let's not have a scene."

She gave him a sidelong look and a flare of nostrils, and he returned to his effort of reaching a higher polish.

Antonio Nuncia adorned his chair like a splayed wet rag. His head was lowered, his eyelids fluttering, his face gone as pale as last week's *formaggio*. In his chest his heart hammered, but otherwise he was already dead. And yet…when Lupo approached and sliced the cords of the ball gag, ripping it from his mouth, Nuncia's eyes opened wide and he gasped for air as if struggling up from the bottom of the sea.

He smelled heat and felt its wash on his face, and then the hot tongs winnowed sizzling into his mouth and gripped his tongue, and too late he tried to cry out…too late…for the pain of his burning tongue was a searing stone in his throat, and then Lupo with his amazing strength wrenched at the piece of smoking flesh, stretching it out almost to the point of tearing, and the hooked blade flashed out through the root of Nuncia's tongue and it came away bloody and black in the grip of the wolfman's pincers.

With the torrent of blood from Nuncia's mouth, the man's eyes rolled back in his head, his body shivered violently and he was still…which suited Lupo well, for the wolfman moved leisurely as he picked up the axe from the brazier's red-glowing coals.

Lupo set his feet on the bloody stones. Someone cried out from the gallery…not a cry of alarm, but an exclamation of expectancy. Beside the Grandmaster the woman gave a soft moan, which made her brother spear her with the look of a drawn blade.

The axe lifted, hung at its height, and slammed down.

Nuncia's right hand was severed at the wrist, along with the armrest beneath it. A gout of blood flew out for two seconds before the hot iron seared the exposed tissue. The renewed agony brought Nuncia up in a teeth-gritting rictus, and then—as bleached as the ghost he was to become—he fell back again into the void. Lupo spent a moment burning the axe in the brazier once more, as the underling worked with the bellows and Nuncia's unconscious body trembled in its chains. When the wolfman determined that his instrument of retribution was ready, he cut off Nuncia's left hand, which flew across the floor and grasped at the mist-bloodied air until one of Lupo's boots stomped upon it.

Done.

Who first began applauding? Was it Conti, Amadasi, or the Lady Bonacorso? It was indeed one of those, but the applause quickly spread around the gallery with shouts of *Bravo* and *Fantastico*. For their approval Lupo leaned on his axe and gave the assembly a bow, which he repeated for the brother and sister twins whose ancestors for generations had governed the *Famiglia Dello Scorpione*.

When the acclaim had ceased, the Grandmaster stood up. "Thank you for your actions, Lupo. Justice has been served. Now: Master Trazini, we expect results. This mirror must be found, and we'll determine then if what has been claimed about it is true—or not—and how it can be used if indeed…well…we shall see, won't we?"

"Yes," answered Trazini, whose skin crawled under his expensive suit for he understood the penalty of failure. "My crew will find it."

"And," the woman named Venus said, also standing up beside her brother, "find the son. Do you hear?"

"I hear, Grandmistress."

She looked down upon Lupo, the carnage and the corpses. "Take those to the swamp and throw them in," she said, addressing the underlings who would be tasked with the disposal. "And make sure *his* body is on the bottom of the pile."

Thus, with the night's business ended, the group began to gather their coats and hats and depart from the event to their coaches waiting outside. Lupo walked into the deeper darkness where the torchlight did not reach. The violinist returned his instrument to its case and closed the latches. Those who were expected to do the job rolled the brazier and rack of weapons away, unlocked the chains that secured Nuncia to the splintered chair—his body sliding down onto the floor like a gutted fish—and hauled the remains of husband, wife and children upon another cart wheeled in for the task. The severed hands were tossed in as easily as one might throw away a pair of unwanted gloves. When the cart was pushed away through the alcove that led to an outside exit—and the morass that lay a hundred yards beyond—two men stayed behind with mops and buckets. The night's business was not yet ended for them, for they would stay scrubbing until the red was gone, and all that remained was the gray coloration of the stones.

At last the torches would be extinguished, the doors secured with heavy locks and the underlings gone home to their families with their secrets guarded behind lips sealed by the respect for power and the fear of horrific execution.

And for a time, dark and silence would reign over the realm of the scorpion.

Yet in truth, as all those involved knew so very well…the scorpion never, ever slept.

THREE MONTHS LATER

One

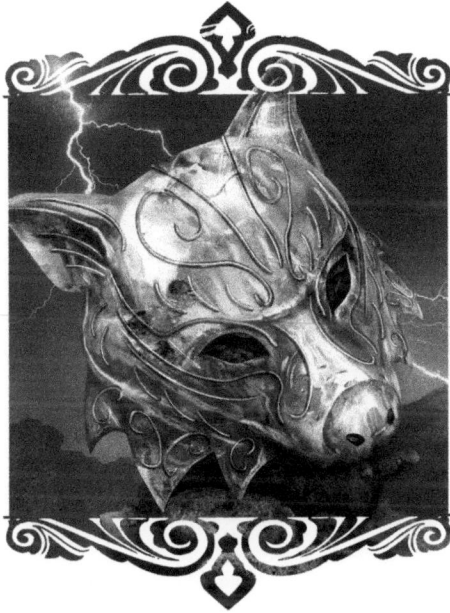

Down Among the Dead Men

ONE

MATTHEW CORBETT WALKED THROUGH A CEMETERY.

It was a large expanse of gravestones on a grassy hill overlooking the town of Alghero on the northwestern coast of Sardinia. The town's roofs of red tile and its fortress walls of yellow stone shone brightly under the noonday sun of August in the year 1704. It was a very hot day, here at the eastern edge of the Mediterranean Sea. Below the cemetery hill and beyond the town and harbor the ocean gleamed green in the shallows, blue in the depths, and gold with the shimmer of Italian *sole*.

Except the correct term, as Matthew knew, would be the Spanish *sol* since at the present time Spain owned the island of Sardinia. And since the Spaniards were the sworn and deadly enemies of all things English and all persons English—whether they be colonials or not—well, Matthew mused as so often he had, that was the sharp end of the stick, wasn't it?

It was fortunate, he thought as he walked amid the stones, that sharp sticks of another variety—Spanish swords—or Spanish muskets had not done away with himself and the others the first day of their arrival. As it was, cannonfire from the parapets had erupted the sea at the bow of the *Triton* as it made its way to the harbor. The ship was already crippled enough not to be able to withstand a single hit, but the white flag raised up to the topmast had urged cooler heads to prevail among the guardians of Alghero. Thus longboats filled with armed soldiers had come rowing out to meet the visitors, and no blood was spilled though it was a close enough call to have made all the *Triton*'s crew—as well as Matthew, Hudson Greathouse, Professor Fell and Cardinal Black—sweat at the idea of the reception they would receive once their boots set heel on Spanish earth.

Today, on his walk up the hill to the prison that stood atop it in all its faded yet still grim medieval glory, Matthew had seen a figure kneeling on the ground before one of the graves. He knew who was buried there, the resting place marked with a simple wooden cross, and who was paying his respects—as the man so often did—and so Matthew moved nearer him to have a word.

"I have heard you English are insane," the broad-shouldered man behind the desk had said to Matthew in his office the first morning of their arrival at Alghero, "but I never understood you were damnable fools as well." He had shoulder-length curls of black hair shot through with gray at the temples, a black mustache, a hawk's-beak nose and dark eyes that held as much amusement as angered incredulity. To accentuate his position as military governor of Sardinia, Henri del Costa Santiago was wearing an indigo-hued tunic crossed by a red sash adorned with a half-dozen medals of various sizes and shapes, his high collar an artistic work of lace, the tunic decorated with silver-threaded designs and ending in large red cuffs similarly decorated with silver threading. On either side of his desk stood a uniformed steel-helmeted soldier who rested hands on swords in their scabbards, while Matthew had no use of his own hands since they were securely tied before him. He was unshaven, dirty and quite the picture of an impoverished prisoner.

"Am I speaking your language well enough for you?" Santiago's black brows went up.

"Yes sir, well enough."

"I *detest* the language; it is the tongue of heathens."

"Yes sir," Matthew repeated, feeling very much like one wrong word would bring the swords out of those scabbards with unfortunate results. "May I ask how you come to speak it?"

"My governess thought I should be a man of the world. I haven't spoken this tongue in years and I shall no longer speak it after you dogs are executed by firing squad."

Matthew understood his position on this dire precipice of life but the man's demeanor nettled him, even more so since what he and the others had just experienced on the island of Golgotha nearly two hundred miles distant. He might have thought twice about what he was to utter, but it spilled out anyway. He lifted his chin. "Am I supposed to bark, or to whine?"

Hands went to swords. The soldiers might not speak English but they recognized an enemy's arrogance.

"*Fácil,*" Santiago said quietly. "*Este pequeno cachorro se cree un bulldog.*"

One soldier laughed and the other smirked, but their hands left the weapons.

"What's the joke?" Matthew asked.

"*You* are." The governor leaned back in his cowhide chair and steepled his fingers before him. The sunlight that streamed through the large oval window at his back afforded a view of the harbor with its array of several tall-masted trading ships and war vessels and glinted off his many jewel-adorned rings. A brass spyglass on a tripod was positioned for a closer examination of the marine traffic. "Since you have been chosen by your patriots as the spokesman for your little expedition into Spain's territory, I suggest you begin speaking."

"Compatriots," said Matthew.

"*What?*"

"The correct word is *compatriots*. Meaning friends...allies... countrymen."

"*Dead* men," Santiago said. "To which soon-to-be ghost am I addressing?"

"Matthew Corbett, born in New York in the colonies...lately in England, and more recently from an island of the damned."

"Do you enjoy mouthing riddles?"

"I have a story to tell if you'd care to hear it. You might not believe it, but it's all—" Matthew stopped talking, because he'd noted in a corner of this ostentatiously decorated chamber a small table with two chairs facing each other. Upon the table was a very nice chessboard and pieces formed of dark and lighter wood. "True," he finished.

"I'm listening." Santiago glanced over in the direction of the young man's gaze. "What are you looking at?"

"Your chess set."

"Do you play?"

"I do."

"*Interesante,*" came the reply. "I am a master at the game."

"I've been known to hold my own," Matthew said.

"*Señor* Corbett, you are not here to discuss chess. I watched you and the crew of that wretched-looking craft come across the gangplank: among them a large man carried on a stretcher, a feeble old thing who had to hold onto your shoulder in order to walk, and a tall thin scarecrow dressed all in black...what the devil are you doing here?"

Everyone mentioned—Hudson Greathouse, Professor Fell and Cardinal Black, along with Captain Brand and all the others—were currently behind bars in a rough-stoned gaol a few streets from the governor's gated mansion. "The Devil does have something to do with it," Matthew admitted. "As I said, you might not believe my story, but what I will tell you is the truth."

"The truth from an Englishman?" Santiago glanced back and forth at the bodyguards. *"Este cachorro yace con su primer aliento!"*

Whatever that was, it caused further smirks on the two otherwise impassive faces.

"All right," said Matthew. "Before I say anything more, my friend Hudson Greathouse—on the stretcher—was badly wounded by a sword. He's running a high fever and is delirious. He needs not a gaol cell but an infirmary bed. I tried to tell this to your soldiers at the harbor and again at the gaol but none could understand me."

"Some could. They chose not to."

"Nevertheless, I'm telling you now. *Asking*, I mean. Will you please get him some medical attention?"

"It matters not to me if an Englishman dies. Why should it?"

Here was the crux of this particular problem, and there seemed only one possible solution. It was worth trying. It *had* to be tried. "I have hidden somewhere on the *Triton* a pouch holding a small fortune in gold coins…enough, I would hope, to make my friend's life matter. It's yours if you help him." It was the pouch given to him by Maccabeus DeKay on the last day, when DeKay refused to board the ship and announced to Matthew's amazement that he was staying on Golgotha. DeKay himself had seemed deranged…of course, due to an attack by the island's tainted atmosphere that had also caused periods of memory confusion and loss to Matthew. Matthew had hoped to use the coins to hire a ship for the rescue of King Tabor and his subjects—as well as Maccabeus DeKay—but that idea of an Englishman hiring a ship from the Spanish now really seemed deranged and was probably instigated as much by desperation as by the fumes of Golgotha.

"The pouch of gold coins to get my friend medical help," Matthew prodded to the governor's silence. "What do you say?"

"I say," came the acidic response, "that I need no gold coins because I am currently the wealthiest man on this island, and my men will tear that ship apart and find it anyway…or I could have you taken to a place where within ten minutes you'll be telling me not only where the pouch is, but where all the gold is being stored in your London town. Is that a proper answer?"

"No." Matthew squared his shoulders. "You might have thought Englishmen insane and you might be right…but I never thought of the Spanish as being *inhuman*."

There was no reaction but for Santiago tapping his fingers in a staccato rhythm on the desktop, time after time. Then: "Where is the pouch?"

"Where is the infirmary?" Matthew countered.

Santiago might have allowed himself a faint smile, but if it was there it was gone in an instant. "You're a brave young fool, aren't you? Did you earn that scar on your forehead from such brave foolishness?"

"It was an unavoidable attack by a bear that had nothing to do with either bravery or being a fool." Though, Matthew thought, one could argue the latter.

"Obviously you survived," said Santiago. "To end up here before *me*. You might wish the bear had taken more than a little flesh before we're done." He spoke to the soldier on his right, who nodded and left the room through its set of polished pine double doors. "Very well, your friend will receive medical attention. Now where is the pouch?"

"Wrapped in an oil-cloth and pushed down to the bottom of a box of books next to my hammock. It will be easy to find, since I was the only one with a box of books."

"I trust it will be there. In fact, I believe it will be. I'm waiting now for the rest of your story."

Matthew nodded. In for a pouch of gold coins, in for whatever lay ahead. "We were on our way to Venice. A mishap caused our ship to drop anchor off an island called Golgotha—"

"Never heard of it," was Santiago's quick response.

"About two hundred miles away," Matthew continued with as calm a demeanor as he could summon. "Not its original name, if it ever had a name. To our distress we learned after a time that a chemical in the island's air caused memory confusion and in many cases complete memory loss. The island is ruled by a man who has taken the role of 'king', and who basically reinvented the entire island's population and agriculture. Unfortunately that mind-robbing chemical has leeched into the crops, into the sea…everywhere, so all the food and drink is tainted. The island is also threatened from time to time by the possible eruption of a volcano, and—"

"Ha!" said Santiago. "You've been reading those pulp English…what are they called?…oh…*magazines* of yours. When one was smuggled into Alghero I had the offender whipped and salted."

"A remedy for intellectual curiosity, I'm sure," Matthew said dryly. "If you care to listen to the truth any longer, I'll tell you that there are nearly five hundred people on that island…fishermen, merchants, farmers…the same as any community. I don't know how many were born there, but I do know many arrived by ship and were overcome by the atmosphere. They lost their memories of who they'd been before, where they'd come from, and certainly their nationalities. I'd venture to say citizens of your own country are likely there, with no memory of having originated in Spain. Their language seems to be a mix of Italian, Spanish, Greek and probably other tongues that have been drawn into the combinations. I can tell you that these people are all in danger of destruction if this volcano does erupt. I've seen it myself, and I've witnessed the power of the island's...shall I say...*corruption*. The thing is, it's a beautiful place. I think on the last day I got through mentally to King Tabor...I believe he might take to heart the idea that as a true benevolent ruler his vow is to protect his people. If he's reached in time before the atmosphere takes him under again, he might agree to getting everyone off the island."

There was a long pause in which Santiago simply sat staring ebony-eyed at the scruffy young man standing before him. Then: "What are you saying...*exactamente?*"

"I'm saying that if you are also a benevolent ruler you might..." And here was the moment of truth for which Matthew had been preparing ever since boarding the *Triton* in Golgotha's harbor. "You might consider saving the lives of those people by sending ships to take them off."

The moment hung as if strangled by time.

Matthew chose to power forward in this disturbing silence, if just to keep himself from losing his nerve. "Consider the benefits, sir. You would be adding to your commerce and your agriculture as well as your population. You must know that at some point in the future the Italians may wish to take Sardinia into their own kingdom, so it might behoove you to—"

Santiago began to laugh.

But it was an ugly laugh, without true mirth, and it made Matthew's skin crawl because he knew what would follow it.

"*¡Loco! ¡Una verdadera loco!*" The governor leaned forward and slammed a fist upon his desktop, which made a small stone paperweight and his quill and silver inkpot jump. "You *are* insane after all, aren't you?" he managed, nearly sputtering. To this outburst the remaining soldier again put his hands on his sword. "And you *dare* to say that Spain cannot hold Sardinia against any hostile power? *¡Dulce madre de Dios!* I'll have you shot first thing in the morning!"

Matthew stared at the floor's polished boards. His heart was hammering and fear nipped at the back of his neck but he had to go on. Home and Berry never seemed so far away, and chances of survival so very slim. "Well, if you don't wish to be both personally enriched far beyond a pouch of coins and acclaimed far beyond your position here," he said, "I'll say now that my last request is a good beef dinner."

Santiago had lifted his fist for another indignant strike against the innocent desktop, but it paused in mid-fall. "What?"

"Personally enriched and acclaimed," Matthew repeated, and now again lifted his face into the sunlight that streamed through the oval window. "As in receiving more gold and much acclaim from grateful families. I'm not positive about this, but I do suspect that some of Golgotha's population is Spanish…possibly once-wealthy merchants from wealthy houses in your country's cities. Likely there are those on the island who were Italian merchants—even counts or barons—whose households would show gratitude for their return." He added, against his good judgement: "Even to the Spanish governor of Sardinia."

"You walk on a very thin floor," Santiago said, stone-faced.

"Still," Matthew said, "it *is* a floor."

"The notion of my sending ships to an island I've never heard of, and which is likely on no nautical map, to bring five hundred unhinged persons under my discipline is…how do you say…ludicrous?"

"Oh, our captain—Brand—could find it for you. And I see you have some very large ships in your harbor…particularly the one I'm looking at right now. I'd say that one alone would carry three hundred or more. You might bring the whole lot over with a single ship. Of course, there are the herds of horses to consider."

"Horses?"

Matthew summoned a half-smile. "Didn't I mention horses?"

Santiago's mouth was a grim line, but there had ignited in his eyes a small flame; Matthew had reasoned that the fact of available horses—to pull carriages, coaches and wagons, or cannons and plows for that matter—would receive such a reaction. Matthew went a step further on this very thin floor, hoping it would not break under the weight: "Even if it proved none of your country's citizens were right now on Golgotha, horses are always worth their weight in gold, particularly on an isolated island… are they not?"

"For your information, young pup, this is not a mere isolated island, it is the *kingdom* of Sardinia, with allegiance to the Bourbon house of Spain and all the glory it provides!"

"Understood," Matthew said, though he realized he had much to learn about this place, if he lived long enough. "Still…all kingdoms need horses, don't they?"

Santiago was perhaps about to explode again, but he rubbed his chin and seemed to be pondering the situation. Before he could reply, there came a knock at the doors. *"Entrar,"* he said.

Into the chamber strode a tall helmeted soldier in the indigo tunic with the red sash but only three medals, his polished black boots clattering on the boards. He crossed past Matthew to the blue rug upon which rested the governor's desk, and an arm thrust out to offer in its hand an object that turned Matthew's knees to water.

Santiago took the aged, dark brown volume, its covering riddled with cracks like demonic skin. The soldier spoke to Santiago in the native tongue, Santiago answered and, frowning, opened *The Lesser Key of Solomon*, to peruse what Matthew had feared would be found sooner or later aboard the *Triton*.

Here was the damnable book open to the eyes of the military governor, and whose eyes were widening to the depicted woodcuts of the various denizens of Hell, their particular powers and the spells used to both raise them and protect oneself from their deadly aggravations at being summoned from their furnaces of repose.

It was a long time before Santiago looked up from the pages; all the while the soldier who'd brought it in—a man in his early thirties, perhaps, with the chiselled face, jaw and aquiline nose of an aristocrat and cropped light brown hair exposed when he removed his steel helmet—simply stood staring at Matthew with iron-gray, accusing eyes.

Santiago and the soldier had a brief conversation, after which the governor took stock of Matthew as one might regard a *Triton* rodent before crushing it with a cudgel.

Matthew cleared his throat. His first words came out in a harsh jumble unrecognizable as any language. He tried again: "Where did *that* come from?"

"Your black-clad scarecrow *compatriot* had it hidden under his cloak. Not very well, for his left armpit was deep but not unfathomable."

Matthew clenched his teeth. Cardinal Black! That Satanic sop would have them all killed!

What have you done with the book? Matthew had asked Professor Fell when the first cannon shot from Alghero's fortress walls had erupted the sea at the *Triton*'s bow.

I've hidden it in plain sight on the bookshelf in my cabin, was Fell's reply. *When they come aboard, they'll not know it has any significance.*

Matthew had thought they should instantly toss the thing overboard but didn't speak it. And turning away from the professor, Matthew had nearly bumped into the odious Cardinal Black standing just behind.

Matthew silently swore. Black must've gotten into the professor's cabin just as they were being approached by the longboats and everyone else was on deck. Had the skulker overheard Professor Fell telling Matthew where the book was? Or...and this was equally crazy to consider...if that supposed *compatriot* of his own he called Dominus was a *real* entity that guided him to the bookshelf? No! Of course not! Black—or Dominus, whatever the thing was—must've reasoned that once the Spanish took control of the

Triton everything aboard would be seized, locked away or burned, and that was probably true even down to the books. But still…damn it all and damn that tall, thin drink of bile!

Santiago had closed the volume. He slid it away and rubbed his hands together as if to wipe them clean. "Would you care to explain why you are travelling in the possession of a book that will see you and everyone aboard your ship hanged within twenty-four hours?"

What could Matthew say? He didn't know. Something came out anyway: "Do I still get my beef dinner?"

Now, three months away from that encounter, Matthew Corbett walked across a cemetery to the side of the little man who knelt before a gravesite's simple wooden cross.

As Matthew's shadow fell across the resting place, which had begun to sprout new grass and was near enough to a stand of lemon trees to afford the citrus aroma to anyone pausing here, the white-bearded and white-haired Uriah Holloway looked up from his devotion.

"Good afternoon," Matthew offered. He noted fresh flowers arranged on the grave.

Holloway—who on the island of Golgotha had been known as Fratello, King Tabor's closest assistant and most possessive protector—nodded but returned his gaze to the marker.

"I saw you here," Matthew said, which was totally unnecessary but yet seemed important.

"So you did."

"I've seen you here many times since the funeral. You often bring flowers, don't you?"

"Is that a surprise?"

"No. You were loyal to him in life, and as loyal as you can be in—"

"Oh, shut up!" Holloway growled, and his seventy-two-year-old wiry body struggled up with the help of a grip on Tabor King's marker. Standing, he was only about three inches over five feet but his character was that of a thorny, six-foot-tall, bare-knuckle scrapper; Matthew had long figured that in his prime Holloway could've likely given even Hudson Greathouse a black eye and broken tooth. "Save your false sentiments for someone who *believes* you," the man said, nearly spitting up into Matthew's face.

"They're not false."

"You've even deceived yourself, then! Out of my way!" He brushed past Matthew and started up the hill back toward the prison. He was dressed similarly to what Matthew wore: a light shirt and tan breeches, suitable for the hot climate. Then again, Matthew thought Holloway always seemed to be simmering under the collar.

Now Holloway stopped, spun around and advanced once more toward Matthew. He stopped at the edge of Matthew's shadow. "Tell me what *good* came of Tabor's decision!" he demanded. "We had lives on Golgotha! We had homes! What do we have now?" He pointed toward the yellow stone castle-like structure atop the hill. "We traded Golgotha for *that*? And don't pretend you don't realize Tabor died of a broken heart and spirit, after you and that damned governor talked him into abandoning our island! I wanted to stay and many others did, but...oh no...under yours and that Spanish peacock's influence Tabor gave it up! And for what? You're supposed to be so smart, what's the answer?"

"He gave it up," said Matthew, "for the reality of the truth. Yes, he was a fine man...and no finer than when he made that decision to vacate the island for the safety and sanity of his people. Deep down, he always knew that life there was a fantasy...and a dangerous one, as well."

"*Your* opinion."

"Don't you understand that he *freed* everyone? Yourself included? And also—very importantly—ended that charade of sacrificing lives to a non-existent monster, which lived only in his misshapen memory."

"*Freed* everyone?" Holloway gave a harsh laugh. "Oh, yes! We've all been freed to be prisoners of the Spanish! By the way, how goes your basket weaving?"

To this, Matthew had to stifle a harsh laugh of his own, for all from Golgotha who could work—shoemakers, farmers, fishermen, horse breeders, seamstresses, carpenters, wine makers and the like—had been given jobs as suited their talents, but as it turned out the only thing Matthew was suitable for on Sardinia was weaving baskets down at the harbor for a few hours every morning alongside a group of elderly men and women...intellectual problem-solvers here were not especially in demand.

"Prisoners at the moment," Matthew replied, though many had actually found homes and those who remained situated in the old medieval prison were free to come and go as they pleased. Really the cells were not so bad; they were never locked, there were no guards, and the straw bedding on the cots was better than a hard stone floor. Also the local food was good as long as payment was offered, and this was why Matthew had found a job with the basket weavers. "We won't be here forever," he added. "And Santiago tells me that none of us are either worth a ransom or worth the gunpowder for a firing squad, so it's just a matter of time before those who wish to leave will be handed over to the Italians."

Holloway grunted. "What, after many years? And you're a young man." He motioned toward the grave of the deceased King Tabor. "I'll be resting alongside him soon. And maybe that's how it ought to be. I have no family in England...I was always a ward of the sea. So..." He shrugged. "Fate," he said. "A fickle thing, isn't it?"

With that, Holloway turned to trudge up the hill, but Matthew stopped him by saying, "One moment. I asked Tabor this and he couldn't tell me, but perhaps you can. Do you have any idea why Maccabeus DeKay went into the chapel and drank the poison?"

It was a moment before Holloway answered. He looked up toward the sun, squinting, and then toward Matthew again. "Maybe I do. He asked me who'd drawn the red shell. I told him it was one of the seamstresses. You know he looked with favor on that girl with the child...the seamstress Apaulina and Tauri."

Matthew nodded. Drawing the red shell had been the crux of a lottery that chose a sacrifice for the so-called golgoth monster of Golgotha. The young woman Apaulina was now a seamstress in town and had already earned a nice cottage for herself and the child. "Was it Apaulina who drew the shell?"

Again Holloway paused, this time staring at the earth. Then: "I didn't like the man. Or...rather...Fratello did not like him because...I suppose Fratello did not like very many who he thought threatened the order of things. I told him that as a means of torment, since I presumed he would be leaving with all of you when I saw the *Triton* in the harbor. No, it was not Apaulina. It was not even one of the other seamstresses." He looked up, his mouth twisted. "It was a farmer, aged even older than myself."

"So," Matthew said, "he drank the poison thinking he might be saving Apaulina?"

"I suppose he did."

Matthew recalled his last conversation with DeKay, and the man who wore the magnificent mask to hide the horror of a face saying, *I can't leave Jenny, now that I've found her again. You see?*

Whoever Jenny was—or had been—would forever be a mystery, but perhaps with the drinking of the poison DeKay had come to some sort of peace in what had obviously been a life both tormented to himself and by his deeds tormented to others. A gift of life...for a life.

"Don't blame yourself," said Matthew.

With a faint sneer, the old Fratello resurfaced: "I wouldn't think of it." Then he turned on his heel and strode away through the cemetery toward the prison beyond.

Matthew let the little man go on ahead. He pushed away the idea of being captive here for years until the Spanish decided what to do with them, because it simply caused him pain. Would Berry be a married older woman when he finally got back to New York...if ever? She couldn't wait forever for him, and there was always Ashton McCaggers waiting in the wings.

When Holloway was a distance further, Matthew started up...but he stopped when he heard the harbor bell tolling below, and he saw a three-masted ship flying the yellow and red Spanish naval ensign just coming in between the breakwater walls. It appeared that Santiago was about to have an official visitor of some kind, and Matthew hoped it was not news that the governor was going to be recalled for another military ruler because Santiago had proven to be a stern but fair "warden" of his kingdom.

But Matthew had another concern that was more pressing, and this involved someone much closer to him.

He turned away from the harbor and continued up the hill on his way to keep his appointment with a frail, infirm man who feared to touch a sword, and that man's name was Hudson Greathouse.

TWO

"¿*Buenos dias, Matthew, como estas?*"

   "¿*Estoy bien, profesor. ¿Y tu?*"

   "¡*Muy emocionado! Creo que he descubierto—*"

Matthew lifted a hand. "Please, professor! English! I'm not as advanced as you are."

"Ah!" Professor Danton Idris Fell nodded and offered a smile from the aged mulatto face, which had become a few shades darker due to his hours spent under the sun. Behind the oval spectacles his owl-like eyes gleamed; they seemed more golden now in color than the smoky amber hue they had been in times past, and Matthew perceived that his entire demeanor was certainly more animated than the sullen, angry wretch he'd been on Golgotha. He was wearing a wide-brimmed straw hat to protect his scalp, and around the hat the white clouds of hair bloomed again like the wings of an owl. "I forget! But Spanish is a beautiful language, is it not? I never dreamed I'd be speaking it!"

Neither had Matthew dreamed it, but the fact of life on Alghero was that the Spanish military was in charge, the Spaniards had been here for generations and though some Italian was spoken it was predominantly the language of the conquistadors, thus after three months it was a necessity to learn as much as possible. In Professor Fell's case, he was paying a very lovely young woman who worked at the *Primer Lancero* tavern just off the town square to tutor him in the discourse, since it was ascertained she did have a knowledge of English.

Matthew had been just about to walk under the prison's stone archway into the interior, where there was a large courtyard and a number of steps leading up to the three levels, when the professor had come through, carrying his usual equipment of small easel and around his left shoulder a leather bag containing his paper, pens, inkpot, brushes and his little corked clay cups of watercolors. Fell was clean and shaved, having access as Matthew did to soap, a razor and water from the prison's well.

"I was saying," Fell went on, "that I am very excited because I think—no, I am sure—I have discovered a new species of *hippocamus*, a short-snouted variety I have never seen nor read about in any journal on marine life. I found two in a small tidal pool yesterday, but as the light was fading I did not have time to sketch them. I hope today I might find them again and do a proper job."

"Excellent," said Matthew. "But...what is a *hippocamus?*"

"A seahorse, my boy! Wonders of nature!"

Matthew's experience with a seahorse was being roped by Jack and Mack Thacker to one made of stone and pushed off a balcony into the sea below Pendulum Island, but that was happily in the past. "I'm glad you've made this discovery," he offered.

"You'll have to come with me some afternoon, I found a fantastic nest of sea urchins I'd like to show off." A physical wreck on Golgotha, Fell was now in the playground of life.

"I'll be happy to, some afternoon."

"Ah. Well, I'm off. Oh..." Fell's expression lost much of its good humor. "How goes the task?"

"Not much improvement. But there's always today."

"Yes. Always today. You know, I've come to have an affection for the rugger. I mean...I wish him well and hope all can be as it once was."

"Honestly," said Matthew, "I don't see that happening."

The professor grunted, and it was obvious this conversation had gone as far as it could. "Give him my regards, then," Fell said, and he started off along the road of old stones that led down the hill, past the cemetery, to the town and to his various favorite places of exploration along the coastline.

For a moment Matthew watched him go—a thin figure in his straw hat, his baggy brown breeches and a loose white shirt, his easel in his arms and his treasures strapped around his shoulder, looking like a spry old man off to seek adventure—and then it struck him.

My boy.

Had Professor Fell really spoken those two words of…what?…*endearment?* Matthew had the sensation of being back on Golgotha and having his mind robbed of all practical sense.

It was hard to believe, but Matthew knew: the old man was no longer Professor Fell.

At least, no longer the *criminal* Professor Fell. He was the Professor Fell he'd started out to be many years ago, before his son Templeton was beaten to death on a London street by a band of rag-tag ruffians and set him on a course for revenge that had turned out to be a voyage of the darkest heart. No longer was he the spider spinning its web, the tiger stalking prey through the jungle or the shark following a trail of blood in the water; he was now simply a scholar of various organisms, with a specific interest in marine life.

Matthew noted that Fell's voice and mannerisms were still somewhat palsied, but not to the degree of his condition on Golgotha. Neither was he lethargic nor embittered. Here Fell was energetic and involved in day-to-day activities, he took long walks even when he wasn't going out to sketch something of interest or another, and it seemed he very much enjoyed being in the company of the young lady at the *Lancero*, who had to be forty years his junior.

This seachange had begun, Matthew thought, when Santiago had taken charge of *The Lesser Key of Solomon*, and that was the last seen of the book. Hangings had been averted when Matthew had told the whole truth and nothing but, about Professor Fell's history, Cardinal Black's involvement and of course about Ciro Valeriani's mirror, its legend of being a doorway to the underworld, and the group's journey to Venice, which Matthew said he reasoned might be a starting point in search for the son, Brazio. At least Santiago had not laughed at this tale of woe and near madness; in fact, he had opened the book in Matthew's presence and had begun going through it page by page with a quizzical expression.

Matthew thought that when Santiago had taken the book, the searches for both Brazio Valeriani and the mirror were over. And when Professor Fell had realized the same thing, the scales had fallen from his eyes. There was no point in even thinking any more about the mirror, and though Black might fume and curse about somehow getting it back, they all knew a finality had been reached.

And in the loss of the book the professor had found a kind of freedom. He was loosed from the bonds of his past. All his endeavors and properties were long ago and literally far away. He had gotten hold of a quill, an inkpot and some paper and started sketching various things around Alghero, particularly the harbor and thereabouts…and here was the stroke of luck, for Santiago's wife Isabelle was strolling under her huge yellow parasol one morning and paused to watch this strange old Englishman in his straw hat sitting on a coil of ropes and drawing some of the ships anchored out upon the blue. One struck her fancy and not only did she wish to take it back to the governor's mansion, but she paid Fell a few coins for it. Which was a good thing, because up until then Fell—as well as many others being "guests" in the prison—had to depend on the soup, bread and wine brought up to feed them by ladies of Alghero's *Sociedad de Bienestar Madre de la Misericordia*, which translated roughly to the Mother of Mercy Welfare Society.

Isabelle Santiago had become the professor's patron of the arts and in turn others in the higher Alghero society—primarily the wives of prominent Spanish officers—had likewise asked Fell through the governor to do sketches of various local scenes. When the professor graduated to watercolors in the last two weeks his artwork of one of the old stone Spanish towers—watchtowers on the coast built to guard against foreign raids, of which there'd been many over the generations—granted him enough coins from the wife of Colonel Calzada to make him a relatively wealthy citizen.

But Fell's real attraction was toward the marine creatures he discovered in the little tide pools and shallow inlets on either side of the harbor, and his scholarly good nature and curiosity in documenting his finds caused the governor to one day ask Matthew if he was absolutely certain this man was the one he'd described as an emperor of crime in England.

"Yes," Matthew had said.

Santiago's reply was: "Impossible!"

It was the damnedest thing, Matthew mused as he walked under the archway into a small tunnel that led to the courtyard. Professor Fell had caused the murder of dozens of victims. He had ordered the murder of Richard Herrald, Katherine's husband. He had financed the school for young criminals in New York and used Tyranthus Slaughter as a hired assassin. He had financed as well the production of the White Velvet gin that had certainly sent many to the asylum and caused murders and violence untold. He had sent Matthew a blood card, which threatened impending death from "the man who never forgets". He had created an entire village to both punish his enemies and shield his cohorts-in-crime. His had been the eyes and ears of the criminal underworld…once upon a time…and now it seemed that he had forgotten his own past, but not like the memory loss on Golgotha; he had rationally and logically put his past into the past, and closed his own book of devils.

My boy.

Danton Idris Fell was now only an old man with a touch of palsy who enjoyed his walks in the sun, his explorations for seahorses, and his watercolors of harbor scenes.

Because the book was gone, the mirror would never be found, and Fell's dream of visiting his dead son in the flesh as a demonic gift was never to come to pass…and thank God for that, Matthew thought…if one believed in the power of the mirror, that is. Which he did not and never would. His main concern now was talking Santiago into turning himself and whoever wanted to leave this place over to the Italians and arranging a voyage back to New York if he had to hang onto the figurehead all the way across. Time was passing, Berry was waiting for him, and he was dreadfully aware of the wasted hours.

He came out onto the wide courtyard with its expanse of brown paving stones. The structure made a circle around the area and was open to the sky at the top. This place had been built for the same reason as the Spanish towers; Santiago had explained that from antiquity Sardinia had been a prize valued by both barbarian tribes and civilized warriors, and the many invasions and possessions under different flags had resulted in a need for the vanquished to be housed somewhere until the hangman's rope or the executioner's axe could dispense with the excess population.

Hudson Greathouse was just coming down the stairs from his quarters on the second level. Matthew stopped his approach and watched, but found himself ready to leap to his friend's aid if indeed Hudson stumbled and fell, for that poorly his balance seemed to be.

What had happened to the man who seized upon action and adventure as a bulldog might grip a blood-wet bone? What had happened to the strong man, the man of great deeds and greater exaggeration of deeds, but amazing deeds all the same? The warrior…the cavalier…the musketeer…the man Matthew could count on to always be there as a companion and not least of all as brawn when the situation demanded such.

Since his sword wound at the hands of his wartime comrade Brom Falkenberg, Hudson had lost over thirty pounds, and for the size and muscularity he'd been before he was gaunt to the point of emaciation. He descended the stone stairs—precarious for any man since there was no railing—as if each step was an exercise in pain…moving slowly, deliberately, his head lowered, his shoulders slumped. His light blue shirt and tan-colored breeches flagged on him. The shade of his skin was a sickly gray, for even though one of his enjoyments was fishing and Matthew had tried to get him a place on one of the boats that went out every dawn, Hudson rarely left the prison and shunned the sunlight. His quarters were on the second level, next to Matthew's, for the reason that—regardless of the dangerous stairs—coming up and down was the only exercise Hudson got except for the program Matthew had devised to give him what he thought might be a reason to live.

For the reality as Matthew saw it was that Hudson Greathouse wished to die, and was committing a slow suicide. It was the killing of Brom Falkenberg that had pushed Hudson toward this edge, not only because the wound struck him by Falkenberg's blade had resulted in an infection that had nearly finished him off in the Alghero's infirmary, but for the reason Matthew had deduced: Hudson was by nature extremely loyal to his friends and those he viewed as worthy, so being put in the position of hunting down Falkenberg in the Golgotha swamp and having to slay him there since Golgotha's evil had turned the man into a maddened killer had taken Hudson apart both physically and mentally, and Matthew feared he could never again be made whole.

And there was something else as well…something that seemed to be eating the man up from within, and Hudson had even said so and started to speak it but had stopped because it was as if it caught in his throat like a stone. What was it? Matthew had wanted to pursue the question but he reckoned that Hudson would tell him, in time. Time, however, was a strict and unforgiving master, and Matthew thought that Hudson did not have much time remaining on this earth.

The craggy face was downcast, his gray-shot beard allowed to grow like an entangled thicket, the black-tarpit eyes now muddy and sunken in dark hollows. He was a walking wreckage.

"Have you eaten today?" Matthew asked when Hudson reached him.

"Soup," came the quiet answer.

"No bread?"

Hudson shrugged, and even this seemed to be an effort.

Matthew felt a mixture of anger and frustration rise up and flame his face. "How long are you going to continue this march to the grave?"

Hudson gave no answer, but in the man's set and solemn expression Matthew read the reply: *Until I get there.*

"You had to do what you did," said Matthew. "I've told you that time and again. It was the island that corrupted Falkenberg, but you had to stop him from killing any other innocents. When will you understand that?" And he went a step further: "Whatever else is burdening you, I've also said you should get it off your chest. While you still *have* a chest, I mean."

That brought a faint smile to Hudson's mouth but it turned into a smirk. "Are we doing this today, or not? I'd just as soon go back to my cell."

"You carry your cell with you." But even that stab was not enough to bring the reaction that the old Hudson Greathouse would've shown: a swift cuff to the face. "All right," Matthew said, "let's get on with it."

He walked to a bucket set against one wall, with Hudson following like a beaten dog. Standing in the bucket were two practice wooden swords of middle length carved in a medieval style, the kind known in England and the colonies as a "waster", and also the kind Santiago said was used to train fledgling Spanish recruits when they were twelve years old. Matthew took one waster and gave the other to Hudson, who accepted it but looked at it as he always did, with revulsion and…yes, the impossible thing…apprehension, his mouth tightening and something in his eyes going inward to a scene unshared and unknown.

Matthew took his position and lifted his sword. "Are you ready?"

"Flail away," Hudson said, his tone completely devoid of interest or emotion.

Matthew attacked. Hudson parried the blow, stepped back and—slowly, too slowly—tried for a sideways slap at Matthew's right leg that Matthew easily turned aside. Matthew thrust forward and Hudson gave the younger man's sword a lazy *pop* that brushed it away, but even with this opening as wide as the Broad Way he would not come in for the attack. Instead, Hudson retreated.

"Come on!" Matthew urged. "Do *something!*"

"You're the master here," Hudson answered…again, an impossible thing. "Do what you please."

Matthew drove in again and again Hudson cracked the strike aside, effortlessly but with no conviction. Hudson had shown some mustard a few days before when they'd done this exercise and Matthew had hoped some spark was returning, but today only the shell was in action if one might call it such. Hudson refused to attack; he simply brushed the wooden sword to one side or the other, his boots rooted in one stance. How different this day was, Matthew thought, compared to the day Hudson had drilled the new recruit of the Herrald Agency in the art of self-defense and attack with an edged weapon; indeed, there was no comparison. This was no longer the same man.

At last, after several minutes of this literally pointless endeavor, when Matthew drove in Hudson struck down the blow and then listlessly flung his own waster aside. It skittered away across the stones, and Matthew said, "Have you no will left?"

He heard mocking laughter from above. Looking up he saw a few of the fifty or so residents of the prison—all Golgothan refugees who were yet to find permanent dwellings—standing up on the ramparts watching the display…but the laughter came from a thin, tall figure in a raven-hued cloak who grinned down upon the scene with obvious delight. Before Matthew could throw a vocal dart, Cardinal Black retreated into a shadow and was gone from view.

Matthew picked up Hudson's discarded waster. He drew a long breath of frustration, let it out and then returned the wooden items to the bucket because the exercise this day was obviously finished. When he turned back to Hudson, the man was simply standing there staring at the ground.

Matthew said, "Is there anything I can do to bring back the man who used to be? You're no longer in physical ill health. I believe you know you had to stop Falkenberg, and that was a noble thing. Terrible, yes…but noble. Hudson, what is it that's killing you?"

Hudson was silent and Matthew thought he was refusing to speak, but then Hudson's mouth opened as he continued staring downward and he said, "Kill them all."

"What?"

"Kill them all," Hudson repeated, his voice soft and yet hoarse at the same time.

"What does that mean?"

And now Hudson lifted his gaze and looked at Matthew but Matthew thought he was looking somewhere else…through himself, toward a place only Hudson knew but he would not divulge.

"It means," said the once Great One, "that I am a lie."

Matthew had no idea what Hudson was talking about. Was the man feverish? A horrible thought: was he losing his mind? Put on a stretcher and taken away from Golgotha, Hudson had been in bad shape, then at death's door here in the Alghero infirmary, and *now*…?

"Corbett!" someone said, from the tunnel that led out of the courtyard.

Matthew knew that voice: a Spanish accent. He turned toward Captain Izan Andrado, the same soldier who had brought Santiago the accursed book on that first day. The slim, aristocratic Andrado wore his usual uniform but had on a yellow peaked cap with a red band. From what Matthew had gathered of the man, he despised all Englishmen, all things English, and spoke not a word of Queen Anne's language.

"Santiago," the captain said, and as he motioned for Matthew to follow he regarded both men with his cold gray eyes.

"*¿Santiago me quiere?*" Matthew asked. *Santiago wants me?*

Captain Andrado simply turned and walked back through the tunnel, but he stopped to wait for Matthew under the entrance archway.

"I am called by the governor," Matthew said to Hudson, whose feelings for the Spanish mirrored Andrado's for the English. "Listen to me. You and I are going to have a talk when I get back. Do you understand?"

"Talk all you like," was Hudson's sluggish response.

Matthew had to get away from Hudson before he himself went mad; whatever his friend's anguish was, it had to come out before it killed him. Matthew followed Captain Andrado out beyond the archway, where he halted in surprise. Before him, drawn by two white horses of obviously noble breed, was Santiago's own personal red coach with its elaborate and ornate gilt trimming. The uniformed driver sat up top waiting for his passengers. There was nothing to be said to Andrado, since Matthew's grasp of Spanish was not yet that firm, but this was a highly unusual occurrence; in fact, it had never happened before. Whenever the governor wished Matthew to come to the mansion for one of their games of chess, he always in the past had sent a simple wagon. So Matthew's curiosity was instantly heightened, and the question was: *Why?*

The two-mile ride down into town in the biscuit-hued leather interior was a pleasure, and the coach still smelled a bit of the very nice spiced perfume used by Isabelle Santiago. As the coach reached the winding, narrow streets of Alghero, Matthew saw citizens taking off their hats and standing reverently as the team went past, of course thinking that either the governor or his wife was making the rounds. It was fine with Matthew, who found himself enjoying this unaccustomed moment of luxury.

He'd discovered that Alghero was a beautiful town. *City* was more the apt description. It was a huge place, far larger than New York. Santiago had told him that Alghero was founded in the twelfth century and now boasted a population of almost ten thousand, though not quite as large as the capital of Cagliari down at the island's southeast. There were warrens of streets, courtyards, gardens, markets, broader boulevards, a myriad of shops, and structures of all shapes and sizes though they all retained the principal construction materials of yellow stone and red tile roofs…the Spanish colors. The harbor was always busy, and was now enhanced by the fleet of small fishing boats that had been towed under sail back from Golgotha.

Matthew had strictly warned Santiago that no one aboard the ships sent to Golgotha on the recovery voyages—of which there were several—should eat or drink anything from the island, and to guard their vessels with muskets if need be. King Tabor was compliant to the initial force that appeared that morning three months ago, but some of the farmers who had invested heavily in their land and crops had refused to leave even under Tabor's urging, and Tabor had made the statement that he was not leaving if there was even one person under his domain still on the island. Santiago's solution had been to set fire to the farmhouses and crops, which settled the problem. Fortunately there was no loss of life on either side. The grandest gift that Golgotha gave the Spaniards of Alghero was the more than two hundred horses brought back to serve their flag.

Another gift was the money and political status gained by Santiago in returning several Golgothans to their families. When his memory returned, the Golgothan Dr. Lucanza realized that he was Dr. Frederico Benedetti, a renowned physician in Padua and a professor of anatomy at the University of Padua. His last clear memory was of being on a ship bound back from Barcelona to Venice after a medical conference. The name "Lucanza" had turned out to be the name of the street on which he, his wife and three children lived.

Among the others was an Italian count who had been a common fisherman on Golgotha, a tailor who made expensive clothing for the Greek aristocracy in Athens, and a Spanish duke who had found employment in King Tabor's horse stables as a groomer. Therefore, all praise to Governor Henri del Costa Santiago, the current hero of Alghero as noted by his superior, Viceroy Count Ruiz de Castro in Cagliari.

The gates to the governor's estate were opened and the coach passed through along a crushed-stone drive lined with short palm trees and other ornamental vegetation. The drive made a circle in front of the imposing two-story mansion, constructed also in the style of the other Alghero buildings but with wide windows edged with stained glass in a variety of colors. Matthew had visited this mansion many times as a guest of the governor, for the purpose of playing chess as Santiago admitted that the Englishman presented a challenge he had not experienced with the other chess players in his social circle.

Thus Matthew and Captain Andrado departed the coach, it continued on around the circle and out through the gates again upon the thoroughfare *Guerrero*, and in another few minutes Matthew had ascended the grand staircase to the second floor and waited behind the captain while he knocked on the by-now-familiar polished pine double doors.

"Entrar," came the also-familiar voice, and Andrado opened the doors for Matthew's entrance.

The governor, uniformed as usual with his sash and medals on display, his long hair freshly curled, was already sitting at the small chess table behind the white pieces, which was always his choice. He was smoking a long, curved clay pipe, the fragrant blue clouds drifting toward the vaulted ceiling. At his right side was another small table supporting a bottle of wine and two cups, again one of the governor's habits. "Come in, come in!" he said with exuberance, and to Andrado in Spanish that Matthew could understand, "Thank you, Izan, you can leave us."

"I appreciate the coach," Matthew said when the captain had gone and the doors were closed. "May I ask why the luxury and not the usual wagon?"

"It's a very warm day, is it not?"

"Yes, but there have been other very warm days."

"Dear Matthew, are you telling me you did *not* enjoy riding in my coach? Oh, you half-mad Englishmen! Can nothing please you?"

"Freedom pleases us. Have you given any consideration to my request that whoever wants to go should be turned over to the Italians?"

Santiago puffed on his pipe and smiled around it. "Now let us not get off on the bad boot this afternoon! I want to avenge that last loss! Come on, take your chair!"

Matthew sat down on a red velvet cushion with his black army facing the white. Santiago might want revenge for a loss, but the truth of it was that the governor was far ahead of Matthew in the winning column. Occasionally Matthew found a way to win, but always he gave Santiago a good game.

"I begin!" Santiago announced, with the two square advance of a king's pawn. A cloud of smoke blew into Matthew's face like the opening not of a chess game but the beginning of cannonfire.

Matthew moved one of his own king's pawns two squares forward. It was just a matter of a few moves before Santiago would get his knights—his *lanceros*, he called them—into the action. He was a very aggressive and confident player, but sometimes wildly aggressive and over-confident, which always accounted for Matthew's victories.

Pieces were moved, the board was studied and the smoke clouds rolled.

"How old are you?" Santiago suddenly asked, but it was a question spoken as if simply something to inquire while Matthew deliberated with his queen's bishop. Immediately Matthew smelled not only the pipe smoke but possibly a rat in the walls.

"Twenty-five," he said.

"Ah! Such a young man to have seen so much and been in so many difficult situations, if what you've told me is true!"

"It is, and sometimes I don't feel very young. I believe I'll take that pawn you're so eager for me to grab so you might further develop the center, but I'll risk it."

"Your entire life has been a risk, hasn't it?" A rook moved to threaten a knight.

"I suppose so."

"And here you are, when you should be back in New York with your bride-to-be. Bonnie, is it?"

"Berry." Matthew reached out to move the knight and then looked through the roiling fog into Santiago's face. "What's the game?"

"Chess, of course!"

He moved the knight to threaten both a pawn and a bishop. He would get one or the other, most likely the pawn because the bishop would be moved halfway across the board. "I mean the *real* game today."

Santiago moved the bishop, but not quite as far as Matthew had expected. The white pawn went down like a valiant but ultimately doomed soldier. Then Santiago began to work his king's knight into a dominant position at the board's center.

"I am curious," Santiago said as he smoked and surveyed the board like a Spanish god from on high. "About your Professor Fell. He has an ample wealth of money from his drawings. Why does he choose to remain where he is instead of finding a cottage? There are some available for a small price, which he could easily afford."

Matthew decided to let the *your Professor Fell* go. "I think he enjoys having no responsibilities."

"Ah, I see. Is his ambition that much gone?"

Matthew was about to move the knight to a more agreeable position because he'd seen the beginnings of the trap Santiago was setting. He paused, his hand hovering over the piece.

"You're getting at something other than winning the game. What is it?"

With another puff of the pipe, the governor said, "We have a visitor who has come from Spain on the new ship you probably saw, and after a brief conference here was escorted to the Marquesa Lorianna Inn to oversee the unpacking of various trunks and baggage. You will meet our visitor directly. Viceroy de Castro himself will be here later this evening. You know you've left that knight right where it should *not* be, don't you?"

"What visitor?" Matthew asked. To blazes with the knight and this sham of a chess game! Something was up! "Who is it?"

"Play on, play on," Santiago urged. "We are civilized gentlemen, are we not, and do not need to fret ourselves into making amateurish mistakes. I will tell you—as you reach for that knight who will be destroyed in three moves—that I had your book sent to Viceroy de Castro in Cagliari."

"*My* book? It's far from being mine!"

"Well, pardon then...*the* book. Viceroy de Castro found it so interesting that he had it wrapped in a package and shipped to Spain."

"All right." Matthew decided against moving the knight. He brought a rook up to aid in the defense. "May I ask, what of it?"

Santiago didn't answer for a while. He relit his pipe with the burning stub of a red candle, blew smoke like a caul over Matthew's head, and said, "I realized, dear Matthew, that you never told me why you had decided to search for this Brazio Valeriani in the area of Venice." He offered a slight smile that showed his teeth. "Would you tell me now?"

Many times in his career with the Herrald Agency Matthew had felt the world give way under his boots: when he'd realized how he and Berry were to be chased down and murdered by the young criminals-to-be at the Chapel estate, when he'd discovered the real identity of the woman known as the Queen of Bedlam, when he and his Indian guide Walker In Two Worlds had found Tyranthus Slaughter's murder victims in the isolated farmhouse, when he'd realized what ingredient made Mrs. Sutch's sausages so spicily appealing, when the supposed automaton of Professor Fell had appeared on Pendulum Island, when he'd learned that Minx Cutter knew he was not Nathan Spade and that Nathan Spade was the traitor Fell had "hired" him to uncover, when the swamp-dwelling Indians up the River of Souls had a game using severed heads as game balls and he'd realized his was the next ball in the game, when it was clear the hunting party in the swamp was being hunted by a creature of hideous shape and ferocity known as the Soul Cryer, when he'd awakened to find himself the servant of the evil Prussian swordsman Count Anton Mannerheim Dahlgren, when the toadish and demented Mother Deare had put a bullet through the forehead of Rory Keen, when he'd found Berry being turned into a drug-addled substitute for the dead daughter of the mayor of Y Beautiful Bedd, when the detested Cardinal Black had shown up at the mansion of Samson Lash, when Dippen Nack had recognized Matthew just before Nack was slashed to pieces by RakeHell Lizzie, when the Autreys' inn was surrounded by the ambuscade of killers and there seemed no possible escape, when he'd had to watch Berry leave for New York on the *Lady Barbara* and he was bound to the search for that damnable mirror, when Hudson had been found wounded near death by a Golgothan farmer, when he'd discovered the other side of the island and realized what King Tabor's true story was, and...

...now, here...another jolt because he had put all thought of Brazio Valeriani, *The Lesser Key of Solomon* and the quest for the sorcerer's mirror away...it was all done, all over, and the important thing was to convince Santiago to give himself and Hudson to the Italians, to get himself back into the arms of Berry and offer Hudson a reason to live...but now, here... it was not over. Governor Santiago's intense stare through the pall of smoke said...no, it was not over.

There came a knock at the door.

"*Entrar.*"

The doors opened wide and Captain Andrado entered first, but he paused to motion the second person behind him into the room.

Santiago stood up. He smiled and gave a quick respectful bow to their visitor from Spain. To Matthew he said, "Here is the witch-hunter."

And across the threshold walked one of the most striking women Matthew had ever seen.

THREE

MATTHEW WAS STRUCK MUTE AND IMMOBILIZED. HE UNDERSTOOD that as a gentleman he should stand up when a lady entered a room, but if the red velvet cushion under him had somehow been enchanted into a bed of hot coals he would still be sitting there paralyzed by both the woman and the moment.

Here is the witch-hunter.

Had he really heard Santiago say that, or was he still on Golgotha with his brain moldering away until there would be nothing left in his skull but gray slime?

The governor dismissed Captain Andrado, who left the room and closed the doors behind him, and then Santiago spoke to the woman in their native tongue: *...this is the young man...his story...the book...*was all Matthew could get of it, but it was enough.

He hauled himself up on weakened knees. "What is this?" he croaked.

"This is not a what, but a who," Santiago answered, with a little haughty snap in the voice. *"Señorita Espaziel, conozca a Matthew Corbett,"* he said to the lady, who turned upon the young Englishman eyes as green as signal lamps.

"I am Camilla Espaziel," she said, her voice low and quiet. She offered a hand that was shielded by no glove and bore no rings. "I have heard much about you."

Matthew had no idea what to say. The woman spoke excellent English, though with a pronounced Spanish accent. Before his mind could shut his mouth's door he said, "I haven't heard anything about you until this moment."

She gave a slight smile, her eyes yet to Matthew's opinion nearly incandescent. "We'll remedy that," she said, her hand still offered.

Matthew took it. He'd expected she had a strong grip and he was not disappointed; after all, though the woman was slim—sinewy might be the better description—she was at least six feet tall and had a no-nonsense air about her that might make even the rough-and-tumble Minx Cutter back up a few steps.

Her complexion was a tawny shade of olive, her chin strong and riven by a cleft, her nose long-bridged ending with a graceful upward tilt. Her age was difficult for Matthew to ascertain, because though she had nearly no lines on her face underneath the dark green riding cap she wore—adorned with what appeared to be a raven's feather—her shoulder-length hair was almost all white except for a few currents of gray in varying shades. Her dark green cloak was worn over a gown of deep violet edged with green lace and lace of the same hue wrapped at the throat. All in all she presented a formidable and beautiful figure, and the way she stared at Matthew made him feel as if he was being dissected by a master—in this case, mistress—surgeon.

"Matthew Corbett," she said, releasing his hand. He saw that her other hand held a black leather valise close to her side. "You seem to have travelled quite a distance for such a young man…and I mean that in the terms of experience. And here you are, an Englishman on Spanish earth."

"I would wish to be an Englishman on English earth," he said, as his wits had gladly returned to him. He frowned. "How is it you speak my language so well?"

"I speak several languages. As for the English, my father was a great admirer of your country's Shakespeare and wished to learn to read the plays in the hand they were written. He was especially interested in the tragedies." Just like that, her focus released Matthew and turned upon the governor. "I have the book," she said, "which I have read several times over," and unlacing the valise she brought forth the accursed thing, set it down upon Santiago's desk and left Matthew nearly staggering because…oh my God! he thought…here was the damned compendium of demons, the powers they commanded and the spells used to summon them and…oh my God!…what was next to come, he dreaded to think.

What came next was Santiago saying, "I have just inquired of *Señor* Corbett why he presumed to search for this Brazio Valeriani—the son of Ciro, the alleged sorcerer—in the area of Venice, and I am still waiting for an answer."

Camilla Espaziel turned those piercing eyes upon the young man. "I would like to hear the answer as well." Her dark brows went up, accenting the governor's previous and damning question.

Matthew felt himself shiver inside from all this definitely unwanted attention, but he steeled himself, lifted his chin in a small display of defiance and said, "Hold on, let's not let the coach run away with the horses. Please don't tell me that you—or someone directing you—is interested in Valeriani's mirror."

He let that hang and felt he was being hanged in the silence that followed.

"No!" he said incredulously. "Are you…both of you…have you lost your minds? Have Viceroy de Castro and some other official in Spain… have they become unhinged by this book? You're a *witch-hunter?*" he said, daring the steady green glare. "What does that mean?"

The slight smile returned. "It means I hunt witches and I destroy them however I can, as my father did and his father before him. I presume you've never had experience with either a witch or someone like me?"

You'd be surprised, Matthew thought but didn't speak it. His gaze went to the book. "And that has brought you here? To do *what?*"

"To hunt," she replied, and added, "Naturally."

"If you believe the mirror is real, I regret your lack of sanity," Matthew countered. "It's not real. It *can't* be."

"Spoken by a young man who has ventured a long distance to find something he believes cannot be real," said Santiago. "The question remains: why Venice?"

Matthew gave a quick glance at the bottle of wine. Might it be Amarone? The irony of ironies, if it was. When Matthew was confined to Fell's village of Y Beautiful Bedd in Wales, a remark by the Italian opera star Alicia Candoleri's makeup girl Rosabella—who was also Ciro Valeriani's niece—had sparked his curiosity. At her uncle Ciro's funeral in Salerno, Brazio had asked Rosabella how old she was and she'd answered "thirteen".

Brazio's reply, according to Rosabella, was: *Thirteen is a good age, especially for Amarone.*

Amarone, Rosabella had told Matthew, was a very strong red wine. To Matthew's further question of why she thought Brazio might have mentioned Amarone, she'd said, *I have no idea, unless he works in a vineyard somewhere.*

And Matthew's continued thought was: A vineyard worker? Or a vineyard *owner?*

From Giancarlo Di Petri, Madam Candoleri's manager, had come the information that Amarone originated from the province of Verona, the Veneto region near Venice.

Thus: Venice was a starting point in the search for Brazio Valeriani. It might add up to nothing, and possibly Brazio had mentioned Amarone to

Rosabella because he'd intended to get drunk on it after his father's funeral, but still…a starting point.

"You can have a cup of Tempranillo after you've spoken." Santiago had noticed Matthew's glimpse at the bottle. "Go on, the *señorita* and I are waiting with the bated breaths!"

Matthew's head swam as if he'd already downed a bottle or three. His mouth opened and what emerged—the fourteen horrible words he could not believe he was hearing—was: "If I told you, why would you need me to find him for you?"

The governor regarded him with heavy-lidded eyes and the witch-hunter simply retained her specter of a smile. After a pause, Santiago said, "You jump ahead."

Matthew motioned toward the chessboard. "Well, I've already lost this game, haven't I? I ought to at least hold onto a pawn."

Camilla Espaziel approached him. He had to force himself not to retreat before her, because to him her mere presence seemed nearly as powerful as a force of nature, and possibly just as dangerous. He smelled the orange-and-cloves scent she was wearing. A hand came up and a forefinger stabbed him in the chest with undeniable strength.

"I have a feeling," she said, "that even if you were to tell us everything you know, we would still need you to find him. Am I correct, governor?"

"I think you might be."

"I *know* I am," she replied, with her finger still on Matthew's chest. The hand moved away. "Now I'd like to meet the other one. The one who calls himself Cardinal Black."

"Just a moment!" Matthew protested, once again fighting for balance on unsteady earth. "That man is an evil maniac! And he's a lunatic as well! He believes he has a familiar he calls Dominus that only he can see!" Instantly he knew that was the wrong tidbit to reveal, because he could detect a further gleam in the woman's eyes.

"Thank you for that," she said. "He's currently in the prison?" This query was directed to Santiago.

"He is."

"Then we shall go there and visit him immediately."

Matthew realized that any more protest to a stronger degree was futile. In a few minutes he, the witch-hunter and Santiago were in the governor's coach retracing the route that had brought Matthew down from the hill. In Camilla Espaziel's hands was the book, and she remained silent as she looked out the window on her side of the coach. Matthew was also silent but his mind was full of cacophony; all right, it seemed he had talked himself into continuing this farce of a quest now for high-born Spanish interests rather than low-handed English ones, but to involve Cardinal Black in it once again? The man—the *creature*—was evil personified! Would that Santiago had had Black hanged as soon as the book was discovered, but a noose would probably have wrung the necks of all of them if Santiago had decided to put Black to the rope. Matthew was sure Dominus Boy would exalt over the attention he was going to receive from the witch-hunter, unless—hope of hopes—she decided he was a warlock unfit to live another day, and thus justice would be done for the spirits of the Black-Eyed Broodies the twisted Cardinal had so brutally murdered.

Matthew noted that the coach passed a straw-hatted figure walking jauntily up the hill, carrying his easel and leather bag of art supplies, and it surprised him that even after all the threats of death, the indignities done to himself, Berry and Hudson and all the rest of Fell's hand in the criminal world, he felt a pang of sorrow for the old man. With the return of the book of demons and this insanity about finding the mirror for the Spanish, Fell's idyllic repast here on Sardinia was about to come down with a resounding crash. But then again, perhaps he'd ceased to care and that would be all to the good. The test would be when the professor set eyes on that book, and what his response would be when he realized the witch-hunter—oh, the stories he could tell to that woman to curl her silvery tresses!—was interested in Cardinal Black.

As the coach neared the prison's entrance, Santiago began explaining to *señorita* Espaziel that most of those taken off the island of Golgotha had found residences in the city, but fifty or so remained for their own reasons where they were and if they did not have occupations were tended to by Alghero's benevolent societies. At least this is what Matthew gathered, since Santiago had chosen to proffer this explanation in Spanish.

After this was finished, the woman looked across at Matthew and asked, "What is *your* occupation?"

"Novice basket-weaver," Santiago said, to drive a particular nail through what was left of Matthew's dignity, and also Matthew figured the man was swaggering a bit before the lady. "He is coming along, though," the governor added, his kindness on full peacock display. "Soon he'll be at the level of our most senior citizens."

She ignored the comment, which Matthew appreciated even though he knew it was a statement of truth. "I understand," she said, "that in the English colonies you were what is known as a problem-solver?"

"Yes, and that's what I'll be when I get back as well."

"Indeed." She gave him that intense stare he thought was seeing right to his soul. "I too am a problem-solver," she said. "The problems I face are of the spectral realm. Do you believe there are such creatures as witches?"

"No."

"A quick and forceful answer. Are you attempting to convince yourself?"

He matched the stare as best he could though in actuality he was no match. "How have you convinced yourself that there are?"

The question caused a strange reaction. Her expression seemed to go blank for a few seconds. Her eyes became unfocused, along with a tightening of the mouth. Matthew thought a cloud was passing over the sun, for suddenly it seemed darker in the coach. He had another second to wonder if Camilla Espaziel was the one who needed convincing…but how could that be, if it was her—dubious—profession? Then the strength returned to her face, the sudden darkness was gone…and yet, there remained something in the luminous green eyes that was…what? Sadness? Regret? One of those, he reasoned…or at least both his instinct and his imagination told him so.

"At some future time," she said, her voice composed and quiet, "I shall impress my belief upon you." And she added: "From one problem-solver to another."

The driver reined his horses in and set the brake. Shortly Matthew, Governor Santiago and *señorita* Espaziel were ascending the prison's steps to the second level. It interested Matthew that the woman had mentioned her father having read Shakespeare's plays, because the prison—which actually in ancient times, according to Santiago, had been a fortress—made Matthew think this might have been what Hamlet's castle looked like: uneven and sloping walls of rough stones, the treacherous winding stairways, ledges that jutted out over the courtyard and up at the top battlements like jaws of broken teeth.

As reluctantly as anyone could be in this life, Matthew led the others along the corridor to the chamber occupied by Cardinal Black. He knocked at the heavy oak door, which was unlocked per the generosity of their hosts but currently closed per Black's desire for privacy. Matthew had to knock a second time before an answer was given.

"Who is it?"

"Me."

"Get away from my door."

"I've brought you visitors. You might want to see them."

"I want to see no one. Now go away."

Before Matthew could respond, Camilla Espaziel moved past him, gripped the door's iron handle and pushed in.

The grim cardinal looked up with an expression of annoyance but if he was about to speak the sight of the woman stayed his tongue. He was sitting on his straw cot polishing one among his collection of silver rings embossed with skulls, bizarre faces and arcane symbols, the rings arrayed before him on a small round table and an oil lamp offering adequate illumination for the task. Like Hudson, Black had lost considerable weight during their stay and his already long, lean body had truly taken on the appearance of a walking skeleton. He had removed his customary black cloak, had folded it on the cot and was wearing dark brown breeches and a pale gray shirt afforded him by the benevolent society. Matthew had wondered how they'd found such a scarecrow in length for the proper donation of size. On his feet were scuffed black boots. His beard had grown out, mottled brown and scruffy gray, and his deep-set ebony eyes set first upon the woman, then upon Matthew and the governor as they both entered.

"What's this about?" came the angered demand.

Camilla said, "We wish to speak with you."

He gave a mocking little smile that made his skull-like countenance appear even worse than usual. "I don't speak with just anyone."

"I think you might be interested in what we have to say."

"Madam—whoever you are—the only interest I have is—"

He was interrupted when the book of demons came down upon the table, scattering his rings with little tinkling silver sounds to the stones and making the oil lamp jump and sputter. Camilla had withdrawn the tome from the folds of her cloak and tossed it forward, and now she lifted her brows and said, "The only interest you have is *that?*"

Black stared at the book. He started to touch it and then drew his hand back. "The only interest I have is getting back to England," he said, but he frowned—again, to Matthew's eyes a horrifying sight. "What are *you* doing with this and who are you?"

"All in good time. What you should know now is that we do share a common interest…in Ciro Valeriani's mirror."

When Cardinal Black stared at the witch-hunter, Matthew thought he detected a glint of scarlet down deep in the dreadful eyes but then again the oil lamp was still spitting red. "The mirror," said Black, and something about the mouth with the sharpened teeth moved as if he was sipping honey…or, in Matthew's opinion, the elixir of the damned. "Oh yes," Black added, with a little nod. "That *is* a subject of interest, isn't it?" His gaze shifted quickly toward Santiago. "*Official* interest? From the Kingdom of Spain? Or let us say whoever is commanding the empire at the moment." This, Matthew knew, was a reference to the fact that—as Santiago had explained to him—Spanish Habsburgs were at war with Spanish Bourbons over who should rule the empire, and their fight—since members of the Habsburg and Bourbon clans ruled nearly every country in Europe—had spread like a wildfire across the civilized world, including northern Italy, with many kingdoms in the balance. "You're a Bourbon, are you not?" Black waited for Santiago to nod. "What, then? You want the mirror so you can destroy your enemies? Governor, the shame of it! Trusting a Satanic hand to do your dirty work? What would the Pope say?"

"The Pope isn't here," Camilla asserted. "And I have the impression that if anyone knows how to do dirty work, it's you."

Never was there a truer statement, Matthew thought but he kept his mouth shut.

"Very well." Black laced his long thin fingers together and smiled up at Camilla like a cat intrigued by a wandering mouse. "What dirty work may I do for you?"

"First you can get yourself cleaned up," said Santiago. "You too, Corbett. I'll not have my dining room smelling of unwashed Englishmen."

"Your *dining room?*" Matthew was newly aghast. "What does that mean?"

"It means that at seven o'clock my coach will arrive to pick you and Black up and bring you to dinner with myself, *señorita* Espaziel and Viceroy de Castro. Here." The governor brought a pocket watch out from a coat pocket and offered it to Matthew. "Seven o'clock *sharp*, as you English like to say."

"Me? Have dinner with *Black?* Are you out of your mind?"

"Guard your tongue, Matthew. I consider you a guest in my city and I have enjoyed our games of chess, but you'll do as you're told. Understand?"

Matthew did. Whatever was going on, it was no game; it was very serious business. He took the watch.

"A dinner with the high-ranking *funcionarios?*" Black asked, demonstrating that he had indeed picked up some of the native language himself. "Dominus and I shall be delighted!"

Matthew couldn't resist this little comment. "And just where is Dominus at the moment?"

"Standing right behind you, of course."

Santiago twisted around but neither Matthew nor Camilla took the foul bait. The governor exhaled a small whuff of disturbed air and straightened his coat about his shoulders since it had gotten a bit crooked in his abrupt movement. "Seven o'clock," he said to Matthew, and he departed the chamber, his boots *clack-clacking* away along the corridor.

Camilla retrieved the book, but Black's hand hung in the air as if yearning either for the tome or for the touch of flesh. "Have you read that?" he asked, all innocent grace.

"Several times through."

"I see. We really do have *many* things in common, don't we...*sister?*" His sharpened teeth glinted in the lamplight.

"I'm ready," she said to Matthew, and she walked out. Matthew backed away from Black, who at last sight was standing up to gather his rings, and then he closed the chamber's door and quickened his pace to catch up with the woman.

"You understand what I mean now, don't you?" he asked her as they walked side-by-side along the curving corridor to the stairs, which obviously Santiago had already reached and begun his descent. "That about Dominus. The man is *insane*."

She stopped, Matthew stopped, and she looked at him with a quizzical half-smile. "Insane?" she asked. One hand rubbed back and forth over the book's cracked front binding. "Young man, before Black mentioned his Dominus the back of my neck prickled. There *was* something standing behind us."

Matthew was about to ask if she too was insane but it stuck in his throat.

Sister, Black had called her.

Did Black in his demonic fevers realize something about this woman that the others did not and *could* not?

Witch-hunter?

Or *witch*?

She turned away and walked on, with Matthew following a few steps behind. Then she stopped again short of the stairway because another figure stood in the corridor before them.

She approached Hudson Greathouse, who Matthew figured was coming to see him because his own domicile—not much, but somewhat larger than his dairyhouse home in New York—was near the stairs. The woman was nearly as tall as Hudson but of course many times more healthy. Matthew saw her look the bearded, emaciated man up and down, while the once-Great One stood gaping at her as if he'd never seen a woman before... or, at least, never a woman like her.

"Who is *this* sad thing?" she asked Matthew.

"My friend Hudson."

Camilla stared into the man's face for a silent time, and then she waved her free hand back and forth before her nostrils. "Don't you people ever *bathe?*" she asked, and she stalked briskly past him and away.

"Who the hell was *that?*" Hudson asked when Camilla had started down the stairs.

"The witch-hunter." Or the witch, Matthew thought.

"*Who?*"

"Never mind. I'll tell you later." Matthew started after her to see her and Santiago off, but before he went down he was stopped by Hudson's voice...which, somehow, had a little more force to it.

"Matthew!"

"Yes?"

Hudson shambled toward him and looked along the stairs at the descending figure. "Maybe...I *should* clean up. Do you think?"

"I do."

"Well…can you get me some soap? I mean…whenever you can. And…" A hand came up and touched the tangled beard. "Maybe…some shears and a razor?"

"You can use mine," Matthew answered. "I'll bring them to you." He started down to follow Camilla Espaziel to the governor's coach, and half-way to the bottom he realized that whether she was a witch-hunter or a witch…the woman had already set a spell on Hudson, and it might well be one powerful enough to save his friend's life.

FOUR

Matthew had learned that wild boars were plentiful on Sardinia, thus the centerpiece of dinner at Governor Santiago's mansion was a large silver platter of roasted boar meat, nearly blackened and accompanied by various sauces prepared by the kitchen staff. All in all, quite a feast of pork, fried pigeons, baked anchovies and an array of vegetables was presented on the long oak table in the large and opulently appointed dining room, which was decorated with various framed emblems of honor, oil paintings of glowering old dead dignitaries who looked very surly indeed that they were only invited to the meal in spirit, and collections of swords, axes, spears and the like arranged on the blood-red walls beneath a huge chandelier of at least fifty candles, as if to remind the young Englishman of his place in the scheme of things.

And the scheme of this dinner was what Matthew was interested to know, for as yet—through three courses and a bottle of Tempranillo—the only matters of inquiry were questions presented to Matthew concerning how things went in the colonies, what the weather was like in that part of the world, what the businesses and interests were there, and other time-killing soft subjects. Matthew took the opportunity several times to remind his host that his wife-to-be was waiting for him in New York and the sooner he could get back, the better. Santiago ignored these comments, and occasionally shot out a remark about the "hungry and foolish" aims of the English military and the government's "greedy and childish" politics, which had to be translated to Viceroy Francisco Gines Ruiz de Castro, who understood not a word of the "heathen's language". De Castro, natty in his dark blue velvet suit adorned with gold buttons, many medals and accented with yellow cuffs and a high lace collar also in yellow, was a small, slender man in his fifties with a trimmed gray goatee and gray moustache waxed so that each end was formed into a curlicue. He sat at the head of the table, with Santiago and Camilla Espaziel on his right and Matthew and Cardinal Black on his left...the sinister side. Matthew noted that de Castro avoided gazing too long upon Black, who was wrapped up in his ebon cloak, his dark hair plastered down with some kind of pomade he'd gotten hold of, and his freshly shaven face similar in glowerance to the portraits on the walls. Black had eaten his meal at a slow tempo, pausing many seconds between bites, but so far had neither spoken a word nor been spoken to. Matthew had to wonder if Black thought Dominus occupied one of the other four chairs at the table, for from time to time a little flickering smile flashed across the ugly mouth as if he was well aware of something the others were not. To his credit and display of wisdom, Santiago had not invited his wife to this occasion, as evidently he thought she might be repelled by Black and certainly would have little appetite in his ghastly presence.

Noted also by Matthew was that Camilla Espaziel—who had changed into a sea-green gown that further accented the intensity of her eyes— seemed to keep quite a watch on Cardinal Black. She had brushed her silvery hair back, exposing a pronounced widow's-peak, and pinned the tresses in place with tortoise-shell combs. Once again Matthew thought she made a formidable—and not to mention, beautiful—figure even at repose here at the dinner table. Matthew was waiting for someone to tell him the when, where, why and what was expected of him, but in the meantime he was thoroughly enjoying this feast, as he'd not experienced the like of this in a very long time.

Still the small talk went on. De Castro conversed back and forth with Santiago and the woman and Matthew tried to hold onto it but he could only get bits and pieces so he gave up the effort and poured himself another cup of wine.

The servants brought in platters of vanilla cake, sugared cookies and small individual bowls of some foodstuff Matthew had never seen before. It looked like pieces of puffed yellow something drizzled with honey, and when Matthew dared to take a taste with his fork he found it appealingly crunchy, a bit salty as well as sweet, and quite good.

"May I ask what this is?" he inquired of the governor.

The reply was: *"Palomitas."*

"Yes, but what is it?"

"Hm. I suppose in your language it would be 'popped corn'."

"*Corn?* It doesn't taste like any corn I've ever had before."

Santiago gave Matthew a look he might have reserved for the most ignorant citizen of Alghero. "Our great champion and noble Lord Hernan Cortes brought this seed of corn and the process of cooking it to Spain after his conquest of the Aztec empire, in the 1500s. The Aztecs ate this and used it in their religious ceremonies. Such as they were," he sniffed. "We have refined the process and instead of using pans of hot sand, as they did, we have special steam kettles. I appreciate that you find it of interest."

Black suddenly gave a barking laugh, which caused both Santiago and de Castro to jump in their chairs. The unholy cardinal's eyes glinted in the candlelight along with the rings on his fingers. "I knew the Spanish were a clumsy breed," he said, "but I never imagined they could foul something as simple as corn." He pushed his bowl away. "This is *hideous*."

"Your opinion is noted," said Santiago in the most dismissive tone, "and instantly discarded."

Viceroy de Castro caught some of this and started slapping the table to get a translation, which the governor supplied. De Castro fired off a spittle-fueled response which caused Camilla to put a hand up before her mouth, but Matthew saw that her eyes found great humor in the rather chaotic moment.

Matthew finished his cup of wine and set it down on the table with a solid little *thunk*. It was time. "Sirs and madam, I thank you for the feast and for the obvious effort at softening what evidently is to come. May I ask that it be presented now?" He held up an index finger before Santiago could speak. "And I already know you want Brazio Valeriani and his father's mirror found. I'd like to know *why*."

The governor took a long drink from his own wine cup before he replied. "Authorities above those present seek to lay claim to the mirror, to have it transported to Spain and locked away in a vault."

Again there came the ugly blast of Black's laughter. "A *Bourbon* vault, I presume! And to what purpose? To finish this little disagreement by destroying all vestige of the Habsburg empire? For that you'll need the demon Marquis Marchosias, I would think, or perhaps Count Mathus might do. Yes…Count Mathus…to send spirit armies out who can destroy but not be touched by mortal weapons. Of course, once you uncork either of those and don't know how to put them back in their bottles they will run through Spain and everyone in that country like this wretched popped corn will surely run through a person's innards…so by all means, destroy the Habsburgs and yourselves while you're at it…and most likely put a demonic torch to the entire world…thus the *end* of all wars and the end of all humans as a great benefit to civilization."

Santiago went about translating this diatribe to de Castro. Matthew understood from the governor that the king of the Spanish empire, Charles the Second, had died in 1700 without leaving an heir. Charles had been a Habsburg, but now the Spanish Bourbons were making a claim to the crown. What had begun as a political battle in Spain had drawn into the fray Habsburgs and Bourbons across almost the entire European continent, as the power of other rulers might be diminished according to which "house" commanded Spain and that country's trading routes. Thus, as Santiago had explained over one of their many chess games, had been pulled into what he termed a "world war" was the Dutch Republic, Prussia, France, Scotland, Bavaria and, on the Habsburg side, England. Fighting was currently going on in the north of Italy, precisely in the area above Venice and where Matthew had presumed to begin his search for the son of Ciro Valeriani.

De Castro made some snappish comment when Santiago's translation was done, and Camilla said to Cardinal Black, "I gather that you would consider yourself able to control these entities?"

Matthew had heard enough. "Am I sitting in the company of absolute *lunatics?* I know Black's out of his mind, but let's have some sense on display here!" He looked back and forth from Santiago and Camilla. "Please don't tell me you actually believe this mirror is a doorway or a gateway or whatever to the underworld! That is *ridiculous!*"

Camilla's gaze was steady. "Can you be certain of that? My father spent his life involved in what you might call ridiculous circumstances, and I can tell you that he—"

"Yes," Santiago interrupted, "we understand the work of your father's life, *señorita* Espaziel, and thank you for that statement."

Instantly Matthew saw again a dark cloud pass across the woman's face. This time it did not dissipate so quickly as before in the coach. Her green gaze moved away, and she reached for her own cup of wine.

Santiago stared across at Matthew. He lifted his chin. "Are you religious, young man? Do you believe in the Holy Bible? The life and work of Jesus Christ?"

"Yes, but what does that have to do with anything?"

"It has to do with *everything.* If one believes in the Holy Bible and in the written word of the life of Christ, one cannot…how would you say in English?…*pick and choose* your items of belief or disbelief. I refer to the temptation of Christ by Satan. You're aware of those passages?"

"I am."

"And do you believe or disbelieve in the truth of those?"

"Well, I…" Matthew was for the moment a little befuddled. "It's in the Bible, I know, but—"

"So you believe in the Holy Father and His Son but not Satan? Is that correct?"

"I don't choose to discuss my religious beliefs."

Santiago gave an impish smile and clapped his hands together. "Ah! The truth of it! You *avoid* these thoughts, do you not? You deny the power of Satan in this world? You deny even the existence of such an evil creature?"

"What I know," said Matthew with a force that surprised himself, "is that there's enough evil done by *men* in this world to have to bring Satan into the discussion."

Black laughed quietly. The sound made the flesh at the back of Matthew's neck crawl and he had to wonder if Dominus stood behind him with an outstretched claw...just about to touch.

"Now *here*," said Santiago with a nod in Black's direction, "is a man— and I use that term with some hesitancy—to whom the name of Satan is not unfamiliar. I might say this man is the keeper of darker secrets than any of us care to know."

"Yes," Matthew said, "and he's adept at gouging out eyeballs and putting them in gin bottles as well."

This caused a long silence, and to his good sense Black did not laugh or register any reaction because Matthew still had a knife beside his plate.

Santiago cleared his throat—a nervous noise—before he ventured on. "My meaning here, Matthew, is that one cannot take what one considers to be true and discard what one deems false in the holy word."

"I'm not saying that."

"Oh, but you *are*. In my country such divisions of belief and disbelief in the holy word have led to—"

"Tortures that brought a smile to the face of any demon who heard the screams," Black interrupted. "Corbett is correct on one count: why should Satan labor, when men do all his best work?"

De Castro slapped the table again, wanting to know what was being said, but Santiago nodded at him and waved a hand for patience before he returned his attention to Matthew. "*If* there is a mirror," he said, "and *if* this mirror has indeed been enchanted by a sorcerer likely influenced by the Devil...don't you agree it would be the wisest thing to find it and lock it away for all time?"

"All time meaning as soon as the next Bourbon king of Spain decides to increase the empire?" Black smiled coldly as he worked the rings on his long-nailed fingers. "Yes, do let amateurs dabble with those forces, and there shall be a crater in the earth where Spain used to be."

De Castro's slapping started up once more and Santiago translated what had been said. Then the viceroy began speaking, directing his remarks toward Matthew and Black. He went on for several minutes, his voice rising and falling in such a fashion that Matthew discerned his speech was of emotional importance to the man. At last de Castro finished, his eyes glassy and his face gone strangely pale, and he looked to the governor to translate in the other direction.

"The viceroy wants you to understand," Santiago began, "that he is of humble birth. When he was a young boy, in the village a short distance from his own a woman was accused of witchcraft. It was found that in an unused barn she had constructed a...*shrine*, you would call it...to honor Satan. She had begun by offering up small animals on an altar...chickens, rabbits and dogs, at the beginning. It progressed to goats and progressed further to... well...several young girls. She lured them in with pretties and cut their throats, and the viceroy recalls that she was found to have bathed in the blood. This woman was caught, tried and hanged in the village square, but not before she vowed vengeance on every soul who lived there."

Matthew said, "She was a madwoman but not necessarily a witch."

"Let me finish with the viceroy's tale. After this woman was hanged, her head was cut off, as were her arms and legs and the body parts burned, the ashes salted and buried in a pit covered over and sprinkled with holy water. The viceroy says that nearly one year to the day of that witch's death, a plague struck the village. He recalls that it was an attack on the blood, in that the villagers were retching up gore, that their bodies were twisting as if they had been bewitched into infernal puppets. He knew this because his father was a physician who tended to all the villages in the area, and his mother was a midwife. The viceroy says his father entered that village to tend to the afflicted before a plague was determined, and he heard the tales told about the ones who first perished. In time, nearly all the citizens of that place had died in most horrible agonies. No one knows why or how, he says, but a fire started that burned everything there to the ground. But that wasn't the end of it. For years afterward—until the viceroy's family moved to Madrid—he heard travellers through that valley report seeing what appeared to be a village on fire, and one could hear the screams of the burning souls. In addition, on some nights could be seen not only the fire but figures capering in and out of the flames...an unholy dance that might well be going on to this day. Viceroy de Castro says he never returned and he will *never* return, but this is why when he saw the book and realized what it depicted...and also after you told me the tale of it, Matthew...you can understand why he had it sent to our superiors in Spain."

"And they replied with this so-called witch-hunter?" Black shot an evil glare at Camilla. "To what purpose? Making the denizens of the underworld convulse with laughter?"

"I have experience with such forces," was Camilla's calm reply.

"You *think* you have!" Black answered, with a derisive snort. "I was schooled in these matters by a very demanding and accomplished master, and I can tell you that whatever you believe you've faced in the past, it was like an ignorant tot playing in her toybox."

"Spoken," said Matthew, "by someone who has a history of child sacrifice. I haven't forgotten that little scene either."

"*Pah!*" Black waved a dismissive hand. "You know nothing. None of you know what you're dealing with, if you intend to go after this highly dangerous object without *my* aid."

"I intend to enjoy the remainder of the feast and forget any of this..." Matthew paused to find the right phrase. "Infernal gibberish ever happened." He speared a gaze at Black. "Professor Fell wished to find the mirror in order to say goodbye to his son who was murdered on a London street. I assume DeKay was after it to restore his face. Tell us, then...why are *you* after it?"

Black stared at his hands before he replied, his head lowered. "*My* business," he said, in what Matthew considered an uncharacteristically reserved tone.

"And now," spoke up Santiago, "it is *our* business." He talked to the viceroy for perhaps half a minute. De Castro nodded. Something had been settled. Santiago's attention returned to Matthew. "Young man, you have impressed me with tales of your work as a...as you've called it...problem-solver. I think you've experienced much more than you've revealed. Thus our proposition to you: since you seem to believe you can find this sorcerer's son, we're going to allow you to do so...working for us, of course. You, *señorita* Espaziel, and this man Black are going to be put aboard a ship along with Captain Andrado and four men he will pick as...shall we say... guardians. You will be—"

"Wait!" Matthew interrupted, as what the governor had just said sank in. "Me, go with *this?*" He jabbed a finger toward the cardinal. "No!"

Santiago went on. "I have had the opportunity to speak with this man several times concerning the book, and while I consider him disgusting and abhorrent I believe he knows his..." He searched for the word and found: "Craft. Furthermore, both the viceroy and I want him off our island, as a precaution against whatever he might delve into. Matthew, I am offering this: seek Brazio Valeriani. If you find the mirror, it will be brought here and you and Black will be given over to the Italians to return to England. *This* will help the endeavor." So saying, he brought from a coat pocket the white leather pouch containing the small fortune in gold coins presented to Matthew by Maccabeus DeKay and set it down beside his plate. "In addition, if after a reasonable amount of time you do not locate Valeriani—and that determination will be up to *señorita* Espaziel—it will be considered a closed issue and the reward for your effort will be as stated...giving you and Black to the Italians with this bag of gold and our compliments."

Matthew considered it. The whole thing was absolutely crazy...wasn't it?

To Matthew's silence, Santiago said, "If the mirror is actually what it is claimed to be...better to lock it away under Spanish protection rather than have it under the key of...say...the Dutch, or the French. Or any other world power, as it were. If it is not what it's purported to be, so much the better."

Camilla tapped her finger on the table to get their attention. "The young gentleman is pondering the situation," she said. "He is unsure, but he does not discount the *possibility* of the mirror's power. I would think that in your exploits, *señor* Corbett, you have found yourself a time or two in circumstances that defy logic and reason. If all are truthful, most people in their lives have. Am I correct?"

Still Matthew didn't answer. She had indeed hit on the truth; there had been several instances in Matthew's career as a problem-solver that had shaken the foundations of his rational beliefs and left him wondering about the presence of spectral or otherworldly forces...and he'd labored to lock those away in as much of a vault as these people now intended to do for the mirror, if they really intended to do so.

He found himself staring at the pouch of gold coins. "That's not enough," he said.

"What? You want more money?" Santiago prodded.

"No, it's not that." He lifted his gaze to the governor's. "I want every Englishman on this island who wants to return to England put into the care of the Italians."

Santiago spent a moment speaking with de Castro. While that conversation went on, Matthew realized something very important: if he left Hudson here while he went on this escapade, his friend would likely be dead by the time he returned.

"And," Matthew said, stopping the discourse between the other two, "I want Hudson Greathouse to come along."

"From what I've seen of him, he's in no condition to travel," said Santiago.

"I'll get him in condition." Matthew thought that having a purpose might be a strong incentive for Hudson to rouse himself, or at least to begin. "How long before we leave?"

Again the governor spoke to de Castro, who seemed to be listening carefully before he nodded.

"Very well," came Santiago's reply. "Every Englishman who wants to leave will be handed over. You'll have a letter signed by myself and the viceroy to get you through the Bourbon lines, if you happen to have any trouble there. We would like to begin this expedition by the end of the week, so if you hope to ready your friend you have five days. From here to the port of Venice is a ten-day journey."

"All right. The first thing I would ask of you is to have your kitchen staff wrap up some of the meat that was left on the platter. Also as much of everything else that wasn't finished."

"Simple enough." Santiago reached for a small silver bell at his elbow and rang it to summon a servant.

Matthew's eyes were caught by Camilla's.

"Your friend means much to you?" she asked.

"Much."

"You'll have to tell me about him sometime."

"I'll tell you about him *now*," said Black. "He's a stumbling shell of what he used to be, and will be of no consequence on this trip."

Matthew paid the killer of children and gouger of Black-Eyed Broodie eyeballs no heed. "My friend is a very loyal and courageous man," he said to Camilla. "I'll be glad to tell you all about him."

The servant appeared and preparations were made for the leftovers to be wrapped. As a celebration of sorts to Matthew's acceptance, Santiago ordered another bottle of wine. Matthew didn't feel like drinking another drop; he already felt light-headed with the idea of a further quest for this damned sheet of glass.

"More wine!" Black said, with a twisted smile. "Excellent!" He glanced back to where the purple-robed-and-hooded, faceless figure of Dominus stood directly behind Corbett, and he thought that only he and Dominus knew why he wanted—desperately wanted—to get hold of the mirror, and not until much too late would the others discover that desire.

Much, much too late.

FIVE

It was a tale of two worlds.

The first: when Matthew sat with Hudson in the latter's chamber and presented him with a platter of meat and vegetables that had been wrapped by Santiago's kitchen staff, the newly shaven and freshly bathed man stared for a moment at the meal and then asked, "What was the occasion?"

Matthew told the tale, during which Hudson made no response though he did begin to eat the pork. Matthew finished with, "If it means getting back to Berry, where I'm supposed to be, I would find the Holy Grail for them." He eyed Hudson's new efforts at cleaning himself up and added, "By the way, *señorita* Espaziel suggested I bring you this dinner."

"Hm," said Hudson, with a mouth full of fried pigeon. He gave no other reaction.

"She also suggested," Matthew continued, casting fate to the winds, "that you come along with us."

Hudson's chewing stopped. He swallowed, sat still for a few seconds, and then began eating again.

"What do you say to that?"

Hudson finished a few pieces of roasted onions before he replied. His tone was low and wistful, and he sounded so old it nearly broke Matthew's heart. "I'm used up," he said. "I can't protect you anymore."

"Who's asking you to? I can take care of myself very well indeed, thank you."

"That I know." Hudson managed the slightest of smiles. "And who taught you?"

Matthew leaned past Hudson and turned up the wick of the oil lamp that stood on a table beside the man's cot. "Listen to me," he said, as the brightness grew. "You're only used up if you believe you are. Don't you understand by now that you *had* to kill Falkenberg? Golgotha had robbed him of his senses. You saved the lives of people he might've murdered because he imagined he was back on the battlefield. So if this lethargy and—I have to say—self-pity continues, it is for naught and does a disservice to you as a man."

By the lamplight Matthew caught a quick flare of red in Hudson's eyes that might have been anger from the old Hudson about to burst forth, but it dwindled quickly away and when it was gone there was a silent return to the dinner.

"So that's it?" Matthew asked, near exasperation. "After all this, you're just giving up?"

Hudson didn't reply.

"Well, you didn't clean up for my sake, did you? It was for the woman, wasn't it?"

Hudson finished another swallow and then said, "The witch-hunter. How ridiculous. But she *is* a fine-looking woman, isn't she?"

"Very fine."

"Spanish," Hudson went on. "Not too fond of Englishmen."

"I'm telling you, she said I should bring you the food." In this instance a lie was the best option Matthew could think of. "There's got to be some reason for that. If you could just put aside what happened to Falkenberg, and—"

"I did what had to be done." Hudson lifted his grim gaze from the platter. "I regret it, it was…horrific…but it had to be done. The thing is, Matthew…Golgotha clouded my mind in one way, but it opened something else up. It was…an event I have tried very hard over the years to forget, and I had been successful at that, until Golgotha."

"What was it?"

Hudson shook his head.

Matthew tried again: "What did you mean, when you said you were a lie?"

"Just that, no more and no less."

Kill them all, Hudson had said, and Matthew had feared his friend was losing his mind. "This has to do with your experiences in war?"

Hudson closed his eyes for a time. When he opened them he was looking past Matthew at the wall. "I know your intention is to rouse me into some kind of action, because that's what you expect of me. The strong man. The soldier. The cavalier. The Great One, you call me. Yes? But I don't deserve your praise and respect. Do you understand that?"

"No. The only thing I understand is that I need you along with us to find Brazio Valeriani and the mirror. If I go—even if I'm unsuccessful—we can get back to England and then New York. You don't want to die here, Hudson. By God," he said with a fierce twinge of anger both at Hudson and at God, "I won't *let* you die here."

Hudson stared blankly at Matthew. He blinked and slowly...slowly... gave a smudge of a smile. "The moonbeam," he said quietly, "has suddenly acquired the strength of the sun. Its heat too. Or did it happen little by little, and I never saw it?"

"Finish your food," Matthew answered, feeling the pulse of warmth in his cheeks. "Tomorrow you're going to get to work—real work—with the waster. You're going to start eating like...like a strong man...like a soldier and a cavalier. In five days you're going to board the ship that is taking us to Venice and you're going to do your part in the search. Do you hear?"

"I hear a lot of *goings*."

"Good. Remember them." Matthew stood up from the chair next to Hudson's cot. He started to go out but stopped for one very important statement. "I expect you to help me finish this task. Don't let me down."

Hudson lifted a hand to hold Matthew's presence for another moment. "Did the woman really tell you to bring me the food?"

"No."

"I thought not. She *is* good-looking, though. Got something about her that appeals to me. *Witch-hunter.* Can you believe such a thing?"

"She believes it. Evidently so do the governor and the viceroy."

"Insanity," said Hudson, "is not only a quality of the English. But let me ask you this: have you told the professor about the trip?" To Matthew's silence he raised a teacup-scarred eyebrow. "You have to. I know he's happy because he's found his little paradise...but you have to."

"It's late. I'll tell him tomorrow."

Hudson shook his head. "You should tell him now. Or would you rather Black told him?"

A valid point had been made. It could not wait. "Tomorrow, you and I on the wasters first thing," said Matthew. His morning job of basket-weaving would have to wait. He left Hudson's chamber and went along the corridor, where an occasional oil lamp on a wall hook afforded light for the darktime wanderer.

The second: Matthew approached Professor Fell's chamber on the lower level, and knocked at the oak door that served here as the entrance, the same as all the other cells but again by the grace of Governor Santiago left unlocked. Soon the door creaked open and the professor peered out, his owl's wings of white hair topped by a dark blue Spanish-style beret decorated with a red tassel.

"Ah, Matthew!" he said, and the sun-browned, healthy-looking mulatto face showed a smile. "What may I do for you?"

"We need to talk."

Did the smile falter just a bit? Possibly. "I was wondering when that would happen." Fell opened the door wider. "Please come in."

Matthew entered and Fell closed the door. The professor's domain would've been a dream of all dreams for any real prisoner locked in here. Two oil lamps shone a golden glow upon a nice rattan chair facing Fell's easel, which was set up holding a watercolor in progress. There stood a chest of drawers bought from a furniture maker downtown, as well as a small desk with a second rattan chair. Atop the chest was his water pitcher, shaving bowl, hand mirror, razor and other implements for personal grooming. Fell's cot was covered with a spread in stripes of green and blue, the feather pillow encased in blue velvet. The professor wore a long caftan the color of dark red wine—Amarone, perhaps?—and on his feet were slippers in a shade of tan, the toes embossed with little shiny round metallics in a golden hue. All in all, Fell was making his stay on Sardinia a profitable venture due to his artistic abilities.

"Sit, sit!" Fell motioned toward the second chair. "I have some lemon water, if you'd care for a cup."

"No, thank you." Matthew sat down. His gaze wandered around the chamber and he recalled a question the governor had asked. Perhaps Matthew had intended to inquire about this before, but now seemed the proper time. "You've certainly done well here. Tell me...you have enough money to move out and go wherever you please. Why don't you?"

Fell sat down before the easel, which supported a canvas displaying the impression of a large convoluted-looking seashell being depicted in sea greens, marine blues and browns. The professor gave a soft laugh. "Why do I stay here? Well...it's quite humorous, really. To *myself*, I mean." He leaned forward, closer to Matthew. "Of all the things I have done and been part of, I finally find myself in prison...and yet, I am as free as a bird to come and go and enjoy this cell as if it was my long-lost home. What do I need with more than this?"

"You might find a cottage nearer the sea."

"I enjoy the view from the battlements. I keep a chair up there, you know, where I can watch the sunset. And I enjoy the walk back and forth down the hill. The exercise has been beneficial to my health, don't you agree?"

"I do." To Matthew it was actually amazing. On Golgotha Professor Fell was a scowling, scrawny, bitter shade of what he presently was, and though his hands did tremble from time to time the slight palsy did not seem to affect his artwork, nor was the condition so pronounced in his speech as it had been on that devil's island. The old man was eating well at the various taverns in town and every morning it seemed he was up with the sun and eager to get at the joy of the day.

How different was the professor's world to that currently torturing Hudson, Matthew mused. He never would've believed such a difference was possible, but it seemed to him that Fell had found a great purpose in living, while Hudson was intent on killing himself for some secret sin he would not reveal.

And this thought brought him to the terrible news he had to share.

Fell was already ahead of Matthew. He said, "You are here because of three things. The new ship that came in today, the fact that the governor's coach passed me on the road with you and a woman in it—and those windows are very large indeed, so there was no mistaking you sitting there—and then the governor's coach came back to pick up you and that detestable vermin near nightfall, for I was sitting up on my perch and saw the both of you leave. So: you wished to tell me something?"

Matthew stared down at the stones of the floor, which in the case of this chamber were partially covered by a throw rug the soft green of seagrass.

"Oh my God," said the professor. "Don't tell me Santiago has decreed the sun won't come up tomorrow. Is it that bad?"

Matthew looked up into the face of the man he had once feared more than any presence on earth, and he dreaded what he was about to say because Fell's perfect world here was about to be cracked to pieces. His mouth opened and it came out. "They want Brazio Valeriani and the mirror. They want me to find it."

Fell was silent, but already with those few words his body had tightened, his smile faded away, his eyes darkened, something nearly imperceptible creeping over him like a gathering of inescapable shadows.

"*They,*" Matthew went on. "Santiago and Viceroy de Castro. The Spanish. I suppose from a high authority. The book was gone through, and that got the attention of the woman you saw. Her name is Camilla Espaziel and she's a…" Could he actually speak this last term? It was a difficult thing. "Witch-hunter," he finished.

The professor laughed. It was a horrible, hollow sound without mirth that made Matthew almost physically recoil, and in truth he did feel something inside himself draw back.

"*Witch-hunter,*" Fell repeated, nearly like a curse. "Did she arrive to see Black hanged?"

"Black is going along," said Matthew, who immediately regretted speaking it but Fell would find out anyway. "I'm taking Hudson too."

"Oh." Fell nodded; his amber eyes had gone dark and almost lifeless. "They think he can control whatever is drawn out, is that correct?"

"He's made that boast himself. Another point is, Santiago wants him off the island."

"And knowing you, I believe you had a choice. Why then, have you agreed to such a thing?"

"I did have a choice. I chose to agree because Santiago and de Castro have vowed that if I go—and even if I fail to find Valeriani or the mirror—every Englishman on the island who wishes to return home will be put into the care of the Italians. There's no animosity between England and Italy. I'll be given money enough to charter a ship. And you know why I need to get back to New York. If I don't do this…who can say how long I'd be here? And Hudson, too. He needs a purpose, something to shake him out of his lethargy, which could be the end of him if I'm not here. That's why I agreed."

For a time the professor stared silently at his watercolor of the seashell, as if seeing in its swirls and convolutions a pattern of the future. "I thought it was over," he said at last. "I thought it was all going to be marked off as a strange fantasy and forgotten. But as you say, someone of higher authority must learn whether it's real or not, for their own purposes." He cocked his head to one side. "Do you think I've used too much blue in this picture? I think possibly I have. I'll need to correct that. Tomorrow. Now…it's late, isn't it?"

"Yes."

"When are you leaving?"

"Five days."

"Do you believe Hudson will be able to travel?"

"I'll make it so."

"Your task is before you, then." Again Fell studied the picture. "Too much blue," he said. "In reality there was not that much, but I like the color. It soothes my soul." He offered a cold smile to Matthew. "Good night, then…and thank you for this information."

Matthew stood up. Before he left the chamber he turned again to the professor, who still sat as before. "I'm sorry about this," he said quietly. "It should've been marked off and forgotten."

"But it wasn't," Fell replied, without looking away from his artwork. "And that is the reality, is it not?"

"Yes."

"You made a sensible choice. You've always been a sensible young man. In my position I would have done the same. Sleep well."

"Thank you, sir," said Matthew, and he left the professor to question the use of too much blue to soften the sharp and hard edges of reality.

In his small but made-comfortable chamber on the second level, Matthew put on his long red-checked nightshirt, lay on his cot by the light of his lamp and wished for sleep—well or ill—that did not arrive. Too much crowded his mind. Every time he tried to find an answer to one question, another demanded attention. Should he actually expend effort in trying to find Ciro Valeriani's son and the mirror, or should he lead the group in pointless circles when they reached Venice? So much the better to have the witch-hunter call the search off sooner than later? Did that thought mean he might have some iota of belief in the mirror's unholy powers? What was Black's purpose in finding it? What role did the witch-hunter have in this, and was the claim of the Spanish wanting to seal the mirror in a vault really the truth? And Hudson…was this quest a way to rouse him out of his downward spiral? Matthew noted that Camilla Espaziel's comments to Hudson about his lack of cleanliness had at least caused the man to shave and bathe, and he considered it a hopeful sign that his friend's fires might have dwindled to embers but they still warmed the hearth.

Five days, and then ten days aboard a ship in the presence of Cardinal Black, and though he appreciated Black's efforts to help him escape Golgotha on that ill-fated little boat voyage, he still planned to do his best to have the beast hanged when they got back to London.

And Berry, waiting for him in New York. And waiting and waiting, with Ashton McCaggers probably circling the Grigsby house, coming in occasionally for tea and pleasant conversation, and never refraining from mentioning that poor Matthew had been gone a long, long time and wasn't it a shame that Matthew might be lost either in a shipwreck or some mis-adventure—and you know, dear Berry, that he has a knack of getting into unfortunate misadventures—that has claimed the fellow?

Surely McCaggers wouldn't go so far as to plant *that* in Berry's mind. Surely not.

Matthew sat up. Damn it, he had to get home and the only way was to go through Venice! To actually search for Brazio Valeriani and the mirror? That was the real question.

He got off the cot, put on his shoes and left the chamber with his lamp in hand. There was a better place to consider these questions, and it being a nice warm night he thought that Professor Fell's chair up on the battlements would at least be a place to sit and relax his brain from its current and rather fruitless gyrations. He ascended the nearest set of steps, past the third level and up onto the highest part of the prison, where under a starry sky and a luminous full moon he found the chair and settled himself into it facing down the hill toward the sleeping town.

If he was not in a distraught hurry to leave this island and return to Berry and their life together he would've thought this was one of the most beautiful places he'd ever seen. A few torches flickered at the harbor where the tall-masted ships—elaborately ornate vessels as was the Spanish style—pulled gently on their ropes and anchors with the soft swells that rolled in through the seawall's entrance. Moonlight shimmered on the water like metallic silver. Further out, small streaks of blue phosphorescence marked the progress of some kinds of schools of fish that the professor could surely and easily identify. He could see an occasional lamp or candle in a cottage window, and also a red-lensed moving lantern held by one of the town's watchmen making his rounds. The calm breeze brought to him the aromas of orange groves and cedarwood, and all seemed at peace in the world.

Matthew thought that someday New York might be similar to Alghero, if not in size then in temperament. He was going to do his best to get back there not only for Berry's hand in marriage, but to witness the town's hopeful progress as the years went on. So…there was no choice but to lead this expedition…but again, should he lead them in circles until Camilla said "enough"?

After perhaps twenty minutes of both deliberation and enjoying the Sardinian night, Matthew noted a figure carrying a lamp down below, walking away from the prison. He watched as this person left the road and wandered into the cemetery, moving in no particular hurry, shifting the light back and forth as if reading the names on the stones.

Matthew recognized the figure's form and gait. He watched for a few minutes more, and then his curiosity compelled him to find out what Professor Fell was doing, down among the dead men.

He came up quietly at an angle to the professor so as not to startle the man. Fell wore his bedtime caftan and the Spanish beret, and he seemed intent on studying stone after stone.

Matthew made sure his own footsteps made a crunching noise on a portion of grainy earth, to alert the professor to his presence without alarming him, and then lifted his light so Fell could see his face when the professor looked in his direction.

"Can't sleep?" Fell asked when Matthew reached him.

"No. I see you can't either."

"Correct. Too much to think about."

"The same," said Matthew.

Fell began his wandering once more, with Matthew walking alongside. The professor's light washed against the names on the stones…some faded, some more recent. In another moment Fell said, "I was asking myself if I wished to be buried here. My answer is: no."

"What does that mean?"

Fell stopped and aimed his lantern at Matthew. "Do you know that I have a favorite place to sit and observe the ocean? It's perhaps half a mile to the south, amid some rocks. From there I can see another group of rocks that jut up from the water. I have seen that on every third or fourth wave, the exocoetidae leap up, five or six at a time. They soar over those rocks, toward the land, but they never reach it. They glide back into the waves, which is their rightful destiny."

"Exocoetidae?" Matthew frowned. "What is that?"

"Pardon the scientific term. Flying fish. They seem to realize that the air is only a temporary domain, and though they exult in it for a short and precious time, they return to the sea where they live. I find that very interesting, Matthew, and very telling for myself."

"I'm not following you."

"We were speaking in my chamber about realities. In reality, I have been a human exocoetidae, living on this large island rock, when my destiny is elsewhere. Oh, I have exulted in my days here. You know I have. But...I must return to what I am...what I have made myself, over all these many years. That is why, when your ship leaves this harbor for Venice, I will also be aboard."

"No, sir," said Matthew. "You can't be."

"So you're commanding *me* now?" Fell's smile showed his teeth in the lantern's backwash. "Save your orders for Hudson. I am what I am, and no watercolors can alter the shade. Number one: I cannot sit here twiddling my old thumbs and playing at art and marine physiology while I know Cardinal Black is seeking to get his hands on that mirror. You might question the power of that object, and I might also, but who can say for certain? I also have concerns about the motives of this so-called witch-hunter. And number two: I got you into this, over time and circumstance. I will not allow you to continue without my presence. If you go into harm's way— which I predict you shall—I will be there, as my conscience dictates."

"Who's commanding who now?"

"It doesn't matter. I'm telling you that I'm going and I expect you to arrange it."

Matthew opened his mouth to continue the protest, but was there any use? A measure of the old Professor Fell had reappeared, in the strength of his voice, the rigidity of his posture, the sharpness of his gaze, and even now his free hand had curled into a fist.

"Do me this favor," Fell said, though the way he spoke it did sound like a command to one of his criminal cohorts. "You will, won't you?"

"If this is what you really want," Matthew answered, "I will."

"Good. And if I know your abilities, I shall be back in London before autumn fogs the Thames."

"I'm not certain I'm going to lead the group anywhere except chasing wild geese. Santiago promises we'll be given to the care of the Italians even if I don't find Valeriani or the mirror. The woman's going to decide how long we search before calling it quits, and Captain Andrado and four soldiers will be there to enforce it."

"You want to stretch it out, then?" Fell shook his head. "Matthew, she could insist it go on for *months*." He paused before he added, "Are you that fearful of finding either the man or the object?"

"No! Of course not! I just—" Matthew stopped, because again there was no use in protest to the sharp-eyed and sharp-minded listener. "Possibly I am."

"In for a shilling, in for a pound," the professor replied. "And…aren't you the very least bit *curious?*"

"I once read a comedy by Ben Jonson called *Every Man in His Humour*," Matthew said. "In it is a line I have never forgotten: *curiosity killed the cat*. It has also nearly done me in many times, as you well know."

"Ah," said Fell, "but you're simply another form of exocoetidae, just like myself. You might reach for some other purchase, but you know your realm. Isn't that true?"

It didn't take long for Matthew to deliberate the question. "Yes."

"Then let us bask in the next few days here, before we revert to our true natures," said the professor, and he actually set a hand on Matthew's shoulder. What amazed Matthew more was that he allowed it to remain there.

They walked together through the cemetery, under the stars and the luminous moon, while the soft swells rolled into the harbor, the torches flickered in the breeze, most of Alghero slept and in a suite at the Marquesa Lorianna Inn a woman with silvery tresses marked a particular page in the book of demons.

Two

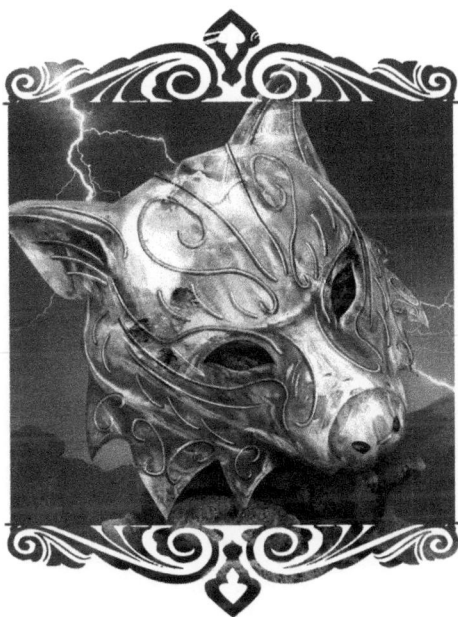

Harm's Way

SIX

"TELL ME," SAID CAMILLA ESPAZIEL.

She was sitting across from Hudson at the galley's table, with the night's finished supper of corn soup, roasted sardines and biscuits between them. Also at the table on the Spanish caravel ship *Estrella del Oeste* were Matthew and Professor Fell, both nursing wooden cups of beer mixed with lime juice.

Camilla's previous question posed to Hudson had been: "What is tormenting you so badly, that you can't even bear to speak it?"

Hudson remained silent, staring at his hands clenched on the tabletop.

The ship—all seventy-five feet long of it, far short of galleon-size for the passengers and crew—was four nights out of Alghero and with a fair wind in the triangular sails making good time around the Italian boot toward the Adriatic Sea. Matthew was relieved that Cardinal Black rarely made an appearance in the galley with the others, taking his meals with the crew. It was bad enough that Matthew, Hudson, the professor, Captain Andrado and his four soldiers had to sleep in the same below-deck quarters with Black, all of them stretched out in hammocks strung up from the beams, but even there Black had moved his hammock away from everyone else and so far toward the bow he might've been sleeping under the figurehead, which was a carving of a woman holding a star aloft.

Governor Santiago had arranged with the master of this ship that Camilla have the single available cabin, which Matthew figured held a nice bunk but otherwise had barely enough room for her to open the large trunk she'd brought aboard. For the rest of them, their clothing had been wrapped in bundles and stuffed into bags of sail canvas. The austere, stone-faced Captain Andrado could be seen striding back and forth on the deck in his uniform as if marching impatiently on an imaginary parade ground, but otherwise he spent most of his time playing games of dice with his soldiers down below. Occasionally could be heard a shout as one or another either lost the prize of the copper coins they were playing for or had rolled a winning number.

Thus it had been, these past four days. The sun rose and set, the moon shone and stars gleamed, the ship's timbers creaked, waves hissed past the hull and sometimes gave a thump like Neptune's adamant fist, scores of seabirds flew round and round in white pirouettes from their nests on Sicily, the *Estrella*'s lean gray-bearded master incessantly smoked a pipe the sweet-scented tobacco of which smelled to Matthew like a woman's perfume, which made him constantly think of Berry—the warm aromas of her hair and her body—and kept him in constant mental turmoil. The master and no one of the ship's crew spoke a lick of English and neither did Andrado nor any of his soldiers, but Andrado did speak Italian and Camilla had revealed that not only did she have a solid grasp of English but she was also well-versed in Italian and Portuguese, with a smattering of French.

Quite a creature, that one was.

And now she had set the green eyes that smoldered like embers in a spectral fire upon Hudson Greathouse.

Hudson felt that. This woman was trying to pry the head off him and get into his mind. He thought maybe she already had, because there was something compelling about her that honestly gave him—dare he even admit this to himself—the shivers all the way down to his knees, bony as they were. Witch-hunter or witch? Had she already put a spell on him, for it seemed to him that even the most pious witch-hunter had to understand something about witchery, and he had the sensation that this dame was as far from piety as midnight from noon ten years hence. Yes, a spell was already on him, he reasoned. Why else had he the desire to shave and clean himself up from the first minute she'd approached him in the prison? Why had he at least tried to work harder with the exercise of swinging wasters with Matthew, though the idea of holding a real sword made him sick to the stomach? Why indeed had his appetite returned, so much so that he was eating double anyone else on this cruise and driving the galley cook to mutterings of likely Spanish profanity?

Why?

And now this woman was waiting for him to speak, and it was apparent from her demeanor that she was not going to let him get up from this table without hearing what lay as heavy as ten-ton anvils on his soul, and the damnable thing was that Hudson could look across the table into those piercing green eyes and *want* to reveal his soul, and it was as if no one was in this galley but her and himself, the images of Matthew and Fell being only ghostly specters that hung like gray mist in the air.

"Who are you?" he asked, and heard his voice as if in a hall of echoes.

"I'm the person who's going to hear your story," she answered.

And Hudson knew it was the truth.

"That island," he began, as he felt the foundations of his resistance collapse. "Golgotha. Matthew told you about it." This was a certainty, since Matthew had told Hudson that Camilla wanted to know how they'd reached Sardinia and why, and she'd gotten much of the information from Santiago. "It changed some peoples' memories and distorted others. Erased some, even. For me…it did the same, but…it made me remember a night I have tried to forget for thirty-one years. It brought that memory back in every detail. I could see it all just as it happened, and it made me remember that I am a lie."

No one spoke. Were Matthew and the professor still in the galley, even as wraiths? Hudson didn't know, for his focus was split between his mind's eye and the face of the woman across the table, illuminated by the compartment's two oil lamps that rolled on gimbals with the motion of the ship.

"A lie," Hudson repeated. "I present myself—*think* of myself—as the noble warrior…the dutiful soldier…the honorable cavalier…but fair to the code of war…to the horrors of violence. I have killed, but I never lifted a weapon to anyone who wasn't trying to kill me first. Oh…you see, that's the lie. And there in the swamp knowing I would have to kill my friend…it all came back to me…and now it never lets me rest."

Did he expect her to speak? Again, he didn't know. Was he in a hole? A cave? A tunnel? There was nothing else in the world but the two of them at this table and even the double lamps seemed to have been lowered to fitful sparks.

"I am a lie because for thirty-one years," Hudson went on, "I have presented myself as this man I am not. I am in fact…a murderer of the worst kind, and that island…that island tore open the lie and brought the truth home…what I had done and what I had *caused* to be done, eagerly and of my own free will."

"What was it?" Was that Matthew's voice? But Hudson saw Camilla look to one side and put a finger to her lips, and then she returned her gaze to him and waited in silence, her expression betraying no hint of emotion… repugnance or otherwise.

Hudson hesitated. Why was he telling all this to a stranger when he could not even bear to tell Matthew? But still it seemed that the woman was urging him to speak, was open to hearing him and from her there would be no judgements made because he had already judged himself guilty. To go on, or not? The moment hung and twisted, and then Hudson said, "I was a young mercenary. The Dutch War, 1673. Fighting on the French and Swedish side, against the Dutch. My friends and I...all mercenaries...were separated from our unit after a battle. We were lost in a land of woods and swamps. Lost...with the enemy all around. We dared not rest or light a fire, because we'd seen what the Dutch did to mercenaries. Sometimes they were shot on the spot...sometimes cut to pieces by a dozen men with sabers...a slow game of it...sometimes roped to the muzzles of cannons and blown to pieces. We kept going, with all that horror around us...the woods dark... cold...trees burned to stubs and corpses lying where they'd died. The animals tearing at them." Hudson's eyes were dark and heavy-lidded. "Once," he said, "I stepped on something in the mud that...well...I knew what it was. Part of a man's brain. That was a common thing, after the cannonfire. To find arms and legs...heads...the guts hanging from branches twenty feet high." He suddenly caught himself, blinked and said to Camilla, "Oh. I'm sorry. It's just...that's how it was. How it *is*."

"It's all right," she answered, the picture of peace. "Go on."

A long silence passed before Hudson found the power to continue. "We had been through a battle that raged a day and a night. So many killed... our comrades. But I know...so many killed on the other side too. We had no commander...no map, but we knew there were other stragglers out there so we set out to find them. We went on and on...and then we found we were so far behind the Dutch lines we came across a gunpowder storehouse and..." Here he hesitated again, a muscle in his jaw working. "An orange tent," he said. "A hospital tent, full of the wounded and the dying. We got in there. Looking for fresh water...food...medicine for Philippe Battencourt's infected leg. Two doctors were inside who both went for their swords. A few of the patients rose up. Others tried. And I heard someone shout in a strangled voice...a noise like those animals out in the woods tearing at the corpses. The shout was *'Kill them all'*. For an instant...I thought it had been Brom who shouted it, but it was not. No. It was not. The island made me remember. Out in that swamp, going to kill my friend...I remembered it was me. And we killed those doctors and we killed the patients who tried to fight, and then the blood in us—in me—was insane with the killing...the spilling out of rage, of hate...and we turned our swords on those who lay on the cots. Boys younger than I was...old men broken by their wounds... and I remember...how some of them could not move their shattered arms and legs but we kept slashing. How some of them just lay there watching us kill the others and knowing they were next. Watching in silence...waiting for death. And we gave it to them, with cut throats and stomachs gashed open. Oh yes, we gave it to them because I shouted out *kill them all*. And afterward when the blood ran across the ground and the air was thick with it we ate the food we found there, drank the water and then we blew up the gunpowder."

He showed Camilla a sick smile, his eyes like hollowed-out holes. "That was not war. It was murder. I killed four defenseless men. One a boy, really...seventeen if that. And a man whose face was wrapped with so much bloody gauze that he likely never knew what was happening until my blade went in. When none of them were moving I went back and slashed the dead bodies again because in that moment I was nothing but a ravening animal myself...tearing at corpses. And *that* is why all my posturing as a noble warrior...a dutiful soldier...an honorable cavalier...is a lie." The sick smile slid away, leaving a totally blank expression that Matthew found terrifying. "In the civilian world," Hudson said to Camilla, "I would have been hanged four times. In the world of the mercenary, we just clenched our teeth and told ourselves we had done what was needed. Another lie." He turned his head as if with a labored effort to look upon Matthew. "We can play with those wasters all you please, but remembering what I have kept locked away...I can't ever hold a real sword again. So...of what use am I in this world anymore?"

Matthew had to force himself to reply. "Your usefulness in this world is not dependent on your ability with a sword."

"Ah," said the once-Great One. "Now who's lying?"

When Matthew didn't—or couldn't—answer, Hudson took the final biscuit from its platter, used it to mop up the last of his soup, ate it in two bites and then stood up. "Time for the hammock, I suppose," he said quietly. He gave Camilla a quick glance and then away again. "Goodnight," he offered, and then he left the galley.

After a minute more during which no one spoke and Matthew looked at neither the woman nor Professor Fell, the problem-solver who found this problem of Hudson's history unsolvable got up from his chair, wished them both a good night, left the galley and went along the passage to the aft ladder, which he climbed up and through the little double doors at the top and onto the deck.

It was a warm night with a gentle breeze filling the sails. A lamp hung back further aft by the first mate at the wheel and two burned up at the crow's nest, one with a red lens to mark the port side and another with a green lens to mark the starboard. Until one reached the bow and the lantern that burned there, the deck was dark, yet the moon was out and though past full and waning still afforded adequate illumination so Matthew did not trip on a coil of rope and break his neck as he moved forward. In truth, his head was spinning as if he'd had many cups of wine too many. He realized he could've told the others he was coming up here for "a breath of air"—a lame statement—but the reality is he simply needed to find a quiet place to sort out his thoughts away from Hudson and everyone else.

He continued forward almost to the bow and then turned toward the portside railing, which he clenched so hard either the strong Spanish oak or his fingers might break.

The ship moved gracefully across the sea, the waves parting obediently and at least for tonight not throwing up angry plumes of salt spray or hammering the hull. Matthew saw the lamps of two more vessels off to the north, one travelling west and the other east. Out across the water at not too far a distance was the bootheel of Italy, all dark at the moment... yet not quite, for another mark that civilization was being approached was a reddish light that Matthew figured must be the fire at the high point of a lighthouse, guiding the ships around shoals or whatnot. Venice was getting nearer hour by hour and mile by mile, and then would come the test of whether his curiosity would win out or he would lead this group in circles. One unfortunate knot in that intellectual rope: he understood that the master of the *Estrella* had been instructed by Santiago to heed Camilla's orders determining how long the ship was to be at harbor, and to prepare for at least one month in Venice.

One month. At least.

"Damn," he said.

"If swearing ever solved problems," said the woman who had come quietly across the deck behind him, "no one would ever need your services, would they?"

Matthew had nearly jumped out of his boots, stockings and undergarments but maybe it was his hard grip on the railing that saved his dignity, because he kept his face toward the sea and the land of Roman emperors beyond.

"Your friend will survive," Camilla said to Matthew's silence.

"I never thought he wouldn't."

"Yes you did. Every time you looked at him you thought he'd died a little more. But I think releasing all that helped him a great deal. Oh, it's going to take time for him to return to what I understand he was before, but you see he's eating better."

"He was doing that before tonight."

"I noticed. Also that he is interested in keeping himself shaved and clean. I wonder what caused those changes?"

You did, Matthew thought but he chose to keep his mouth closed.

"Now tell me," Camilla said, "what your plan is when we reach Venice." To Matthew's continued stony countenance, Camilla leaned against the railing and stared out toward the distant land alongside him. Then she said, "If you're considering leading us all in circles that go nowhere, I would say

that it's not in your best interest. Or Hudson's either. You're a highly intelligent young man and you must realize that the sooner we bring this search
to a conclusion, the sooner you both can get home. And I understand you
have a very specific and pressing reason to want to get back to your New
York as soon as possible, is that not true?"

There was no use in denying the obvious point. "True."

"So. What is your plan? And I believe now might be a proper time to
tell me why we are in particular going to Venice."

She was right, Matthew decided. The search had to be carried out in a
professional manner, because he *was* a professional, because the sooner he
got himself and Hudson back to New York the better...and also because,
as crazy as this was, he did have a mounting sense of curiosity about the
mirror. He said, "The owner of the first tavern I walk into might tell us what
we need to know."

"How is that?"

"I believe that Brazio Valeriani either works at a vineyard or owns one.
I believe also that this vineyard produces Amarone, the grape of which is
only grown in the area of Venice. Why I believe this is a long story I won't
go into but you'll have to trust me." Camilla made no comment on the
statement, so Matthew went on. "The owner of a tavern might tell us where
those particular vineyards are, since his business is dependent on the product. Valeriani might have kept his birth name or changed it for the reason
of putting distance between himself, his father and Ciro's creation. But it's
a start, do you agree?"

"Certainly."

"Now you tell me something." Matthew turned to face her. "How do
you get away with calling yourself a witch-hunter when you and I both
know there are no such things as witches? I had an experience a few years
ago with a woman who was suspected of witchcraft. It turned out she was
being blamed for murder by simply evil men. There were no devils involved
but the human kind, and I suspect that anyone who presents himself or herself as a warlock or witch is not sane enough to grasp reality. Like Cardinal
Black, for one. He may believe he has a demonic friend no one else can see
who guides him, but I can tell you that *his* hands do the dirty work."

Camilla met with a faint smile what Matthew considered daunting ac-
cusations of fraud and cruelty to the mentally infirm. "Of *course* the human
hands do what you call the dirty work," she said. "That's the whole point
of it. The continual fight from the beginning of time has been good against
evil. The saints, the bishops and the holy men do their labors—yet sometimes they are seduced by forces that take advantage of chinks in their armor—and on the other side is...well, you've gone through *The Lesser Key*."

"Which is some madman's fantasy of Hell."

"It might be," she agreed, which further surprised and intrigued Matthew. "Do you know much about the book?"

"Enough to consider it beyond belief."

"Many *have* believed in it, over the generations. It's not exactly on everyone's bookshelf, but not as rare as you might think. My father had a copy. No one knows when the book was written—or let me correct that to say when the *information* was collected—or by whom."

"Not by Solomon?"

"Some scholars believe it was many hundreds of years old before the time of Solomon, and it was known by many names. Solomon's name is in the title currently because of his dealings with the demon Ornias."

"You're joking!"

"You haven't read the Testament of Solomon?" She arched an eyebrow. "In it Solomon recounts receiving a ring from the angel Michael in order to bind demons to his bidding, and the first he binds is Ornias. You should read that tome, it goes into much detail on the denizens of the underworld and Solomon's experiences with them."

"And you believe that?"

Camilla's smile became a bit broader. "Matthew—if I may call you that?—why is it that people put faith in the story of a man who performs miracles, walks on water, had his own temptations from Satan and was raised from the dead, but turn a blind eye and ear to the subject of darker powers that the Holy Bible spells out quite clearly? Is it that people believe what they wish to believe, no matter that all this information is in the *same* book?"

"I don't know about that," Matthew answered, feeling more than a little uneasy about this conversation. "But I do suspect this kind of talk would bring a witch-hunter after *you*." He frowned at her continued bemused expression. "How many witches have you caught? Did you have to spell up your own broomstick to chase them down?"

"Three," Camilla said. "No broomstick needed. I will tell you that before I answered this summoning, I had been a teacher of languages at the University of Barcelona. When the war began, it turned Spaniard against Spaniard and has affected all walks of life, thus the loss of my position."

"*Summoning?*" Matthew asked, putting a note of irony in his voice. "Don't you mean to use the word 'calling'?"

"I spoke it as it is."

Matthew recalled her saying *I hunt witches and I destroy them however I can, as my father did and his father before him.* It was a family's "summoning" then, he thought. A disturbance in the mind and the blood, is what he considered it to be.

But there was something else too, underneath all this. He remembered Santiago speaking somewhat curtly to her: *Yes, we understand the work of your father's life,* señorita *Espaziel, and thank you for that statement.* It had caused that cloud to pass across her face. Why?

"Speaking of languages," Camilla said, breaking Matthew's process of thought, "I haven't asked before, but do you speak or understand Italian? It would be helpful."

"I know Latin and I can speak and understand some Italian if I can relate what's being said to that. As far as being proficient, I am not, especially to anyone speaking the language at conversational speed. I'll leave the translating to you." At this, she nodded assent.

Matthew was ready for the hammock. He saw that the two ships he'd been watching were nearly out of sight. Six more days and the *Estrella* would be towed into the harbor at Venice by the pilot longboats. Then… yes, Camilla was right; there was no need to waste time on an errant and misguided search. He would do his job.

"I appreciate your philosophies," he told her, "but I've had enough for tonight. As for the demons in the testament of Solomon, I would think that entire tale is an allegory to represent Solomon's power during that time."

"An allegory," she repeated. "Then you think, of course, of the entire Holy Book as a compendium of allegories."

"I didn't say that."

"Picking and choosing, Matthew. Truth here, allegory there? Who can say which is which?"

"I suppose only Solomon can say. And he's quite dead, isn't he? Good night, and thank you again for the—" He paused, summoning up his own wisest statement which came out as: "dagger to the brain."

"Better a dagger to the brain," Camilla retorted as Matthew started to walk away, "than a claw to the face. If that mirror is what it's purported to be, it's a literal opening up of Hell…and I don't speak in allegories."

Where was Solomon when you needed him? Matthew mused. He continued along the deck to the aft ladder, thinking that Hudson was already locked into his own version of Hell, Cardinal Black was playing at having a Hellish "friend", Professor Fell had reentered the world of Hell his actions had created, Camilla Espaziel and the Spanish power she worked for had too much Hell on their minds, and as for himself it was Hell being away from Berry for so long. And no end yet in sight.

He was going to change that as soon as they reached Venice. But if at the end of a month and a determined search no Brazio Valeriani and a supposedly enchanted mirror could be found, to hell with it.

SEVEN

IN THE MORNING SUNLIGHT, UNDER AN AZURE SKY, MATTHEW'S FIRST glimpse of Venice was as of a golden cloud shimmering on the aquamarine sea. As the *Estrella* drew nearer to the harbor's entrance past the breakwater, Matthew was aware of the immensity of the city. As large as London? It seemed so, with all the buildings and the towers of cathedrals and other edifices, but whereas London in his memory was colored in slate and charcoal grays, Venice was indeed a city of vibrant orange, lemon-yellow, russet-red and gold. He was joined at the bow by Hudson and Professor Fell, who both seemed to be getting along amazingly well since their histories had been so wretchedly wracked though they kept their silence around each other. A glance back along the deck showed Cardinal Black observing the approach, and beyond him Camilla, Captain Andrado and the soldiers. In another few minutes, with the favorable breeze pushing the ship along, they were suddenly part of the city's maritime traffic: a veritable fleet of scows, cutters, gondolas, private and ostentatiously decorated yachts, lumbering cargo schooners and perhaps every other manner of water vessel under the Italian sun coming and going or back and forth at what sometimes appeared dangerously close spaces. What seemed to be a confusion of navigation was simply the order of life in such a marine-dependent city as this, which Matthew understood had been built on a series of islands in a swamp so as to protect the early farming settlers from barbarian raids. All in all, it was quite an astonishing sight.

In accordance with what was evidently Venetian rule, the *Estrella*'s captain had the anchor dropped well before the harbor proper and at the same time ordered a green flag hoisted up to the mainmast's top as a signal to the harbor master that the ship was ready for inspection and—if that was positively resolved—the pilot longboats to row them the rest of the way in. It took another hour or so for the official boat to sail up to them from its berth, during which Matthew on the sun-splashed deck luxuriated in the sight of so much activity, also thinking that Berry would have enjoyed this vista as well.

In time the ship was given its passage, the longboats arrived, and the *Estrella* was eased into a harbor slip, followed by the anchor going down again and the usual throwing of many ropes to secure the vessel. By the time the gangplank was dropped afternoon had arrived, and thus next the crew was tasked to bring off baggage and various crates of goods that had been brought along for the city's merchants, these to be loaded onto wagons ready for such transport. Then had to be found shore accommodations for those setting foot on Venetian paving stones, and for this job Matthew, Camilla and Captain Andrado went off in search of an inn that could lodge for a night or two everyone who chose not to remain on the ship, which in fact was all but the *Estrella*'s master and his men though the crew did understandably go off in search of their own misadventures.

"One moment," Matthew said to Camilla as they and Andrado walked along a narrow street approaching a bridge that arched over one of the canals. He had seen off to his right a sign that read LA TAVERNA IMPERIALE. No translation was needed for what this place was. "We should start here," he suggested, and they entered what might have been any tavern in New York except that it was a hundred percent more clean, airy and brightly painted in yellows and blues within.

"Ask the bartender if they serve Amarone," he told Camilla, who approached the elder gentleman behind the countertop. The man gave Andrado a sharp, hard glare due to the fact that the captain wore his Spanish army uniform with its sash and medals but had replaced his silver helmet with a dark blue beretlike cap. After a short conversation in Italian, Camilla reported, "He says they normally do but it's difficult to get now because the vineyards that produce it have been affected by the fighting just north of here."

"All right," said Matthew. "Now please ask if he knows the name of Brazio Valeriani."

This query brought a shake of the bartender's head.

"Ask him then if he can tell us the names of these vineyards and where they are."

The conversation went on a little longer this time. At the end of it, Camilla turned her luminous eyes upon Matthew. "He says he has no contact with the vineyards and neither do most of the tavern owners. All the wine served comes in barrels bought from merchants who specialize in the product. He says his wine is bought from the most powerful and respected merchant in Venice, whose name is Ottavio Meneghetti." She cocked an eyebrow. "I think e's doing a bit of bragging."

"Ask him when this man can be found."

The question was delivered and the answer was, "He has an office in the *sestiere*—neighborhood—of Dorsoduro, on the Calle Forno two miles or so from here across the Vidal bridge."

Matthew nodded. "Thank him, give him some money for the information and then ask where the nearest inn might be."

The *Palazzo dell'Amicizia* stood two streets past the tavern, on the edge of one of the canals. It was a layer cake of a white three-story structure with intricate multicolored mosaic designs etched below the red tile roof. At the clerk's desk in a lobby area that Matthew thought outdid the Dock House Inn by quite a few overstuffed dark red chairs, cowhide sofas and hanging chandelier lamps, Camila carried on a lengthy negotiation with the white-suited, five-foot-four inp of a manager that ended with five rooms granted and the exchange of a sum of money from the purse of Viceroy de Castro's treasury. Before they returned to the ship, it had to be worked out among Matthew, Camilla and Andrado who was in rooms with whom, the difficulty being that Cardinal Black was no one's idea of a congenial roommate. Thus the final agreement which would be presented to the group on their return: two soldiers and Black in one room, Andrado and two soldiers in another right next door, Matthew and Hudson together, and Camilla and Professor Fell in single rooms simply because it made sense that way.

Twilight had arrived before all was in order at the Palace of Friendship, all the baggage sorted and meals taken at the nearest tavern, which was the same that had first been approached. Andrado and his soldiers drank more wine than they consumed food, Hudson ate beef brisket like a starved bear, the professor and Matthew tried some kind of deep-dish bready thing that was smothered in tomatoes and spicy circles of meat, Camilla kept to a bowl of chicken soup and Black sat as far away from everyone else as he could while wrapped up in his ebony cloak and chewing a porkchop down to the bone. Matthew had to wonder if the creature imagined Dominus sitting with him at his table, for it seemed that only a phantom of the mind could entertain that fiend as a companion. The tavern filled up with locals, there was more wine, women and song with the addition of a wandering violinist, a couple of Andrado's soldiers started spoiling for a fight with some Venetian roughs who looked as if they were eager to break Spanish heads, and it was time for Matthew and Camilla to herd everyone back to the inn without anyone being hospitalized or behind bars for the night.

Dawn came without further incident and in the bright sunlight of morning Matthew left Hudson sleeping in their quarters and he, Camilla and Andrado were again moving through the streets on their way to the office of Ottavio Meneghetti, directions to the Dorsodro neighborhood and Calle Forno having been supplied by the inn's clerk.

On the way, Matthew found Venice a fascinating city not only because of the ornate and quite beautiful architecture but also because the place was simply a beehive of activity. Shops of all varieties stood along the streets, taverns seemed to be on every corner, workmen were up on scaffoldings either repairing old buildings or painting newer ones in vivid hues of yellows and reds, carts aplenty stacked with crates and barrels were being pushed hither and yon, dandies and damsels in their finery and high wigs were on parades of wealthy display even though the day was hardly begun, dancers twirled and leaped above tricorn hats upturned to catch a passerby's change, street musicians with violins, trumpets, drums and cymbals put up both appealing and raucous noise, dogs ran yapping around as happily as any Venetian could be, and the occasional washtub of water was overturned from a window or balcony above and came splashing down upon this carnival of rich, poor, musical and canine. Andrado barely missed having an unwanted bath but for Matthew spotting an old woman heaving the bucket out her window a few footsteps ahead and pulling the captain to dry safety, in thanks getting only the same stone-faced expression the man always wore.

Another thing Matthew found of interest about this city was the difference in aromas between Venice and New York. Whereas New York's smells were of newly cut wood, marine odors and unfortunately the nose-wrinkling rank of a multitude of horse figs, Venice was the myriad perfumes both woman and men seemed to be wearing, plus the aromas of spices and flowers being sold by vendors on the streets. All that was well and good until one got a whiff from a canal, and then…bring on the horse figs!

If their inn's building was a layer cake, the two-story white stone structure that had a brass plaque by the door reading simply MENEGHETTI E ASSOCIATI was a wedding cake, with its intricately etched ornamentation around windows shaded by sea-green awnings and below the roof, and there at the four corners of the peaked roof stood statues of women that appearing to be pouring out from upturned vases wine for a thirsty city.

Before they entered the building, Andrado made some comment to Camilla, who translated it to Matthew as, "The captain says this man must be as rich as the governor."

Within the cool marble-floored lobby there were beautiful hanging paintings on either side, most of them showing artists' depiction of vineyards. A young and very attractive woman sat at a desk before them, and as they reached her she looked up from some writing she was doing with her quill pen, her expression as cool as the lobby and perhaps also as hard as the marble when she regarded the Spanish captain.

"We'd like to see *senore* Meneghetti," said Camilla in Italian, and when the young woman answered in a quiet but firm voice Camilla said to Matthew, "I am told he sees no one without an appointment."

"Tell her it's very important we speak to—"

"*English?*" the woman interrupted. Her face had instantly softened and her eyes taken on a shine.

"English, yes," Matthew said.

The woman nodded and spoke again to Camilla before she stood up from her chair and went through a door behind the desk. Camilla said, "She says she'll see what she can do though *senore* Meneghetti is very busy today. She says it's rare to have an Englishman here and the *senore* might wish to see you."

"Well bully for England," said Matthew. "Hopefully that'll get us somewhere."

It was a few minutes before the door opened and the young woman motioned for them to follow. They went up a flight of stairs in a passageway lined with hundreds of multicolored glazed clay tiles, again emphasizing the wealth of this wine merchant. At the top of the stairs there was another door leading into a red-carpeted hallway with other doors, the one at the far end marked with a second brass plaque of O. MENEGHETTI. The woman knocked at it, a man's voice from within said *"Avanti,"* and their escort opened the door to a large, white-walled office with a balcony to the right overlooking the street below and the nearest canal under the Vidal bridge. Facing the door across a rich red and gold Oriental carpet was a huge oak desk, its occupant seated behind it and in front of a well-stocked bookcase. He stood up as the visitors entered. *"Avanti, avanti,"* he said, waving them in with a smile on a genial suntanned face, though Matthew noted that his smile did cool a few degrees when his bright blue eyes grazed past Captain Andrado. He appeared to be in his early fifties, his hair dark brown, curly and allowed to grow down around his shoulders. He had a waxed mustache and a slip of a goatee centered on the rather large chin, and he was wearing a light brown suit with brass buttons down the jacket's front, a white shirt and a brown patterned cravat adorned with a gold stickpin.

Meneghetti spoke to the office girl, who left the room and closed the door behind her. Then, to Matthew, "An English! I speak English! Little bit!" He held up two fingers nearly pinched together, his smile incandescent.

"I'm Matthew Corbett, this is *señorita* Camilla Espaziel, and—"

"I do not wish to know the name of a creature of war," the man interrupted, though his smile had not faltered. "For the likes of him, my business pains." He motioned toward two black leather chairs. "Please, please, care to sit! You and the lady beautiful, the creature can stand."

"We won't take up much of your time," said Matthew.

"Oh, time is of nothing! Sit, sit!"

Matthew and Camilla took the chairs. With an indignant snort, Andrado stalked out onto the balcony and the wine merchant settled himself into a high-backed black leather chair that had carved ram's heads on the ends of the armrests. Before him the desktop held a small stack of papers topped by a small brass monkey paperweight, a polished gold-toned inkwell and a stand of three quills. Beside the desk stood a little table supporting six decanters with different shades of red and white wines and four crystal glasses. Meneghetti noted Matthew's glance at the decanters. "You would care to try the wares?"

"No, thank you, it's early in the day yet."

"Too early for *vino*? Cat grab the tongue!" He looked from Matthew to Camilla and back again. "Well! The last time I am dealing with English, it was…oh…seven years ago. I am remembering I sold much Chianti and Valpolicello to that gentleman, I am sure to be served in the best taverns of your London. What interests you today?" He clapped his hands together in expectation of a very rewarding deal.

"Um…we're not buying wine," Matthew said, and saw the man's eyes form the slightest sheen of ice though the smile remained. "We're wanting—*needing*—some information."

Meneghetti remained silent.

"I—we—understand that you buy Amarone from the vineyards to the north," Matthew continued. "Do you know the name Brazio Valeriani?"

The merchant frowned. "Who is this name?"

Camilla spoke up. "*Senore*, we're looking for a man who may either work on a vineyard producing Amarone, or actually be the owner of one. We take it that the Amarone grape is grown most successfully and most plentifully in the district north of Venice."

"The Veneto *region*," Meneghetti corrected with emphasis. "Which is very large. You are speaking then of the Verona province, which you are now standing in. Also where the creatures of war from your country, lady beautiful, are at labor destroying each other and my business." He swept out a disdainful hand. "What do I know of this name?"

"We were hoping you did know it," Matthew said.

Meneghetti stared at Matthew for a few long seconds, his blue eyes in the tanned face now frosty and careful. "You wish to do business behind my back? Why do you seek this man? As the contracted agent of all those vineyards and their owners, I have the right to hear it."

"It's a private matter, but not anything to do with the wine business."

"You *say*." The man offered a smile that this time was a shade mocking. "A young English, a Spanish lady, and a creature of war coming in here asking a name. What am I to be thinking?"

"That it's important we find him," Matthew answered, "and that's all we can tell you. Still…" He hesitated, wondering if he should play this particular card. "Still, we can offer you a reward if you—"

"Stop foolish talking!" Meneghetti's voice was a hard slab of granite crashing down upon yielding earth. "I am not a shopboy to be thrown a coin or two!"

"I meant no disrespect," Matthew amended. "It's just…well, considering that you are—we understand—the most preeminent and knowledgeable expert on wines in this city, that—"

"Cease the flower talk," came the riposte. But Matthew thought that this small thrust of flattery might have done some good, because Meneghetti drummed his fingers on the desktop and then said, "I don't know of this name, and that is all. However…yes, I am the best knowing of the wines and the vineyards, it is of truth." He opened the top drawer of his desk and produced from it a clean sheet of paper. One of the quill's tips was dipped into the inkpot. "This name is spelling how?"

Camilla offered the spelling and Meneghetti wrote it down.

"I will ask my sources. You are staying where?" Camilla told him and he wrote this down as well. "That inn is very nice. You *do* have money, it seems."

Before the man's mood might turn darker again, Matthew said, "Another thing, if you please. How many vineyards are in that province producing Amarone?"

"Six. Some many miles from here. As I have lately heard, two have been destroyed by the tramplings of soldiers. Dutch and French fighting each other, as I hear."

"Would it trouble you too much to give us directions to those vineyards?"

"*Si,*" was the quick reply. But then he frowned, drew circles on the paper as if using them to come to some decision, and when he regarded Matthew once more his smile had returned though somewhat less of Venice's strong sunlight. "I believe you when you say you are not trying to rob me. You look…how would you say?…the sincerity? You have come a great distance to find this name, whatever it means to you. I will give you this. I will have the office girl bring to your inn tomorrow a map to show your way. Is that an agree?"

"Yes, that would be fine and much appreciated."

Meneghetti stood up, and so did Matthew and Camilla because it seemed this meeting was at an end. "Never let it be said that Ottavio Meneghetti is an unreasonable man," said the merchant. "And for the

English, I do this. *Senore* Corbett, is it? You tell them back in London how fair you are treated here, and maybe you say at the taverns how much you like the Italian *vino?*"

"I'd be glad to, and thank you again for your help."

"Ah, *il mio piacere di essere d'aiuto!* Good day to you!"

The wine merchant returned to his chair and his visitors departed.

After ten minutes—time enough for the three to be out of the building and gone—Meneghetti stood up once more and looked at the paper in his hand with the written name. He reached for his quill and added the names of the young man and woman as he remembered them: Matthew Corbett and Camilla something Spanish, then he went to a wall peg, retrieved his cream-colored peaked hat, adorned with a hawk's feather, where it hung and put it on, cocked just so. He left his office, descended the staircase and in the lobby said to the young woman at the desk, "I will be out for the rest of the day." His voice was tight. "Send any more visitors up to Bernardi."

She nodded and asked softly, "Will I see you tonight?"

"If I can get away." He folded the paper and put it into a coat pocket while regarding with hooded eyes the supplicant before him. This one was becoming tiresome. Without another word he turned his back on her hopeful expression and left the building, walking briskly to the north in his very expensive knee-high crocodile-hide boots shipped from Egypt. He brushed through the busy streets as quickly as possible without raising a sweat, because he hated to sweat and it was a very warm day. Crossing the Vidal bridge, he continued in a northeasterly direction and over the della Verona canal at the Calle del Cristo, past numerous flower stalls and tailoring shops. He worried that he'd been too fast to offer the map, but he had to get them out of the office. Would that be noticed or remarked upon? The woman with the piercing green eyes had given him *i fantasmi*—the spooks—and she seemed to be staring right into his soul. Still, that couldn't hinder his progress though he was a careful man and such things bothered him like a thorn in a bedsheet.

In time he reached a small but elaborately fronted shop with windows displaying various equally elaborate gowns in pink, violet, white and pale green. At the bottom of one window was painted in dignified white lettering SIGNORA BONACORSO.

Of course when he went in he saw she was in the showroom section of her shop speaking quietly to one of her high-wigged society hags, their heads close together and the hag's tongue wagging. When the little silver bell over the door announced Meneghetti's presence the Lady Bonacorso immediately put a finger to her ruby-painted lips, as if the secrets and intrigues she had expertly cultivated from this particular client were never to be revealed in one hundred lifetimes yet if they were important enough for blackmail or some other form of pressure they would be on their way within the hour to a higher ear. It was her specialty.

"Good morning, sir!" said the lady, as if she'd never before seen Meneghetti. "A gift for your wife, I presume?" And for the benefit of her client she swept a lace-gloved hand toward the display of women's hats decorated with rhinestones, feathers, gold and silver threading and other ostentatious materials.

"Only the best for her," Meneghetti replied, and he gave the departing hag a brief bow before she left the shop. When the little bell's ring had silenced, he took the paper from within his coat, unfolded it and handed it to the lady. "Do you recognize this name?"

She produced from her Vesuvian bosom a pair of small round spectacles, put them on and perused the paper. The Lady Bonacorso was in her late fifties, quite elegantly slim, and attractive in a way that only a miracle of makeup, bosom lift and bustle could create. Her extravagant and voluminous gown was a pale peach color with pearls stitched at the cuffs and the throat. A cloud of white lace wrapped several times around her neck was the same hue as the hair that was brushed upward toward the heavens and secured with pearl-studded clasps.

Her sharp-nosed face lifted toward the visitor and the spectacles came off before she spoke. "This is the name of the man Master Trazini was tasked to find."

"Exactly. After more than three months he found nothing, and today... well, there it is. Not an hour ago I was visited by a young Englishman—a boy, really—a Spanish woman and a Spanish soldier wanting to know if I knew this man."

"Why should you?"

"According to the woman, they think Valeriani's son has something to do with a vineyard growing the Amarone grape. I told them I had no idea who they were talking about, but they wanted directions to those six particular vineyards to look for themselves."

"You gave directions to them?"

"I said I'd have the office girl take them a map tomorrow. They're staying at the Palace of Friendship."

"Hm," said the lady. She put the spectacles back on to reread the paper and the two additional names. "Matthew Corbett and Camilla with a Spanish name? There was a soldier?"

"I saw no need for his name." Meneghetti took a deep mental breath before he added, "I should see the Scaramangas. Will you give me permission?"

The Lady Bonacorso deliberated that request before she returned the paper to Meneghetti's outstretched hand. She motioned for him to follow through a curtain at the back, along a short corridor and to her neatly arranged office. There she opened a desk drawer, took from it a small red box and then from the box an old antique key painted black. She held it before him. "You have my permission, but be careful with them. You'll be searched at the gate, so carry no weapon. And I know you so I say do not ask for a reward. If one is offered, fine, but let them consider the situation."

He took the key and put both it and the paper back into a pocket. "Agreed," he said.

Retracing his path back to his own building, Meneghetti kept striding past it and to his carriage house a street beyond where he kept his coach and the coachman on duty. Within a short time the team was readied and the coach trundled out, headed through the narrow, rather torturous streets and across the many bridges toward the Santa Croce district and the ferry pier. The fee was paid, the coach rolled across the ramp onto the next ferry barge sailing to the mainland, and Meneghetti sat back to await the destination.

His mind went to the scene that night when justice had been done to the traitor Antonio Nuncia, and the Scaramangas had ordered Trazini to find Brazio Valeriani in connection with this strange mirror that had caught their interest. Unfortunately Trazini was no longer among the living due to his failure to uncover after three months any trace of this man; it was unknown what had happened to him since he'd simply disappeared one night from his villa, but it was common knowledge that likely a wolf had slipped into the house or been waiting patiently for the moment to strike. No one but the Scaramangas knew the executioner's identity, which meant it could be anyone in the universe the Family of the Scorpion commanded…even the coachman now sitting up atop the vehicle. But no, that man wasn't big enough and whoever Lupo was, he was quite a formidable beast.

The Family of the Scorpion! In Meneghetti's opinion the organization had been named by an overdramatic idiot but since the title had come from the Scaramanga bloodline, to challenge it after all these years meant a visit from Lupo. The story was that the original Scaramanga was a petty thief who'd been stung by a scorpion while burying a bag of stolen silverware and lay in a state of fever and anguish for three days, during which his hallucinations had shown him a plan to waylay a heavily guarded wagon carrying a shipment of gold from Venice to the city government of Padua. With a rag-tag band of recruited thieves who must've been insane or desperate—likely both—the audacious and imaginative attack using a counterfeit road sign to an area of mud that had locked up the wagon's wheels had been successful and the gold seized with only a few deaths to pay the bill. Meneghetti understood that the old strongbox was now an altar of sorts in the palatial villa he was on the way to visit, for with the opening of that the Family of the Scorpion—*ghastly!* he thought, but actually well-named—had begun its first chapter.

There came the thump of the ferry mooring to the pier across the bay at the harbor of Mestre. The ramp was lowered, the coach and the ferry's other passengers departed, and Meneghetti sat rehearsing in his mind what he was going to say as the coach's team trotted through Mestre's old Roman-designed streets and then in a westerly direction toward the town of Mirano some ten miles distant.

Two miles past the last villas and rolling green hills of Mirano, the coach turned off on a road to the south. A few minutes afterward, the coach stopped at a black wrought-iron gate that guarded an estate surrounded by an eight-foot-high wall of rough stones topped with broken glass. There was indeed a stone guardhouse on the other side of the gate, and as Meneghetti approached it two men on duty came out, one with his hand resting on his holstered flintlock and the second with his pistol already cocked and raised for potential trouble. The black key was shown, taken and closely inspected in case of forgery, and the gate was unlocked. After a thorough search of jacket and breeches pockets, Meneghetti was allowed to begin the walk up a long, curving white gravel drive with ornamental foliage, blooming flowers and small barrel-trunked palm trees on either side, as the coachman had been instructed to wait where he was.

The white stone villa with its roofs and turrets of red tiles was in view beyond a stand of palm trees. The structure might have been the fortress of an ancient Roman emperor, and in fact the brother and sister who inhabited this domain were regarded with the same allegiance. And, of course, fear. It was said that somewhere on this property also lived a wolf, called to prowl by day or night.

Meneghetti continued walking up the drive. The villa grew nearer and more imposing, and to the wine merchant's irritation he realized he was sweating not just from the walk in the midday heat, but for the fact that as he was a lesser partner in the scheme of things he'd never before been face-to-face with Mars and Venus Scaramanga, and what to expect from the forthcoming introduction was unknown.

EIGHT

IF HE FEARED A BROAD-SHOULDERED WOLF MIGHT ANSWER HIS USE OF the iron knocker against the door, Ottavio Meneghetti was gladly mistaken. The door was opened by a short, slight, white-haired grandmotherly looking woman Meneghetti reasoned was easily past sixty. She wore a dark red caftan-like gown with long sleeves and a high white ruffled collar, and nothing at all was threatening about this small, nearly frail figure.

"I'm here to see the Scaramangas," he said, his tone that of how he spoke to any citizen of Venice…a shade haughty.

She said nothing and did not move, her solemn gaze peering through him as if he were made of transparent glass.

He realized what she wanted. He held up the black key. At this she opened the door wider and motioned him in. Before he crossed the threshold he caught movement to his left, glanced in that direction and saw the man watching him, standing there with one hand on a holstered pistol and another on the grip of the sword in its scabbard.

His nerves again on edge, Meneghetti went in. The doorkeeper shut the door at his back and silently motioned him to follow. If he was expecting a sinister interior to the manse as befitting the reputation of its residents he was once more gladly mistaken because the marble-floored foyer and the rooms he passed through were all bright, airy and decorated with ornately framed paintings, gold-hued chandeliers and leather furnishings similar to what he prided in his own villa. He was led into a windowed room with many books on many shelves, the walls of polished pine, a thick gold-colored carpet on the tiled floor, and a sofa and chairs arranged around what appeared to be a small, square dark brown slab of a table that stood out for its obvious hard usage and age. It took him a moment to note the markings etched into the old wood, and thus to register that here before him was the fabled stolen government strongbox, which he stood staring at as the elderly woman left the room through another door.

Did he dare touch it? This symbol of the organization's beginnings? No, he decided he should not, and in fact he decided he should not take a chair until he was invited to do so. He removed his hat and waited. He could see through an oval window a well-tended garden behind the villa where butterflies flitted in the sunlight hither and yon among flowers of yellow, crimson and violet, and he was watching their rather soothing motions when a dark bird of some kind swept down and got one in its beak, then was gone in an instant.

"You wished an audience," came the man's quiet voice behind him.

Meneghetti nearly whirled around but got himself in check and so turned as smoothly as a surprised and trepidatious man could do. "Yes, Grandmaster," he answered with a bow of the head. "If you please."

They stood looking at each other.

Mars Scaramanga said with a hint of annoyance, "Well, sit down then. *That* chair." He pointed, and Meneghetti took it. Scaramanga settled himself on the sofa before the legendary strongbox. "You're...Maneghetta, aren't you?"

"Meneghetti, sir. Ottavio. I am a member of Master Crisafi's crew."

"He gave you the key?"

"No, sir. I asked permission from the Lady Bonacorso. Master Crisafi sailed his yacht to Rimini two days past."

"I know he keeps his concubines there for the sailors. All right." Scaramanga swung his waxed black boots up onto the strongbox with a solid *thud* and crossed his ankles. "What is it you want?"

Here was the moment. Meneghetti was still taking in his impressions of the Grandmaster, for though he'd seen the man at a distance, being this near—in the same room, and just the two of them alone though Meneghetti figured eyes were fixed on them from somewhere in the walls—made him feel almost lightheaded. For one, Mars Scaramanga was a very handsome young man...no older than thirty-three, was the wine merchant's guess, which made him younger by far than most of his subjects. A youthful emperor, he thought. King of all he surveyed...and all of *who* he surveyed. It was the power, too; Meneghetti could feel the energy of it coming off the man like the sun's noon heat from August pavement.

Scaramanga was slim and tall, probably an inch or two over six feet was Meneghetti's guess, and he had the air of a born patrician—an *aristocratico*—which of course he was. His cheekbones were prominent and sharp, the brows above his attentive coal-black eyes fashionably thin and arched, yet his high forehead was furrowed by some concerns over low subjects. The upturned tip of his nose made it appear the nostrils were either breathing in some exotic perfume of the wealthy class or disdaining the dung odors of the impoverished. His clothing was of the finest Italian linen, royal blue in color with double rows of silver buttons down the front and a silver-gray cravat wrapped around the throat. His hair was—

—and here was the thing that might either be said to be a flaw (no one dared) or a mark from God to identify Mars Scaramanga as one chosen for special deeds in this world (as many did)—

—so black it held hints of blue, glossy, sleek and trimmed caplike to the scalp, yet on the left side of the head there grew a burst of red hair that might have been a bloody wound delivered by a bestial claw. This hair had a different texture than the rest, and was as rough as a washerwoman's scrub brush. Tendrils of this scarlet thicket trailed from the temple nearly to the back of the head, and stood out only to be tamed by a sharp pair of shears but never by any comb or brush known to man.

"What are you looking at?" Scaramanga asked, because Meneghetti had indeed for the moment been entranced by the red roughage.

"Nothing, sir," was the quick answer. And to cover the uncomfortable moment, the wine merchant said, "I bring news concerning the where-abouts of Brazio Valeriani."

Scaramanga sat very still. It seemed to Meneghetti that the man had ceased breathing.

Finally, a word emerged: "Explain."

Before Meneghetti had gotten very far in the explanation, Scaramanga said, "Stop," and stood up. "I want my sister to also hear this." He turned away and left the room, going through a corridor and up a flight of spiral stairs.

Through another corridor and two more rooms, he advanced into a bathing chamber with crimson walls and a floor of black marble. Instantly the thirty-pound gray lynx lurched up from its resting position, a hideous hissing coming out, the mouth opening to reveal two-inch-long fangs, its black-tipped ears up high and its yellow eyes yearning for murder.

"Venus," Scaramanga said, "control your pussy."

The woman in the copper tub filled with cow's milk looked up lan-guidly from her repose. "You're such a twiddle. Can't you see Nyx has her collar on?"

The black leather collar studded with metal prongs was fixed to a leash that was itself wrapped around a towel rack and knotted. That Nyx was securely bound didn't prevent the big cat from crouching down as if about to spring forward in attack on the bath-time intruder.

"That thing hates me." Scaramanga moved forward with caution to the edge of the tub. "It hates *everything*."

"Except me, dear brother."

"Mark it, some day that thing will turn on you."

Venus Scaramanga showed a slight smile in which her fine white teeth glinted. "Never. My Nyx loves me. Don't you, darling dear?"

"Get dressed, we have a visitor with important news."

"I've only been in here an hour."

"News," Mars said with emphasis, "about Brazio Valeriani."

"I thought that was a closed subject."

"Put aside," he answered, "but not closed. I want you to hear what the man has to say. It's Meneghetti from Crisafi's crew."

"Who?"

"Never mind. Just get dressed and come downstairs." When she didn't move, he added, "A *request*, humbly made." Avoiding any further approach to the lynx, Scaramanga left the bathing chamber, went downstairs and returned to the room where Meneghetti was waiting. When he walked in, he found the wine merchant on his feet gingerly touching the old crate stolen by great-grandfather Adolfo. Instantly Meneghetti flew into his chair as if his shoulders had sprouted wings.

"I don't care if you touch it," the Grandmaster said as he took his place on the sofa. Again his boots thudded up on the fabled item. "It's a comfortable footrest to me, nothing more, but my sister is the one who wants to keep it. So we keep it. Now hold your story, she'll be down in a few minutes." He cocked his head to one side as he examined something that had interested him. "I admire your boots. Where did you get them?"

It was at least twenty minutes before they were joined by Grandmistress Scaramanga, during which Meneghetti explained about his delivery of the boots from Egypt, and also he gave his host the piece of paper upon which the names were written. Venus Scaramanga came in wearing a long purple-and-gold printed silk gown and preceded by Nyx on the leash, the lynx appearing to be continually on the prowl for a throat to seize. Meneghetti restrained himself from drawing back as the woman passed him—smelling of a pungent spice-tinged perfume—and took her place on the sofa with the animal at her feet. Then she regarded him with the same coal-black eyes as those of her twin. She shared the same handsome characteristics though in truth much more so and even viewing her from afar Meneghetti had always seen she was a very beautiful woman. Now, this near, he might call her as he might term his finest wine: exquisite.

Venus shared a singular trait with her brother, though as an opposite. Her long, well-brushed tresses were as black and sleek as the man's, but on the right side there were streaks of the same nearly garish red from temple toward the back of the head in a pattern that strangely resembled a spider's web. Meneghetti did not fail to notice that though there was ample room to sit on the right side of Mars Scaramanga, the woman had chosen to sit on the left side, therefore the red-riddled sides of their heads were closer together. He had heard whispers—never to be spoken in more than a whisper—that in the womb Mars and Venus Scaramanga had a third sibling and they had consumed the new flesh, their mother passing into death during the labored birth.

Would that third sibling have had flaming red hair?

Only whispers, and best to remain so.

"This man looks frightened," Venus said, and she crossed her legs to display one smooth calf as the gown parted.

"With a beast in the room, who wouldn't be?" Mars offered her a ghost of a smile. "I mean the lynx. Or I suppose I do." His smile disappeared as he returned a hard gaze upon the wine merchant. "Your story from the beginning."

Meneghetti told it, complete with descriptions of the trio.

At the end, Mars studied the paper once more before he asked, "If you say these visitors have assumed for some reason that Valeriani either owns a vineyard or works in one, do you have any idea who this might be?"

"No sir, I don't. I would have heard if one had changed ownership over the last few years, but this man might be working in any one of several capacities."

"How many vineyards?" the woman asked.

"Six. Well…I understand that two have been destroyed by the war, but families still live on the properties."

"And all to the north?" she prompted.

"Yes, mistress. All along the Piave River. We're speaking of an area stretching from thirty to fifty miles."

"Matthew Corbett and Camilla with a Spanish last name," Mars read from the paper. "You say also a Spanish soldier? Did they mention others being with them?"

"No sir, they did not."

"I find it quite fascinating," Venus said, "that an Englishman should be allied with the Spanish in this search."

"Fascinating?" Mars's thin brows went up. "I find it disturbing." He regarded the paper again. "Staying at the Palace of Friendship. They have money to spend." His gaze went to his sister, to Meneghetti and back again. "I don't like this. It smacks of the Spanish government being involved, but how did an Englishman come into it? And the larger question: why do they want the mirror, because that's exactly what they want." He spent a silence in thought. Then: "Meneghetti, I assume you would wish for advancement?"

"Of course, sir."

"I'm giving you the opportunity. By all means, have your girl take them an accurate map in the morning. Then I want that inn watched and those three followed when they leave. I would recommend using Gallo, Lamacchia and Rossone from Divittori's crew. I'll have a message sent to provide them to your office." Mars stood up, strode to one of the bookshelves, pulled aside two volumes and unlatched a cubbyhole hidden behind. He returned to Meneghetti and held out the black key he'd retrieved. "Yours," he said. "Earn it."

"Thank you sir! Most kind, most kind!" As he took the key and this increase in both responsibility and respect, Meneghetti felt a small twinge at the back of his neck, knowing that if he failed in any way in what he was assigned, Lupo would come calling as the executioner had with Trazini. He had to also dare to ask: "Would I be going with them, sir?"

"Your task is to organize the search. Get their supplies and make sure they know their purpose. But first...I admire your boots, Master Meneghetti. Do you think they might fit me?"

"Sir?"

"The boots." The voice was a shade more demanding. "Fit me."

"Oh...yes. Of course!" Meneghetti got them off. Mars removed his own, sat down on the sofa to the right of his sister while studiously avoiding Nyx, and put the wine merchant's boots on his own blue-stockinged feet.

"A little tight," was the judgement. An affable smile followed. "But no matter, I'll break them in."

"Yes sir." All Meneghetti could do was return the smile as best he could.

When the bootless wine merchant had been shown out by the housekeeper, Mars stopped his sister from departing the room with her Nyx by saying, "I have a task for you."

"Really? Does he think he gives me *tasks* now?" This was said to the lynx.

"Don't play as if you're no longer interested in finding Valeriani and the mirror, because I know you are just as I am. I want you to go have dinner in Venice tonight. I'll send Lorenzo with you."

Venus almost said *I'll go alone* but she knew from the family's history that it was not an issue to be debated. "What's the purpose?"

"After you have dinner, I want you to go to their inn and find out how many are in the group. I have a feeling there are more than three. Put on your charming face and speak to the clerk."

"You can send Lorenzo," she answered, "but I don't want to see him or know he's there. Send him in a separate coach. I mean it, Mars. I want to pretend I'm at least a *little* free."

"Free," Mars repeated with a bitter twist of the mouth. "Pretend all you like but he'll be shadowing you every minute."

Venus nodded. She didn't like it, but it was necessary and certainly it kept her brother from his overuse of the opium pipe. If there was a chance of finding the mirror, this might be it. "All right," she said, her mood now deadly serious. "I'll go."

Thus, at nightfall, dressed in a black gown trimmed with red and in her red lace-up boots with the high heels, a red hat with a circular brim on her head, Venus Scaramanga entered the coach that came for her from the estate's coachhouse, and started on her task.

"Flamboyant tonight, are we?" Mars had asked at the door. "You were not supposed to attract attention."

"Dear brother," was her reply, "attention is my life."

In the city she left her coach in the Scaramangas' private coachhouse and walked a quarter mile to the *Saleria*, one of her favored restaurants, where she dined on peppered pasta with black mussels and enjoyed a glass of Verdicchio. If Lorenzo was near—which she was certain he was—she saw no trace of him, not even a shadow from the one being shadowed. When she departed the *ristorante* she stopped in a bookshop on the Calle Lunga and bought there a tome she'd been wanting to read, the famous gambler and mathematician Gerolamo Cardano's book on games of chance and his theory of probability. From there she continued through the busy, lamplit nighttime streets across the Vidal bridge and the Grand Canal to the Palace of Friendship. At the inn she decided to bide her time before approaching the clerk at his desk as there was much coming and going of people in the lobby, so she settled herself in a nice brown leather armchair in a corner, turned up the reading lamp on the small round table at her side, and read for a while with one eye on the desk about twenty feet away.

As Venice was a center of commerce for the merchants and business-men of many countries, the number of people moving through the lobby at any one time was quite interesting to her. Within ten minutes of situating herself she was approached by a rather large, ruddy-faced gentleman in an expensive-looking suit who said in poor Italian strained through an accent that sounded Slavic, "Madam, may I—"

"No," she said without looking up further from her book, and the man went away. In another twenty minutes an Asian businessman came up to her with a hopeful expression, which she immediately caused to freeze on his face with her hand motioning him to politely go fuck himself. Then the ice walls around her chair seemed to solidify because no other unwanted intruder approached though many gave her more than a glance as they passed. She had in her head the descriptions Meneghetti had provided. In half an hour of watching she saw no one who met them. The time moved on, the lobby began to become less populated due to the later hour—after eleven by the ornate silver clock on the wall above the clerk's desk—and Venus decided she would wait until eleven-thirty and then approach the clerk with a question about a young Englishman she had happened to meet that afternoon. *Matthew Corbett is the name,* she would say. *We were talking of all things about books and I mentioned this particular volume as one he might enjoy, though I'm not sure he's very proficient in our language. Are there others travelling with him who might be able to translate? Of course I'll leave it for him, I wouldn't wish to disturb him if—*

"I demand my own room! Do you hear me?"

Venus looked up from the pages. A very tall, thin man in a black cloak and a black tricorn hat was at the clerk's desk making some kind of commotion, and most importantly he was speaking in English, which she knew enough to speak and read at an acceptable level, the Scaramanga's governess—a Swiss woman—having made sure the two children were well-educated in regard to languages, including Spanish and a foundation of Latin.

"I can't sleep in that room!" the man was protesting...angrily, almost a snarl. "One of those soldiers snores like a beast!"

Soldiers, Venus thought. She very softly closed the book.

The dismayed but unruffled clerk held up his hands in the universal attitude of not understanding the problem, which seemed to make the black-cloaked man even more belligerent. "I can't sleep in there! Don't you understand me? And I'm on a cot that breaks my back!" To the clerk's silence he slammed a fist down on the desktop. "I'd rather sleep on a public bench than in there! Damn you!" he fired at the clerk, as he stalked toward the doorway. And with a last enraged, nearly choked "Damn all of you!" he was out the door and into the night.

Venus stood up. This man did not fit any description Meneghetti had provided...but, still...

Soldiers.

She followed him out.

This very tall, gaunt and pallid-faced man walked with an angry purpose through the streets, which were quieter now except for a few late-night revelers usually strolling in groups. He must indeed be searching for a public bench, of which there were many, but none appeared to fit his extraordinary length. And a strange thing, as well: every now and then on this trek he seemed to be speaking to himself, yet his face was turned to the right as if addressing a person really there. She watched him stop at an intersection and, his hands on his hips, might be deciding which way to venture further. Again he spoke to the air. Infirm in the head? Venus wondered.

An Englishman, with soldiers in his room. It had to be tried.

She picked up her pace. At the next junction of streets under the yellow glow of a municipal lamp he paused once more, and as Venus was almost upon him she said before he could move away again, "Wait."

The man quickly turned his face toward her, and perhaps she wished he had not because in truth the long jaw, the deep-set dark eyes and the cadaverous cheekbones under the ebony tricorn gave her the impression of a skull barely covered by pale white flesh, the angle of his shoulders making the cloak spread out like the wings of a black crow. Her confident steps faltered.

He spoke…a raspy, still-angered voice: "What do you want?"

Venus approached. The man's ugliness was repellent to her, and yet… was there something about him that was oddly fascinating? "I overheard," she said, keeping her expression calm and composed. She knew Lorenzo had to be nearby, in some doorway perhaps, watching with his hand on his sword.

"Overheard what?"

"I was sitting in a chair in the lobby. At the inn. I overheard your—" What was the correct English word? She hoped she'd found it: "Discomfort."

"What?" The man still seemed stupefied, or simply stupid. "You followed me from the inn?"

"I did."

"Why?"

It was time to put on her charming face: an easy smile and a gentler, almost flirtatious expression in the eyes. She did not fail to note the silver rings on the man's fingers engraved with skulls and strange but interesting symbols, and also the long fingernails that could well serve as claws. She decided in that instant that this creature—as repulsive as he appeared—was her drink of Chianti. Was it time to also push forward?

Yes, it was.

"You're searching for Brazio Valeriani," she said.

The moment hung as if frozen in the warm, sweetly scented night air.

"The mirror," she continued fearlessly. *"Si, e cosi?"*

With what appeared to be a real effort, he got his mouth working. "Who are you?"

"I am Venus Scaramanga. And you are?"

Cardinal Black suddenly had the impulse to turn and flee from this scene. He looked left and right, backwards and forwards to see if anyone else was lurking nearby but there was only the purple-robe-clad and faceless Dominus standing beside the woman.

"There's no one else," she said, reading his motions. She felt he was on the verge of bolting. "Only you and I. And I would care to know your name."

A soft voice drifted to him.

:*Tell her*,: said Dominus.

"Are you sure?" Black asked.

The question had been aimed at Dominus, but the woman—smiling easily, her dark and attractive, nearly mesmeric eyes fixed patiently upon him beneath the wide brim of her crimson hat—said, "I am certain."

"Adam Black," he replied. And, still flustered: "I am Adam Black."

"One of you is enough, I think. You are very long and tall aren't you?"

"I suppose…some say."

She nodded. "I like long and tall."

Cardinal Black was aware that his heart was beating very hard. Could this woman detect it? Surely she could, for it was the pounding of a hundred kettledrums in a cavernous music hall where only he and she stood alone. But…this was madness! And dangerous as well! Who the hell *was* she? And how did she—

"You are travelling with a young Englishman named Matthew Corbett and a Spanish woman named Camilla," Venus said to his obviously discomforted silence. "And a Spanish soldier, I believe? More than one soldier, yes?"

:*Wake up*,: Dominus commanded.

It was true. Black realized he was acting as hazed in the head as a staggering sleepwalker. Him, the master of his own world, the avenger of his mother's death-in-life, the worshipper at the temple of souls that had been his when the aged, blind and brain-softened Gavin Flay had taken an unfortunate misstep down a flight of stairs helped by a firm young hand, the challenger to the kingdom of the wretched Professor Fell, the voice that had given the order to kill…how many? Fifty? Sixty? At least that many enemies of the empire of Cardinal Black, put into their graves if any of their corpses were to be found. The intelligent mind that knew of secrets and powers beyond the ken of ordinary men. And here he stood, reduced to near childish stupor by this woman who had appeared from nowhere. He wasn't having it; it was time to take control.

"I know where Valeriani can be found," she said, before his resolve could move from thought to action.

He felt some last barricade within himself crack and begin to crumble. "Where?"

"First…you're searching for a place to sleep, are you not? I doubt you can find a public bench that would suit you. My coach is kept not far from here and my villa is across the bay, an hour's ride."

"*Where* is Valeriani?" Black's voice had recovered a measure of more force, but the woman just continued to smile.

"A vineyard, of course," Venus answered. "To the north. Now: we'll talk further at my villa, and then you can have a good night's rest in a real bed."

How did this woman know? It was a mystery he had to solve, and if she really did know where Valeriani was…it changed everything, didn't it? He said, "We're supposed to start off in the morning."

"I'll deliver you by dawn. Trust me."

Still Black hesitated. The woman was so beautiful. Enticing, even…but in a way she frightened him, and it had been a very long time since he'd felt that crippling emotion.

He looked to Dominus for advice. "Trust?" he asked.

His phantom companion nodded, at the same time Venus Scaramanga took his cold right hand in her warm left and said, "By my word…with your life."

She led him away.

NINE

ADAM BLACK STOOD IN A DARK ROOM WITH NO WALLS AND A FLOOR OF brown stones. He was dreaming. He knew he was dreaming. It was a dream he'd experienced many times before, and each time seemingly more real. As he walked forward across the stones he saw a shimmering in the air before him, and in another moment he was standing before a huge mirror in which he could see his own reflection.

And yet there was something else in the glass. Figures swirled around his reflection. Nothing was clear, but he could catch impressions of what might be a head, a pair of shoulders, an arm, a torso…all darkened in the glass, all shadowy and indistinct yet there all the same.

They were waiting for his summons.

He watched them move as if they were made of liquid, emerging from the greater depths. His mouth was dry and he felt the sweat of expectation at the back of his neck. He knew who he was to call forth, and had known for what seemed all his life.

The Seventieth Demon depicted in the book…the mighty Prince Seere, who governed a host of twenty-six legions, and would perform whatever was commanded if the seal of his summoning was correctly inscribed on the floor before the glass, along with the proper incantation. He had locked both into his memory, and he was ready.

Prince Seere…the first command to destroy every enemy who had ever turned a hand against him, to wipe every slate clean…to turn to immediate ash everyone who had wished him hurt, which included Danton Idris Fell and a certain young man named Matthew Corbett, among a host of others.

Prince Seere...the second command...

Adam saw himself as a fourteen-year-old boy by candlelight, awakened by his mother Hester in his small, gray-walled room at the house of his father the Vicar Black in the village of Colquitt, after the incident in which he had accidentally blinded the tormenting boy Davy Keeler, the mayor's son.

Now listen to me, his mother said. *I'm going to bring a bag in for you. It already has some money and food in it. I want you to get up and pack some warm clothes, and I want you to be very quiet.*

Pack? Why? he asked.

Because you're going to your Aunt Sarah's. While you get ready, I'm going out to the barn to hitch Mavis to the wagon. You know the way to Sarah's, don't you?

But...it's nearly forty miles, the young Adam Black said.

No matter. You have to get there. Most important...you have to leave here. *I'll not have my son punished any more than you already have been. No gaol, no stocks. Now get up and I'll fetch the bag.*

A vital question followed from the boy: *What about Father?*

What about him?

He'll be even more angry.

I'll manage that, said Hester. *Get up and get moving.*

And here what Prince Seere would give him came into reality, because it was the gift of both seeing the future, going back into time and changing what the years had wrought.

You are going with me, Adam said, and he spoke not as a boy but as a man who had been shown what was to be.

I can't. I must stay.

If you stay, I stay. Because if I leave and you don't, the man who calls himself my father and your husband will become so enraged that in time he'll put you into an asylum for the insane, and I will have to kill you to release you from your misery.

I don't—

Listen to me, mother. Under his hand you will suffer as no saint ever did. I love you, and I won't leave you to be destroyed by either him or by myself, years from today. Now pack a bag for yourself, because we both have to leave this place.

Prince Seere. Giver of death to those who deserved such, and of second chances to those who begged them. And Prince Seere was the spirit that would save his mother's life.

"Penso che stia tornando."

Who was that? Who had spoken? A woman's voice. Not his mother. He was a heavy weight upon himself, his mind full of mud. He was lying on a very hard bed, that he knew. But where? He remembered...what?

His eyelids were opening, beginning to admit light. It was lamplight…
flickering, he thought. Abruptly the light stung his eyes as they fully opened.

A hand bearing silver rings hung in front of his face.

"They're very pretty, don't you think?"

It took him a few labored seconds to realize they were his own rings.

The woman's dark-eyed face came into focus. "Now," she said, "we can
really have a nice talk."

Another figure stood beside the woman and peered down at him. This
creature was a large, broad-shouldered form with the face of a wolf. A mask,
he realized. A man wearing a silver mask, metal of some kind. He could see
the human orbs in the mask's eyeholes. The man had on a dark blue jacket,
his throat wrapped by a white cravat. Then the figure drew back, and Adam
Black tried to sit up on this very hard bed but found he could not.

Pain throbbed at his wrists and ankles. He felt the abrasion of rough
rope. His arms were spread wide above his head, his legs spread wide beneath him on this flat wooden platform.

And suddenly, as more consciousness returned, he realized he had been
stripped completely naked.

Fear caught him and shook him like a wet rag. He could lift his head
only a few inches and even that was a strain on his neck. His heart pounded
so hard he thought his eardrums would explode.

"…is this?" he heard himself cry out, because the *what* was still lodged
in his throat like a sharp-edged stone.

The woman said something in Italian, presumably to the man in the
wolf mask. Black could see a yellow plaster ceiling above him, and the glow
of lamplight. He thought from the strength of it that many lamps hung on
the walls.

He tried again: "What is this?"

It was a moment before she granted him an answer. "This is…oh, the
English word. What is it, I can't recall. This is…*oh*…this is an *interroration*.
Is that correct?"

Interrogation, she meant. He squeezed his eyes shut but when he
opened them again the plaster ceiling was still above his head, the lamps
still made their patterns of dancing light and the ropes still burned his wrists
and ankles.

He remembered now, or thought he did: entering the guarded front
gate and then the villa with the woman, who had been silent on the ferry
trip and then the coach ride. *My brother and I are important people*, she'd
told him as he'd been led into a sumptuous parlor with pale blue walls and
white leather furniture. *I think you must also be important, sí? Excuse me
while I go speak to Mars…my brother. I think he would like to meet such an
important person as you.*

She had returned about ten minutes later, without her brother and without her hat, and he'd noted the peculiar and to him quite interesting difference in her hair from one side of her head to the other. *Sleeping*, she'd said as she'd settled herself on the white sofa next to him. *I won't wake him, he is not the night owl I am.* She had put her hand on Black's arm and leaned in closer, and she must have applied fresh perfume because he could smell her like a fine spicy mist. *You search for the mirror.*

Yes, but first we have to find Valeriani. You say you know where he is?

Let us trade information, she'd countered. *You say "we". How many are you?*

He had looked across the room at the silent figure standing in the corner. Dominus had given a brief nod, the unspoken message being: *Tell her.*

Nine others, he'd said.

Then tell me, Adam…do you believe in the power of this mirror?

I do, was his firm answer.

And why do you? Because you wish to believe?

Because I've been shown that such powers exist beyond this earthly plain and beyond the understanding of the human kind.

Who showed you this? she'd asked, and now her face was very close to his, her perfume nearly intoxicating his senses and making his head swim.

Another glance at Dominus, and another nod of assent was returned. *Experiences in my life*, he'd replied. *And I have a familiar. A spirit who walks with me and informs me of these things.*

She'd paused and he could see her pondering this statement. Then she'd asked, *An evil spirit?*

A spirit who suits my needs. I call him Dominus, and he is standing in that corner yonder.

She didn't look, as he'd expected she would. *I think*, she'd said, *that I believe you. Why are the Spanish interested in the mirror?*

I understand they want to lock it away.

A small laugh had resulted from these eight words. She'd said, *I'm sure they will…after, if the power of the mirror is real, they have delivered to themselves a fleet of ships…made of iron, perhaps, that yet float and sail as easily as any in their armada. Or they might simply desire whirlwinds and plagues to decimate any other country on earth. Would that be possible?*

With the mirror and the book under one's control, Black had replied, *anything is possible.*

And now her gaze had taken on a sharper edge. *The book? What book?*

When he'd given Dominus another glance, the familiar did not respond yay or nay; it was up to Black to tell more, and he feared he'd already revealed too much. It was time for his own revelations. *I want to know where Valeriani is.*

A vineyard to the north, as I've said.

What vineyard?

The Bonacorso estate. Now…I want to know about this book.

She was a very beautiful and persuasive woman, Black had thought. Perhaps too persuasive? He made a decision. *I'll keep that to myself for the present.*

As you wish. Her smile had not faltered. She'd reached to a table for a small golden bell situated there and rang it. *A glass of wine for you,* she'd said. *Then sleep.*

I should get back to Venice. I'll find somewhere.

Oh, there's no hurry. I told you I'd deliver you before dawn, and I shall.

Into the room at the summons of the bell had come an elderly white-haired woman in a green robe. She was bearing a tray with two glasses of red wine, one with a silver band and one with a gold, and Black had noted that the old woman's face and eyes were puffy as if she'd only recently been roused from her bed.

I took the liberty of arranging this after I saw to my brother, Venus had said. *A glass of wine to help you sleep, sí? Then when you're rested, we'll continue our pleasant talk.*

I think I should—

Humor me, the woman had insisted, and as one hand ran up and down his sleeve the other reached for the glass with the gold band and offered it. *You should drink. It's of a vintage you might never experience again.*

Had Black caught a whiff of danger beyond the aroma of exotic perfume? When he cast a questioning look toward Dominus, again the trusted familiar made no motion. The woman was sipping from the other glass and the servant was walking away. Danger? There was no hint of it from Dominus. Why would there be danger? In the villa as far as he knew were only the woman, her brother—so she said—and the elderly servant. The coachman had taken the coach and team away behind the villa. Still…the man who had come to be called Cardinal Black was on edge though he did not know exactly why.

Venus had tipped her glass against his to make a soft chiming noise before she took another sip.

Black had asked, *How come you to know about the mirror?*

Let's allow that to rest for a while. Tell me about your great city of London.

What is there to tell?

Paint me a picture, she'd said.

Black had taken a drink of his wine. It was a little bitter, but strong, rich and satisfying. He'd decided that if Dominus was giving him no warning there was nothing to fear. And why should he fear this woman? In fact, she could help him get to the mirror long before the others might find it.

He knew the proper seal and incantation by memory, so he no longer need-ed the book. Yes. He'd decided he could use her very well indeed.

And so he did paint her a picture of London, but it was done in a chro-ma of grays verging upon ebony, a panoramic portrait of the grim world he inhabited with its appalling and yet addictive vices, its secret chambers where violent men planned their deeds of vengeful murder against their enemies, the damp cellars and shadowed garrets that saw innocents reduced to hollow screams, the backstreets and dead-end alleys where no man dared to wander either by starlit night or fog-shrouded day. His London, and he'd told her all this because he wished her to know the truth about himself and it had seemed by her expression and the quickness of her breathing that she had become herself enraptured by this painting and she was silently urging him on and on, into deeper and darker revelations, and as he drank the wine down in his glass some nearly lost thing in his heart sang and rejoiced because here...*here*...was a human being who not only did not turn away from his recitations of brutality and avarice in all its twisted forms but who actually...*actually*...relished the telling.

Here, he'd thought as he'd strangely begun to feel so very tattered and tired, his vision of her blurring because indeed he was in need of sleep and would be so glad to find rest away from those wretches who were in essence chaining himself to them...

Here...

...was his soulmate.

And he was still rejoicing as the almost-emptied glass had fallen from his nerveless fingers, a streak of the red wine had spilled across the sofa's white leather—a thing he was aware of only dimly, but something he decid-ed he must apologize for—and his eyes had closed.

Now, awakening to the reality of being stretched out and roped at wrists and ankles, stripped nude upon some hard flat surface, Adam Black tried to thrash against his bonds but there was not a quarter inch of give in them and all that resulted was a further abrasion of the flesh. He heard the woman speak in her language again to the man in the wolf mask, and then her face once more hovered above him.

"Easy, *mio caro*," she said, and she tapped the center of his thin chest with a long fingernail. "Don't strain yourself for nothing."

"What's happening?" A ridiculous question but it had been blurted out in desperation; he knew what was happening was that he was in deadly danger. But why had Dominus not warned him?

"I told you," she answered silkily, "that I liked long and tall. We're going to make you longer and taller yet." She gave a nod to one side. There was a creaking noise followed by the sound of gears ratcheting. Immediately the ropes at Black's wrists and ankles pulled him in different directions...

with only a beginning twinge of pain at his joints and up his spine…but he realized with the hammering of his heart and a burst of terror sweat that he was stretched out upon a torturer's rack and the huge wolfman's strength was at the spoked wheel.

Venus leaned over him, watching the darting eyes in a ghastly pale face that knew there was no escape. And yet…he might *hope*, mightn't he? She had suspected that at some point he might decide to withhold information from her, and so when she'd gone to invite Mars to the party and found her brother sleeping under his usual administration of the tincture of opium, she had used just a little of his valued liquid in the golden-rimmed glass and instructed Edetta the housekeeper to be ready to bring out the tray. Perhaps she'd used too much, for this tall thin cretin had been unconscious for four hours. But time enough for Lupo to shoulder him and bring him down to this chamber below the villa to prepare him for the real party.

Her chamber. Mars rarely came down here. Not that it disturbed him, but that he understood why she needed it, as a release. It had been a while since she'd experienced a release, and she desired one. She stood looking down upon this thing who called himself Adam Black with her glorious collection arrayed in the chamber around her, among them the Iron Maiden, the Knee Splitter, the Pear of Anguish, the Judas Chair, the Scavenger's Daughter, the Iron Spider, and hanging saws and chisels and files and axes and knives and knives and knives.

Her chamber.

"I think you don't want to tell me something I wish to know," she said quietly. "About this book. What does it have to do with the mirror?"

He was an instant late in responding. She gave a nod toward the wolfman, the wheel was turned another degree, the ratchet gears ground against each other and Black gave a gasp of increased pain as the joints of his body were further stretched.

"Wait! Wait!" he cried out. "The book! It's about the demons…the spirits! It gives…gives the names of the devils…describes their powers… shows the seals used to call them and protect the caller…and the incantations. All the incantations."

Venus tapped his damp forehead. "Very good. And where is this book?"

"The woman has it. Camilla Espaziel, the witch-hunter."

A slow smile moved across Venus's face. Looking across at Lupo, who stood with his hands ready for more pressure on the wheel, she said in Italian, "Lupo, they've brought a witch-hunter! Isn't that amusing!"

It was difficult to know what Lupo found amusing or not, for though he lived in a dwelling behind the villa she had never seen him without the metal mask and the mask bore only one expression: a frozen rictus of ferocity.

"We don't need the book!" Black had begun to jabber, his lips glistening with saliva. "I have it by memory who I'm going to call. We don't need it!"

"That's so touching, the way you say 'we'," she answered. "So. This witch-hunter has the book that will call demons from the underworld, and nine people are going out in the morning from the Palace of Friendship to search for Brazio Valeriani and the mirror. Is that correct?"

"Ten," Black said, his voice tightened as the ropes had tightened. "Ten of us."

"*Nine.* You know I can't let you leave here. Oh, what a fool I would be! No, I promised I would deliver you by dawn, and so I shall because the sun is almost here. Deliver you to Hell, I mean."

"No! Please! Listen! You need me!"

She nodded, still offering a vapid smile though the dark eyes in her beautiful face were dead. "I do need you, dear Adam, though not how you might expect."

Black felt a shout come up from his throat. It exploded through his mouth: "Dominus! Help me!"

There was no response. He lifted his head as much as he was able, and there he saw his Dominus standing beside Venus Scaramanga. And as he watched, he witnessed with soul-crushing horror the phantom familiar place a bloodless gray hand upon the woman's shoulder.

He knew.

If he had reached the mirror and summoned Prince Seere, and Prince Seere had given him what he desired…if he had either talked his mother into escaping with him or if he had stayed to accept his punishment… he never would have met Gavin Flay and been drawn into the league of Satanists…he never would have gone to the asylum atop Brierly Hill and delivered a merciful death to the wreckage Hester Black had become…he never would have tracked Enoch Black down and murdered the creature and the others in that mansion…never would the cross on the wall have tilted upside-down under the weight of a falling body to show him the hideous path that lay ahead…and Cardinal Black would never have existed.

And neither would have existed the entity he knew as Dominus.

Dominus. A spirit from Hell or a specter of his own mind?

Whatever it was, it refused to be blanked from existence.

Venus said, *"Lupo, fatelo a pezzi."*

Lupo, tear him apart.

The wolfman's muscles worked against the wheel. The ratchet gears moved and moved and moved with a harsh clattering noise.

Adam Black screamed.

His joints were being pulled apart, his spine stretching…stretching… something snapping there with a fiery agony he felt at the base of his brain and he screamed and screamed while the woman stepped back sweating and she also began to moan and cry out because this was her only release, the sound and vision of torture and more and more and more…

The wheel turned, the wolfman putting more power against it. In this realm of Hades on Earth where all hope was lost to those who entered, Adam felt his left leg break from its socket, and then the right arm. His teeth chewed through his tongue and broke themselves against each other. Still the wheel turned and the ratchets clattered, the ropes thrummed in their tensions, Adam's left arm cracked at the elbow joint before it tore loose at the shoulder and he shrieked and wept as his body involuntarily convulsed, fighting against what could not be overcome.

Through a crimson haze Adam saw the woman over him, her face sweating and drawn taut by the energies of her own body, and she was showing him something…a bowl…something in it…meat…bloody pieces of meat…in a bowl…

She poured the bloody meat over his testicles, and then she stepped aside as Lupo locked the wheel down, picked up the thirty-pound Nyx off the floor, and set the animal between the shattered legs of the screaming and insane thing that had been Cardinal Black.

The fangs went to work in a frenzy. Lupo returned to the wheel. There were more noises of bones cracking and a sound of flesh splitting like old cloth being ripped apart by clawed hands, but of a human voice there remained only a faint guttering like a candle about to go out.

Until at last Venus Scaramanga drew a ragged breath as she leaned against a wall beside the Iron Maiden, and then silence reigned.

She needed to go have a strong drink, take a bath and rouse Mars from his stupor. They were going to have a conversation about how to get a certain book from nine fools who had wandered into territory they would never leave again…especially some *cagna* who called herself a witch-hunter.

Lupo would clean up this mess and clean Nyx as well. He always did.

She felt light-headed, yet vibrant, powerful and energized…more alive than an hour before. The torture room and her collection of toys always gave her the blessing of release. Yet as she started to climb the stairs out of the chamber she thought there was something new in the rejoicing of her body and senses, for…

…was there a figure in a hooded purple robe standing there in the corner?

Now gone.

Dominus! Help me! the man had cried out.

Interesting, she mused in the cold cavern of her mind, and she spent a few seconds admiring her new very fascinating silver rings. Now she really did need a strong drink, and she left the room as Lupo began to remove the mutilated corpse from the rack's embrace.

TEN

Two rented canvas-covered wagons each with a four-horse team had been sailed across the bay by ferry and had rolled off the departure ramp onto the pier at Mestre. The time was just past two o'clock on an afternoon where a few slow-moving clouds drifted across the eastern sun. Driving the first wagon through the streets was Captain Andrado, with a second soldier sharing the bench seat and another man in the back. The remaining soldier had taken the reins of the second wagon, Camilla had elected to sit up on the driver's seat, and in the back on more bench seats were Hudson, Professor Fell and a young man who thought the very air tasted like the most bitter wine on earth.

It galled Matthew's soul that Cardinal Black had escaped punishment. At six o'clock this morning, when it was reported from the soldiers that Black had stormed out of the room before midnight and not returned, Matthew and Hudson had gone out in search of him knowing he was not going to be found. Evidently Black had taken the opportunity to wrap himself up in his ebony cloak and perform a disappearing act. But it was the damnedest thing! Matthew thought. There was no doubt Black had wanted to find Valeriani and the mirror for his own nefarious reasons, so why would the creature simply leave the inn and the search party? Had Black decided to go off alone in pursuit? But the map drawn by Meneghetti hadn't arrived until after nine o'clock, so how would Black know where to search? And the book was still in Camilla's possession, so he'd left that darkly instructive volume behind as well.

It made no sense.

They had waited as long as both Matthew and Andrado had figured to be a reasonable time, thinking perhaps that Black would show himself at the latest before ten o'clock. That time had come and gone and by then Andrado and Camilla had secured a pair of suitable wagons and horse teams. Supplies of dried ham and fish in gunny sacks, baskets of oranges, apples, peaches and figs were gathered as well as potatoes, cooking utensils, a keg of fresh water and bedrolls for all, as the journey ahead would necessitate camping. Some of the items could be roped to the sides of the wagons, but with their baggage of clothing aboard Matthew reckoned the wagons' interiors were going to be as tight as a rum-drunk tick.

As this was put together Matthew suffered a severe pang of anxiety, for he realized he was simply pursuing Brazio Valeriani's supposed connection with a vineyard due to a few words spoken at his father's funeral. It hadn't been much to go on back in England and now seemed even less so, and as Matthew watched all the elements being readied for this search to the north he feared—or secretly hoped?—it would all be for naught.

But there was the matter of the vanished Cardinal Black. When one applied cold logic it was no mystery, really; Black had decided his freedom and life were worth more than the mirror, and Matthew would have strenuously pursued justice for the murder of his Broodie gang companions and by extension the brutal execution of Rory Keen. Matthew would of course have wanted legalities to be properly maintained, but he felt robbed of seeing Black stretched by a rope around the neck. Evidently this future stretching did not meet the grim Cardinal's approval, and so like a black crow into the night he had flown, to become a stranger in a strange land.

¡Adios! Matthew thought as the wagons trundled onward. *And fare not so well!*

One other thing also troubled him.

As they'd been readying to leave the inn, Camilla had come up alongside him and said, "Matthew, tell me this: how will you find Valeriani if he does not *want* to be found?"

"What do you mean?"

"It's a question you've probably asked yourself, but you know nothing of the man's description, you have no idea what false name he might be using or really even if he's anywhere in the north of this country, so how shall he be found even if we're looking him in the face and he doesn't come forward?"

To that and to her steady and unnerving gaze, Matthew had nearly stammered his reply. "I suppose we'll have to convince him somehow… possibly intrigue his curiosity."

"*If* he's out there," she'd answered. "*If* he reveals himself to us, and *if* he can be convinced." She'd given him a truly withering glare. "Too many *ifs*."

He'd recovered his fortitude enough to brashly say, "You'll recall I didn't volunteer for this. We can turn around right now and board the ship back to Alghero for all I care, but I would trust that Santiago and de Castro will carry through on their part of this agreement as I'm doing on my end."

Camilla had given a soft little *whuff* of air to this rather bold assertion, but Matthew saw in her face a quick-passing smile that said she respected his manner if not his method.

The two wagons rolled on through Mestre, raising small whorls of dust beneath the hoofs and wheels. There was nothing for Matthew, Hudson or Professor Fell to do but try to withstand the jostling and back-and-forth motion that was inevitable in a vehicle such as this. The professor stretched out on a bedroll as best he could among the assemblage of supplies, all necessary for the trip but hardly offering comfortable space. Matthew and Hudson remained on the slim seating bench on the wagon's right side, pinned in between a basket of figs and a grain sack of dried sardines.

They were silent for a while, listening to the discordant creaks and groans of the wagon's timbers, and then Hudson said, "What do you make of her?"

There was certainly no need of asking to whom Hudson was referring. "A little frightening," Matthew said.

"Maybe. But a strong-minded woman, for sure. I don't know." Hudson shrugged. "Do you think she's got her own purpose for finding this thing?"

"Possibly," said Professor Fell, who the other two had thought was sleeping because his eyes had been closed, and were still closed as he spoke. "I don't trust any of them. They *are* Spanish, after all."

"The woman." Hudson seemed determined to make her the center of conversation. "She's…" He paused, seeking a word.

Before Hudson could hunt it down, the canvas between the interior and the driver's seat was suddenly pulled open and Camilla peered in at the three. "She's *what?* You don't think I can't hear you up here?"

"She's got big ears," Hudson said.

"Spoken by a large mouth," was her retort.

"Powered by a large brain," he answered.

"Please," she said, and Matthew nearly said the same thing at the same time. With that remark—made as if to a particularly annoying child—Camilla let the canvas fall back into place.

"We'll watch our tongues from now on, your highness!" said Hudson in the direction of the closed canvas, and he gave a wink and a smirk to Matthew.

Matthew smiled, but he wasn't fooled. He'd noted the way Hudson looked at Camilla Espaziel. In what kind of way? Appraising, for one, and admiring for another. Matthew had also taken note that on the ship's ten-day voyage from Alghero there wasn't one day Hudson hadn't shaved and made himself presentable, even with that long-ago terrible day of bloodshed weighing so heavily upon him. So Hudson was now winking and smirking as if to say he could take this "highness" or leave her for she was simply a bother, but Matthew wondered if his friend wasn't actually…

What?

Appraising, admiring, and *attracted?*

Hudson had gained back some sturdy weight and was far more energetic than he'd been in the prison but he still had a long way to go to return to his past self, if that ever was to be. Though he was clean-shaven and *clean*—relatively speaking—Hudson's eyes were yet haunted and deep-shadowed by this inner torment. Last night in the room they'd shared Hudson had twice cried out in his sleep, and also Matthew had awakened to find him sitting in a chair at the window in the early light of dawn, just staring out into the world as if he no longer felt a part of it. He was eating better, that was true, and on their search for Cardinal Black his stride had been quick and unflagging, yet…he was distant from the man he used to be. Oh, he tried to mask it, tried to clothe himself in the winks and smirks of the old Hudson Greathouse but it was no longer a good fit. Would it always be so? Matthew thought that Hudson was on a path to become a different man, but who that man would be no one—not even the owner of the body, soul and name—could guess.

All Matthew could do at the present was try to make himself comfortable in this lumbering vehicle. The Italians might be great artists and architects, but as far as comfort in a wagon or coach was concerned, he thought the English won the award. But beyond that, Captain Andrado had possession of the map Meneghetti's office girl had brought to the inn, and it was calculated that they would reach the first vineyard depicted there, at the village of Sante Vallone, around ten o'clock that night. Failing to discover Valeriani there, the next stop would be past what Meneghetti indicated on the map with a large "X", a war-destroyed vineyard near the village of Pappano, and to the still-thriving one beyond at Balanero…and so on, many days ahead. And yet more days away from the ship that would take him back to Berry!

As Matthew listened to the sounds of the turning wheels and the creaking language of the wagon, he mused that there were questions he had yet to pose to Camilla: who were the three witches she said she'd discovered and caught, and…

…Matthew remembered her saying *I hunt witches and I destroy them however I can, as my father did and his father before him.* But he also recalled Santiago speaking somewhat sharply to her: *Yes, we understand the work of your father's life, señorita Espaziel, and thank you for that statement.*

It seemed to him that there was some displeasure on view concerning Camilla's father. Santiago's tone had caused that brief cloud to pass across her face.

Why? Had it possibly been...*shame?*

It was yet to be seen, but Matthew's innate and sometimes damning curiosity had been raised on its mile-high flagpole.

By nightfall, Matthew, Hudson and Camilla had all taken their turns spelling the soldier at the reins while Professor Fell lay back in the wagon like a lazy potentate, chewing on a fig from time to time. At his stretch on the driver's bench—a hard and splintery perch, to be sure—Matthew saw the landscape become more hilly and forested the further they got from the coast. They passed farm fields and hamlets with a few houses and the occasional small church. The road was dirt and dusty; gray clouds were beginning to congeal to the north. The aroma of pine woods fermented the air, so thick were the trees on either side, and reaching a hilltop that sloped into a summer-green valley the wilderness was its own verdant sea. Still the wagon teams labored on with short periods of rest and water, until with the soldier at the reins again the vehicle came to a halt. Sitting up beside the driver, Hudson drew aside the canvas and announced to Matthew, Camilla and the professor in the lamplit interior, "Sante Vallone. We're here."

Disembarking from their wagon, Matthew, Camilla and the professor were not met with the sight of a vineyard. Both wagons had drawn up in what appeared to be the village itself, with a few small cottages scattered here and there showing lamp light in the windows, a couple of barns, horses standing in a corral, a general store, and the central point of Matthew's attention: a brown stone structure with light blazing from the windows, a sound of raucous merriment rolling from the place into the street, and a hanging sign above the door that read in weather-beaten letters Riposo del Gallo.

"Rooster's Rest," said Camilla, standing between Matthew and Hudson. "Obviously a tavern. I'm going to find out from Andrado why we've stopped here." She marched off.

"Gentlemen, I could do with a drink of wine," Fell said, straightening the tasselled cap atop his head. "Surely we can indulge a bit, since we're here."

Hudson said, "Sounds like someone's having their own festival in there." The noise of laughter—however rough—was an enticement after the long hours spent in that cramped wagon, but no one took a further step toward the place until Camilla returned. They could see Andrado and his soldiers already going in, which caused a sudden halt to the laughing and brought on an ominous silence.

"What's the tale?" Matthew asked.

"It seems," said Camilla, "that we went past a vineyard just short of the village but there were no lights in any of the buildings."

"I saw that," Hudson said. "I thought Andrado knew where he was going."

"He saw the lights here," Camilla continued, "and so decided to—" She was interrupted by a shout from the tavern that made them all jump. It was not one shout, but roared from many throats that rattled the windows in their frames. Immediately afterward, the noise of hilarity picked up again at an even higher pitch.

"Good Lord!" Fell exclaimed. "Did they murder the soldiers?"

"Let's find out." Hudson started for the door with Camilla right behind him, Matthew and the professor following both with severe trepidation that there would be five Spanish bodies lying on the barroom floor, since it was likely any soldiers in this area would not be greeted with friendly hands.

Within the place, oil lamps hung from the pinewood rafters, sawdust covered the floor and pipe smoke fumed the air, there was a long bar behind which stood two large kegs and a shelf holding a variety of clay cups, there were ten or so scarred and well-used tables and the current occupants in appearance and clothing went along with the Rooster's roughness. Matthew calculated a crush of about fifty people gathered there, mostly men but a few women, and they gave the new entrants a look but otherwise they were banded around Captain Andrado and the soldiers, whacking Spanish shoulders with one burly hand while reaching for the bartender's pitcher pour of brown ale with a cup in the other. A gold coin was briefly seen upon the bar before the tavern keeper snatched it up, and Matthew realized that Alghero money was funding ale for the house, a wise decision from Andrado to keep the peace.

Ale but not wine? Matthew wondered.

Of course. These were workers at the vineyard, and either they had had their fill of *vino* long before or they knew that every drop of it leaving Sante Vallone for Venice or points south added up to livelihoods for themselves and their families, so ale it was.

As Matthew and the group moved forward into this crush, a couple of men who obviously had nearly drowned in their own cups staggered toward Camilla as if to grab her up in an embrace, until—astoundingly— Hudson put an arm around her and herded her away from the approaching bears. Astoundingly also to Matthew's sensibilities was that Camilla neither showed irritation at this presumption nor did she move to shake the arm away. It was only when they sat at a table with four chairs in a corner of the merry maelstrom that Hudson's arm again became his own.

Matthew stared at him for a time after they'd seated themselves. Hudson looked the other way.

The bald-headed and heavily brown-bearded tavern keeper adjusted his rather dirty apron and pushed through the hubbub to their table. Camilla spoke up in Italian: "We'll have four ales in clean cups, if you please." She showed an agreeable smile to this softly stern command.

"Yes, miss," he answered in a guttural dialect. He was so snaggle-toothed that his *sì, signorina* came out a bit wet. "Can I ask where you're from and what you're doing here?"

"From Venice. Passing through to the north."

His square face folded in a frown. "Oh, miss! I wouldn't go so much further up that way. I've heard from travellers coming south that the French and the Dutch are at it day and night."

"I understand that." She offered no more comment on the subject of warfare, but she took a quick look around at the boisterous throng. "Are most of these vineyard workers?"

"Yes, miss." He started to draw away, then paused. "The harvest starts next week, so they're doing their finest before the hard work demands." *Vendemmia* was the word for "harvest" he'd used. "And I dare to say, it's a good night to be here."

"Why is that?"

"We'll have some entertainment before long, and you've never seen such."

"Entertainment? Of what sort?"

He showed an impish grin. "You'll have to wait and see."

When the man had shuffled off, Camilla translated for her companions. Fell shifted uneasily in his crooked chair and said, "I never dreamed I'd be among such rabble as this!"

"Relax, professor," Camilla answered. "It's good for the soul, and according to what Santiago told me about you, your soul needs some goodness."

"My reputation has been—" *Untruthfully stretched*, Fell started to say, but on reflection of his past life he decided it was best to let that sleeping dog lie silent.

Their cups of ale came on a battered wooden tray, and Camilla paid from the money pouch she kept tucked in a pocket of her dark blue high-collared jacket. Clean cup or not, Matthew drank deep though the sturdy stuff nearly set fire to the tongue. Fell reached out his cup to clink some kind of toast with Hudson, which the latter completely ignored. Hudson's drink went down the hatch in two gulps, while Camilla sipped hers and kept regarding the revelry with obvious quiet interest.

Matthew decided to broach her quiet in favor of knowing her interest. "What are you thinking?"

"We have here a tavern full of vineyard workers," she said. "Among them might possibly be Brazio Valeriani. Don't you believe we should interrupt this festival to—"

She herself was interrupted by the tavern keeper banging two pans together in a godawful clamor. There followed an immediate hush but for a murmur of what must have been anticipation. The keeper began to bray something out to the others gathered around, which Camilla translated as he spoke.

"He says the betting is about to begin, and as usual he will write the bets down in his wager book," she explained. "There will be payments either in coin or in credits, and he says you all know the rest of the procedure." She paused while the keeper went on, and then she said, "He tells them to step up and place your wagers, and good fortune to all." After that, the crowd broke once more into raucosity and jammed themselves around a big clay pot set up on the bartop. The keeper started dipping his quill in an inkpot and scribbling furiously in a little book while one after another someone hollered out what was obviously a wager and dropped coins—*plink, plink, plink!*—clinking down into the pot.

"What in *blazes* is this all about?" Fell asked.

"I don't know," said Hudson as he stood up, "but there's something going on over there." He motioned toward the far side of the tavern.

Matthew also got to his feet. He saw tables being cleared away and the chairs pushed back from one table in particular but that table left where it stood. Two men were hanging a round object on pegs that had previously been driven into the wall. It took him a few seconds to make out that the object was a cross-section of a pine tree with bark still attached, nearly perfectly round and about twenty inches in diameter. The men were placing it six feet or so off the floor and perhaps ten or eleven feet distant from that table where the chairs had been removed. The strange thing about the cross-section was that rings had been drawn on it in red paint in emulation of the natural rings, with each one becoming smaller until the center was hardly a circle at all but simply a red dot in Matthew's estimation little more than an inch across, and the rest of the circle painted off in triangles numbered also in red.

"What in the *world?*" Camilla said, standing at Hudson's side.

Matthew knew what he was looking at. It was of the same roughness as the people and the place, but its purpose was clear.

"It's a dartboard," he said.

Coins continued to clatter into the pot. Now even Captain Andrado and the four soldiers seemed intrigued by this renewed vigor, for they started pushing their way toward where the crude dartboard had been mounted.

Professor Fell was standing up. "Well, I have to get closer," he said, and he began making his way past the bar toward this center of activity, as the area around that lone table was getting jammed with bodies.

Not to be outdone in either curiosity or audacity, Hudson followed, and then Camilla a few steps behind. Matthew took his last swig of the mouth-scorching ale and approached the hollering tumult in expectation of one devil of a game between dartsmen, or women as the case might be.

When he reached the group and was close enough to see what was happening, he witnessed the same two men who had hung the dartboard now lifting what appeared to be a bundle of rags up onto the table. No! Matthew realized in another instant. The bundle of rags was actually a gray cloak wrapped around what appeared to be a thin body, for the bundle had a head of long sand-colored hair and a gaunt, pallid face freighted with a thick darker brown beard. This man rested upon his elbows atop the table while he seemed to be surveying the dartboard, all the while the congregation around him hollering what must have been shouts of encouragement, for Matthew caught no derision nor sneering in the voices. The two men went about removing the boots from the trousered legs of the figure atop the table, revealing his bare feet. When that was done, the tavern keeper came forward with a leather arrow quiver, which he placed in the hands of one of the men. Then he backed away, gave a shout and a pump of the fist into the air which caused further pandemonic yelling.

As Matthew watched—rather spellbound by what seemed a ritual everyone already knew—the figure on the table smoothly brought his right leg back...back...and back at an angle that appeared agonizingly about to pop it from its socket...and the man with the quiver put an arrow—cut shorter by about half the length of a regular shaft—between the big and second toes of the right foot with its sharp point aimed toward the dartboard.

There was a short pause. The figure on the table stared with intensity at the board and moved his leg just slightly to the left. Then with amazing speed—and power, as well—his leg shot forward, the arrow flew from between his toes...and struck into the board perhaps four inches to the right of the center red, in the triangle numbered twenty-seven.

"*Ventisette!*" the tavern keeper called.

There was a whoop and more shouting from those who Matthew perceived must have placed bets that the arrow would strike the board in this particular triangle...and then the man on the table brought his left leg back...back...and back, a second arrow was placed between the big and second toes of the left foot and obviously tightly gripped, the leg powered forward in very nearly a blur, and the arrow's shaft was suddenly quivering a few inches almost directly above the center red, in triangle number fifteen.

"*Quindici!*" came the cry.

Again there was much shouted joy among the winners along with some miserable bleats of anguish from those who had seen their money lost. The man's right leg came back once more at that incredible joint-snapping angle, the foot positioned far behind his head, and a third arrow was placed in preparation for firing.

Matthew could clearly see the outline of the man's elbows against the table through the folds of his cloak.

But he realized quite suddenly that this bizarre archer had no hands.

ELEVEN

Not since he'd witnessed Professor Fell's giant octopus snatch up the severed head of Jonathan Gentry during his adventure on Pendulum Island had Matthew been as awestruck as what he experienced at this moment in time. He simply could not turn away nor hazard a blink for the idea of missing one instant of the handless archer's amazing performance. One after the other either the right or the left leg was used to fire arrows from their grip between the man's toes to strike with impressive power into one of the board's many numbered triangles. Matthew had never seen the like of it. Each strike brought a new chorus of triumphant winning cries and gasps of lost wager anguish. Matthew surmised that in this game the chances to wager were which triangle would be hit and what foot would be used to deliver the arrow, a choice that was apparently strictly up to the archer, as he did not necessarily go from foot to foot during the spectacle.

Was there room for cheating in this endeavor? Matthew reasoned that though this interesting man had not seen the wager book, someone might have informed him of a particular bet and to which triangle the arrow should go and which foot should cast the bolt, but still…it was a remarkable show of skill and bodily control, and Matthew thought that even though the cries of the losers were well-played, the winning or loss of a copper coin or two was not the point here: it was the entertainment, which everyone—even the criers—were obviously enjoying far more than their cups of ale.

The archer sent nine arrows into various triangles with the tavern keeper shouting out every number. The tenth arrow—carefully aimed, it seemed, with the left foot—went flying through the air and struck smack in the red center, the response to which Matthew feared was going to bring the roof down upon their heads.

At that literal point, it appeared the game was over. The two men who'd helped the archer up onto the table replaced his boots and helped him down, while another figure Matthew had not previously noticed due to the compelling commotion—this one wearing a tan-colored cloak and with shoulder-length white hair and a long white beard—got up from his chair in a shadowed corner, came forward and went about gathering the archer's cloak a little better around the man's shoulders in an act of companionship. Matthew noted that this figure wore a black patch over the left eye.

In the meantime, the tavern keeper had begun to consult the wager book and dip into the pot as the winners crowded around. Matthew saw Hudson and Professor Fell getting up closer to the bar to watch the proceedings, and there were Captain Andrado and the soldiers as well, but where was—

Bang! went something that nearly sounded like a gunshot, and caused all the noise of joviality to instantly cease. Matthew spun around, for the sound had come from behind him, and saw Camilla standing next to one of the tables. She repeated the sound by slamming a cup down upon the wood so hard it surely nearly cracked the thing in two, and then when all attention was directed to her she put aside the cup and held up two gold coins, one in each hand.

She spoke to the throng in their language, which Matthew struggled to understand but he had the feeling he already knew what she was saying.

"We have come in search of a man named Brazio Valeriani," she announced, looking from left to right and then the center. "We understand he has a position at a vineyard. Possibly the one here. Why we choose to find him is our business, but I will tell you that it's very important. If he's here somewhere, he should know that we have no ill will toward him. It's a complicated matter that he might already grasp. Now: I have a gold coin for anyone who tells me that he knows Brazio Valeriani and where he is to be found…or I have *two* gold coins for the man himself, if at this moment he steps forward."

No one moved or spoke.

"Well?" Camilla prompted. "No one wants this gold?"

The silence stretched. Suddenly a voice broke it: *"Lo sono l'uomo!"*

Matthew's heart jumped, for his knowledge of Latin now paid off as this was not so very different: *I'm the man.*

Here came a veritable black-bearded beast of a gent staggering through the crowd. He stopped short of Camilla and weaved back and forth on his feet. Frowning, he gave a horrible belch and, blinking as if the shine of the gold stung his ale-addled eyes, asked her, "Who did you say I am?"

This caused another blast of laughter that almost lifted the roof from its joints. "Rocco!" the tavern keeper shouted, his grin showing the snaggled teeth in a crooked display, "don't taint the air around this beautiful lady!" He said to Camilla, "He's touched in the head, miss, and unfortunately he's my brother-in-law!" Then he put his hands on his hips and addressed the crowd. "Anyone here know that name? If you do, speak up and take your gold, I can use it when you lose it in the game next time!"

There was no answer from the gathering. Camilla looked at Matthew and shook her head to guide his understanding. She returned the coins to her money pouch. Matthew regarded the assembly and thought that indeed Brazio Valeriani might be among them, but if the man didn't want to reveal himself how would he ever be found?

The villagers began returning to their drinking and general carousing. Hudson and Professor Fell made their way over to Matthew and Camilla, Captain Andrado took one last swig of ale and then he and the other four— one who had tippled a bit too much had to be supported by another— joined them and it was obviously time to leave. A campsite for the night had to be made, the teams unhitched, and sleep found for an early morning return to the road.

On her path to the door, Camilla was suddenly stopped by a figure lurching in front of her, and it was such an abrupt halt that Matthew nearly crashed into her back.

Standing before the witch-hunter was the handless archer. The man's bearded face was heavily lined and the pale brown eyes sunken in hollows the color of bruises. He opened his mouth to speak but all that emerged was a gasping, nearly strangled sound.

A hand fell upon the man's shoulder.

The white-bearded and white-haired companion spoke quietly to the man, who continued to stare at Camilla and make that harsh gasping sound. All saw that the companion himself—an aged gent who appeared to at least be in his middle sixties—was not without a prior injury. His right eye was dark blue but the left was covered by a black leather patch that bore an outline of the Christian cross burned upon it. A jagged scar marred the flesh two inches below the patch and cleaved up nearly into the hairline.

At that moment, Matthew forgot himself. He said to both men, "I've never seen such a demonstration as I've witnessed tonight."

The companion's single-eyed gaze snapped toward Matthew. His mouth opened.

"You are *English?*"

"Yes."

"*English,*" the companion repeated. "I have not heard that spoken for...oh...many years."

He spoke it well enough himself, though with a decided Italian accent. "All of you are English?"

"No," Matthew said. "My friend there and the older man." He motioned toward Hudson and the professor.

"And you are here searching for this Brazio Valeriani? Why?"

"Just a moment," said Camilla. "Who are you?"

"Forgive, please. I am Silva Archangelo, the priest here." He was softly stroking the other man's arm as if to calm him, because for some reason the handless archer appeared disturbed and he kept up that gasping sound, his face twisted into what was nearly an expression of agony. "Shhhhh, Trovatello," the priest said quietly. *"Cerchiamo di essere rispettosi nei confronti di questi visitori."*

He'd said *Let us be respectful to these visitors.* Camilla asked, "His name is *Foundling?*"

"Trovatello, *si.* I did find him, little more than three months ago on the road from Venice. I was returning from a conference. He was covered with mud, and…well…you see he has no hands, and neither does he have a tongue. I take care of him as best as I'm able, and I can tell you, young man, that he enjoys his demonstrations far more than anyone else. Also, it's good exercise for him and to be honest the church partakes in just a bit of the pot."

Trovatello had ceased making any noise, and now simply stood staring down at the floor.

Hudson had come forward to stand beside Camilla. He looked Trovatello up and down. "No hands and no tongue? What happened to him?"

"He has no memory," said the priest, "but I can assure you that he is not…how would you say…afflicted in the mind."

Another voice spoke from behind Matthew: "A traitor of some kind in one of the organizations over here. This is their punishment, and then he was left for dead."

Everyone but Trovatello directed their attention to Professor Fell.

Fell shrugged. "I know how it's done."

After a short pause in which he seemed to be digesting that comment, Archangelo said, "It's more than likely true. In this country we unfortunately are burdened with such criminal groups who would do such a thing: The Brotherhood, The Family of the Scorpion, *il Braccio Lungo,* The Knights of the Apocalypse…and all at war with each other as well. As if we don't already have enough war on our doorsteps."

Matthew was fascinated by this handless archer's history but—alas!—there was no time to pursue it. "How do you know he has no memory if he can't coherently speak?"

"He can write," said Archangelo. "With a quill between his toes. It's rudimentary but legible. Or at least *I've* learned to read it. The last thing he can remember is…now this is strange, but…the last thing he can remember is a wolf that walks like a man. Before that and after, nothing."

To this, Trovatello—whose hearing seemed not to be impaired, and though he might not understand English must comprehend the thrust of the speech—let go a soft whine from the depths of his throat and perhaps the depths of his soul, his glassy stare still fixed upon the floor.

"Calmati." Archangelo rubbed the poor man's shoulder. *"Non ne parleremo."*

Captain Andrado said something to Camilla and indicated the inebriated soldier who was now being supported by two comrades.

"Oh, you must be going, I'm sure," said the priest. "And we as well. But may I ask why you seek this Brazio Valeriani?"

"A private matter," Camilla replied, and Archangelo nodded in understanding that it was not to be revealed.

Andrado and the soldiers moved past the others and out through the door. Camilla and Hudson followed, but Matthew and the professor lingered for just another moment.

"Sir?" said Professor Fell. "How is it you speak such fine English?"

"Long ago…*very* long ago, I was a cabin boy for several English captains on vessels carrying spices from Italy to England," was the priest's answer. "I learned the language in that way." He managed a grim smile and touched the eyepatch. "I also learned, in a shipwreck, what a single flying shard of wood can do. After that, I learned to love both the land and the Lord. Come, Trovatello," he said in their language, "we must allow them to be on their way." Then again in English: "Good fortune to you all."

There were at least a dozen questions Matthew wished he could ask of both the priest and Trovatello, but in this case his inflamed curiosity would have to burn itself out into embers. As Archangelo urged his charge out the door with a gentle hand, Trovatello suddenly lifted his head and stared into Matthew's face with an intensity that seemed to be a blaze of pure white-hot rage, so forceful it nearly rocked Matthew back on his heels. In that moment Matthew realized that the horror of what this man must've endured had prematurely aged him, for behind the deep furrows in his face he might've been only in his thirties, as there was not a trace of gray in the hair or beard though his countenance was old and—yes—broken.

And yet…

…there was certainly a living fire in the man's eyes…almost as if some message was trying to be conveyed…and then, gone in the next instant as Trovatello looked away and both he and the priest left the tavern into the warm night air.

Though somewhat shaken by this silent encounter, Matthew recovered his wits enough to say to Fell in a chiding tone, "So you know how it's done?"

"Of course. I had it done as necessary. In my other life, I mean."

"Did you ever plan on doing it to *me?*"

"If you were paying attention, dear boy, you would understand that it is a punishment for *traitors* to the organization. Cut off the offending hands and remove the offending tongue. Then...possibly there would be other things done that I shall not mention. After that, the traitor is left for dead somewhere. In my case—as you well know from your escapades on my beloved and lost island, the thought of which nearly brings me to tears—I had traitors taken care of quite neatly. Now I suggest we get off this line of conversation because it does neither of us any good. Suffice to repeat: I know how it's done."

Outside the tavern as the others were getting up into the wagons, Matthew watched the priest and Trovatello walking away, Archangelo's hand on the other man's shoulder. Trovatello glanced back once, then continued onward toward wherever he was living. Again, Matthew wished he had time to explore their history, but it was not to—

"*Signorina?*" someone said.

Camilla had been about to climb up into their wagon, and she paused now to see that a slim dark-haired man had emerged from the tavern and was approaching. "*Si?*" she asked.

He stopped and said in his language, "Pardon, but...you were asking about this man?"

"I was. Do you know him?"

"Well...not that name, but...I know a man named Brazio."

Hudson had been about to help Camilla climb up. He, Matthew and Professor Fell all heard the name and instantly turned their attention to what was going on.

"Continue," Camilla urged.

"The name," said the man. "A year ago I was working at the vineyard in Pappano. The fighting destroyed it. The soldiers...their horses and the cannons...crushed all the vines before the harvest. There was a man who worked as a bookkeeper by the name of Brazio Nascosto. A strange name, I know, but he was a good fellow though very quiet and he kept to himself. After the vineyard was destroyed, I came here for the work. I don't know where he went, but not here."

"Nascosto," Camilla repeated. "You're sure of that?"

"Oh yes, miss. I am wondering if he maybe went to the west, to work at the vineyard at Balanero. That would be a few hours journey past Pappano. I mean to say, what is left of Pappano. The village too was destroyed."

"Balanero," Camilla said. It was clearly marked on the map from Meneghetti's office. "Thank you, that's very helpful." In fact, so helpful it had caused her heartbeat to pick up.

"You are welcome." He cleared his throat before he spoke again. "Would I receive the gold coin for this information?"

Camilla made the quick decision. She took a gold coin from her pouch and held it out. "Thank you again," she said. The man took it, plunged it into a pocket and returned to the tavern.

"What was that about?" Hudson asked.

"He says he worked with a bookkeeper named Brazio Nascosto at Pappano, which was destroyed by the war, and this man might be at Balanero. We have to go through Pappano to get there...and that's where we should go, as quickly as possible."

"Why?" Matthew had come to Camilla's side. "That's not who we're looking for."

She showed a slight smile. "Nascosto is a name but it's also a word, meaning 'hidden' or 'unseen'. As I say, we should get to Balanero and hope this man is there. It could be Valeriani, or not. We'll only know if we find him."

Once more, Matthew was struck by the fact that this entire search hinged upon what was really only a "hunch". But it was all they had to go on, and so on through Pappano to the vineyard at Balanero, for better or for worse.

The wagons moved on a few miles past Sante Vallone until Captain Andrado found a clearing in the pines off the road where they might make camp. The teams were unhitched, watered and allowed to graze, the bedrolls were rolled out, a fire was made and some of the dried food, apples and such were eaten. Matthew observed that clouds had obscured the moon, and the following day might be overcast. A threat of rain? They would see.

About half an hour into their encampment, Hudson came back from one of the wagons where he'd gotten a handful of figs. He sat down on his bedroll between Matthew and Camilla and quietly said, "I'd estimate that two miles back someone else has a fire going. I just saw the flicker. Then it was probably either doused or somebody put a shield around it. A little too late, but gone dark nevertheless."

"What does it mean?" Camilla asked.

"It means," said the once Great One who was steadily and noticeably becoming better in all ways, "that we're being followed by someone who doesn't want to be seen." Then he bit into a fig and held one out to her, which she accepted from his hand.

TWELVE

IN THE HOURS AFTER HER RAPTUROUS EXPERIENCE IN HER TOYROOM, Venus Scaramanga drank half a bottle of Chianti and regarded on the white sofa the crimson stain Adam Black had left there. The sun was coming up, and soon the butterflies would be flitting back and forth among the garden's flowers. She enjoyed watching them, particularly when she was so relaxed. But her relaxation was a passing thing, because someone else—nine of them—were after the sorcerer's mirror, and added to that there was a book that had to be taken.

Nyx was still with Lupo, back in his dwelling behind the villa. He would have to clean and handle the lynx carefully and wearing thick leather gloves, because the odor and taste of fresh blood made the animal's wildness rise to the surface, and while she considered Nyx never fully tamed—an attribute she admired—the creature was a threat even to her while the blood smell remained on its breath. So Lupo would bring Nyx back after a time, he would put on the stout collar and the leash, and she would have her pet under control once more.

She had told Mars that attention was her life. So, too, was the thrill of danger.

Which was why she'd been galled at having Lorenzo track her through the streets of Venice last night. Lorenzo was of course an accomplished bodyguard. He knew his business. They all did. But the idea of strolling about open to an assassin's strangle cord or knife...it appealed to her in a way she could not fully convey to her brother. No, he had his opium to dream on and make himself feel safe. She did not wish to feel safe. She wished to live on the raw edge of uncertainty, and challenge those fears that death was always lurking in a shadow.

For it was. It might come from the Knights of the Apocalypse, the Brotherhood, or *il Braccio Lungo*…the Long Arm. They were perpetually fighting over territorial rights, just as the Family of the Scorpion fought against them as well. Just last month a high-ranking member of the Brotherhood had climbed into a coach with his wife and young son on their way to dinner in Bologna, and the coach had never arrived. In fact, it was never found. Scorpion blades had cut their throats along with those of the driver and the bodyguard on top, the corpses cut into pieces and thrown into a lake along with the bodies of the horses, the coach dismantled down to the wheel hubs and those elements given over to one of the water-powered sawmills in the Family's employ.

One coach and a Brotherhood *tenente*…vanished.

But of course they knew it had been an assassination, but they did not know from whom it had arrived.

It was the world into which Mars and Venus had been born, and now through family heritage and obligation expected to preside over.

She got up from the sofa and walked back into the spacious kitchen, where she told Chiara the cook to prepare a pot of the strongest *caffe* she could brew. While that was working, Venus climbed the spiral stairs, then into her red-walled bathing chamber where she stood appraising herself in the full-length mirror there with its gilded frame and carvings of the visages of beautiful women, none more beautiful than herself.

She opened her jacket and blouse to expose her high, tight breasts with their dark brown nipples. She ran her hands across them in appreciation of the youth that still pulsed there. The rings caught her attention, and she brought them closer to her eyes to examine the skulls, strange carved faces and even more bizarre symbols. She wondered what kind of man Adam Black had been. Perhaps she wished she had hesitated in her decision, but then again no…it had been a most satisfactory release.

Venus looked again into the mirror, and to her horror she saw it happening once more.

Her face was changing.

The flesh was tightening, the cheekbones jutting out like sharp blades, her lips and chin sagging, the fiery flame of the eyes dimming, her neck corded and thickened. As she watched in this transfixion of terror she saw the lines deepening across her face, the wrinkles rising up as if in an old pale cloth, her hair turning to gray in an instant but for the red on the right side which became dull and rusty, bags of loose flesh growing beneath the eyes, her breasts falling, loosening like small burlap bags, the cords of the neck now grown thick, her lips nearly thinned away and—

With a stifled cry she put a hand over her eyes and stood trembling.

When she dared to look again, the exquisite beauty of Venus Scaramanga had returned and she drew a deep breath of relief though she trembled still. This apparition…this horror…was happening more often. It was the only assassin she truly feared.

Time.

And now as she peered into the mirror she realized there was a figure standing behind her in a far corner of the chamber beyond the copper tub.

It wore a hooded purple cloak, and in the darkness of the hood it had no face.

She heard it speak. It was a whisper in her mind rather than in her ears…a quiet voice, carrying neither the tone of male nor female but rather as if a cold night wind might speak.

It said, :*Do not trust*:.

When she spun around she realized she was entirely alone, for that corner of the chamber was empty but for a rack of towels.

Or was she alone? Her trembling had now become nearly violent. It was terrifying enough that she regularly had these visions of creeping time, of old age falling upon her like a deadening cloak, and though she despised men, no longer would any man look upon her with hunger for a feast they could never have, and year after year what she saw in the mirror would come true in a failing of flesh and bone and mind, unless…

…unless the sorcerer's glass could change all that.

But now…this vision as well…this message from the unknown.

Do not trust.

In a deep place never to be revealed to anyone she thought that perhaps she was already losing her mind, that the responsibilities of the Family she shared with Mars had overtaken her, and all her steely resolve was a sham. But no, no…she could not let doubt cripple her…could not let any failing crack the strong stone villa she had constructed around herself. Weakness could not be tolerated in anyone, and particularly not in the grandmistress of the Family of the Scorpion.

Never.

But this vision…this hooded figure, now twice seen…

I have a familiar, she remembered Black saying. *A spirit who walks with me and informs me of these things.*

She'd asked: *An evil spirit?*

A spirit who suits my needs. I call him Dominus, and he is standing in that corner yonder.

Venus again studied the silver rings. There was a Satanic influence at work here, she thought. The idea gave her both a chill and a thrill. Dominus? *A spirit who suits my needs.*

Was this more evidence of the slippage of her mind? Or was it possible that whatever this thing was…after the death of its master, it had attached itself to *her?*

Do not trust.

What did this mean?

She thought she knew. This spirit—if it was real, and it seemed real enough to her—was now at work suiting her needs. The need to get hold of that book and consequently power over the sorcerer's mirror.

Yes.

She buttoned herself up and went back downstairs, not to the kitchen but to the front door, where she pulled a bell cord that hung next to the entrance as it hung the same in other rooms. She heard the bell ring up in the turret. Within seconds the door opened and Ivano and Raimondo, two of the several bodyguards who roamed the estate day and night, came in with their hands ready to draw the swords at their belts. Ivano, he of the slim and wiry body and eyes like small bits of ebony ice, also had his other hand about to unholster his flintlock pistol.

"No emergency," she told them to ease the moment. "But an urgency. *You.*" She pointed at Ivano, who she considered the more capable of the two since in April he'd killed a pair of would-be assassins who'd managed to get over the wall using ropes attached to grappling hooks. "Go to the office of the wine merchant Ottavio Meneghetti." She gave him the exact address. "Tell him I want the same map he gave to his visitors. Get there as quickly as you can and back as quickly. *Go.*"

Without a word the two men departed, closing the door behind them. On horseback Ivano could reach the ferry within the hour, and then soon after to Meneghetti.

Venus went to the kitchen, had Chiara put the *caffe* pot and two cups on a tray, and then she climbed the stairs and strode along the corridor to the door of her brother's room. Inside the huge chamber with its massive paintings on the walls and its luxurious cowhide furnishings, Mars lay sprawled naked amid the twisted sheets of his gilded bed with its high, ornately decorated headboard. She put the tray down on a white marble table next to the bed and went about opening all the curtains to let the morning sunlight stream in through the barred windows.

"Wake up!" Venus grasped his shoulder and shook him but there was no reaction. His mouth was partway open. She could pour a little hot *caffe* into it, that might do the trick. She shook him again and this time his mouth closed and he made a muttering sound. "Wake!" she demanded. When he shifted in the bed and tried to pull the sheet over his head, she poured a little *caffe* into a cup and turned it over on his chest through the sheet.

That brought him up with a shout that turned into a wheeze. His drug-swollen eyes searched for the offender.

"Get your tail out of bed," she told him.

Mars sat up, rubbing his chest. He blinked in the strong eastern light. "Have you..." He tried again, in as much of a forceful voice as he could manage. "Have you gone *mad?*"

"Get up, drink a cup of *caffe* and listen to me."

"What? Oh...now you're giving *me* commands?"

"Take it however you please." She poured him the cup and held it out, but he just sat there staring at it. "Tell me again," she said, "who you sent after those people."

"What people?"

"If you don't take this and drink it in three seconds it's going into your face."

Mars knew his sister meant it. When they were children she delighted in torturing him with such things as the little coach whip she'd convinced their father to gift her. That and the tarantula spider under his pillow. He had no doubt hot *caffe* in the face was a possibility. But he was listening now through the last of the opium fog, because there was some rare immediacy in her voice. He took the cup, and she waited until he'd put most of it down.

"Tell me again who you sent to follow those people who visited Meneghetti," she said.

"Wait...I'm thinking. All right...well, you were there...don't you remember?"

"Refresh my memory." She poured herself a cup while he gathered his brains.

"Rossone, Lamacchia and Gallo from Divittori's crew," Mars said. He held out his cup for another pour, which Venus obliged. "Good men. I sent the message to have them available to follow—"

"Divittori is an idiot and his crew are idiots," Venus said.

"Your opinion, dear sister. Divittori has shown his abilities again and again." Mars blinked at the nearest window. "What time is it? They're probably already on the job, if those people have left the inn."

"On the job," Venus repeated with an air of sarcasm. And again: "*On the job!* You've given one of the most important tasks in *our lives* to these men!" *Do not trust*, she thought. It was a message worth heeding. "You might trust them, but I do not."

"By the mercy of Mary, what are you going on about?"

"Listen to me." She sat down on the bed at his side. "While you were having dreams of flying bullfrogs or whatever it is you see in that stuff, I discovered that these people are not only after the mirror, but that they have a very important *book*. Don't give me a look like that, I'll slap it off your face! This book, dear brother, gives the names of the demons, their powers, shows seals to invoke them and protect the person calling them along with incantations. And right now that book is in the hands of a Spanish witch-hunter by the name of Camilla. Are you understanding what I'm saying? The mirror is important, yes, but the book is just as vital! And you've sent off underlings to be on the job! What happens if they get hold of this book? And the mirror as well? Dear brother, I don't wish to be alarming anyone within earshot on this happy morning, but if those men decide it's in their own interest to betray us and use the mirror and the book…it would be an assassination of a very different and very efficient kind. And don't tell me that the odds are against those people finding Brazio Valeriani! I don't care about odds! The possibility is there, and I'm not going to sit here sweating about it night and day, wringing my hands and letting you sleep this crisis away! Because you *cannot!*"

"Wait, wait!" Mars held up his free hand. "This book. A witch-hunter. How did you find out about all this?"

"My little mission in Venice last night. I happened to meet one of that group. And no, the others had no idea. I brought this fine gentleman home to the toyroom and we had a nice conversation. Also he left me some gifts." *And possibly more than these*, she thought as she turned her own free hand into the light to make the rings gleam.

"Where is he?" Mars asked.

"Don't make me laugh."

"I hear what you're saying," Mars continued, "but we don't even know if this Brazio Valeriani is even in—"

Venus stopped him by picking up the pot in a threatening gesture. "I swear I'll brain you with this if you speak another stupid word! No, we don't know *this* and we don't know *that!* We know only what that supposed sorcerer said: Leviathan! What does it mean? We don't know that, either! We could die not knowing, while the mirror and the book are found and that would be the end of us! I say it's worth one thing: that we should go after these people ourselves."

Mars sat as if stupefied.

"Yes," Venus said. She drank her *caffe* down and set the cup and the pot aside. "Hear me out. We take the coach. I've had Ivano go get from Meneghetti the same map he gave them. We take Ivano, Pagani and Lorenzo with us. And Lupo too, we might need his talents. If we get on their trail, we can catch up with them. They have to be travelling in at least in one wagon and probably two, so we'll be faster. But we don't attack…at least, not yet. We follow them, and for the time being that is all."

Mars still had no answer.

"Ivano, Pagani and Lorenzo," she emphasized. "Also Lupo. All right, it's a risk getting out of the house and going on the road like that. Yes, it is… but I do not trust anyone but *us* to get hold of Valeriani, the mirror and the book. Are you going to speak or remain forever dumb?"

A further, deeper darkness had come into the eyes of Mars Scaramanga. He said in a quiet voice, "Don't push me, sister. You have reached your limit."

Venus stood up. Like Nyx, her brother could be unpredictable when truly angered and in this moment it would do neither of them any good.

"Control your emotions," he said, still in that quiet and very dangerous voice. "Give me time to think."

"Our time may be running out," she dared to reply.

His stare upon her was unwavering. "And what about Divittori's men?"

"We release them from their *job*." Again, it was a daring response. "If necessary, they can be disposed of." She tried another angle. "We take the coach and bodyguards every month to the gathering. What's the difference?"

"Ten miles as opposed to…what?…thirty? Fifty?"

"Do you not understand that this is our chance to be *free*? And my chance to get what I want? Mars, either we believe in the power of this glass or we don't. And if we *do* believe, we can't leave it to the hired help."

He was silent, but Venus could tell this was beginning to sink in.

"The coach," she repeated. "Lorenzo, Pagani and Ivano with us at all times. Lupo can ride a horse behind the coach to watch our backs."

"We won't be safe," Mars answered. His voice was hollow. "We can never be safe."

She touched his face with gentle fingers. "Safety," she said, "is only in the mirror."

He lowered his head, and she knew she had won.

"If we start arranging now," she told him, "getting our baggage together, some food and whatnot—a couple of tents in case they're needed—we can start off around midday. That won't put us but a few hours behind them and we can catch up. The map will be here soon. Can I have an answer?"

His answer was: "Leave me."

Venus nodded. Mars knew. He was intelligent; he knew. Best now to let him come to her decision on his own. She leaned down, kissed his cheek, and left the bedroom.

For a long while he sat where he was, his head lowered with the sheets twisted around him. The thought of leaving the house and travelling that distance even with three bodyguards and Lupo drove a cold spike through his heart. Was there any other sensible way? The mirror…the book…the freedom both combined could give himself and Venus! Oh, she courted death like a lover but he cringed at the idea of going down with his slashed throat spewing gore like…

…like their father had been murdered.

Eight years ago, the fourteenth night of October. All the regal coaches pulling up to the front steps that swept to the entrance of Venice's *Teatro San Cassiano*, the beautiful opera house where—alas—only four hundred people could find seats to hear the magnificent Madam Alicia Candoleri singing in Jacopo Corsi's *Dafne*. And within, all the lamps lit and the little flame lights flickering across the front edge of the stage, while Mars Scaramanga and Venus Scaramanga sat on the front row, center stage, on either side of their father Vittorio, Grandmaster of *il Famiglia Dello Scorpione*. All the audience being the upper class of this city of art and architecture, the men in their finest suits and some in powdered wigs, the ladies in their voluminous pastel-hued gowns and hair styled to the heavens. Behind and around the Scaramangas sat their bodyguards, hard-faced men armed with pistols and daggers under their silk-lined cloaks, their eyes never resting upon the activity on stage, their ears never hearing the thrilling notes cast up to the highest point like stars of amazing light from the madam's throat…no, not just the throat, but the soul.

Vittorio so loved the opera. *Scorpione* money went into its management. And after the opera was over, after all the roses had been thrown, after Madam Candoleri had basked in applause after applause and invited the entire cast and conductor of the orchestra upon the stage, after that…there was a walk down the steps in the cool night air to the waiting coach, and as usual there were the street violinists playing and the beggars in their hooded cloaks calling for money with upturned cups of the roughest clay, and then from one of those cloaks came a pistol…a shot followed, gasps and screams following that, the crowd in confusion, the beggar lying dead on the steps, shot through the head by a *Scorpione* bodyguard before his own hammer could fall, and then Vittorio pushing his son and daughter into the coach and himself being pushed by another bodyguard when a snake of an arm belonging to a second beggar impostor came out of a cloak bearing a small hooked knife—and here Mars remembered the glint of it by the coach's interior lamp, how small it was, how insignificant to the wealth and power of the Scaramangas—and for all its diminutive size, only long as half a crooked finger, it got past the man pushing their father in and it cut the throat of Vittorio Scaramanga as if the flesh was made of wet parchment and all the blood…all the blood sprayed upon the twins in flying streams that Mars remembered looked to him in that instant before the horror set in like red paper confetti thrown by wine-drunk revellers at the merry *carnavale*.

Still Vittorio tried to get into the coach, his widened eyes upon his children, as if not yet fully aware that beneath the square chin and the trimmed black beard his throat had been sliced open like a gutted cod. Mars could still hear his sister's ragged high-pitched scream in the bloody confines of the coach, and she would not make another sound again for almost a month. Two more shots cracked out, aimed at the assassin. One of the balls blasted through the side where Mars was sitting, showering him with splinters and shreds of padded gray leather. The assassin was hit in the back but survived for further interrogation, and so it had begun.

Nothing could prepare one for such a life, such a responsibility, nor armor one against all threats. Indeed, great-grandfather Adolfo, his wife and younger daughter had been burned alive in a coach when a thirteen-year-old boy in the employ of a rival family threw a firebomb that also burned him to a screaming cinder, for whoever had instructed him had evidently withheld information on the bomb's power. Adolfo's surviving son Maximus had faced death several times but had escaped until the dark angel found him in his bed at the age of sixty-eight.

Mars's first order of business had been loosening the wounded beggar's tongue when the man had recovered enough to speak. One afternoon Venus came back from town with an item she'd bought in an antique shop that sold such things: something called a thumbscrew, large enough to crush all five fingers at once and with the added implement of piercing spikes. She wished to speak to the assassin down in the wine cellar beneath the house, joined by others from the family and by Lupo, who had served Vittorio and the organization so well as an executioner in the last three years of Vittorio's life that the Grandmaster had presented him the guest house behind the villa and the vow that his face was never to be seen without the mask.

And with the thumbscrew, Venus's collection had begun.

A traitorous bodyguard was discovered, implicated in Vittorio's murder. He was traced to where he and his family had fled, an apartment in Rome. Man, woman, three children and dog were killed on Mars's command. As it was, the neighboring family also had to be killed, for the man had come over to take his new friend for their weekly game of bocce ball while the heads were being axed off by Lupo, who among the unsuspecting public always wore a hooded cloak when not the metal *domino*.

Nothing could prepare one for such a life. Yet it had to be lived. Mars understood very well indeed that with riches and power came those seeking to rip it away. He had heard someone put it succinctly: *E quello che e.*

It is what it is.

He got up from the bed.

Freedom? Release from this mental torture of perpetual fear?

Venus had spoken it: *Safety is only in the mirror.*

The sunlight burned his eyes. He must now get dressed and have Edetta do his packing, because he and his sister had a journey to take.

THIRTEEN

A WOLF THAT WALKS LIKE A MAN.

It was the second thought Matthew had upon awakening, the first being the fact that he had to find a place in the woods to pee.

As he stood against a tree at a distance from the group—in particular, from Camilla—and found relief from last night's ale, he recalled another creature he'd encountered on his voyage up the Carolina colony's River of Souls in pursuit of a murderer. It had been called the Soul Cryer and described as a panther that walked as a man. In reality, it was a panther deformed by a fire in the swampy forest that in its agony did shamble upright for short periods of time. But a wolf that walks like a man? And this a grotesque memory from a poor individual whose hands and tongue had been severed? A traitor to his organization, the professor had suggested. More than suggested; the professor knew how it was done.

Matthew buttoned up his trousers. When he returned to the group he caught the bemused expression on Hudson's face that he knew was a precursor to a statement such as *Everything come out all right?* but considering that Hudson was trying his best to appear a gentleman in front of Camilla, nothing was said. Anyway, all of them would have to visit the woods before they continued toward Pappano, the lady included.

Before his eyes had closed last night, Matthew had watched the lady sitting before the fire and removing the book from the small leather valise she kept it laced up in. The need for sleep had prevented him from a long observation, but he'd seen her reading some of the pages with what appeared an intense interest, and this wasn't the first time. He wondered again what the Spanish wanted with the book—other than that ridiculous attempt at convincing anyone they wished to lock it away for the good of the world—and in particular why they'd sent her on this mission. A university teacher of languages, turned into a "witch-hunter" as her father and grandfather had been. Was that entirely true? What was it about Camilla Espaziel that the Spanish—at whatever level of authority—considered her qualified to put her hands on the mirror and deliver it to them? She was a forceful personality and seemed highly intelligent, true, but he had the distinct feeling that something else was at work. And he was determined to find out, though it might take some time and a quiet approach.

There was another element that intrigued Matthew as well: several times he'd caught Camilla staring with that equal intensity at Hudson, though she quickly averted her gaze when Hudson glanced at her. An attraction, yes, and it was returned in Hudson's desire to clean himself up and attempt to break free from the haunting episode of his soldiering past. But was that all there was to it? Again, Matthew wished to find out more but it was—suffice to say—a tricky subject.

This morning, a thick pall of gray clouds covered the sky and a firm breeze ruffed through the tops of the pines. Matthew could smell dampness in the air. Food and water were taken by all, the bedrolls packed away, the teams hitched back into their traces and the wagons remounted, again with Andrado at the reins of the leading vehicle and one of the soldiers—the same one who'd gotten a bit dazed in the head last night, but now happily recovered—up on the driver's bench of the second. Professor Fell took a turn seated next to the Spaniard, and they were ready to resume their progress.

They had been on the road—a goat track, at the very most—about ten minutes when Hudson said to Camilla, "Do you have any idea who might be following us?"

"No. If indeed we *are* being followed."

"It could be simply travellers heading in the same direction," Matthew offered.

"Could be," said Hudson. "Who else knows about this mirror?"

Camilla shook her head. "I have no idea."

"This wine merchant you two visited. Spaghetti."

"Meneghetti," Matthew corrected.

"Whatever. You only asked if he knew the name Brazio Valeriani, correct?"

Camilla gave him what Matthew considered the evil eye. "Hudson, we're not fools."

"But he's the only one you spoke to?"

"The only one."

"Well," Hudson said, his mouth crimped and his eyebrows raised, "that only leaves fifty or more people in that tavern. I hope Andrado and the soldiers didn't spout anything off in there…particularly our ale-loving driver."

"They're not fools, either," Camilla replied, now with a slight air of indignation. "They know how important this is."

Hudson shifted his attention to Matthew. "You know who else it could be."

"Who?"

"You know. Black. It's possible he got himself a horse or he's hired a wagon."

"A remote possibility," Matthew said. "He doesn't speak the language and as far as I know he didn't have a single coin in his pocket…but then again, he did have his silver rings."

"Exactly. He might have met someone who speaks English. And what would stop him from robbing a person on the street for money? Or killing somebody, if it came to that? You have to admit, it's very strange that he turned his back so quickly on finding the mirror, since it tickled his Satanic ass so much…pardon to the lady, but it did." Hudson moved through the supplies and bags to the rear of the wagon. He parted the canvas and peered out. The landscape was hilly and covered with dense forest. Because the road curved back and forth he could see less than a quarter mile of it. "Did Andrado bring a spyglass?" he asked Camilla.

"I assume he did, but it would be with his belongings up front."

Hudson gave a quiet grunt but maintained his vigil. Matthew wondered if indeed Cardinal Black might be on their trail. If true, there was yet a chance he could see the demoniac stretched at the end of a rope.

After a while, Hudson let the canvas fall into place and returned to where he'd been originally sitting. "Can't do anything about that right now, but I'll keep an eye out." He looked around the interior, obviously searching for something but not finding it. "Too bad we don't have cards or dice, I could use some entertainment." He gave Camilla a sly smile. "Unless you want to hear all about my ex-wives."

"I'm sure she does *not*," Matthew said. And to her: "The scar across his eyebrow is from a broken teacup."

"And the one across *his* forehead is from one hell of a bear," Hudson ventured. "Oh, between us we could really rattle your cage."

"I'm unaware of being caged," she said.

"It's a figure of English speech. No disrespect meant."

She made no further comment on his comment. The wagons rolled on with their slightly inebriating side-to-side sway. Perhaps ten minutes passed during which Hudson retreated again to the rear of the wagon and then returned once more, having spied nothing but pine-forested hillsides, lowering gray clouds and the lonely road.

When Hudson had situated himself, Camilla said, "How many wives have you had?"

"What?" The question had caught him totally off-guard, and Matthew as well.

"Wives. How many. Had," she repeated, speaking to the largest child she'd likely ever encountered.

Hudson made a show of counting ten fingers. Then he held up three. *"Tres,"* he replied.

"I take it you're no longer in the state of wedded bliss? Did you abandon the ladies or was it done legally? I presume in England there is some procedure a refined gentleman like yourself would follow."

"Yes. I mean *no*. All legal, and thank you for the compliment." He smiled but Matthew saw the fox behind the teeth. "Have you ever been married?"

"No."

"Oh, playing the proud virgin, are you?"

The green eyes gave him a withering look. "I said I'd never been *married.*"

Matthew had to aim his gaze down at the floorboards on that one, and it was a long moment before anyone spoke again.

It was Camilla: "Do you have children?"

"Huh? Oh. No, I don't." Hudson made a whuffing sound. *"Me* with children! A father! I can't imagine it! Can you, Matthew?"

Don't drag me into this, Matthew thought. He assumed they'd left the wooden practice swords far behind in Alghero. But just to be wicked he said, "You'd probably make an exceptional father."

"Are you—" No telling what foul epithet was going to follow, though Hudson caught it back before it spilled out. His smile stretched so hard one could almost hear the face creak. "Thank you kindly."

"I agree," said Camilla. "I'm sure your experiences would be a valuable cautionary tale for any impressionable youth."

"Did she just insult me?" Hudson asked of Matthew.

He shrank down on the bench seat a little further. It seemed to him that in lieu of cards or dice these two had found a way to entertain themselves and each other and at the moment Matthew felt like a third wheel, a fifth horseshoe and an eleventh finger. He decided retreat was the better part of valor, and so he said, "Pardon me," and went out to spell Professor Fell his seat next to the driver.

The day moved on so did the wagons. The rolling landscape became even more so, hill after dale, the forest thick and thicker, the road a challenge to the teams and the sky threatening rain. When there came time for a stop to rest the horses from this perpetual and ever more hardy labor, Hudson asked Camilla to inquire of Captain Andrado if he might borrow the soldier's spyglass, which Matthew saw was greeted by one of the sour captain's most saturnine expressions, but the polished brass instrument was given up with Andrado's warning not to drop it or otherwise foul the focus.

They got underway once more with Matthew again up beside the driver, who though not as dour as the captain was wont to mutter in Spanish what sounded like sincere curses from the lowest alleys of Madrid. On this day the sun was never more than a somewhat lighter blot in the sky. With the first blue tinge of twilight came a steady rain that made Matthew wish for a mariner's oilskin coat but alas he only had his landlubber's garb which was soon soggily uncomfortable, the driver beside him equally wet and voicing his curses at a louder volume.

Over another hill where the clouds hung like shreds of torn white tapestry among the trees, and there in the valley before and below them was the village of Pappano and its vineyard.

Rather, Matthew mused, it had *been* a village and vineyard, for as the teams pulled the travellers onward it was clearly seen that most of the small houses constructed from wood had been burned to ashy debris and the few that were formed of brown stones had suffered broken windows and collapsed roofs. Around the ruins the forest showed signs of a ravenous fire, the black skeletons of trees now dripping with rainwater that would not nourish life again here for a very long time. Indeed, though this area had been destroyed by some battle or another at a distant time, Matthew yet caught the odor of gunpowder and scorched earth. What appeared to be the vineyards covering a hillside about three hundred yards from the village was a crumpled area of ugly ground now producing nothing more valuable than weeds and scrub brush, everything wet with the rain but dark with the tragedy and senselessness of human conflict...in this case which regal family—the Bourbons or the Habsburgs—ruled the Spanish crown, and in so fighting had drawn into the war nearly the whole of Europe.

Matthew saw a few buildings out amid the wrack, but they too looked to be wrecked. Still...through the twilight's mist he could make out a larger structure with a gabled red roof that stood almost at the top of the hillside and was surrounded by a tangle of forest. A villa, he took it to be. Likely the house of the vineyard's owner, who obviously had a taste for finer living and had been doing well enough financially to afford such a place.

"Good-sized house up there," said Hudson, who was looking out from the wagon over Matthew's shoulder. "I doubt if anyone's home, though." He took a gander through Andrado's spyglass. "Broken windows and a couple of big holes in the walls. Cannonfire, I'd think. Looks like—"

At this point with a low rumble of thunder the rain began to come down so hard it made the horses jump and shiver as if they'd been smacked with whips. Against the canvas of the wagons it sounded like a hundred drummers all vying for the most generous coin. His hair and face streaming, Hudson closed the spyglass with a *snap* and finished his thought: "Looks like shelter for the night."

What there was of the road had turned to ebony mud. Andrado halted his team and came sloshing back through the increasing downpour. He called for Camilla, who when she pushed her head forth from the wagon's canvas was almost instantly reduced to a mess of silvery hair and a nearly drowned face. Andrado and Camilla talked back and forth—or rather shouted back and forth due to nature's noise—and obviously the captain had seen the vineyard's villa because he pointed at it. Camilla nodded, Andrado returned to his wagon, and both wagons started up the hill between the devastated rows of what used to be healthy and profitable grapevines, now sodden and sad under the deluge.

And deluge it was. Partway up the road there came a flash of lightning, another crack of thunder and the horses of Matthew's wagon began to lose their footing on what had become a sluice of flowing water. Matthew, who was completely drenched up beside the dripping driver, Hudson, the professor and Camilla in the back all sat with bated breath, the rain hammering the wagon's canvas, until the vehicle halted behind Andrado's in what appeared to be the villa's overgrown and desolate courtyard.

The effort was undertaken to remove their bags of clothing and some supplies from the wagons into the house. Andrado's first entry through the blasted and char-edged opening where the front door had been caused the two deer that had taken up lodging within to leap through a gaping hole in the far wall and flee for the forest. Chocks were set up under the wagon wheels to prevent the things slipping down the hill but there was the question of how to handle the teams in this severe storm. The nearest structure was a small outbuilding that might have been a gardener's shed, far too small for the horses, and beyond that the debris of a burned barn. Andrado and another of the soldiers had an argument that Matthew perceived involved whether the jumpy teams should be unhitched and perhaps run away or left in their traces and drag the wagons with them if the thunder and lightning caused them to bolt. Andrado's position evidently ruled, because the horses were left hitched in trust that if they ran the wheel chocks wouldn't let them get very far.

The villa, which had a once-beautiful high-ceilinged foyer and a staircase with a wrought-iron railing, still retained some furniture but most of the pieces were ruined either by soldiers, the elements, or animal invasion. Andrado got one of the wagon's lamps burning with his flint-and-cotton tinderbox. By its illumination could be seen water streaming through holes in the cracked ceiling above what had been a spacious parlor that yet had a mosaic of—appropriately at the moment—fish swimming in a pond upon one of the fully intact walls. The decision was made and seconded by all the near-drowned survivors of this torrent to find shelter deeper in the villa's interior. A room toward the middle of the house was chosen as it contained a large white stone fireplace and beside it a copper pot holding eight logs of what was found to be dry pinewood and a half-dozen pine-cones, all suitable for burning.

Having to wage strategic warfare against the water that dripped steadily down the flue, Andrado got the fire started. Matthew discovered a standing candelabra with three stubs remaining, and these were lighted to provide at least a triad more of cheer on this dismal night. Two of the soldiers ventured out again into the storm to bring back another pair of oil lamps, a third and fourth soldier brought back two leather chairs from other rooms, the bedrolls were laid out upon a floor covered by a sand-colored rug, and those who wished to get out of their wet clothes were given the opportunity to take a lamp, retire to a place of privacy—in accordance with the presence of a female—and do so.

Hudson elected to let his clothes dry on him by the fire, while Matthew and Professor Fell each found another chamber in which to change, the pro-fessor returning with the discovery of a clay jug that when uncorked—and the liquor-loving soldier taking the first swig—turned out to be what would be called in England "applejack". There was enough for all to warm what the fire could not reach. Camilla came back wearing a dark brown dress, white ruffled blouse, a black riding jacket and a pair of high-topped black boots with crimson laces, which prompted Hudson to lower the jug from his mouth in interruption of his drink and ask, "Do you always dress like you're about to go to a royal garden party?"

If she intended to fire back a witty riposte she was second-best to a blast of thunder. She strode past Andrado and the soldiers, the professor and Matthew, took the jug from Hudson and put down a slug, and then she gave it to Matthew, settled herself on one of the leather chairs and stretched her legs out.

Matthew declined to drink and so passed the jug to Professor Fell, who gulped down a bit and in turn passed it on. Rain beat steadily on the roof, thunder boomed and lightning cracked, but the fire was a fine warmth and illumination and for the moment this room in the villa was home sweet home.

"If the storm passes soon enough and the road isn't completely washed out, we should reach Balanero around noon if we leave at first light," Camilla said from her memory of the map.

"I wouldn't count on any of that," said Hudson. "Ask Andrado what he thinks."

Andrado's opinion was inquired. The captain paused his second drink of the jack to give a scowling reply.

"Is he always this sour?" Hudson asked Camilla. "I swear the man sweats lemons."

Camilla spoke to the captain, who answered back once more in his usual bitter tone.

"He says he has a right to be sour." Professor Fell was exhibiting his learned knowledge of Spanish. "He says his wife is expecting their third child and here he sits on what he calls an idiotic mission."

Hudson nodded an assent. "It *is* idiotic…but we're here, so we might as well do the job and get it over with."

Camilla turned her gaze on the professor. "Do *you* think it's idiotic, sir?"

His answer was a pause in coming. Then he said, "In my old life, I thought it was the most important thing on Earth to find. The mirror, I mean. Now…I wouldn't care if I never set eyes on either Valeriani or the glass."

"And what caused that change?"

A low rumble of thunder preceded Fell's response. "I came to my senses. Rage had me blinded and quite insane. Rage over the death—the murder—of my son. I won't go into that, it pains me still…but what pains me even deeper now is how I have allowed my life to be tainted by it. First that, then…power. For whatever that's worth." The seamed mulatto face stared into the flames. "I just cannot believe I was that man…that I did all those things. The killing…the intrigues…the petty revenges and…all of it. That I actually put together an organization of that size and for those hideous purposes. That I built a village to hold my enemies in the stupor of drugs… or, murdered them outright. Was I really that man? My God…*was* I?"

"Well," Hudson said, "whoever you are right now, you might be interested to know that before we left the Emerald Inn in London I wrote a letter to my friend and ex-Herrald Agency associate Gideon Lancer, now the sheriff of a little hamlet called Whistler Green. You met him, Matthew, on that jaunt you took with Julian Devane. So in this letter I described Y Beautiful Bedd, where it was and why he should get there and do what was needed to take those people out. By this time—if all went well, and I'm pretty certain knowing Giddy that it did—your village is deserted but for a few seagulls and all the men who worked for you are behind bars or six feet under."

This was the first Matthew had heard about it, and he was absolutely amazed. "When were you going to tell me?"

"I was planning to, but Golgotha got in the way. And I was going to let the professor find out about it when—if—he ever got back there."

Matthew looked to Fell for a reaction, but the professor just steepled his fingers together and gave a half-smile.

"You're an enterprising gentleman, Mr. Greathouse," Fell said. "I suppose everything works out in time, doesn't it? Anyway, after Julian Devane killed Firebaugh and destroyed the book of potions there was no method of keeping control, so...good for Sheriff Lancer. Tell me, Matthew...did you know where Devane went after he left the village?"

"Away," said Matthew.

"And good for him as well, I suppose. Devane had his reasons, I'm sure. You might not believe me, but I hope he finds peace."

Matthew nearly laughed. *Peace?* For Julian Devane? The man was like Brutus the bull that had destroyed the pottery shop of Hiram and Patience Stokely in New York...Julian could always be counted on to leave things in pieces. But perhaps he *had* found a higher purpose, and that was the saving grace of every man.

Rain continued to pound the roof and thunder continued to boom. It sounded to Matthew as if this might go on all night.

Suddenly Professor Fell said, "It might interest both you gentlemen—and you also, Miss Espaziel—that I have no intention of returning to England. I have decided that when this is over I am going to make my home in Alghero, if Santiago will allow it."

Matthew recalled the professor stating that he didn't wish to die on Alghero. Obviously he had changed his mind...and why not? It seemed to him that for someone interested in marine life, Alghero was a perfect place to live out one's remaining days. And Matthew thought that the professor had begun to realize the value of the days remaining.

"A wise decision," Hudson said. "If I had as many charges against me for murder and crimes against humanity as you do, I'd hide out on Spanish territory too."

Fell nodded. His fire-lit expression was placid. "Thank you for that thought, but I'm not running *from* something. I'm running—as well as an old man can—*toward* a new life. Being there, returning to what I was before I became *him*...it restored my sanity. Of course, being sane...one looks back and clearly sees the path one has taken. While I was researching the marine life there, and doing my art...I asked myself if I would ever long to be Professor Fell again...the feared 'mastermind'. What did they call me, Matthew? Oh...the emperor of crime. Me...a professor of biology, come from the study of mollusks and eels, codfish and squid...to what I turned into. I was good at what I did. 'Good' being a relative term." He tried to smile but it slipped away. "All those things. The worship of gold and the worship of the blade. Don't fret, Hudson, that I have ever forgotten or ever will forget that I ordered the murder of Richard Herrald. Oh, those blood cards…wasn't that an overly dramatic effect? Don't fret that sanity and a new life will assuage my mind from those past deeds and absolve my conscience…which the old Professor Fell locked into what he thought was an unbreakable vault. Oh, no. Will a new life bring all the dead out of their graves? Again…no." He shrugged. "Santiago might order me out of Alghero and off Sardinia. I might find myself back in London after all, if I don't decide to jump overboard on the way. There I'm sure I should be hanged a hundred times over, but—alas—I have only one neck to give to my country. In lieu of a strangling knot I should like to live out rest of my life doing what I started out to do…simply being in wonder of nature. Does that sound so strange to any of you?"

"You make that sound almost believable," Hudson replied. "I've held myself back on this trip, but you can be damned sure I remember every-thing you did to me…as well as to Matthew and to Berry. So I'm not so sure the old Professor Fell is as dead as you're making out."

"Believe what you like. A man can change, can he not?"

"Some men can."

Fell's head slowly turned until he was looking straight-on at Hudson. "Can you?"

"We're not talking about me."

"In a way, we are. If there were no more villains to face, battles to fight or causes to pursue, where would Hudson Greathouse be? Because you see, what we're really talking about is the future…and new beginnings, for ev-eryone. Matthew has a very wonderful young lady waiting for him in New York. His future, and hers. I have the hope of Alghero, my studies and my art. Of slowly sinking into the sunset, and enjoying the warmth. So tell me…what is *your* future, Mr. Greathouse?"

Hudson didn't answer. He stared into the fire with darkened eyes. Matthew remembered him saying *I can't ever hold a real sword again. So… of what use am I in this world anymore?* It was evident that Camilla's pres-ence had had a positive effect upon Hudson's desire to live, but as to the purpose of living…Matthew thought that his experience with the Dutch wounded in the orange tent yet weighed heavily upon him, and how was that to be overcome?

Food was taken from one of the bags. Matthew had never been a fan of dried sardines, and after this venture he thought if he ever saw or smelled another one it would be all up with his stomach.

Andrado and the soldiers settled in to sleep, as did Camilla. One of the soldiers began snoring so loudly he was banished to another room. Matthew, Hudson and the professor remained before the fire, which Matthew tended to with the other pine logs to keep the light and semi-cheer going.

But there was a question Matthew's curiosity felt the need to ask Professor Fell, and now was the time to do so, as the rain continued to thrash against the roof and walls, the fire hissed as drops of water sizzled there down the flue, and thunder crashed in the heavens.

"You're being in England," he said to Fell, "how did you find out about the mirror in Italy?"

"I'm surprised you haven't asked about that long ago."

"We have not always been on such amicable terms. I'm asking now."

"Fair enough. But I dread the distaste of recounting all this, because as I say I am not the same man. Must I?"

"It would be a benefit to me."

"Of course." Fell gave a knowing smile. "The problem-solver, ever at work. All right then, if I must." He angled his face in a way that made Matthew remember the keen and haughty expression the emperor of crime had given to Judge William Atherton Archer—alias the golden-masked marauder Albion—during the bizarre dinner in Fell's house at Y Beautiful Bedd.

"It began years ago," Fell said. "Long before you entered the picture. When you were but a stripling, no doubt. A shipment of White Velvet was waylaid by a no-account gang of amateurs. Naturally they were quickly caught and brought to the village for a public execution. One of them was an Italian who begged for his life. He had information to trade, he said. Before he came to England he did odd jobs for a man in Salerno…a thief, a forger…but again, by all reasoning an amateur. This man also made money by providing items such as grave dirt, skulls, fresh fingers cut from corpses, dead owls and the like…for the supposed sorcerer Senna Salastre, who had his workshop—I suppose you could call it that—just outside the town. This Italian who'd been captured asked if on my honor—ha—I would spare his life if he told me what Salastre had been doing. I agreed, simply because I also have a curiosity."

Here the professor paused, watching the fire burn. A pinecone popped with a quiet little squeal. "Salastre," Fell went on, "was helping a man named Ciro Valeriani create a mirror. Oh, not just an ordinary glass, but—"

"Now the ridiculous part," was Hudson's dry comment.

"But a very *special* creation," Fell said as if Hudson's voice had been a sound of the rain or a distant peal of minorly annoying thunder. "You know the rest: a passageway between the earthly realm and the underworld, able to present to the incantor a demon to serve any wish. I took all this with a large mound of salt, of course. After I heard the Italian out, I had his hands and feet cut off and his body thrown from the cliffs into the sea."

"I thought you agreed not to kill him," said Matthew.

"Dear boy," was Fell's smooth response, and in it Matthew thought the old professor still lived, "*I* didn't kill him. The sea did, unless he learned how to flip-flop himself to shore."

Matthew had no return for this, as it was the same defense he'd used when he was accused of the murder of Count Anton Mannerheim Dahlgren and tossed into Newgate prison.

"I go on," said Fell. "As you might suspect, what began as a splinter in my mind became a thorn. I found myself...well, obsessed would be the proper term. And you know why...wishing to communicate with my dead son. Was that insane? Yes, but when one is in such a state it seems like rationality. I wanted to know more about the subject of such mirrors...if anything could be found indicating their true existence. In a little bookstall in London I came across not only a Flemish account of such a glass, but a tome written on the subject by Salastre himself. You might be amazed that this subject has come up from nearly the beginning of history as we know it to be...from the Assyrians, the Greeks and forward. I found an interesting account concerning an evidently talentless French portrait artist named Roberte Barbet in the 1600s who got hold of a supposedly enchanted mirror, and suddenly was able to create the most wonderful paintings of his grateful and wealthy patrons. Unfortunately the man was found in his study by a servant one night with his face clawed off and a symbol of some sort chalked on the floor before a dark-glassed mirror. Was there any truth to the tale? If one believes in such things, the man must've made an error either in the demonic symbol or the incantation involved. Such errors, it seems, can be deadly."

"Posh," said Hudson.

Again the professor ignored the intrusion. "In my ramblings amid the bookstalls I found a copy of *The Lesser Key of Solomon*, which I instantly recognized as having value if indeed I desired to investigate the Italian's story. In fact I bought every copy I could find, just to make sure no one else got hold of one. When Simon Chapel visited my house in London and we were devising that particular school near New York—you know the one, Matthew—he saw a copy, expressed an interest, and I gave it to him. Otherwise they were all mine. Then I determined I had to find both Salastre and this Ciro Valeriani, so I sent a pair of trusted men to Salerno. By the time they located Salastre, Valeriani had killed himself and Salastre—a very old and infirm man at this point—knew not where the mirror was. But he thought that the son Brazio might know. Now...where was Brazio? I had given instructions to pursue the matter as necessary. My men discovered that Brazio had attended his father's funeral in Salerno. The family connection that came up most quickly and easily—from the church's priest—was that a celebrity had also attended the funeral. Her name was Rosabella and she was the makeup artist to the famous opera star Alicia Candoleri. My men returned with this information and the fact that there were five other persons at the funeral but the priest did not have those names. They also visited Rosabella's house in Salerno to speak with her mother and father, under the guise of being lawyers representing an interest in buying Ciro Valeriani's vacant house in the hills. Where, incidentally, they found no trace of the mirror. The good mother and father could offer no further information on the son, though saying he'd sent a letter from Florence thanking them for their support of his father through many trying circumstances. No address was added to the letter. You know, Matthew, that on Pendulum Island I challenged others to find Brazio, thinking that their many contacts in other countries might offer a clue. As far as I knew, Valeriani might no longer even be in Italy. Of course…" Here his mouth gave a bitter twist. "Mother Deare was also feeding all this to Cardinal Black without my knowledge."

"Black certainly knew the whole tale," said Matthew, remembering how the demoniac had spouted it all out at Solomon Lash's mansion.

"Rosabella's mother and father did offer something of interest," Fell continued. "When they learned my men were originally from England—though they all spoke fluent Italian—they could not help but tell them that their daughter was currently on a country-wide tour with Madam Candoleri, and—the most marvelous thing!—she would within the next year be travelling to England on the summons of a certain Earl of Canterbury, who wished to sponsor a series of operas in that country. Therefore, I realized Rosabella was coming to *me*. I ferreted out the particulars of their arrival, the name of the ship and such. Did she have any knowledge of Brazio and the mirror? I had to know. And there you have it."

Matthew nodded, but he still had to ask: "Did you need to kill everyone who came to pick up Madam Candoleri at the harbor?"

The professor gave a soft little laugh, and in it once again Matthew heard the recently wicked Danton Idris Fell. "Dear boy," he said, "did I have to eat lamb stew for supper that day? Did I have to clean my teeth with a wooden pick, or arrange what remains of my hair with a tortoise-shell comb? You ask me to look back through different eyes. They were problems that had to be solved, nothing more."

"Well said for a heartless bastard," Hudson replied.

"Heartless, yes. Bastard, no; I had two loving and legally wed parents, thank you. But neither of you grasp that I did what I did—what *he* did—in what now to me seems like peering into a dark-glassed mirror. I know I stand before it, but I cannot see my reflection."

Hudson stood up. "I appreciate all these frightening bedtime tales, but I'm going to get some sleep. Sounds to me like the rain is tapering off, so maybe we *can* get on the road early." Thunder followed as if in defiance of his confidence, but it did sound muted and distant. Hudson gathered up his bedroll and found a comfortable corner.

It was time also for Matthew to get some sleep. He left the professor sitting before the fire, took his own bedroll and spread it out in an area across the room. Within a few minutes he was asleep, his last recollection of the evening being another faraway thump of thunder.

He came suddenly awake.

Sitting up, he looked around the room. The fire had burned itself out, yet the dim blue light of dawn was creeping in. Professor Fell was asleep on his side nearby, curled up with his hands under his head.

Then Matthew heard it: a closer boom of thunder, yet this seemed more hollow and different than what he'd heard before. He blinked the last of the sleep from his eyes and realized both Hudson and Captain Andrado were standing a few feet away, both of them appearing tense and listening to…what?

The thunder crash came again, followed by another right after it and then a third, the noise echoing between the villa's walls.

"What is that?" Camilla was awake, and now the other four soldiers were on their feet and Fell was beginning to stir.

"It's not thunder," Hudson answered, his voice tight, as yet a fourth blast reverberated through the rooms. A cracked mirror on one wall shivered.

Hudson said, "It's cannonfire."

FOURTEEN

To Camilla Hudson said, "Stay here." He, Andrado and the soldiers were already moving out of the room toward the front foyer. Matthew would not be left behind; he pulled himself up and followed, and at his back the professor called out, "I shall remain with the lady!"

Outside in the blue dawn, clouds still plated the sky though the rainfall had ceased. Not so, the sounds of thunder and this time—if Hudson was correct—it was man-made. As Matthew followed behind Hudson, Andrado and the four soldiers through the tangle of woods toward the top of the hill, he could see smoke spinning in the treetops and smell the bittersweet, sulfuric odor of gunpowder. Now could be heard a multitude of musket shots, shouting, the scream and squeal of horses, and as the hilltop was reached the view to the valley below showed that the war was in full battle only a few hundred yards away.

Smoke whirled across the figures of infantry in lines firing at each other, and beyond them flames shot from the muzzles of cannons facing toward the forested hill upon which Matthew and the others stood. A cluster of cavalry charged forward, muskets blasted and the cavalry fell back, wounded horses staggering and men limp in their saddles. Here lines of soldiers rushed together and bayonets stabbed, there gouts of earth were thrown skyward by the cannonfire, everything a cacophony of noise and a cauldron of confusion. To the right Matthew saw flags bearing a yellow *fleur-de-lis* on a royal blue background—the French—and to the left flew Dutch banners of striped orange, white and blue. These troops were not new to warfare, because Matthew took note that nearly all the flags were tattered and shell-holed.

The booming noise of the cannons seemed to crash against the hillside. To his horror Matthew could actually see bodies being torn apart by the murderous barrage, pieces of human beings and horses flying in all directions. Still some lines of infantry fired upon each other while others rushed to close-quarter fighting with their bayonets, and as the cavalry troops of both sides rushed in, swords were swung, sending more flesh and blood spewing into the air above the smoke-stained carnage. The noise of battle— ragged shouts, mangled screams, the yelling of officers' commands through mouth-horns, and further back on both sides the blare of trumpets and pounding of drums as if this was only a maniacal military parade—was its own language, delivered to ear-grinding volume and effect.

Back and forth went the waves of soldiers, a sight that transfixed Matthew with both its deadly advance and even more critical retreat, for as the boots struggled back through an earth of clenching mud men lay writhing and agonized beneath them, their once-gaudy uniforms already the same color as their graves.

Abruptly there was a startling movement on the right. Matthew saw maybe fifty cavalry riders bursting from amid the trees just below where he and the others stood. Their leader was holding a French banner and they all wore plumed helmets and metal breastplates over their uniforms. As they started across the hillside in what Matthew thought must be a circuitous maneuver meant to strike into the Dutch flank, Matthew heard a quick series of three cannon shots and just as suddenly twelve of the riders including the leader were torn into bloody shreds. Huge chunks of flesh flew from their horses and one's head was nearly ripped from its neck. At the same time Matthew heard a high-pitched hissing and a strange buzzing noise and the trees around himself, Hudson and the others were struck as if by a hundred wooden bats.

With a shout of "Canister fire!" Hudson grasped Matthew's shoulders and went to the ground atop the younger man as a new deluge of leaves, pine needles, bark and branches spun down from above. Hudson realized that Andrado had opened his spyglass and he and the other soldiers were still standing only five yards away. "Get down!" Hudson yelled, and Andrado stared at him, hesitated...and hesitated an instant too long.

The next cannon blast of canister, aimed at the cavalry troops but firing high, took a large section of Andrado's head off. Part of his brain burst from the gaping skull as his body was thrown backward by the impact of the canister: a bag that burst open upon firing and dispensed a hail of either round iron shot or pieces of scrap metal, glass and nails. Whatever had been in the canister bag, not only did it remove Andrado's life in a horrible second, but it also hit the soldier standing just to his side, slamming into the man's chest and exploding in a bloody gout of shattered bone and wet pink lungs through his back.

Andrado's body fell along with the other and the involuntary spasm of dying muscles made them writhe and thrash in the gore-wet brush as if enraged at this permanent affront. With no further hesitation the surviving two soldiers turned and fled for their lives down the other side of the hill toward the villa.

"Don't move! Don't move!" Hudson was shouting to Matthew as the canister shot continued to hiss over their heads by deadly inches, slam into the tree trunks and rip off branches as if they were made of flimsy paper. One with considerable weight crashed down across Hudson's shoulders but he remained exactly as he was, pressing Matthew down into the earth.

The canister fire ceased though the cannons were still blasting below and the cacophony of battle yet went on. Dazed by all this, Matthew had the sense to reckon that the cannon or cannons firing such rounds had been turned to keep the cavalry troops a target, and woe to those men because he doubted if one of them had made it down the hill.

How long did they remain on the ground, both fearing another canister attack? At last the sounds of battle began to lessen through the scorched and smoky air. Hudson got up to a crouch, paused there a minute or more, and then stood up. He reached down, grasped the collar of Matthew's shirt and hauled him to his feet.

Below, it appeared that the French troops were retreating though some were still taking a kneeling position to fire their muskets at the Dutch line. A mass of cavalry swirled together, swinging swords, and then broke apart, each pulling back toward their own positions. To the far right, a pair of French wagons were burning, black smoke curling up into what was already a gray miasma. Dutch cannons fired a few more times at the mob, scattering bodies anew, and with those final deadly bursts were silent. The Dutch did not pursue as the French tumbled backward. More shots continued to ring out but less and less until the muskets also were quiet. And then the last of the French lines moved out of sight, the Dutch also retreated, and there upon the mud-churned valley floor remained the bloody bodies of men and horses, while could be seen the wounded or shocked staggering about and horses with lowered heads, shivering as they stood over crumpled corpses.

"My God," Hudson said, in a hushed voice. He was looking out through the slowly shifting layers of smoke. Then he turned away from Matthew, took a couple of steps and almost toppled himself over broken branches on the ground. Matthew watched him approach the bodies of Andrado and the soldier. Hudson got on his knees and began to work the spyglass out of Andrado's clenched right hand. With an effort he freed it, stood up, returned to Matthew's side and peered through the glass into the distance on the left.

Matthew saw what he was looking at.

Through the haze he could make out an orange tent, there among other brown Dutch tents—the encampment that had been attacked—at least a mile away.

A hospital tent, he realized. Bright orange as a beacon for the wounded.

Hudson dropped the spyglass by his side and it fell from his hand to the earth. Then he took a step forward, and another and another, and he was making his way down the hillside toward the carnage with the air of a sleepwalker determined to reach some destination in a dream.

"Hudson!" Matthew called, still in a state of shock. The man did not look back or pause in his progress, and after a few further seconds Matthew followed him among the trees that were marked with deep scars and broken limbs by the canister rounds.

They passed through the area where no less than thirty of the French cavalry troops that had ridden across the hillside lay dead, their breastplates and helmets pierced by the shots. Where the metal had managed to withstand the projectiles it was dented in as if by monstrous fists, and how the canister had cleaved through their bodies and gutted many of the horses—some still kicking in anguish—was a stark, bloody horror.

Hudson reached the bottom of the hill. Matthew trailed him in silence across the muddy, blood-soaked battlefield. Figures lurched back and forth in the smoky gray pall. Sobbing could be heard, and tormented cries reaching to heaven. Matthew realized he and Hudson were both stepping on not only whole corpses but body parts and freshly steaming intestines that were strewn about in weirdly fascinating hues of varied red and blue.

A horse was bucking wildly in front of Hudson with a headless corpse being tossed and dragged along, one boot spur caught in a saddle's stirrup. It righted itself and galloped on, taking its dead rider on a last journey of the damned.

A few more hideous steps into this morass of misery, and Matthew was caught about the shoulders by a blonde-bearded older man in the infantry uniform of a dark blue tunic with Dutch orange piping. The wild-eyed man began jabbering in Matthew's face, obviously asking some question over and over again that Matthew could not decipher. As suddenly as he'd come through the smoke, the soldier released Matthew and rushed off through the mud as if late for some vitally important appointment, and only then did the young man realize there was fresh blood all over the front of his shirt.

To the right, the dead and dying; to the left, the same. Hudson kept on striding forward and Matthew after him several paces behind. A hideous wail reached Matthew's ears through the many cries, and he looked to his right and down to see a pretty young woman—probably a camp-follower—in a blood-stained brown dress cradling in her arms a Dutch soldier whose faded blue eyes were open in death, a bullet hole in his forehead and streamers of gore yet trickling from both corners of his mouth. She was rocking him back and forth, her own face as pallid as if she too was on the cusp of becoming a ghost, her eyes staring blankly as were the eyes of the corpse that in her desperation she was trying to revive.

Matthew averted his gaze, but all around there was only the ugliness of warfare. He felt his courage ebbing away and his soul shrivelling, and he could not take much more of this walk through what any demon of the mirror would rejoice in.

Ahead, Hudson felt a hand grasp at his left leg just above his boot.

He stopped. Looking down, he saw a young infantry soldier whose eyes were open, the tousled, long brown hair darkened by blood and a sword slash across the left side of his face. There was another blotch of blood at the boy's side, likely a wound from a bayonet's thrust. The boy—slim and clean-shaven, eighteen or nineteen years of age at the most, Hudson thought—looked up at him imploringly and then the eyes closed and the restraining hand fell away.

At once Hudson knelt beside the fallen warrior. He put a hand to the soldier's throat and felt a pulse there, however weak.

This was the one he sought.

The one who could be saved.

He took a deep breath, trusted in God that he could do this—and whether God granted him the strength or not, he was *going* to do it—and he braced himself in the mud and started to lift the boy's body up over his left shoulder.

Matthew came in to help.

"No," Hudson said. His tone of voice was nearly menacing. Matthew stopped where he was. Hudson huffed another breath, got the body situated where he wanted it, stood up, and staggered twice before he regained his balance. "Go back," he told Matthew.

"I can't leave—"

"Go *back*."

"I won't," Matthew said.

Hudson's face was grim and as gray as the lingering gunpowder smoke. "I have to do this alone," he answered.

"Do *what?*"

"You know," Hudson said, and with a last shift of his shoulders to further balance the body he turned away from his companion and began slogging through the mud, the blood and the human debris to the distant orange tent.

How far was it? A mile or more by the spyglass, but that was judged from the top of the hill. He decided to call it an even mile. Within the first two minutes he realized he was not the man he used to be; his legs were already trembling with the labor, even though the boy probably weighed at the most a hundred and forty pounds. He'd thrown through windows men who had fifty pounds on this one. Trembling legs and realization of mortality aside, he was going to make this journey and no one on Earth or in Heaven was stopping him.

He felt the warmth of the young soldier's blood on him. The smell of blood tainted the air, but whether it was the boy's or not, it made no matter. Thirty yards or so further on, Hudson nearly collided with a soldier who staggered past with both hands pressed to his stomach, and Hudson thought the man was probably holding his guts in through a gaping wound. To the left there were three musket shots, likely either at an escaping prisoner or from some Dutch soldier deciding live prisoners weren't worth the effort.

Hudson knew this emotion. It was the rage in the aftermath of battle, seeing one's comrades shot down or slashed to death by blades, coupled with the relief at living through the carnage. For a brief time there was a strange exhilaration at having survived, and then the blood fury came with a vengeance. He knew it well, because his own rage and blood fury had brought him to this moment in time.

He had to reach the orange tent with the wounded—dying?—young man over his shoulder. Would it expunge his guilt? No. But if he could save one...just one...it seemed to him the best he could do.

He walked on, boots sinking into the mud, his legs aching, his back now starting to protest. Around him the Dutch survivors moved back and forth, seeking fallen comrades or some kind of organization to this chaos, and though Hudson wore no uniform he was left alone because he was as a ghost amid other ghosts drifting through the pall.

On and on. A mile yet? He couldn't see the tent. Was he walking in the wrong direction? Had he misjudged the distance or the degree? On and on, his lungs working hard now, his knees threatening to lock. He passed a row of three falconet-sized cannons, all lined up and silent after their deadly hail of canister. There stood an ammunition wagon, with a team of six weary men sitting in the mud waiting for some kind of commands from a commander who might well be himself strewn about the field in several pieces.

Such was the other side of the glory of war.

Hudson stepped on something in the mud that caught the toe of his right boot—a discarded pistol, he thought it might be—and caused him to dangerously lose his balance until he got himself under control. He realized that if he fell he would likely not be able to lift the boy again. On and on he went, past figures and faces and other wounded wrecks moving painfully in the same direction.

And then there it was about another seventy yards away, standing toward the rear of the Dutch encampment. Seventy yards. Could he ever have been that strong man he remembered? Now he was nearly used up and literally on his last legs. But he crossed past the other tents, ignoring the soldiers who watched him pass, and entered the orange tent where the bodies lay on stretchers with more stretchers being carried in, three doctors in bloody whites working with what they had available to save the lives of those shot and stabbed almost beyond saving, and a pair of female nurses who had grown old far beyond their years at this duty and whose blankly staring eyes saw everything and nothing.

Two rows of cots had already been prepared in expectation of necessity. Hudson strode to the nearest one vacant and eased the young soldier onto it.

"What are you doing? Who are you?" A bespectacled, brown-mustached doctor came along the row and stared angrily into Hudson's face. Hudson knew enough Dutch from his own wartime ventures to understand both the language and the fact that only the doctors were in charge of who got the cots instead of the floor. "I asked you who you—" The man stopped in mid-sentence as he looked down at the soldier lying between them. Hudson saw the young man's eyelids flutter and then open, focusing with an effort on the doctor.

Hudson put a hand on the boy's shoulder and then he turned away. What he'd had to do was finished. He hoped the soldier would survive, but now it was someone else's task. Would his legs carry him back? They would have to, or else he would crawl, but he was getting back however he could.

Outside the tent, one of the infantrymen at last noticed this intruder at the heart of the camp. "Halt!" He raised his musket, and though it was in need of powder and a bullet the bayonet could still do what was intended. "Halt, I said!"

Hudson didn't look back and kept going, his pace labored. The soldier took two strides after him with the bayonet poised to thrust forward.

He was stopped by a firm hand on his arm.

"Let him go," said the doctor, and he wiped the glass of his spectacles off with a small white handkerchief that bore the first letter of his wife's name. "I don't know who he was, but he brought back my son."

Hudson passed through the camp and began crossing the battlefield. The smoke had started to lift and dissipate. He saw around him the many corpses, the comrades and the camp followers searching for those who had not yet returned from the skirmish, and perhaps were never to be found. As he walked onward, Hudson felt he was leaving something behind. His guilt at the act of murder in the orange tent so many years ago? No, not that exactly, but leaving a battlefield of his own making. The saving of one life…was it so important, in the scheme of things? He thought it was. And though his legs were heavy and he was recognizant of age and diminishing abilities…it was all right. He had been where he needed to be, when he needed to be there, and that was the statement of his existence. He would lift his head and go on with his life, wherever it took him, and perhaps also in the future he would find that this path through war, horrors and now a small redemption in his own soul would lead him gratefully into a new beginning.

But he was weary. The mud clung to his boots, making his tread heavier still. Yet a sense of freedom had come upon him, a rush of relief as if he was taking the first real head-clearing breath he had experienced in a very long time. It was so powerful it nearly overwhelmed his senses and made his head swim, and suddenly under its force he fell onto his knees in the mud, yet he had never felt so clean.

He saw before him a pair of high-topped black boots with crimson laces, and a hand extended to help him up.

He lifted his face and looked into hers. She nodded, the green eyes kind and knowing.

He took her hand, allowed her to take some of his weight as he rose, and he put his arms around her and hung on as if onto a solid rock amid a wild windstorm.

She put her arms around him and they stood together as if one, melded body to body, soul to soul.

And with his head against hers Hudson thought he was having a vision…for there, nearly at the base of the hill, two figures were moving amid the fallen soldiers, both Dutch and French, as Matthew stood to one side watching the scene. One of the figures wore a gray cloak, had long sand-colored hair and appeared to have no hands, while the other had on a tan-colored cloak, had shoulder-length white hair, a long white beard, and wore a black eyepatch over the left eye.

As Hudson watched in amazement, Silva Archangelo was bending down and offering the sign of the cross to one after the other who lay on the earth, speaking quietly and then moving on, as Trovatello followed at the priest's side.

Hudson pulled away from Camilla. "What…what are *they* doing here?"

"They came in on horses just after you left the villa," she said. "Following us from Sante Vallone, the priest said. He said Trovatello communicated that it was important."

"Important? Why?"

Camilla reached into a pocket of her jacket and unfolded the piece of paper the priest had given her. "Trovatello can use a quill with his right foot. The priest said that when they got back to their cottage, Trovatello wrote *this*." She gave him the paper.

Hudson read it.

In spiky, ink-spattered but legible writing was:

Valeriani
Brazio
Brazio
Brazio
Ciro

Three

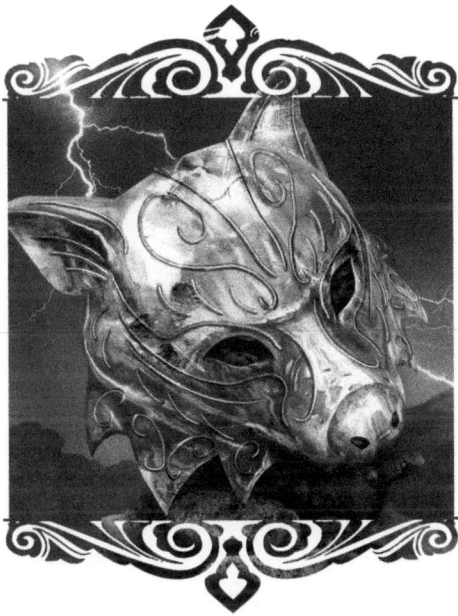

Daughter of The Spike

FIFTEEN

Matthew said, "Ask him how he knows the name 'Ciro'."

"I've asked," replied Archangelo. "He says—writes—that hearing the name 'Valeriani' made him remember a dream. Or...as he explains...a nightmare."

"Let's hear it." Hudson gave a quick glance at Trovatello, who sat in a chair staring blankly into the hearth's newly lit fire.

Outside the villa, another rain had begun to fall but not nearly with as much intensity as the previous cloudburst. This time there was no lightning nor thunder, and no sound of cannonfire. Hudson had changed into a clean shirt, electing to toss the bloodied one into a corner of another room and call it quits, and Matthew had done the same. Camilla and Professor Fell stood by waiting to hear what the one-eyed priest had to say. Up at the top of the hill, Archangelo had spoken a few words and made the sign of the cross over the mangled corpses of Captain Andrado and the unfortunate soldier. As for the other two stalwarts of the Spanish military, the missing wagon with their own belongings and some supplies aboard told the tale: with the death of Andrado and their realization that here the war could snuff them out as easily as might befall any Dutch or Frenchman, the idea of searching for a supposedly enchanted mirror did not hold precedence over preserving one's skin. Therefore, they had likely fled back the way they'd come and certainly not *toward* any further fighting. Upon seeing the single wagon remaining, Hudson had made the comment to Matthew and Camilla that the soldiers might find their nerve and return to their duty, but with their captain dead...probably not. He just hoped—as they all did—that the soldiers would not get back to the Venice harbor, report everyone else dead, and convince the ship's master to high sail it back to Alghero.

"You should understand that I can often 'hear' Trovatello just by his motions and expressions," Archangelo said. "The use of the quill with his right foot began slowly but he seemed determined to at least make his thoughts known and legible. Thus it was that soon after you left Sante Vallone and we reached our cottage, Trovatello became very…the word would be agitated, I suppose. Highly so. He paced back and forth in the room for a time, and then he sat staring into a candle's flame. He motioned for the quill, the ink jar and paper, and he wrote what I've shown you."

"You say he heard the name 'Valeriani' in a nightmare?" Matthew prompted.

"It was one he communicated that he had experienced many times and each time it seemed to him more real. He wrote out quite a lot I didn't bring, but the gist of it was that he was in a room with other men and they were speaking this name. He wrote down that he was a member of some kind of *equipaggio*…a crew, or a team. These men were not speaking of Brazio Valeriani, but he says he heard the name 'Ciro Valeriani'." Archangelo looked back and forth from Matthew to Hudson and then the younger man again. "Does this name mean something to you?"

Matthew ignored the question for the moment. "What was the nightmare part?"

"There was in this nightmare the wolfman using a hooked blade to cut the throats of two lambs. Again, this was something he has seen over and over again and each time…well, he has cried out from his bed many nights, but it was only after he had heard the name 'Valeriani' spoken by the lady that he wrote this down. At the end of that writing, on another sheet he quilled the word 'Lupo' three times, which is our word for 'wolf'."

"And this 'Lupo' means something to him?" Hudson asked.

"It must. On the third time, he bore down so hard he snapped the quill."

"After that he wanted to follow us?" was Hudson's next question.

"Yes. I packed our saddlebags and we left the village only a few hours after you'd gone."

"I saw your fire. You weren't but about two miles from our camp."

Archangelo frowned. "Fire? We had no fire that night."

"No fire? But—" Hudson stopped speaking. His eyes narrowed. "Did you see anyone else on the road?"

"Not a soul."

Hudson regarded Matthew and Camilla. "Someone else is behind us. Probably behind these two as well."

"Just other travellers, possibly," said Camilla.

"It doesn't feel right." Hudson walked over to the fire and held his palms out. He gave Trovatello a sidelong glance before he returned his gaze to the burning pine logs. "Whoever it is, they're likely close enough now to know where we are. I think we should stay here another night. With the rain, the muddy road…and whoever that is following us…I think we'd be best sheltering here and keeping a watch. If Valeriani is in Balanero, he won't be going anywhere anytime soon. Agreed?"

"That suits me," said the professor.

Matthew nodded. It struck him that since returning from the Dutch camp, there had been a change in Hudson Greathouse; his voice was stronger and his eyes had taken on a sharper glint that reminded him of the canny original. If this man said so, it *was* so. Just like before, and Matthew was thankful for it.

Hudson said, "Matthew, we should tend to the horses. Unhitch them and let them graze." The two mounts that Archangelo and Trovatello had come in on were tied to a hitching post out front, the priest's horse being a dun color and Trovatello's a piebald. The saddle of Trovatello's animal had something like a wooden backbrace affixed to it to keep the man balanced and comfortable, and Hudson assumed that Archangelo just held the reins of his foundling's horse or tied them to his own and led it along.

"I have in my saddlebag a leather pouch holding a quill, a small ink jar and some paper," the priest offered. "I thought that if we caught up with you, and Trovatello had anything further to say, he would be prepared."

"He can write with his foot? I'd like to see that!" said Professor Fell.

"I as well," Matthew added. "I have some questions I'd like to ask him."

"In time," said Archangelo. "First…I want to know about the name. Why you're seeking this man. As *signore* Greathouse says, it does not feel right."

"Camilla, will you and the professor explain our purpose?" Hudson asked. "I think he should know everything, it might be helpful to us. Matthew, let's see to the horses."

"If you would open my saddlebag and bring the writing pouch, that would also be helpful," the priest said. "Also if you'll tend to our horses?"

Outside in a light rainfall, as Matthew and Hudson worked to unhitch the horses so they would be free to graze, Hudson stared along the misty road they'd come but could see nothing moving. When he returned his attention to Matthew, he asked, "Are you all right?"

"I think so." In truth he was still shaken by the sight of Andrado and the soldier being blown to pieces, and how close he and Hudson had come to the same fate. "Are you?"

"Better," was the reply. "I don't like the fact that I saw a fire for a few seconds before it was either put out or hidden, and the priest hasn't seen anyone on the road. And as for Trovatello knowing the name of Brazio's father... correct me if I'm wrong, but that name wasn't spoken at the tavern, was it?"

"It was not."

"Don't like it," Hudson said again, with grave emphasis. "If someone else *is* following us, they're being very careful to keep out of sight. And you know the one reason we might be followed."

"Someone else knows about the mirror," Matthew said, "but they don't know where to find Brazio. So...they're hoping we'll lead them to him. But it's a bit fantastic, Hudson! Who else knows where we're going?" The answer came to him an instant after that question was spoken. "The wine merchant, Meneghetti. But how would he know about the mirror?"

"That's the hundred-pound question, and I have not a penny of an answer. Well, for the moment there's nothing we can do but wait and see."

When they'd finished releasing the horses, Hudson went to the priest's saddlebag, opened it and retrieved the leather pouch. Matthew was about to go back to the villa when Hudson said, "Wait a minute," and Matthew stopped.

Hudson hesitated before speaking again, and it seemed to Matthew that something very important was on his mind but he didn't quite know how to express it. Then Hudson cleared his throat, straightened his shoulders and said, "This is going to sound strange, but...it's about Camilla." Again, he hesitated.

"Go on," Matthew said.

"About Camilla," the Great One repeated. "I feel as if I've known her."

Matthew's brows went up. "In what sense?"

"I'm not talking about *that*. From the first minute I saw her in the prison, and she spoke...I thought...I have *met* this woman before. Somewhere. But that's impossible, isn't it?"

"Is it? I'm sure you've had many adventures I know nothing about and wish not to hear."

"I can tell you," Hudson said with some force behind it, "that I have never met Camilla Espaziel in my *life*, and yet...I just have this feeling... this *sensation*...that she is familiar to me."

"It could be that you've met someone she reminds you of."

"No, it's not that. I would remember." He gave a thin smile. "Matthew, I'm not so far gone that I wouldn't."

"I said nothing of the sort."

"I can *read* you. But...do you think it's...crazy to feel this way?"

"I think there's a perfectly logical explanation," Matthew said. "You just haven't come across it yet."

Hudson's smile faded. He shrugged and looked up at the sky as rain-drops dappled his face. Then he turned toward the villa with the writing pouch in hand, and Matthew followed him in.

Trovatello was still sitting exactly as they'd left him, staring somberly into the fire. Archangelo had walked over to stand at his side, Camilla had taken one of the other chairs and Professor Fell was cutting an apple from their supplies with a small bone-handled knife. "Found this in the kitchen," he said, holding up the blade. "Whoever owned this place left in a hurry but they were neat about their departure. Dishes and all sorts of utensils are there in the cabinets."

"Good to know if we wanted to have a banquet and invite our guests who are probably out there in the woods watching," Hudson said. He gave the pouch to Archangelo, whose expression Matthew thought was on the edge between incredulity and shock but after all he'd just heard the tale of Ciro Valeriani and the demonic mirror from Camilla and the professor.

"Can Trovatello write out the answers to a few questions?" Matthew asked.

The priest spoke to his companion, who nodded and stood up. A table was brought over and Archangelo removed from the pouch a quill, a small brown clay bottle of ink and three folded-over sheets of cheap and rough paper. "Bring a chair over," he instructed, his voice hollow. When the chair was situated before the table as Archangelo wanted, Trovatello sat down in it and put his legs up over the table. Archangelo removed the man's right boot to reveal the bare foot. He put down a sheet of paper and held it firmly. Then he dipped the quill in the ink and put it between Trovatello's big and second toes.

"Ask and I will translate," Archangelo said.

Matthew noted both Camilla and Professor Fell coming nearer to watch, with Hudson standing on the other side of the table. Matthew's first question was: "In his dream, where were these men who spoke the name 'Ciro'?"

The translation was made. Trovatello curved his foot downward—again, a motion of the ankle that made Matthew think the man could well have been a contortionist, his muscles and tendons were so supple—and began to write.

"He writes that it was unclear," said the priest when Trovatello was done, "but it seemed to be a meeting place."

"You knew these men? Their faces?" Matthew asked.

The quill was dipped again and returned to Trovatello's foot.

"He writes that they were men he worked with," was Archangelo's reply.

"Worked how?"

The quill, redipped and reset.

"He doesn't remember."

"These men were speaking of the mirror?" Matthew asked.

Writing further, the quill's tip scratching across the sheet.

"Of Ciro Valeriani," Archangelo read. "Of a mirror, he doesn't remember."

Now Matthew had to ask a more dangerous question: "The wolf that walks like a man. You call him 'Lupo', do you not? Does he have another name?"

The quill was dipped once again and replaced.

Trovatello sat without moving, his expression blank.

"Another name," Matthew said. And to the priest when Trovatello remained motionless: "Does he understand what I'm—"

The foot curved downward and the quill's tip met paper.

The priest looked up from the scrawl when his friend was done. "Murderer," he said. "And he writes Beast. Monster. Devil. And one more: *Boia*."

"Executioner," Camilla said.

"Yes." Archangelo and the others realized that Trovatello had begun to shiver though the air in the room was warm and humid. He put a hand on the man's thin shoulder. To Matthew he said, "Must we go on with this?"

"One more. Ask him…in his nightmare, did the lambs that Lupo killed—executed—have names?"

"Please." Archangelo shook his head. "Don't go any further."

Matthew's voice was firm, though he understood this was a realm—nightmare or not—that Trovatello feared to re-enter: "One has to lift a stone to find out what's underneath. Ask him."

The priest hesitated, the eye-patched face downcast. He dipped the quill once more and replaced it. Trovatello's toes took a strong grip. When Archangelo asked the question in their language he spoke softly, as if that might cushion any hammer blow to come.

The foot and the quill did not move.

Trovatello sat staring at the paper as if it had become his worst enemy. Then the foot trembled, the quill fell away, and the man's face contorted in a rictus of remembered horror. From the tongueless mouth there came a harsh bleat that became a hideous wail from deep in the throat, and just that suddenly tears burst from his sunken eyes and he struggled to get out of the chair.

"Facile! Facile!" said Archangelo, who grasped both the man's shoulders as he thrashed. The priest shot a look at Matthew that might have served as one of Trovatello's tavern darts. Then he leaned forward, putting a cheek against that of his friend, and he began to rock him back and forth like a motherless child. Soon Trovatello's frantic motions ceased though he continued to sob. "Come, let's walk," Archangelo said in their language. He put

the boot back onto Trovatello's foot, helped him up from the chair, and proceeded to lead him around through the room and into the corridor beyond.

"What do you make of that?" Matthew asked the others when the priest and Trovatello were out of earshot.

"The same as you, dear boy." Professor Fell walked to the fireplace, threw in a few more pinecones to make the red flames pop, and warmed his palms there. "The man was a member of a criminal gang. As punishment for some infraction, his hands were cut off and his tongue removed. Probably his entire family was killed before his eyes, then he was left somewhere for dead. He is a living testament on how *not* to betray one of these Italian organizations, and likely this wolfman in his nightmare was the executioner. Is that what you perceive?"

"I perceive something else," Camilla said. She had just scanned the paper on which Trovatello had scrawled his answers. "I believe he's trying to help us. He heard the name of Ciro Valeriani evidently from men he worked with, and if it's true that the organization did this to him—and I believe it—then he would probably wish to have some kind of revenge."

Hudson said, "Which also means that they're looking for Brazio and the mirror too. If that's some of *them* out there tracking us...well...they won't be friendly."

"And," Matthew spoke up, "Hudson and I think Meneghetti sent them after us. He's the only one who knew where we were going."

Camilla nodded. "These criminal groups have their hands in many pots. It stands to reason that Meneghetti sent word after we left."

"Wonderful!" was Fell's acidic comment. "I survived years of gang warfare in England, and now when I plan for a comfortable retirement I'm murdered by an Italian gang!"

"Not yet you're not." Hudson came over and took the chair where Trovatello had been seated before the hearth. "Don't fret, Professor! You've got me to protect you."

"Oh, heaven's blessing, I'm sure!"

Hudson watched the fire burn for a while in silence, and then he said, "Matthew, I'm curious about something. If you had a command for a demon in the mirror, what would it be?"

"I wouldn't have one. It's ridiculous."

"Humor me. What would your command be? Mind you, it could be anything in the world."

"This world or the underworld?" Matthew shot back.

"This world. What would it be?"

"Yes, Matthew," said the professor. "You know what mine would've been...only now I decided that the past is left unbothered, and wherever

Templeton's soul is resting he should not be summoned to me by a crass creature from Hell. What would *you* wish for?"

Ridiculous! Matthew thought. But all eyes were upon him, and he felt he should say something to get them satisfied. "I would wish that I was wed to Berry and back in New York on the moment, but I think that should best be served to me by an angel and not any demon from the mirror."

"You're dancing!" Hudson admonished. "From the mirror! What?"

Matthew mused about it and then decided. "I would wish for a library. In it would be every book ever written, and of course I would be able to read all languages, ancient and modern. And…hmmm…I would never have to sleep."

"You rarely do that anyway," said Hudson.

"All right." Matthew turned a hard stare upon the Great One. "You've heard mine. What would be yours? Able to beat ten men with your little finger?"

"I can already do that."

"Dream on. What would it be?"

"Ah," said Hudson. He closed his eyes. "There you have it."

"Have what?"

"I would command—ask—that my dream comes true."

To Hudson's subsequent silence, Matthew prodded: "Well go on, don't leave us hanging! What's your dream?"

The eyes opened. Hudson gave a smile that was not simply a smile, but rather as if his face was a vault behind which rested the most wonderful and glorious secret. "Oh Matthew," he said, "a man has to have a dream that he keeps to himself. In here." He touched his chest over his heart. "To speak it…might make it fly away."

"Has he been drinking anything?" Fell inquired.

Hudson looked toward Camilla. "Since we're all indulging in fantasy, what would be your wish?"

Camilla stared down at the floor. When it seemed she was never going to reply, she spoke in a quiet voice that Matthew detected held undercurrents of both pain and anger.

"I would ask for proof," she said, "that my father was not an insane murderer."

SIXTEEN

From the silence that followed this, Professor Fell said, "Would you mind elaborating on that statement?"

"I do mind. I'm going for a walk." Camilla was already heading out of the room.

"It's still raining," Hudson said but he got no response. "Do you want some company?" Again, nothing. "Don't go very far," he added, but she was gone before he spoke it. He walked after her as far as the open front door, where he stood watching as she crossed her arms before herself and strode on through the atmosphere of looming gray sky and a light rain. She stopped and peered up at the clouds, and then he almost left the villa to join her but he decided against it, as she seemed at the moment to need her privacy.

He withdrew to give her space and time.

As the day drew on, Trovatello curled up in a corner of the room on a blanket found folded in a cupboard and fell asleep. Professor Fell likewise dozed in a chair, and after Camilla came back in she went up the stairs to further explore the house but both Matthew and Hudson reasoned that she was not yet ready to face any further questions. Archangelo discovered a kettle in the kitchen as well as a small bag of tea, and drawing some water from the wagon's keg he set about brewing tea using a hearth hook hanging above the fire. Cups were brought from the kitchen and the priest poured for Matthew and Hudson before he took his own, then he pulled up a chair closer to the fire and sat sipping from his cup and watching the flames dance.

"We should be able to get started again in the morning," Hudson said. "From here the road turns nearly due west, and depending on the conditions—God willing—we'll reach Balanero in about five hours."

"And I hope we see no more war," Matthew said, as he sat on the floor near Archangelo.

"I think we'll have to take our chances with that." To Archangelo, Hudson said, "I trust you'll be safe going back to Sante Vallone."

"Going back?" The priest paused with his cup at his mouth. "We're not going back yet."

"Why not?"

"Because as much as I am repulsed, I am also curious about this mirror. What was described to Trovatello and myself sounds like either the ravings of a madman or something that the power of God should destroy. I am not saying I believe in such a thing, but I can tell you that in my life I've witnessed many incidents and met individuals one might call unholy. More than that: evil." The eye-patched face was painted with red and orange from the crackling flames. "I've found the well of evil to be nigh bottomless. It draws scores of humans to partake with promises of just what this mirror offers. But in the end, the promises are hollow, and they are a further spreading of evil, like a plague from human to human. As a man of God—weak in my own way, but attempting to be both vigilant and faithful—can I turn my back if this thing really exists? No. Therefore…Trovatello and I are going with you."

Hudson shrugged. "I think it's a wild donkey chase, but suit yourself. I'm less concerned about a demonic mirror than I am about who's out there in the woods watching us. *They* must believe the glass is real or they wouldn't be waiting for us to lead them to Brazio Valeriani."

"Who may or may *not* be Brazio Nascosto," said Matthew. "If he's the son, he's come a long way from his father's home in Salerno." Matthew watched the priest drinking his tea. Unable to pose any further questions to either Camilla or to Trovatello though his curiosity was its own fiercely burning fire, he ventured one toward Archangelo: "You may not wish to speak about it, but how did you say you lost your eye?"

"Oh, I can speak about it. I don't even miss it anymore…it was a very long time ago. As I said, a splinter can do a tremendous amount of damage. I suppose I'm fortunate I wasn't killed, but then again…" He gave a shadow of a smile. "I was on my knees praying to God like no boy of sixteen ever prayed, I can tell you that."

"You said you were a cabin boy?"

"On several ships, back and forth from Venice to Portsmouth. The spice trade. You English are excitable about your varieties of pepper, your vanilla, saffron, garlic, cloves…many things."

"I always relish a dash of pepper in my soup," Hudson said.

Matthew snorted. "The last time I tried a taste of your soup it nearly blew my head off." He focused again on the priest. "Shipwreck?" he asked.

"The Devil's own. I knew from experience that storms swept up the Gulf of Venice with sometimes terrifying power. It's where the gulf shallows into what used to be a swamp. This voyage—my fourth—we had a young English captain. I recall he was from Folkestone. He didn't know the waters and the weather as well as he should have. We were pushed along at a tremendous speed, and us trying to man the sails. Even me. We hit the shoals just south of Leviathan. An old Roman lighthouse, but in that gale the fire had blown out, so there was no warning." Now Archangelo grimaced at the memory. "I was praying that if I survived I would turn my life over to the hand of God. Those waves were pitching us up and down, the sails in tatters and then the bow hit those rocks. I don't know how fast we were moving, but it seemed as if the entire front of the ship exploded. My eye was taken. I have other scars, some that don't show." He paused to take a drink of tea, as if fortifying his spirit after these recollections. "There were good, hard-working and honest men on that vessel," he said. "Most drowned. I clung to a galley door and made my way to the beach, we were so close. I'll never forget the ship's name: *Prize of Heaven*." He swirled the last of his tea around in the cup before he shrugged and said, "Then again…what's in a name?"

Night came on. Food was taken: dried ham, the dried sardines of which Matthew refused to eat one more, some apples and figs and a second brewing of the last of the tea. Taking one of the oil lamps that had been brought in from the wagon, Camilla ate her food in another room apart, as evidently she thought she'd revealed too much and was reticent to face the questions that both Matthew and Hudson wished to ask. Archangelo fed Trovatello his meal and drink. In time, as the fire burned into embers, all settled down to sleep.

An hour past that, Hudson stood up from the spot he'd selected on the floor, picked up a low-glowing lamp and moved quietly out of the room. He ascended the staircase with an equally quiet tread and entered a room that faced the road to the south from whence they'd come. It was a bedroom, the blue-canopied bed unslept in for who knew how long. Attached to it was a small balcony, the double doors of which remained intact though some of the glass panes were cracked. Hudson further lowered the lamp's wick, set the lamp aside on a table, opened the doors and stepped outside.

The air had cooled after the rain. He saw that the clouds had cleared. Overhead the stars were blazing in a display of celestial magnificence, but he was less interested in the stars as he was focused on the forest to the south.

He waited, watching.

There was no sign of what he thought he might see. But no matter… he knew they were out there. Soon enough they would—

He realized quite suddenly that someone had joined him, and was standing just behind him in the room.

"No fire?" Camilla asked, her voice pitched as softly as the lamp's wick burned.

He shook his head, and when he turned toward her she was right there in front of him, had taken the three steps necessary to reach him nearly like the drifting of a spirit, and her green eyes looking up at him seemed to Hudson to catch the shine of the stars.

In a voice as muted as hers had been he said, "I think I've found it."

Who kissed whom? All Hudson knew was that their lips came together, her arms were up around his shoulders and his heart was beating like that of a youth's first escapade. The kiss lingered; they drew apart, and again met. He felt dizzy, in an otherworldly realm, as if he were falling into her. In that instant, in her closeness and with her warmth permeating his bones, Hudson thought that through his many encounters with women he had never experienced such an emotion…of wanting to be closer to her, and closer still, and in his honesty he realized it both tantalized him and frightened him as no moment in his life ever had.

And then…who took whose hand and moved toward the bed?

It was Camilla's hands that began unbuttoning Hudson's shirt. He felt as nervous and trembly as if he were the novice of all unschooled lovers. He actually heard a quaver in his voice when he said, "I haven't shaved," which was apparent to all present, brought a smile beneath the intense green lamps but did not pause the unbuttoning for what would've been a New York instant.

As Hudson sought to return the favor he found his fingers turned to jelly. Had he forgotten how to do this, or did Camilla's bodice and skirt possess buttons and clasps that reproduced themselves or rejoined after they were unjoined?

The fact was, he realized he was reduced in this woman's sexual presence to a fumble-fingered, buffle-brained, nearly idiotic stumble-bum, and as they each undressed the other and lay down together in the bed Hudson thought the suppleness and strength of her beautiful body would call his head's-up a quick rouster and done.

But she was not going to let that happen.

Hudson was not used to having a woman be in control. He was used to the rough-and-tumble, the quick thrust, the conquest that sometimes left bruises on both himself and his quarry. This was far different, for this was neither a conquest nor a quarry…this was something else entirely, and he wasn't sure exactly what it was but he knew he liked it.

She guided him into her. Not that he needed guidance, his aim was true enough, but he was there in her warmth and she was kissing his neck and where in this world were they?

Oh yes…somewhere in Italy.

For it seemed to Hudson as his thrusts were not quick but slow, sure and uncommonly gentle that the world and all of time had melted away and nothing remained of any reality but this moment which he wished might go on forever. He could look down into that face and those lamps and think that he and this woman were made for each other, and then all thinking ceased because thinking was a ponderous weight and he was flying with her, free of all land anchors.

Camilla gasped beneath him and thrust upward. She whispered his name as if it were a secret she had held in her soul and was now to be revealed. When his body shuddered in its orgasm hers reacted in kind, and her arms drew him against herself like a gift to be treasured. As he relaxed in the afterglow her hands stroked his sides and shoulders, her fingers moving across all the old war scars that he kept hidden from view. At last he withdrew from her and rolled over on his back, and at once she grasped his chin and kissed him with a fervor that was at first burning fire, then soft cool mist.

When she spoke her voice was hushed, her mouth up against his ear. She said, "I know you."

"I should say," he answered, just as quietly.

She got up on her elbows to look into his eyes. "I mean…I really *do* know you. I thought that when I first saw you at the prison."

"*What?*"

"Yes," she said. "I thought…I know this man. I've met him before."

It was time for Hudson to tell her what he'd been feeling. "I thought I've met you before too, but that's impossible. Where could we have met?"

She didn't answer for a moment, and then she said, "Another time and place."

"All right, but when and where?"

"A hundred years ago," she said. "A thousand years ago. But we've met, and we were together just like this."

Hudson had to shift his position and turn so he could see her face. Her lips were damp and sweat sparkled at her hairline. "Can you explain that statement?"

"Don't you believe in souls?" she asked. "I mean…that souls meant to be together search for each other without knowing, and they find each other over the distance of time?"

"You're over my head now."

"I believe that we knew each other somewhere else…somewhere in the past. Who can say when? I realized being around you day-by-day…it was becoming clearer to me that my first impression was correct because it grew stronger and stronger. You felt it too, didn't you?"

Hudson gave a muffled little laugh. "Oh…like I was an Egyptian king or something, and you were the queen?"

"The other way around."

"You were the king and I was the queen?"

"No!" She put an elbow into his ribs. "We might have both been peasants in a medieval French village, far from being royalty. It could've been anywhere, at any time. A hundred years ago we might have been students in a Prussian school. Maybe we were artists in—"

"Save me from being a Prussian," he interrupted. "One of those nearly killed Matthew. As for being an artist, I can't draw worth a doodle."

"You're not listening seriously. Well, maybe you *were* a king and I was your queen."

"Me a king!" he said. "Go on, I like this part."

"I'm not alone in believing souls live again, after people pass away. It's an ancient belief called reincarnation."

Hudson shook his head. "A king one minute, dead the next! Couldn't you let me enjoy my crown until morning?"

"I suppose I'm thinking aloud in all this, but it's not witchery or superstition, as you might think. It's an honest trust in the future."

Now Hudson was silent for a while. "The future," he said softly. "In my life there were many times I thought I was not going to see another sunrise. That would be my dream…to have a future where hope outshines fear. Oh, I am never afraid. Rarely afraid, I mean," he corrected. And another more truthful correction: "Sometimes afraid, but not often." He conveyed this with a slim smile before he went on. "A future with a purpose," he said. "A path to take, leading to…well, that's the joy of life, isn't it? A shining path to take…going somewhere, the destination unknown, but knowing that wherever you find yourself…it's where you were meant to be."

"That's exactly what I'm saying," she ventured. "I believe in my heart and in my soul that you and I were meant to be together. Right here, right now."

"And the future?" he asked, looking deeply into her green lamps.

"I trust in it," she said.

Hudson lay back on the bed. It was a nice romantic fantasy, though altogether a fantasy. Still…there was truth in the feeling he had that he'd met and known Camilla somewhere else. But in another time? That was beyond him. Did some people really believe in such a thing? She said so and he reckoned she wasn't touched in the head or lying about it, so…

…who could say?

She put a hand on his chest and kissed his grizzled cheek, and then in his ear she whispered, "You're not done here."

Indeed.

At dawn Hudson got up from the bed, spent a moment admiring Camilla as she lay with the past villa owner's fine Italian sheet barely wrapped around her body, and then he put on his breeches and went again to the balcony. The sun was just coming up and the sky appeared cloudless. He inhaled the morning air and stood looking out at the forest to the south, thinking once more of what she'd said about souls searching for each other over the expanse of time. And when they found each other, what then? A night of abandon in an abandoned bed? Or something more lasting? He realized as he mused about this fantasy that a fantasy became real when one wished it to be.

Hudson was interrupted in his thoughts when he saw a brief spark of light from the forest about a half mile away.

He quickly drew back and inside the room, away from whoever had just opened a spyglass the lens of which had caught the sun. He remembered he'd dropped Andrado's spyglass in the woods on the hill and now he cursed himself for not going back for it. The pursuers were up early, or perhaps one or two of them had been up all night keeping watch.

A breeze from the north brought him the scent of death from the battlefield. Soon the carrion birds would come swooping in to tear at the unburied corpses and bits of scattered flesh.

He had the feeling that danger was very near, and maybe this was the day it would close in upon them with its own tearing talons.

It was time to pack up and get on the road to Balanero. If Brazio Nascosto was the hidden Brazio Valeriani, son of Ciro, with knowledge of where the demonic mirror might be, this day would tell the tale.

He thought the watchers out there were equally interested in the telling of this tale, and for that reason he decided he should search the kitchen for anything to be used as a weapon.

SEVENTEEN

WITH HUDSON AT THE REINS AND CAMILLA ON THE SEAT BESIDE HIM, the wagon rolled on to the west toward Balanero. Just behind the wagon on their horses rode Silva Archangelo and Trovatello, the latter's mount being tied to the priest's and Trovatello's back strapped to the support Archangelo had created for his companion's safety and comfort in travel.

The morning was clear, the sky blue and the air cooler as the road ascended into a landscape of even steeper hills and deeper valleys. Here a few villages were passed, mostly a few cottages and farms but no vineyards in the area. In the back Professor Fell sat wedged in between two gunnysacks of supplies, paging through *The Lesser Key of Solomon* that Camilla had taken from her belongings to let him peruse at his request. Near him, Matthew sat eating an apple and watching the professor with a careful eye.

Matthew said, "I hope you're not thinking what I think you're thinking."

"Absolutely not," was Fell's quick reply. "You must admit, this is fascinating reading."

"I don't admit that."

"All these supposed demons, their powers, the seals and the incantations...who in the world could've put this together?"

"Solomon's name is on it."

"Yes, but I doubt King Solomon had the time and inclination to gather all this. I would venture that sorcerers in his court had hands in it and it was written by—shall we say—a roundtable of those who had interests in the supernatural."

"Or warped imaginations," Matthew said with another bite of his apple. He had been eating an apple and drinking the last dregs of his cold tea this morning when Hudson and Camilla had come downstairs. It took no imagination—warped or otherwise—to reckon that the Great One and the witch-hunter had done more than commune in an upstairs chamber. But he was glad for Hudson. Thank God the man was back almost to what he'd been before they'd reached that wretched island of Golgotha, and it seemed also that Hudson's walk to the orange tent with the wounded soldier over his shoulder—quite an amazing undertaking—had freed him of some of what was tormenting his soul. Hudson's eyes were clear, he had regained his healthy color—quite noticeable when he'd entered the downstairs room with Camilla—and all praises for those little miracles.

"How many times have you read that thing through?" Matthew asked.

The professor took the opportunity to remove his spectacles, wipe the lenses on his shirt and return them to his face before he answered. "At least thirty times, but I forget how many. So many that I've committed to memory three of their seals and their incantations. Three entities with the ability to bring the dead back to life: King Paimon, Earl Botis and King Asmoday. You must remember that I was desperate to find an answer to my desire."

"And you're positive that desire is gone?"

"More than positive. I have made my peace with myself, which counts for everything."

Matthew gave a soft grunt. "There must be continual war down in the underworld, with all those kings, earls and such. Peace would be a concept of angels, not of those creatures."

Fell closed the demonic book and put it aside. "I'm going to tell you something...and a year ago I would've cut my own throat before I uttered such a thing. You caused me so much trouble. So much wreckage of what I had constructed. I wanted to kill you a dozen times over in the most horrible methods I could devise."

"Perhaps you'd best keep these heartfelt sentiments to yourself," Matthew suggested.

"No. Listen to me. *Hear* me. I realized..." He paused, and it seemed from his expression that he was having some difficulty going forward. "I realized," he finally said, "that you are a young man the likes of whom I had never met. The idea of you going out with Julian Devane to save your Berry. The steadfast loyalty you have to Hudson. And then...your vow to find Brazio Valeriani, and whatever happened you stood true to that vow. How many times could you and Berry have escaped, there in London? I didn't have anyone following you. It was then I truly knew...you were to be trusted, even by me."

He drew a long, deep breath and released it in an equally long exhalation. It sounded to Matthew as if he were inhaling fresh air and exhaling old ghosts. "I have to tell you," said Professor Fell, the ex-emperor of crime and onetime fierce nemesis of everything that Matthew considered true and right, "that if my Templeton had lived…if he had grown to manhood…I would have wished that he was as strong-minded and…and as *good*…as Matthew Corbett. And that, dear boy, is as high a compliment as I have ever given anyone on this earth."

Dear boy, Matthew thought. He'd considered that somewhat comical when the professor had last spoken those two words. Now…they seemed a wistful reach for the son he had lost so many years ago.

"Thank you," was all Matthew could say. But then he added, "Sir."

An hour or more into the journey, Matthew heard Hudson and Camilla quietly talking beyond the folds of canvas but he couldn't make out what was being said. Whatever it was, it sounded serious. Then the folds were drawn aside and Camilla slipped into the back of the wagon. She let the canvas hang open a few inches, and she said, "I have something to say to you and I want Hudson to hear this as well." Her focus went to Matthew. "You asked me about my task as a witch-hunter. I told you it was my summoning that I hunted witches as my father did and his father before him…but that's not exactly true. I told you I had discovered three witches, which also was not exactly true. And I want to tell you now why I was assigned to this mission by the government of Spain, and why I accepted due to my own motives."

"It doesn't matter to me. You have your own—"

"Allow me," she interrupted, "to explain. It's important."

Matthew waited while Camilla further composed herself. He thought it was more important to her to tell this so Hudson could hear rather than himself and Professor Fell, but so be it.

"You must know," she began, "that the Inquisition is still going on in my country. Oh, not what it was…the torture chambers and such…but there is still a religious attitude of…I would call it a low-simmering frenzy. My grandfather was a member of the Inquisition. My father followed his path, and in so doing lost his compass and his mind. He was Nicolas Sebastian Espaziel, also known as '*La Espiga*'. That translates in your language to 'The Spike'. Which became his favored method of both torture and execution. His most infamous act was in 1678 when he and his small army of rabid followers attacked a Basque village in which he was certain witchcraft had taken hold, and he executed forty-seven men, women and children. The children were hanged, the women were burned and the men hoisted upon wooden spikes and left to slowly die. Then the entire village was set aflame and the ruins salted. Thus my father's reputation…praised by some, reviled by others. In his last years Nicholas Sebastian became un-hinged and feared that his mind was being overtaken by the demonic spirits of those he had executed, and before myself and my mother he blew his brains out with a pistol. She never recovered from the event and died raving against the powers of Satan in a hospital."

Matthew tried again. "Camilla, it's not necessary for you to—"

"I'm trying to *tell* you," she insisted, "why—if we find it—the mirror is not leaving this country."

Matthew was silent and the professor looked on with obvious interest. Hudson was hearing this too but he kept his attention on the team and the road.

"Because of my heritage," Camilla went on, "I have been *summoned*—forced—into a role I would not otherwise pursue. I have been working on behalf of government officials who wish voices of dissent to be silenced, therefore the easiest way is to declare their political enemies to be possessed by demons. It has been my family's history—which is very well known in Spain—that has brought me to this level. I should say, *down* to this level. Matthew, I told you I found three witches. Two were enemies of the state and were executed according to my testimonies. The third was…different. A woman in a small village who was selling supposedly magic potions to anyone who would buy, and who was performing decidedly Satanic rituals. To add to this, she was luring children from other villages into her travelling wagon…I suppose with the promise of sweets, murdering them and using their blood and ground-up bones in her potions and charms. Was she truly a witch? I don't know, but she was calling upon Satan as the hangman's rope was noosed around her neck. She murdered at least eight children that I could discover. So…as I say, she was different."

Camilla was silent for a time, gathering her thoughts, and neither Matthew nor the professor spoke.

Her voice was ragged when she continued and her face stricken with the pain of what was perhaps the thorny emotion of guilt. "The two polit-ical enemies I testified against…ordinary citizens who defied government dictates with their voices and their writings. I was paid for this. And I was told by authorities that if I did not perform the task I would simply dis-appear. I had at first resolutely refused to help them. They took me to one of the old torture chambers down below a very famous cathedral, and they demonstrated with a common thief what could be done to a human body before the mercy of death. It was my name they wanted…Camilla Espaziel, the daughter of The Spike. I did the work."

"Then," she said, "the subject of the mirror and the book came to their attention." She managed a twisted and rather chilling half-smile. "Don't you think it the most hideous of ironies…that the state pursuing so-called witches for the political gain should now be intrigued by an object with which they might actually call forth the powers of the underworld?" Her half-smile faded. "I didn't know what I was going to do about Andrado and the soldiers," she said. "Andrado was commanded to bring the mirror back if it was discovered, and he is—*was*—loyal in the way of a mindless dog. But with him gone and the others as well, I can do what I had planned. Had *hoped* to carry out. If we find Brazio Valeriani and then the mirror...that mirror will not leave Italy. It must be destroyed before any government can get their hands on it. With Andrado gone, I can return to Alghero and inform those who are waiting that the mirror was not found, and indeed we discovered that it was destroyed many years ago. Might they send someone else to search? Yes, they might...which is why we have to make sure it's never found. Do you hear me?" Her voice was a force directed at Matthew. "*Never* found."

Matthew waited until it seemed her harsh breathing had settled and she had relaxed from these obviously horrific recollections. He said, "Then I take it you believe the mirror's powers may actually be real?"

"I reserve judgement on that. But if we find it, I have to test it myself."

"What? *Why?*"

"I told you I wanted to know if my father was an insane murderer. As a child and a younger woman, it appeared to me to be so. Then...after the incident of the woman who killed the children...I thought there is an element of pure evil in this world that I cannot comprehend. Yes, there's human evil as much as anything else and what I've told you about the role I've had to play confirms it. And of course Nicholas Sebastian Espaziel likely executed many innocent souls...but were there some among those he tracked who he rightly perceived *were* witches? Some among that legion who'd made compacts with the underworld, and had secured demonic knowledge in exchange for it? You say that human evil is more than enough to contend with and I agree...but is there something else out there? Something in the deepest dark that pulls the strings? I have to know...if it *might* be real. I cannot totally excuse and hold The Spike blameless...but if I stand before that mirror and am able to have my call answered, I will know that there is a *possibility* my father was not *only* an insane murderer. In essence, I want to look into the face of Hell. Then I want the mirror destroyed, so no human hand can ever touch it again."

"A rousing speech, madam, but there is a fly in your liniment," the professor said. He narrowed his eyes behind the spectacles. "What will your feeling be if your call goes *without* answer? If it's simply a piece of glass that just stands there and looks back at you? Will you lose your mind in that moment and rush to kill yourself on behalf of your father's history?" When Camilla hesitated, Fell added, "I would suggest that his history is not yours.

You share the name, but—to be a bit poetic—you don't share the blame. So if the mirror is only a mirror, what then?"

"Then I go on," was her firm reply. "Whatever my father was, he was. I'll have to return to Spain to make the report they're expecting. After that, I'm leaving there."

"Will they let you leave?" Matthew asked.

To that, she had no answer. She withdrew and returned to her place beside Hudson.

Just past noon, the wagon turned a gentle curve in the road and Hudson announced, "We're here."

Matthew looked out to see a good-sized village, quite larger than Sante Vallone had been, with a central street and several streets branching off on either side. Under the strong sunlight the white stone cottages were made brighter still, with their red tiled roofs and occasional vibrantly hued awnings over courtyards and gardens. A number of residents moving about on the streets noted the wagon's passage with polite curiosity. Matthew saw a sign with the painting of a white dove in flight above the doorway of a structure on the left and considered that it was likely the local tavern. On the right down a side street stood a small church of brown and white stones, topped with a belltower. All in all, it appeared an industrious, prosperous and well-populated village, and thank the stars the war had not touched, torched or trampled the place. A little further on the land hollowed down and the long rows of the vast vineyard were revealed in all their rich green glory climbing up the far hills, large clumps of red grapes hanging ready for—what was the harvest called? oh, he remembered it—the *vendemmia*. The cool air of this higher elevation carried the heady scent of the dark soil, the lush greenery and a faintly musky aroma that must've been the grapes themselves. Matthew thought that one could nearly drink the air, it was so clean and crisp.

Down where the vineyard began a road led to several white structures that should be the storage buildings, the offices and whatnot, and to these Hudson steered the team with Archangelo and Trovatello following just behind. There were a few workers out in the vineyards but they seemed only to be inspecting the grapes. At the largest of the buildings, which likely held the managerial and bookkeeping offices, Camilla asked Hudson to stop, and she went inside to inquire about Brazio Nascosto.

She returned in a few minutes. "I had a little trouble with a secretary in there, but I convinced her I was a relation come to bring him some money from his deceased uncle Pietro's will. He's finished his work for the day and gone home," she reported. "His cottage is further up the hill, its windows are framed in yellow."

With that description, Hudson flicked the reins and the team followed a little circular turnaround which set the wagon back on the main road. Up the hill they went, alongside a pinewood fence that ran the length of the vineyard. A half-dozen cottages stood amid the trees near the hill's crest, and up on the right was the one with the yellow-framed windows, a barn situated beside it and a small corral holding two sturdy-looking horses. Hudson pulled the wagon to a stop before the cottage, put down the wagon's brake and started to climb off the seat.

Camilla touched his arm. "You should stay here for the moment."

"Why?"

"Because you're an imposing presence. We don't wish to alarm him any more than we probably already will, if this is indeed Valeriani. Matthew, will you go with me?"

While Hudson waited on the driver's bench, Professor Fell came between the canvas folds to take the place beside him and the priest, and Trovatello remained on their horses just behind the wagon. As Matthew walked with Camilla to the yellow-painted front door he felt the warmth of the sun through the overhanging trees, heard a symphony of birdsong and mused that if this was their man, Valeriani's placid and peaceful life here was about to be rudely—but necessarily—upturned.

Camilla knocked at the door. They waited.

The door was opened. A slim man with curly black hair and light brown eyes behind a pair of square-lensed spectacles peered out. Matthew quickly judged him to be in his mid-thirties. He had a handsome face with a high forehead, a narrow Roman nose, a trimmed black mustache that had the first beginnings of gray flecks, and at his chin a closely cropped black goatee.

He looked from Camilla to Matthew and back again. *"Posso aiutarti?"*

To the question of *Can I help you,* Camilla said in Italian, "You are Brazio Nascosto?"

"I am, yes."

"I am Camilla Espaziel and this is my friend Matthew Corbett. Do you speak English?"

"English? No." The eyes behind the spectacles found the wagon and the two horsemen. "What is this about?"

"May we come in and speak with you?"

Now Matthew detected that wariness had entered the man's expression. He understood the language enough to decipher the repeat of: "What is this about?"

"A few minutes," said Camilla. "Please."

"I think not," the man said. "Good day." He started to close the door but was stopped when Matthew put his booted foot against it. A little red spark of anger flared in the man's eyes. He said, *"Ho una pistola in casa."*

Matthew understood that well enough. "Ask him why he keeps a pistol in his house. Is the criminal element so dangerous here?"

Camilla decided against going in that direction. "We have come a very long way to find you," she said, her voice urging calm restraint. "You can be sure that if we could find you, others also can." And she added: "Mister Valeriani."

Anger had left the man's face but his countenance was completely blank. "Madam," he said, "I don't know who you believe me to be, but you have the wrong house and the wrong person. Now please...I have a pot of minestrone cooking over the fire, so if you'll—"

"The Spanish government wants your father's mirror," Camilla broke in. "I'm here to make sure they don't get it. I want it destroyed."

"Pardon? A mirror?" The man brought up a look of confused dismay. "My father's *mirror*? What nonsense are you talking? My father owns a tavern in Naples!"

"The name of which is—?"

"The Happy Traveller. Now please go away, I have my soup to tend to!"

Matthew sensed in the air a sudden doubt: his own. Whatever this man was saying, he seemed to be adamant that they had come to the wrong house and the strength of his speech and firm manner fortified the doubt. *Was I wrong?* Matthew had to ask himself. *After all this time and effort, was I—*

"I'm sure you've created a fine and convincing biography for yourself," Camilla plowed on. "This young man beside me had reason to believe you were hiding at a vineyard which produced Amarone. I believe those are the grapes nearly ready for harvest? And your choice of a new name: Brazio Nascosto! The 'unseen Brazio'? Really? Your intent was understandable but your imagination was lacking. And do you still despise your father so much you had to forge this new identity and run all the way here from Salerno?" To the man's absolute silence Camilla said sharply, *"Speak!"*

The eyes were fierce. The mouth curled. "You're mad! If you don't leave my door in thirty seconds I shall go for my pistol."

"Go and get it," she answered. "Make sure it's loaded not just for one or two, but for ten...twenty...fifty. A *hundred*. Ciro's mirror is known now, and there will be many searching for it...and *you*, as well. You would be wise to let us be the first to find it."

"Fifteen seconds," he said. And then he looked past Camilla, and Matthew saw his expression of sullen anger turn to bewilderment. Matthew glanced back and saw Archangelo approaching with Trovatello a few steps behind.

The priest halted just beside Matthew and Camilla. He said gently, "Young man, if you're the one these people have been seeking, you should hear what they have to say."

Matthew saw Brazio Nascosto's gaze go to the priest's eyepatch and linger on the burnt-in image of the cross. There followed a long moment of silence in which a muscle worked in Nascosto's jaw.

At last he spoke with a bitter edge: "I have a good life here. Why did you have to find me?"

EIGHTEEN

BRAZIO VALERIANI SAT AT HIS KITCHEN TABLE CASUALLY EATING FROM his brown clay bowl of minestrone as if his afternoon had been complete-ly undisturbed. He seemed not to give a care that he was surrounded by this pack of unwelcome intruders, including Hudson, Silva Archangelo, Trovatello and Professor Fell, who had found a comfortable cowhide chair to sprawl himself into and had closed his eyes in the attitude of all this rig-marole being beneath the ex-emperor of crime. Whether Valeriani was truly listening or not, Matthew didn't know.

"You realize how dangerous this object is, don't you?" Camilla was say-ing in Italian as she stood leaning against the kitchen's washbasin on the countertop. "You of all people *must* know."

"I don't understand what you're saying," Hudson remarked, "but I'd like to hear if he really *believes* in the thing."

Valeriani paused in his meal to cast a glance once again at Trovatello. "Why does this man have no hands?" he asked Camilla before he continued spooning up his soup.

"Never mind that," she said. "Is the mirror real, or is it not?"

"It's a real mirror, yes."

"You know what I'm asking."

"I know it's best left exactly where it is."

Camilla raised her eyebrows. "And where exactly is it?"

He took two more spoonfuls of soup before he replied. "Where no one can possibly find it…and even if the impossible happened, no one would recognize it for what it is…one mirror among many."

"What's he saying?" Hudson asked.

Camilla translated what the man had said. "Otherwise, no answer," she added.

"Well, make him answer!"

She gave him a baleful glare. "Shall I begin the beating, or shall you?"

Hudson sighed in exasperation. His nerves were on edge. When he'd stepped down from the driver's bench he'd seen another quick flash of light from the village, and peering in that direction he'd seen a man on a dark bay horse positioned in front of the village's tavern with a damned spyglass aimed up at the cottage. Then the man—a scout, of course, for the main group of whoever was tracking them—closed the glass, dismounted and went into the tavern. There he would ask who inhabited the cottage with the yellow-framed windows up on the hillside and likely offer a coin or two for the information. And thus it would soon begin. Hudson touched the waistband of his trousers where the drawstring held the knife Professor Fell had found in the kitchen. Also in Hudson's belongings in the wagon was a good hefty meat cleaver he'd found in a kitchen drawer; he decided he should go out and get it right this minute, and to hell with this Italian blathering.

He left the cottage without a word and saw that the scout and his horse were gone. Opening his bag he took hold of the cleaver. It would scare Valeriani to death, but maybe it would loosen his stubborn tongue. He went back inside to the kitchen, where no one had moved and seemingly from the expressions no progress had been made, and he set both the cleaver and the knife up on the countertop.

Valeriani took another spoonful and pushed the bowl aside. "Are those for me?" he asked Camilla, his tone yet undisturbed.

"What are those for?" she asked Hudson.

"We may have visitors. Professor, I hate to disturb your beauty slumber but would you go outside and keep watch? If anyone starts up the hill, get in here quick. Father?" Hudson turned to the priest. "Would you ride down to the tavern and find out if someone has just asked who lives here? I want to be sure before I start getting too nervous. Get a description if you can and find out if he's carrying a pistol. The keeper will likely speak to you quicker than to any of us. Your patch and the cross, I mean. You won't have to tell him you're a priest. And tie your horse around behind the place, because if they come up while you're there they'll recognize the mount. All right?"

"Shouldn't I stay here to help?" Archangelo asked.

"You can help in the way I've said. Remember: your horse *behind* the tavern. If anyone—and I mean anyone—comes up that road while you're there, I don't want you becoming a hostage. Just stay in the tavern. Otherwise if the road is clear and *only* if the road is clear, make sparks under those hoofs getting back. Understand?"

"I do."

"Needless to say, if you start down and see anyone coming up, get back here."

The priest nodded. "Yes, of course." He started for the door, with Professor Fell leading the way, but before Archangelo could go out Trovatello made a gasping, croaking sound of anguish, threw himself forward and wrapped his handless arms around the priest. "I'll have to take my friend with me," Archangelo explained to Hudson. "He cannot bear for me to be too far away."

"All right, as you please but make sure you move *fast* and mind what I said about your horses."

All three left the cottage. Valeriani stood up from his chair, went past Camilla, took a cup from a shelf, opened a small white jug and poured dark red wine into his cup. He sipped at it and regarded the others in the room with a maddening calm that Matthew certainly did not share.

"Will they come at night?" Matthew asked the Great One, whose ability to make command decisions obviously and welcomely had returned.

"I expect them at any time. They have the information they need, why should they wait until night?" Hudson lifted his chin toward Camilla. "Ask this idiot where his pistol is and if it's loaded."

To the following question and answer, Camilla replied, "He says there's no pistol."

"Wonderful!" Hudson said sourly. "Any weapons in the place besides what I brought in?"

To this query Valeriani said, "In the front room's closet is a ceremonial sword I was given as an award for my work three years ago in Pappano. That's all." He pushed his spectacles up further on his nose and speared a hard look at Camilla. "Madam, have you brought evil to my home?"

Camilla translated the information about the sword before she replied, "Brazio—if I may—the evil is in the mirror. People who wish to do evil want it, and they're coming here soon. Did you really think your father's work would be forever unknown?"

"Not my father's alone. An equal part—or more—of that Senna Salastre. Oh, you should've heard the grand promises and schemes that came out of his mouth!" Here at last, Matthew noted, was a flame of emotion across the barrier of language. "He insinuated himself into my father's work, with his claims for—as I remember he put it so very well—knowing the unknowable. And then urging my father to help him create that *thing*. Oh, what power should come out of it! What riches! What secrets to be learned, that no other man could know!" He set his cup down so hard on the countertop that the red wine sloshed out in a spatter. "My father was guilty of being both human and fatally curious. But it was that sorcerer who enticed him and corrupted him! And now you are here and it seems others are coming with possible violent intent. Yes, madam." He nodded gravely. "You *have* brought evil to my home."

Hudson was on his way to the front closet. He opened it and there propped against the wall toward the back was a rapier with a scrolled grip and the name of Brazio Nascosto engraved in scrollwork upon the blade. The thing looked dulled, but it would have to do.

When Hudson reached for it, his hand began to tremble before it touched the grip. The trembling coursed up his arm and into his shoulder to become a tightness and twitching of the muscles. At once his heart pounded and he felt sweat blooming at the back of his neck. In his mind he saw the scene of battle with Brom Falkenberg in Golgotha's wretched swamp, everything at triple speed like a drug-frenzied nightmare. He could not force his hand to close upon the rapier's grip; the tendons and muscles fought against him. And so did his fleeting power of will.

He recalled what he'd said to Matthew, Camilla and the professor on the ship from Alghero:

I can't ever hold a real sword again.

Was it true, or did his belief make it so? Whichever it was, he could not grasp the rapier.

"Matthew!" he called. "Come here!"

Matthew came to the sound of a broken voice.

"Get that sword," Hudson said.

"What? Why can't you—"

"I *said*, get that sword. You handle it. Hear me?"

Matthew took the rapier from the closet. He had a moment of panic, for Hudson's face had gone sallow, his eyes seemed dazed and a faint sheen of sweat glistened on his forehead. "Are you all right?"

"No questions. You're the swordsman now."

And Matthew understood. It was the memory of having to kill his friend, and Hudson might be past it next week or next month or next year, but at this precarious hour Matthew Corbett was the swordsman.

Hudson made his way back to the kitchen without stumbling. Instantly Camilla saw that he was distressed and she started to speak but he lifted a hand in a motion to deflect her attention back to Valeriani. In the front room, Matthew tested the rapier's tip with a forefinger and found it a good enough ceremonial sword but not sharp enough to pierce a wheel of cheese. He was torn about this situation. Valeriani was neatly dressed in a brown-and-white-striped shirt and brown trousers, white stockings and brown boots. His cottage was also neat: the furniture clean, a shelf of books by the fireplace, everything well ordered. Not married, it seemed, and no dog around. The man had found his place in the world and though it appeared to be solitary he had considered himself far away from the mirror and the memory of his errant father here. And now he'd been discovered, whoever was following was soon to be at the door, and what then? What then, for all of them?

Matthew took the sword and returned to the kitchen, the idea of finding Brazio Valeriani giving him no reason to rejoice.

Outside, Professor Fell watched the priest and his companion come around from behind the tavern where their horses were secured. They went inside, Archangelo holding the door for Trovatello. Less than sixty seconds after that, a large black lacquered coach pulled by four horses came tearing along the road with a hooded rider on a gray horse and another man on a dark bay following. Fell felt something like a punch to the stomach when the coach started up the hill at speed.

He burst into the cottage. "They're coming!" he called out. "A coach and two riders behind!"

Hudson picked up the cleaver and rushed past Matthew to the door. There was no latch on it and the two windows at the front of the cottage were unshuttered. "Get into the kitchen," he told the professor, who moved faster than Hudson could've ever expected. Matthew came up beside Hudson with the rapier that would be about as useful as one of the wooden wasters they'd practiced with at the prison. Less useful, because one could use a waster as a club.

Camilla and Valeriani both came into the room, and though Camilla's face was strained Matthew saw that she was still calm. Valeriani, however, had begun to crack now that these new and possibly deadly visitors had finally arrived, his face pallid, eyes large behind the spectacles and his hands kneading together so hard he would soon be down to the bones.

Through a window they saw the huge black coach pull up on the other side of their wagon. The bald, heavyset driver got down. They couldn't see the coach's door from this angle, nor could they see the two riders Fell had mentioned.

For a moment there was silence except for the huffing of the coach's winded team.

Then there came a knock at the door.

Just a tapping. Almost a gentle sound, as if a small elderly lady was using her fragile knuckles in a kindly visit on a neighbor.

Hudson moved to the far window to get a glimpse of who was standing out there.

He didn't reach it. As he crossed before the door it was kicked in with a tremendous crash that almost caught him broadside, and as he spun toward the entrance a monstrous broad-shouldered figure in a dark blue hooded cloak was lunging in, and instinctively Hudson swung with the cleaver and—*clang!*—the blade turned aside on a metal wolf's mask within the hood. Two black-gloved hands caught his shirt and nearly ripped it off him as he was thrown through the air like a sack of wheat, crashing over a table and an oil lamp that shattered on the floor. He slammed into the wall with nearly bone-breaking force and the cleaver skittered away.

Matthew felt himself nearly stunned into a state of paralysis as the wolfman came upon him like a gigantic whirlwind, and as he lifted the rapier for some prayer of a strike one of the gloved hands batted his arm aside with terrifying ease and the next instant the other hand came down on his right shoulder in a blow that shot pain through every nerve of his body and put him on his knees looking at the floorboards through a red haze. Another hand—did this creature have three?—caught him by the scruff of the neck, picked him up and threw him aside with a disdainful grunt from the metallic face. A black boot crunched down on the rapier, and then in his sprawled position on the floor and feeling like a stomped worm Matthew was aware of other figures coming into the room while Camilla and Valeriani retreated before them.

Hudson sat up amid the broken debris, his mind spinning and his eyes nearly knocked from their sockets. He smelled and tasted blood. A hand to his nose brought away a smear of red, and then right in his face was a grotesque-looking cat with high dark-tipped ears, its eyes fierce with murder, its jaws opening to reveal fangs ready to tear into already-bloody flesh.

"Nyx!" It was a woman's voice. *"Non ancora!"* With that, she pulled the lynx back from the wounded and groggy man on a black leather leash attached to a spiked collar.

Matthew's head cleared as the pain in his shoulder lessened to a throbbing ache. He saw the moving shapes take human form, except for the strange feline on the taut leash held by a black-haired woman in a red jacket and gray skirt. No, her hair was not entirely black; weirdly enough, it was red on the right side of her head. Silver rings flashed on her fingers as she dragged the straining cat further away from Hudson. Those rings...were they familiar? Someone's boots walked past him. He started to get to his feet and someone else pushed him down again, so for the moment he stayed exactly he was.

"So...this is the famous man." Mars Scaramanga was speaking in Italian as he approached Brazio and Camilla. He smiled thinly at her. "And you are the famous witch-hunter?"

Camilla said nothing. The other woman came up close to her face and inspected her at a distance of inches. "Not so fearsome, I think. Lorenzo, you and Pagani check the other rooms in this charming little shithole."

The coach's bald-headed driver and the brown-bearded scout Pagani obeyed, while the slim and wiry bodyguard Ivano and the wolf-masked

Lupo stood over the big man who'd been thrown aside. The first room Lorenzo and Pagani entered—a kitchen—held an old codger with his back against the wall. Behind his spectacles he wore a fierce look of defiance and his right hand gripped a small knife.

"Come on, grandfather," Lorenzo said with a twisted smirk. "Out with the others."

The professor did not understand the language but he fully understood the intent. He stood unbudging.

Lorenzo moved forward. "Don't make this difficult. You're going out."

Two more strides were taken. Before the third could progress, Professor Fell gritted his teeth, slashed out with the knife he'd taken from the counter-top and Lorenzo staggered back with a line of blood rising from the sliced shirt at his chest.

"Ha!" Pagani gave a harsh laugh, showing a silver tooth in the front of his mouth. "The old grandfather wants to play rough!"

"Bastard! My good shirt!" Still, Lorenzo had to echo Pagani's laugh. His cut was a scratch, nothing more, and he had many worse scars to prove his mettle. "Grandfather," he said as he drew his own knife with its seven-inch-long blade, "if you don't play nicely we'll cut your nose off and feed it to you."

The professor was in no mood for joviality, whatever these two fools thought was so comical. With a display of strength born of desperation he upended the kitchen table and drove it onto the two men as both a shield and a battering-ram. Pagani took the brunt of the blow, one edge of the table giving him a solid knock in the mouth and nearly causing another tooth to fly down his throat, while Lorenzo dodged aside, came up behind the old man, got an arm around his neck and—*oh i santi!* it was like fighting a squirming eel!—put the knife to the soft and wrinkled flesh at the base of the skull.

"Don't kill him!" Mars commanded, standing in the short corridor between the front room and the kitchen. "Bring him in here!" He saw the blood on Lorenzo's shirt. "Christ, are you slipping?"

Pagani was now twisting the old man's knife hand, but the damned thing wouldn't open. He struck a fist into the ribs...once and then again. When that brought two wheezes of pain but showed little more effect Pagani leaned forward and put his teeth—silver and all—into the offending hand. The knife dropped but the old man still thrashed while releasing a raging torrent of foreign language that sounded like English, his spectacles hanging from one ear. Lorenzo made a quick but shallow cut across this devil grandpa's right cheek that paid him back for the injury and served to make him understand the continued penalty of resistance. As a further act of small revenge he swept the man's spectacles off his face and smashed them under a bootheel.

With blood trickling down his cheek, the professor sneered, "I only need those to avoid stepping on shit like you."

"Old Englishman!" Mars said in the man's tongue. "Your cursing hurts my ears. Come along and be sociable." To his two men: "Bring him."

Between them they hauled Professor Fell out of the kitchen, not an easy job since the old man dropped to his knees and dragged his boots to make himself as unwieldy as a land anchor.

He was thrown to the floor alongside Matthew. The wolfman stood over Hudson, and Ivano had drawn a pistol from a sheath at his hip. "Watch out for the grandfather!" Lorenzo warned them with a snigger. "He thinks he's a killer!"

Matthew saw the blood on the side of Fell's face. From all that noise of fighting in the kitchen, he thought that the many weeks of roaming the coast and coves around Alghero had surely brought the professor renewed vitality. It was unfortunate that vitality alone would not save the day. He imagined Berry standing in a corner saying *I told you not to do this.* Well, it was done; the problem to be solved now was undoing it, if they lived long enough. First thing was controlling the fear that clawed at the back of his neck as if it were that damned big cat—a lynx, wasn't it?—riding him. He'd read and heard of the things but had never seen one. Supposedly they were as ferocious as hell and who would want to keep one on a leash!

Steady, he told himself. Panic would do no good for himself or any of the others. In fact, any display of fear might bring the lynx on him no matter how hard the woman was restraining the thing. He lifted his face to regard the wolfman, who beneath the hooded cloak wore a double-breasted gold-buttoned jacket in the same dark blue color, a white cravat neatly knotted, a pair of light brown breeches, white stockings over thick legs and a pair of black boots. Quite the dapper monster! He stood with his hands on his hips obviously awaiting further orders from the master of the moment, whose sleek cap of hair was black on the right side and red on the left in direct opposite of the cat-woman's.

With a start, Matthew realized that here was the wolf that walks like a man.

But it was impossible! What connection could there be between Trovatello and this beast in the metal mask?

He watched as the wolfman bent down and retrieved the cleaver…and he had the thought that a sharp, heavy blade such as that would be the right implement to cut off a man's hands.

That or an axe.

The name that Trovatello had written three times on the paper…the third time the quill having snapped under the increased pressure of…what? Not a nightmare, but horrific memory?

The name.

"Lupo," Matthew said, and the wolfman's metal face instantly turned toward him.

NINETEEN

DOUSE THAT FIRE, YOU FOOLS!

It was what Mars Scaramanga had said when the black coach and the contingent of bodyguards had come upon the camp of Divittori's men Lamacchia, Rossone and Gallo on the first night, just north of Sante Vallone. As soon as Mars had spoken, Lupo had torn the cloak off Lamacchia's shoulders and with it smothered the fire where the men were heating their *caffe* after the long day's ride. Before the fire had been attacked by the huge wolfman—burning a substantial portion of Lamacchia's cloak in its fitful departure—the three men had recoiled from the sight of Lupo rushing toward them through the woods. Such a vision had been known to make strong men fall to their knees and beg for mercy without an inkling of their offense. It was whispered by the underlings—the workmen, the ones who actually performed the tasks commanded by the leaders of their crews—that the mysterious Lupo was never seen without the metal mask because his face was so hideously deformed from birth. Or that the mysterious Lupo wore the mask because as the family's executioner he wished to hide his face from God and the saints. Or that the mysterious Lupo wore the mask because his first killing had caused blood to spurt into his eyes, and thus the metal protection. Or that the mysterious Lupo wore the mask because he was indeed part wolf, had been born a bizarre commingling of animal and human, and he realized the sight of his dark-haired, lupine features and his mouth with their tearing fangs would drive any ordinary man to madness. Had anyone ever seen his hands ungloved? It was to hide the coarse animal hair!

After all, everyone knew he only ate the most raw and blood-soaked meat.

Thus: the shock of their lives when the creature came out of the dark and at the command of Mars Scaramanga—another shock, the Grandmaster a few steps behind the beast—sacrificed Lamacchia's fine velvet-lined cloak to the flames. But to protest such a thing? One would be killed on the spot. Further shocks: the Grandmistress on the scene out in this territory of peasants and forest so far from the gleam of civilization, her fearsome cat collared and leashed yet another frightful sight, and bringing up the rear of the procession the men Lorenzo, Pagani and Ivano who everyone knew were the Scaramanga's personal bodyguards. What to make of all this?

It was quickly announced by the Grandmaster that Divittori's team was relieved from their duty and instructed to pack up their camp and leave the area at dawn. No one grumbled about this demotion. At first light they were on the road for their homes, and glad about it. Venus ordered Pagani to ride ahead a short distance, find a hiding place, use his spyglass and report back when the quarry left their own camp.

A peculiar report followed: Pagani saw not only the pair of wagons regaining the road, but two figures on horseback following at a distance. Two men: one with long white hair and wearing a tan-colored cloak, the other…strange, Grandmaster and Grandmistress, but the other seems to be an invalid of some kind. This one is braced up in his saddle and the other leads his horse.

"An *invalid?*" Mars had frowned. "What do you make of it?"

"I'm not sure, sir. I thought at first they might be robbers, but after I saw that something was wrong with one of them I suspect they're beggars following from Sante Vallone."

"Can't be *robbers,*" Venus noted. "Whoever heard of an invalid being a robber? Yes, they must be beggars. And it must simply be coincidence that they're on the same road. Probably run out of Sante Vallone on the threat of tar-and-feathers, and they're just travelling north."

"Yes, Grandmistress," said Pagani. "That's also what I think. But still… it's peculiar."

"Why is that?" Mars had asked.

"They do have fine, healthy horses to be beggars."

"Whoever they are," Venus had replied with a flippant motion of a hand, "they're of no concern to us."

She had been just about to ask this roomful of people where these beggars of no concern were, since they'd been seen joining the group at Pappano, and Pagani had spied their horses up here on the hillside before he'd come back with his report about the cottage being the property of one Brazio Nascosto. But the name *Lupo* spoken by the young man on the floor—the Englishman Corbett, she presumed—had stopped her own speech.

Venus doubled and tripled the length of Nyx's leash in her fist, the better to draw the straining cat closer. Nyx was muscular and heavy but her own arms had become strong enough over time to handle the weight. To Corbett she posed a question in English: "How do you know that name?"

How indeed? he asked himself. His mind raced. "I have a knowledge of Latin," was what he came up with...lamely, he realized.

"I also have that knowledge. You're thinking of the word 'Lupus', aren't you?"

"My mistake," Matthew said, but he knew from the woman's sharp stare that she was not satisfied.

"A strange mistake. One either knows the word for 'wolf' in Latin or one does not. Something is wrong here, but I don't know what it is."

Mars said, "Venus, we're not here for a language lesson!"

"Certainly not, dear brother." Again she aimed her attention at Matthew. "Where are the other two? The white-haired man and the invalid? Pagani saw their horses here."

Invalid. Matthew suspected that though this Pagani had seen Trovatello through his spyglass he'd not realized the man had no hands; he'd simply seen the back brace, which could account for several infirmities. *Executioner*, Trovatello had written of Lupo. Possible—no, probable?—that this creature had cut off Trovatello's hands, wrenched out his tongue and executed... who? The man's family? *Lambs?* Children?

To Matthew's continued silence, Venus said to Lorenzo in Italian, "Cut off one of his ears."

"They were sent away," Camilla spoke up in English, to avoid the cutting.

"Really?" Venus turned her cold smile into Camilla's face. "Strange that we didn't pass their horses on the road, and it's the only way out."

"I sent them down to the tavern," said Hudson. He wiped his bloody nose again and turned himself so he was sitting against the wall. Glass from the broken oil lamp pinched his ass, but that couldn't be helped. Hopefully Archangelo and Trovatello had seen the coach pass—how could they miss it?—and ridden out to safety. "They just took up with us on the road. A priest and—"

"His companion," Matthew said quickly, before any further information could be offered. "We knew there would be trouble and there was no need for them to be involved."

"Trouble!" She smiled in the direction of her brother. "He doesn't know what trouble is, does he? Pagani! *Scendi alla taverna e riporta indietro gli altri due.*" Instantly the man left the cottage, as Matthew reasoned to ride down to the tavern and bring those two back.

He had to change the subject. "Nice rings," he said with obviously false appreciation. "What did you do with the rest of him?"

"My Nyx has to eat."

"I'd say that was the worst meal your cat ever tried to digest." It wasn't the ending Matthew had in mind for Cardinal Black, but winding up as lynx shit…well, it was something.

"Young man—Corbett, is it?—we are not here for discussions of Latin and food for my sister's cat." Mars approached Brazio, and Venus stepped aside. Mars tapped the man's cheek with a forefinger. His next statement was in Italian: "Now you'll tell us where the mirror is."

"What mirror?"

"Oh, this makes me ache!" Mars patted the cheek, this time with all his fingers. "Brazio, we don't have time for nonsense. Be a good boy, won't you? Let's start with this: there *is* a mirror created by your father and the sorcerer Senna Salastre. Yes?"

"I want all you people out of my home. Every one of you."

"He doesn't have much up in the belfry," Mars said to Venus. Next, he lightly slapped Brazio's cheek. The Grandmaster's eyes had gone hard. "You don't realize the difficulties of travel, do you? We have been on the road for far too long, in territory I would much rather have never seen and with war going on around our heads. This was not a pleasure trip. Sharing a tent with my sister is not my idea of a holiday, and with that cat growling night and day…you must understand I am not in the best of moods. I will ask this, then: what does the word *leviathan* mean to you?"

When Valeriani failed to respond, Mars leaned down closer and said in his face, "Leviathan! It means something important, does it not?"

Matthew caught the second use of the word *leviatano.*

Leviathan? Was that the correct translation?

He remembered something Silva Archangelo had said about the shipwreck that had taken his eye: *We hit the shoals just south of Leviathan. An old Roman lighthouse, but in that gale the fire had blown out, so there was no warning.*

And Brazio's statement about where the mirror was hidden, translated by Camilla: *Where no one can possibly find it…and even if the impossible happened, no one would recognize it for what it is…one mirror among many.*

From Matthew's reading and understanding, the old Roman lighthouses used a semicircle of mirrors behind an open signal fire to send the reflected light an adequate distance. Such it had been since the marine traffic of antiquity. One mirror among many mirrors positioned behind the fire. Was that where Valeriani had hidden the glass? *No one would recognize it for what it is.* And the impossible part? If the lighthouse was abandoned.

Still…it was simply a pistol shot in the dark, wasn't it?

If Hudson or Professor Fell had picked up on this, Matthew couldn't tell. Camilla had been out of the room when Archangelo was speaking of the shipwreck, so she wouldn't know. He lowered his head, trying to decipher through his knowledge of Latin what was being said.

"I have no idea what it means." A tremor had entered Brazio's voice.

"You make things difficult." Mars went about straightening the collar of the other man's shirt. "It does not have to be so, but if you wish it that way we'll grant it to you and we'll not even need a spirit from the mirror. Lupo! Escort this man into the kitchen and put that table upright. Seat him. We want our friend to be comfortable. Oh…don't forget the cleaver."

"And *you*," Venus said to Camilla. "There's a book you have. Where is it?"

"What book?"

"You people!" Venus shook her head in mock empathy. "So wishing pain! We'll find the book, don't fret. Come along, all of you! Into the kitchen! Ivano, cock your pistol, put it against the big man's back and march him!" Her ebony eyes turned upon Matthew, and she said in English, "Handsome, will we have any trouble with you?"

"No trouble," was all he could say as he got to his feet. His right shoulder and arm felt dead. It seemed that before he became cat meat, Cardinal Black had spilled everything. Logic said that he was picked up after he'd left the inn—probably by this woman—and taken to a secure location. And who had told these two about the quest for Valeriani and the mirror, so they could be shadowing the inn? It could only have been the wine merchant, Meneghetti.

Also spoken in English by the woman: "Grandfather, get up. No tired old tricks, or we'll have to knock what remains of your teeth out of your head."

Professor Fell stood up and gave her a cold grin. "I have all my real teeth, madam, and when I trick you you won't see it coming."

"Oh, bravo! Shuffle along, please."

In the kitchen, one of Lupo's black-gloved hands shoved Brazio down into a chair at the newly righted table while the other held the meat cleaver down at his side. Then he stood motionless, waiting for the next command.

"We'll wait a bit while the gentleman contemplates his future without fingers," Mars said, speaking to the English captives. "Also for Pagani to bring the other two back."

"I don't know of any mirror!" Brazio cried out, realizing what the cleaver might be used for, but no one was listening and Lupo's grip on a shoulder made sure he wasn't leaving.

"What little band of thieves do you belong to?" Fell had directed the question to Mars Scaramanga while he blotted the blood from his cheek with his shirt's sleeve.

"Don't be insulting, grandfather. You're already in enough difficulty."

"Ah! So it's a large organization? What's the title?"

Mars turned toward Matthew with a pained expression. "Can you make this irritating old *verme* close his mouth?"

"It's an honest question," Matthew answered. "You know *my* name. I'd like to hear yours."

"Why? So you can bless me at bedtime?"

"I am *Venus*," said the woman with a dramatic flair. Matthew supposed he should've known she would like all to hear her name, which she also seemed to think fit her description. "My brother is Mars. Scaramanga."

"Pleased to meet the both of you," Hudson growled. "We'll make sure your names are spelled right on your tombstones."

"Listen to these people!" Mars smiled and shook his head. "Standing without an iota of hope, and yet they talk like they're strutting along the Grand Canal! It's really quite entertaining!"

The so-called entertainment was dampened for Mars Scaramanga when Pagani came back into the room with news that the priest—a white-haired man wearing an eyepatch with a crucifix burned onto it—and the man without hands had—

"*What?*" Mars interrupted. "A man without hands?"

"Yes sir. They both left just after we passed the tavern."

"But we saw no horses!"

Pagani shrugged. Horses or no horses, the two men were gone.

Mars was staring fixedly at his sister. "A man without hands," he said. "Could it have been *him?* You remember: Nuncia."

"It can't be!" Her mouth crimped. "He was thrown in the swamp!"

"But was he *dead?*"

"I don't know if he was or not…but no one could've lived through that!" Venus's gaze snapped toward Matthew, who had no idea what the conversation was about. "The man with no hands! Could he speak?"

Oh, they'd figured this out! Matthew said calmly, "Speak? Yes, he could speak and he prayed many times with the priest. In fact, he could sing very sweetly."

"He's lying," Venus said.

"What the *hell* does it matter?" Mars's cheeks had begun to show whorls of red. "Hands or no hands, speak or no speak, sing or not! I'm not interested at the moment in auditioning anyone for a handless opera! All right, those two got away. What difference does it make? We have Brazio Valeriani and we're going to get the mirror!" He showed a fierce expression to Lupo and he spoke again in the native tongue: "Chop off a finger."

With a hoarse cry Brazio tried to stand but the wolfman's hand on his shoulder pressed down harder still. Before Brazio could clench his own hands into fists the cleaver chopped down and the index finger of his left hand flew across the table in a spurt of crimson. Brazio gave a scream, the sweat burst out on his face, and his head thumped down against the blood-spattered wood.

"He thought we were playing," Mars said to Matthew. "This is not playtime, Englishman."

To the further horror of Matthew, Camilla, Hudson and Professor Fell—though not so much in his case, because he knew how these things were done—Venus Scaramanga picked up the severed finger and tossed it into a corner. At once the lynx was trying to get at it, and the heavy creature nearly pulled the leash out of her grip before she was able to play out a length of it and let Nyx have the prize. The cat got the finger between its fangs and crunched down, and as it ate it swivelled itself in the corner so its back was protected and its blazing eyes staring at those who dumbfoundingly stared back.

"I wouldn't look at her while she's eating," Venus advised. "It makes her angry."

Did anyone's face ever turn so fast in the history of the world? But where to set one's eyes? The bleeding stump on Brazio Valeriani's hand, the red-edged cleaver held by the wolfman, the wolfman's impassive metal visage, the sleek Roman conqueror smiles on the faces of Mars and Venus Scaramanga? *Where?*

Hudson had shifted a few inches away from Ivano and had his eyes on the cocked flintlock pistol. "You should put that away before someone gets hurt."

As this was not understood, there was no response but a slight disdainful curl of the lip.

"Wake him," Mars said in Italian, to no one in particular, and he plucked the spectacles off their victim and tossed them aside.

Lorenzo found the pot of minestrone soup from which Brazio had filled his bowl, and this he poured over the man's head and into his face. Brazio's body shivered, he coughed and groaned and began to come up from the agonized depths to what Matthew knew was a place of further agony.

When the man opened his eyes they were puffed and bloodshot. He looked desperately around the room for some kind of aid but they squeezed shut again as he caught sight of his mutilated hand.

"You can save yourself so much pain," Mars told him, in what was for him a soothing tone of voice. "Just tell us where the mirror is and we'll leave you with nine fingers. Is that such a terrible thing to tell?"

"Please," Brazio managed to say. "*Please.* The mirror. You don't know what it is…what it can do. *Please.*"

"We *do* know what it is and what it can do. Why would we have come to visit you if we didn't? And these people also know. Oh, such a secret it is *not*. Now: you've hidden it somewhere, haven't you? I am asking as one gentleman to another, before things get ugly."

"I destroyed it. It's gone. I swear I destroyed it."

"You did? But our information from Nerio Bianchi, who was a disciple of Senna Salastre, indicates that it cannot be destroyed. At least that's what Bianchi claimed Salastre told him. *Cannot* be destroyed. Didn't your father try to destroy it, and failed? Oh, Bianchi said your father broke it but he was compelled to remake the glass and Salastre helped him. Nerio Bianchi told my sister everything he knew about it before she had his eyes gouged out and introduced him to her Iron Maiden. Why would such an intelligent and talented sorcerer as Nerio Bianchi lie when he was feeling those spikes at his chest? You see, Brazio? No one lies to my sister when she wishes the truth."

And that *was* the truth, Venus mused as she stood watching this pretense of civility. Her heart had begun beating with a harder rhythm in anticipation of what the cleaver would do, and now knowing it was likely soon to be used again she felt as light-headed as if she'd had two cups of wine too many. The mention of what had been done to Nerio Bianchi in the torture chamber brought back all the moments of what she considered a delicious memory. She felt sweat at the nape of her neck, felt it collecting in the hollow just above her hips. Her nerves were firing like little bursts of gunpowder, and then she looked down at her hands.

Beneath the shine of Black's bizarre rings they had become wrinkled, misshapen claws.

A cry of terror tried to escape from her mouth, but she bit down so hard on it she nearly pierced her lower lip. The flesh of her hands had turned the gray of the funeral vault, and as she stared in a silent paroxysm of horror she witnessed the skin crinkling up her wrists like ancient parchment. Up into the sleeves of her silk blouse and jacket she could feel the flesh betraying her, drying out like an old riverbed where liquid life had ceased to flow, and if she dared at that moment to peer into a glass would she see not the beautiful Venus Scaramanga but the hideous creature she might become without the power of Ciro Valeriani's mirror?

She had no illusions about living forever; that was not her wish. But to be forever beautiful even at the lip of the grave…to step into death as one of the most alluring and flawless women who had ever lived…yes, that was the wish…to be magnificent all the years of her life, never to be concerned with the realities of aging…those would be beneath her, and given as the most fantastic gift by the servant she would summon.

As these things whirled through her head she saw the wrinkled flesh fade and disappear, and a few heartbeats later she was as she had always been and with the enchanted mirror always would be. A figure in a purple robe was caught in the corner of her eye, and looking to her right she saw the hooded and faceless figure standing there against the wall…a silent watcher to this interrogation of Brazio Valeriani. Just as fast as she had registered the figure in her consciousness it began to fade. When it had vanished she had the stricken thought that Venus Scaramanga, the beautiful, never to be duplicated Grandmistress of the Family of the Scorpion, was poised on the edge of insanity and perhaps had been balanced on that rim for many years since witnessing the violent death of her beloved father who called her his little Pastiera Napoletana…the most gorgeous of cakes…but then she let that go too…let that go…return to the moment…the cleaver in Lupo's hand, the smell of blood and fear, Nyx crunching on the finger bone, the stark faces of the captives around her, the sensation of power that became for her an overwhelming urge of lust…and all was right with her world.

Valeriani was babbling. "The mirror…please…leave it alone. It killed my father…drove him mad. That monster Salastre cast spells…drew things up from below…showed my father creatures no man should see… he told me…told me they boiled up like things in a kettle and then sank down again…and my father tried to destroy it but a hammer wouldn't…a chisel, no…not even a bullet, which he said bounced off the glass as if it was concrete and left no mark. It could only be cracked by an iron crucifix and then…he could not find sleep because the mirror was calling him… many voices…horrible, merged into one…calling from the mirror…he could not rest until he had remade the glass and he told me all this on his fishing boat…the *Nascosto*…just a little boat so small my mother said other boats couldn't even see it…but we had such happy times together… and then when he told me he sobbed and wept and said he was cursed the mirror had cursed him it had to be destroyed or hidden and after he was gone it would be up to me…up to me…never to let anyone find it… for what it might set loose." He looked up into the impassive face of Mars Scaramanga with tears clouding his eyes and wet on his cheeks. "I beg you…*beg* you…to leave it alone."

"Tell me where it is," said Mars, his voice dead. "You will lose two fingers next."

"I...can't...I..." Brazio put the bloody hand to his face. "All right. Just...all right. It's hidden in a—"

Brazio suddenly bolted from the chair. He twisted his body and got past Mars. Lupo reached out to grasp the man with his free hand but Brazio was upon Ivano and fighting for the pistol. Hudson lunged forward in an attempt to help Brazio and was met with Lorenzo's knife at his throat. In a blur of motion and a fling of blood from the severed finger, Brazio and Ivano grappled for the gun. Ivano put a hand against Brazio's chest to shove him away, the pistol went off with a loud blast and a gout of blue powder smoke, and Brazio Valeriani fell away from the other man with a black-edged hole in his forehead. On the opposite wall his brains had painted the pinewood.

The son of Ciro crumpled to the floor. Matthew nearly jumped out of his boots when the lynx gave a blood-curdling scrowl as if it smelled the beginnings of a royal feast.

Silence in the aftermath. Smoke drifted through the room and mockingly played beneath the sharp-tipped nose of Mars Scaramanga.

"He pulled the trigger!" Ivano had almost screamed it. "I tried to get it away but his hand was slick with blood! I swear to you sir, he pulled the trigger!"

Mars and his sister stood staring down at the body, which continued to convulse in its final throes. At last there was a gasp of death and the open eyes looked heavenward as crimson gore puddled around the head.

Mars spoke. It was not more than a strained whisper.

"Lupo. Kill him."

Matthew hadn't understood much of what had been said, but of this there was no doubt.

The cleaver flashed as it came up. In his state of shock Ivano had no time nor will to cry out. Lupo sank the cleaver into the top of Ivano's head, wrenched it out and struck again into the skull before this second body could fall to the floor. Ivano's legs kicked as if he were trying to outrun the reaper, but he was no match for that onrushing specter.

Someone began to laugh.

Mars, Venus, the wolfman and all the others turned to see Professor Fell evidently enjoying the moment as if he were watching the most comical play ever presented at London's Cockpit Theater on Drury Lane.

"Marvelous!" Fell said, his expression one of jolly grim mirth. "By all means, keep going! Kill your sister next, that should do nicely!"

Matthew thought the next killing would see the professor joining the pile, but before Mars could speak it was his sister who said, "Let that old fool laugh!" She was having difficulty holding the lynx back from pouncing upon the newly dead meat, and to prevent her arm from being pulled from its socket she gave the leash to the wolfman. "Mars, don't be hasty! They got here before us, they might know something!"

"What would they know? That dead bastard wasn't going to talk unless I'd had all his fingers chopped off! Even then…he killed himself to keep from talking, you do realize that, don't you?"

"I'm telling you that he may have said *something* to them." Her voice held a firm resolve that even under the hideous circumstances Matthew found of interest, if one could be interested in homicidal lunatics…only these two were more driven than demented. "A *word*," she went on. "You heard him say *It's hidden in a*—what might that be? A *what*? He might have said to these people a phrase or a word we can decipher to still find it!"

Mars gave a short and bitter laugh. Matthew thought that a darker shade of terror had surfaced in his eyes. Mars said, "Do you really believe that?"

"We'll tear this house and the barn apart, but it won't be here. He wouldn't have brought it anywhere *near* this cottage or this village, not after what he thinks it did to his father. But it's not been destroyed. Do you hear me? It's still out there and we can still find it. Where might one hide a mirror so it would never be found? Buried it? Might it be dug up someday? That's what we have to think upon: where might one hide a mirror in a place it would never be discovered, knowing also it could never be destroyed?"

"These people can't tell us anything."

Venus took the knife from Lorenzo, went the few steps to Camilla and put the blade under her chin. "Where's the book, witch-hunter?" She pressed the knife with more strength, which made Camilla gasp as the blade was just about to pierce her flesh.

"It's in the wagon," Hudson said quickly. "Easy to find, there's no need for that."

Venus withdrew the knife. Still speaking English, she said to Mars, "We'll have the book. We have that word: Leviathan. It may mean something or it may be a sorcerer's muddled mind…but if we can find out *what* it means…all the better. And…we have these people."

"What of them? I say kill them right here and let's get back home."

"Dear brother," Venus said silkily, "you forget how a human being can suddenly recall all kinds of details when I seek them out. We have here four people…one of whom may offer a detail or two that we need, and at the moment this person does not even realize he—or she—has this valuable information."

"We can torture them here," Mars said.

"Oh my Christ!" she answered. "Are you joking? Wasting the—"
Opportunity, she was about to say, but she let it go. "Better there than here.
Trust me."

Mars did trust her. He trusted her to lose her mind in rapture when
she tortured these people in her chamber. But she did have a point: they
might have overheard an item of importance, or they might already know
something of value. Her torture chamber would tell the tale.

There were some issues to work out. Rope to bind them could likely be
found in the barn. If not that, a bedsheet could be cut apart and used. They
would be put in the back of their wagon, with Pagani driving the team and
his horse lashed behind. Lorenzo would continue to drive the coach. Lupo
would bring up the rear on his horse. The missing element: Ivano would
not be seated in his bodyguard position in the special seat at the back of
the coach, just behind himself and Venus. It galled him now that Ivano
was dead, because it meant to him one less element of safety. And safety
was why he wished to find the mirror and call from it a demonic protector...the perfect bodyguard to prevent what had happened to his father and
great-grandfather...the sudden assassin and the murder that came without
warning. A demonic bodyguard would know far in advance who was planning assassination...even contemplating it...and even could be compelled
to destroy all enemies at a distance of many miles between cities.

Yes. As Venus had said, *Safety is only in the mirror.*

"Find rope enough for all of them," he told Pagani.

Matthew had heard it clearly: the word *leviathan*. Brazio was never
going to speak it, no matter how many fingers he lost, but was it on his
mind to say *It's hidden in a—*

—lighthouse?

If they had the name, they had the place but they didn't yet realize it.

How soon would it be before they did?

And Matthew didn't know if the professor or Hudson had registered
any understanding of the word, but if they were going to be taken to a torture chamber somewhere...his would be the detail these creatures needed
to get hold of the mirror. After that...

He dared to look upon the lynx still crouching in the corner. Their
eyes met, and was it his imagination or did the thing's tongue come out to
lick the bloody mouth in anticipation of sending him to the place where
Cardinal Black rested in pieces?

He had to figure a way out of this. Not just for himself, but for all of
them. Otherwise, they were already walking corpses.

Had to think. Had to use the chess-honed mind, in what seemed now
like a deadly game that could not be won.

Had to figure a way out of this.

But *how?*

"All of you into the other room," Mars said. "We're taking a little trip."

Venus took hold of her cat's leash from Lupo. She allowed the beast to lick up the blood around Brazio's head, the lynx shivering with excitement and scrowling at everyone to stand clear of the bounty.

Matthew was still mentally thrashing when one of the wolfman's black-gloved hands grasped the back of his neck as if it were a chicken's ready to be beheaded, and pushed him to follow the others toward a decidedly precarious future.

Four

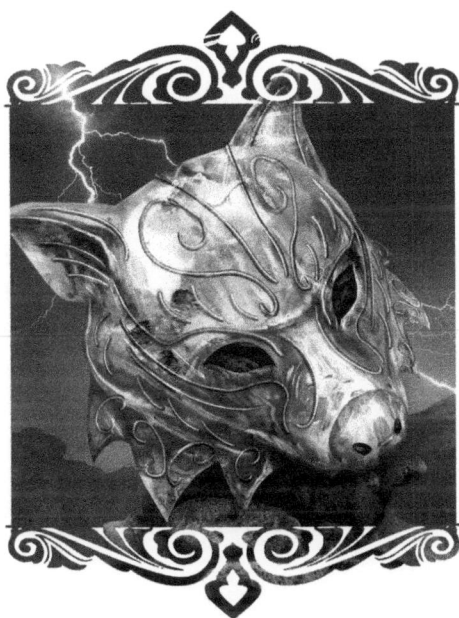

BLACK KEY

TWENTY

MADAM, HAVE YOU BROUGHT EVIL TO MY HOME?

The question posed to Camilla from Brazio Valeriani haunted her as she sat in the back of the wagon with Matthew, Hudson and the professor, her wrists roped together before her as were those of the others. The man known as Pagani sat on the driver's bench. The wagon's rear canvas curtains had been pulled open, and behind the vehicle was tied Pagani's dark bay horse. A few yards past the animal, Lupo followed on his gray horse, his dark blue hooded cloak pulled up so the metal wolf's mask was nearly hidden in its folds, only the upper portion visible.

Ahead pulled by its four-horse team was the large black lacquered coach occupied in its interior of red leather luxury by the Scaramangas and the deadly lynx, with Lorenzo on the padded driver's seat. About two hours previously, the prisoners had been searched for knives and bound by the ropes, Venus Scaramanga had found and taken *The Lesser Key of Solomon*—which Matthew presumed she was now perusing to choose the demonic servant of her choice—and the wagon also gone through for weapons, of which there were none. Then the coach and the wagon had pulled away from the cottage with the yellow-framed windows, leaving two dead men on the floor.

Matthew thought it had been quite a harvest, indeed, though not one of his liking. The problem remained of how to get himself and the others out of this, intensified by every mile the caravan travelled. The ridiculous idea of everyone trying to jump out the back of a moving wagon was quickly abolished. Lupo was watching and the odds of broken ankles and worse were not in favor of the jumpers. In any case, even if successful they wouldn't get very far. So...*how?*

"We killed him," Camilla suddenly said; it was the first time she'd spoken since being hauled up by the wolfman into the wagon. "Valeriani," she added, her face downcast. "If we hadn't led them to him...we killed him. If he hadn't used that name we never would've found him. And you know what he told Scaramanga? That it was the name of his father's fishing boat!"

"Stop that!" Hudson replied. "All right, we led them to him...unknowingly. He killed himself. And you might even cast blame on his father for that, more than anyone else. So stop taking on guilt for something that was going to happen sooner or later." When she didn't respond, he said, "Look at me," and she did. "What's done is done. Right now we've got more things to worry about."

Matthew didn't offer anything to these comments, but he was thinking that a large share of the blame had to be put on Cardinal Black, who even after death had reached out in a show of his macabre silver rings to lead them all to destruction. And not forgetting the wine merchant Meneghetti, who had to be the one who told the Scaramangas the visitors from Alghero were staying at the Palace of Friendship. It occurred to him that Valeriani might have said something else of interest to Scaramanga, of course in Italian. "The mirror," he said to Camilla. "What else did he say?"

"I remember he said his father tried to destroy it with a hammer, a chisel...even a bullet but it could only be cracked by an iron crucifix. Then his father was compelled to restore it."

Matthew nodded. He was conflicted about revealing to the others his suspicions of what *leviathan* might mean and where the mirror might be hidden. Could he himself resist torture? Certainly not; he had been known to shed tears over a stubbed toe. Was there any way he could use this information as a bargaining chip? Again, that seemed a hopeless tactic when one faced being ripped apart by these obviously brutal criminals. So what, then? Just to sit here and give up? Berry had never seemed so far away...and the idea of marriage and living a happy life with her? A dream in danger of fading to nothingness.

He tried the ropes for probably the tenth time. Still locking his wrists together, but at least his arms were in front of him. They hadn't bothered to rope the ankles, because he presumed they didn't want to have to carry the lambs to the slaughter. Lambs? Trovatello's children executed by the wolfman? And his wife as well, most surely. But he was getting off on a tangent, and for the eleventh time he put tension on the ropes. Did they give a half-inch or so? No, they did not. The ropes themselves were not thick or heavy. The coil had been taken from the barn and was the kind used to guide horses…more like sturdy white cords, but more than strong enough to securely bind.

Hudson must've noted him engaged in a small soundless struggle, because he said, "Comfortable there, Matthew?"

"Far from it."

Hudson inched over closer to Matthew, positioning himself between the problem-solver and the professor. When he spoke it was barely above a whisper. "Fell, in a few minutes I want you to shift yourself as if you're trying to stretch your legs or something. I want you to sit behind Matthew and myself so you're blocking Lupo from seeing what we're doing."

"What are we doing?" Matthew's question was equally a whisper.

"In my right pocket is a shard of glass I put there after the lamp broke. Thank God they missed something so small." The search for hidden knives carried out by Lorenzo and Pagani had been at waistbands, armpits and a patting of the pockets though it was already obvious to all that the prisoners were defenseless. "You're going to start sawing on my ropes," Hudson continued. "With luck and care they won't realize what we're doing."

"A fine idea." The professor had whispered it with bitter mockery. "A little piece of glass against these creatures? Ha!"

"A *sharp* little piece of glass against the ropes. Against the others, we'll figure that out later. Matthew, you'll have to reach deep into the pocket, it's down at the bottom. It's going to take time and I'm hoping we have enough."

"Impossible!" was Fell's opinion.

"I know how it's done," Hudson said. "Now shut your trap and do what I'm asking."

In three minutes the professor began to move as if he were stretching a pair of aching legs, after which he completed a shift of position so that he was between the wolfman and Lupo's view of the wagon's interior. Another benefit was that Pagani's horse was tied to the back of the wagon at a distance of about eight feet, further impeding a clear view. After Fell's move, Hudson turned his body to the left to offer easier access to the right pocket, and Matthew dug down as far as he could with his roped right hand…felt the shard of glass…dropped it from between the groping fingers…found it again, and cut himself on it because the little bastard's edge was indeed very sharp…but on this second attempt withdrew it clutched between the index and middle fingers.

The piece of glass was about two inches long and less than an inch in width, not a very efficient cutting tool but it was all they had. Matthew now had to shift the glass to the working area of his thumb and index finger, which wasn't an easy proposition in a wagon that swayed and bounced over the country road, if road it could be called. If he dropped the glass onto the wagon's floor he would need the help of a demon from the mirror to pick it up again. Further complicating the maneuver was a small leakage of blood from Matthew's nicked index finger; all in all, it was an exercise that demanded his most intense concentration and for a few seconds a determined holding of breath.

"Easy, easy," Hudson urged, which was really no help at all.

When Matthew was situated facing Hudson with Hudson's wrists offered, the work began at a place on the ropes just under the central knotting, which itself was a formidable obstacle. Within several minutes Matthew realized that though the edge of the glass was indeed sharp enough and the glass thick enough to resist further breakage the work required to cut through this devil of cordage was going to take steady strength and steadier patience, plus making sure the shard did not slip from his fingers to the flooring, all while balancing the entire act against the wagon's sway.

He'd had an easier time dodging falling fiery debris when the professor's gunpowder warehouse had exploded on Pendulum Island, and here there was going to be no respite of it. Two questions: could this actually manage to either cut through or loosen the ropes enough for Hudson to free himself, and then what?

Soon—and after cutting Hudson twice—Matthew's right wrist simply gave out. The rope had been injured but not parted nor loosened. "Give me the glass," Hudson said. "I'll work on yours. Careful, don't let it slip."

A slip was barely averted as the wagon trounced from side to side. Hudson got hold of the glass and began to saw at Matthew's bonds with stronger effort than Matthew had been able to supply.

Time went on and the afternoon's sun began to sink. The shard was passed back and forth between Hudson and Matthew. For a short while the work paused and had to be concealed when the coach and wagon stopped to rest and water the horses. Pagani looked back from the driver's bench and Mars Scaramanga came around to the rear of the wagon to make sure all was still in order. While Pagani and the wolfman's horses were being watered, Lupo stood a few feet behind the wagon, silently staring at the prisoners through the eyeholes of his metal mask. Then Pagani's steed was retied, Lupo remounted his horse, and the caravan started on again. At once the shard returned to work in Matthew's grasp between aching thumb and protesting index finger.

Less than an hour after the water stop, Hudson whispered with urgency, "It's coming loose. Let me try to break it." He began to work his wrists against the frayed cords. His face reddened. "A few more," he told Matthew, who continued sawing and realized that not only had the rope frayed but the friction was working the shard down to half of what it had been.

Six more? Eight? Ten?

Hudson clenched his teeth and wrenched mightily at the rope. It snapped apart with a soft *pop* and suddenly he was wearing cordage bracelets. He kept his hands low and out of the wolfman's view.

"Now what?" the professor sneered. "A hero's lunge at our driver?"

"I ought to throw you at him, and keep your voice down." Hudson was aware that Pagani had picked up dead Ivano's pistol and loaded it before this jaunt had begun. The pistol was probably under the driver's bench. Was it worth trying to go for it, shooting Pagani and attempting to get control of the wagon? What if the pistol wasn't under the driver's bench? It might be held in the man's waistband, but on which side? Hudson knew he would have only a second or two of surprise because Pagani would be instantly alerted by the noise of the canvas being shoved aside; if he didn't get the pistol fast enough it would be in his face and he might get his hair parted as well as his brain. What good would that do for Camilla? And yes, for Matthew and the professor as well?

He could throw Pagani off the bench. Maybe. But there was Lupo to consider. The man's strength was far more than his own. How long would it take the wolfman to be on him if he was indeed able to take the reins? And the reins themselves…they would fall away if Pagani was pitched off. They might even fall to the ground down amid the team, so if he went for Pagani he would have to consider getting the pistol, making sure he could take control of the reins, and possibly using his own shot to hit Lupo anywhere that would stop the beast.

His verdict?

He didn't have six hands. He needed more before he decided on an action.

He went to work again on Matthew's wrist, using both his fingers and the diminished piece of glass, with the realization that the oncoming twilight and nightfall would help to hide the effort. He thought also it was a lucky thing that the fourth man had been killed, otherwise they'd probably have him sitting back here in the wagon watching over them.

As the blue twilight deepened, Matthew felt the ropes loosening from Hudson's work on what was another devil of a series of knots.

"Almost," Hudson said.

Ten minutes later, Matthew's wrists were free and with a grateful rush of relief he set about rubbing the blood back into them. The caravan suddenly stopped again. Up front, Lorenzo was using his tinderbox to light the four oil lamps that were bolted to the corners of the Scaramangas' coach. Two more lamps were flamed within the coach. Venus put aside the book to feed Nyx from a packet of dried beef, and the half-drowsing Mars opened his eyes to slits to make sure the creature stayed on her side. When the lamps were burning, Lorenzo used the foot rungs to climb back up onto the driver's seat, he gave the team a crack of his whip and they started off once more.

Hudson moved in the gathering darkness of the wagon to set about freeing Camilla, but Professor Fell put his wrists up in front of Hudson's face.

"Mine first," he said.

"I'm doing hers first."

"No, you're not."

"What are you going to do, yell for help?"

In the gloom Fell's smile was enigmatic. "I might. You see, the Scaramangas have no idea who I am. I would venture they might have heard of me, as I've had business dealings with gentlemen from Italy in the past. I'm not so far softened that I wouldn't attempt to strike some bargain with them…maybe a shipment of White Velvet for my life?"

"You *wouldn't*." Hudson's whisper sounded like he was chewing on stone. "If you were thinking of doing that, why didn't you tell them already?"

"Up until this moment I have been counting on you and Matthew to get me out of this. So far I have not been impressed, and the only recourse I may have is to reveal myself and throw the rest of you to…the wolf."

"I'd kill you before they could get in here."

"Well, let's test your reflexes, then. Are you so eager to?"

Matthew had no idea if the old ex-emperor of crime still felt up to the role or if he was bluffing, but before he could offer his two pence—which was to err on the side of sanity and release the professor—Camilla said, "His first, Hudson."

"Damned if I will. It's the principle of the thing."

"We don't have the luxury of principles," she reminded him. "Please. His first."

"I'll work on hers," Matthew said, knowing he might put forth a good effort but he didn't have the digitary strength to equal Hudson's. Still, he'd give it his best.

Muttering a curse that would've made every sailor in the British fleet green-faced with both envy and sickness that anyone could think up such a thing, Hudson roughly grabbed the professor's wrists and started working as Matthew got himself in position in front of Camilla.

"Gently, sir," Fell said. "I bruise easily."

As he sought to loosen the knots that appeared so tight only a sharp blade could do the job, Matthew reasoned they were near or had already passed the villa at the ruined vineyard of Pappano. Night was almost complete. He wondered if the caravan was stopping to make camp or would just keep going as long as the horses could move a hoof. Obviously Mars Scaramanga was in a hurry to get "home", wherever that might be, so it was possible that even if they did stop it would only be for a few hours.

Hudson noted Matthew's difficulty and told Camilla, "I'll get to you soon, don't worry."

"I'm not worried."

"They didn't knot you as tightly as they did Matthew and me," was Hudson's next statement to Professor Fell. And he added: "Grandfather."

"I have had people killed for less than that," Fell said. "You're fumbling. Can't you see in the dark?"

Matthew had to ask the question, albeit still in a guarded whisper: "Even out of the ropes, what do we do?"

"I'm thinking about it," said Hudson. "We'll have to get the reins away from Pagani. He's got a pistol tucked away somewhere, but it's only one shot."

"Wonderful," was the professor's comment. "Who takes the bullet?"

Hudson ignored him. Two of the knots confining Fell's wrists had been undone but there was a third still holding everything together. "We've got to get control of the wagon. Good that it's night, that helps. We'll have to be fast. Hold still, professor, it's coming loose."

"We'll need to get that horse off the back of the wagon," Matthew said, as it was well understood the extra animal would be a drag on their speed.

"When we come to it. No professor, I can't see in the dark and I hope Lupo can't either, because if he sees us grabbing Pagani I suspect he'll be the first to attack. Got to get that pistol, but the hell of it is I don't know if it's on Pagani or under the bench."

Which meant, Matthew thought, that one of them was in danger of being shot. Lupo surely was carrying a weapon somewhere on him, but hopefully not another pistol. *Hopefully*; that word in his mind made him cringe. At the moment, even with freed hands, there was not much hope to be found.

Hudson was at a quandary of what to do as he loosened the final knot from Fell's bindings. His own fingers were rubbed raw to the point of nearly bloody. When the professor's ropes went slack enough for Fell to winnow his hands out of them, Hudson immediately turned his attention to Camilla, pushed Matthew aside and started laboring again on another series of tight knots.

She sensed his indecision, and who could blame him? She had no idea what the next move might be. "We'll get out of this," she said.

"We've gotten out of worse. Haven't we, Matthew?"

Matthew wasn't so sure about that, but he said, "Absolutely."

Up front in the driver's padded seat of the black lacquered coach, the weary Lorenzo guided the team in a steady walk and wished for a rest to his aching back and arms. He dared not express this to the Grandmaster and Grandmistress. He was paid very well for his pain, and also he was loyal to a fault. It was a pity what had happened to his friend Ivano, and perhaps—dare he even think it—the Grandmaster had been rash, but still…one did not question the absolute authori—

His musings were abruptly shattered when the coach came around a forested curve in the dark and suddenly the front pair of horses stumbled, wrenching down on their traces. The second pair was thrown sideways from the momentum and one fell with a high scream of equine panic. The entire coach slewed to the right, tilting so dangerously Lorenzo was almost thrown from his perch. A cry of alarm from Mars met a gunshot cracking sound from the right rear wheel. Behind the careening coach, the wagon's four-horse team collided up on its rear before Pagani could haul back on the reins and those animals were thrown off balance, the leading four trying to avoid the collision and the back four jamming into them. The wagon like the coach slewed to the right before it centered and stopped under Pagani's strength on the reins but the wagon's frightened team jumped and thrashed in their traces and one even snapped at another. At once Lupo kicked his bootheels into the flanks of his horse and galloped around the wagon to aid his master and mistress.

In the confusion of the moment, Hudson recognized an escape route. "Go!" he shouted at Matthew, who had no hesitation in leaping from the back of the wagon past Ivano's horse, the animal bucking and kicking in its agitation. He ran for the forest on the right side of the road, and just behind him the professor clambered over the back of the wagon, got past the horse while narrowly missing being kicked in the head, and chased after Matthew.

Hudson had not finished freeing Camilla, but now he picked her up as he had the wounded soldier. As he turned to get them both out the back he heard the canvas folds come apart with their crackling noise, Pagani hollered, *"Se la stanno cavando!"* loud enough to wake the dead from the watery vaults of Venice and Hudson felt the barrel of a pistol thrust against his spine.

"No no, signore," Pagani said with the confidence of one who held a loaded and cocked flintlock, *"Tu non vai da nessuna parte!"*

Which meant, Hudson reasoned, that he and Camilla were not leaving.

But as for Matthew and the professor…Hudson shouted with his best lungpower: "Matthew, keep going! Don't let them catch you!" For this effort he received a hard fist to the back of the head that put sizzling stars in his eyes but at least it wasn't a lead bullet through a kidney.

He eased Camilla off his shoulder and did his best to offer her a smile though the pistol's barrel was still at his back. She gave him a smile in return even if her eyes were wet with fear, and she kissed him on the lips and said, "Better together," which he understood to mean either in life or in death.

And he agreed.

Mars and Venus were out of the coach, Lorenzo having put down the brake and run back with his knife out to respond to Pagani's shout. Lupo dismounted from his horse, and he and the Scaramangas saw by the light of the flickering oil lamps the mass of thornbrush, vines and tree branches that had been set across the road and now was hung up under the wheels.

"You know who did this," Venus said.

"The priest and the man with no hands. Antonio Nuncia. It has to be him."

There came another shout, this time from Lorenzo: "The young Englishman and the grandfather got away!"

There was no telling which side of the road they'd escaped to. His face aflame, Mars turned and called out, "I know you can hear me! Come back or we kill the man and the woman here and we smear this mess with their guts!" And then quietly to Lupo in their language: "Choose a direction and search for them. I'll send Lorenzo the opposite way."

A black-gloved hand came up and pointed to the right, after which the wolfman strode to his horse, unlaced a saddlebag and withdrew a small axe.

Fifty yards away, Matthew and Professor Fell lay on their bellies in the underbrush and weeds in a thick pine forest that angled down into a gully. Hearing the threat, Fell said softly and dispassionately, "He's bluffing. He won't kill them."

"Can you be sure?"

"I've told you, I know how it's done. They want information. Hudson and Camilla are too valuable to kill. *Yet.*"

It occurred to Matthew that the Scaramangas might not kill the others, but they might start doing some torturous cutting. He hated to think of Hudson Greathouse with only six fingers or lacking a nose, and Camilla the same, but what were they to do? Go back and return to captivity? Hudson would want him to get away, no matter what; he would not say the same for the professor, but here they were, two fugitives verging on a state of fugue. The professor had stumbled over exposed roots and fallen, Matthew had stopped to help him up, and now they lay gathering strength and breath to run again. But to where? Deeper into the woods in this landscape where the nearest village—behind them, for sure—was the dead Pappano? Matthew looked up and through the treetops saw clouds scudding from the south over a nearly full silver moon, so that from second to second the dark and light advanced upon and conquered one another. He could not see the road from his position, but he knew very well that they'd be searching. Who would take the left side of the road and who the right?

Fell had the same thought at the same time. "We have to move."

"I can't stand to leave them."

"Dear boy," the professor said in a voice of the coldest frost, "you've *already* left them. Suit yourself, but I'm moving." He didn't pause any longer. He stood up and in a crouch began to make his way down into the gully.

Matthew asked himself what choice he had. There wasn't any. And as he watched in the direction of the road he saw a sudden glint through the trees that might've been metal catching moonlight before the clouds closed in again. He moved, following the professor down.

TWENTY-ONE

UNDER THE SILVERED MOONLIGHT AND THE OBSCURANT FLEETING clouds, an owl hooted and a second answered in the distance. Two figures struggled on through thornbrush and high grass, the forest primeval now their temple of survival. Matthew occasionally paused against the trunk of an oak or pine to look back and study for movement or the moon's glint off a metal mask, but he detected nothing as of yet. Thus he and Professor Fell—Matthew realized from their history the most unlikely of pursued companions—went on toward an unknown destination, wanting to get as far as possible from the road while clinging to the ink-black shadows.

After perhaps twenty minutes, Fell sank down to the earth against a huge oak tree, its branches spread out and interlocking with others in the canopy sixty feet above. "Let me rest," he said in a still-guarded voice, and Matthew sat at his side. Then, another statement from the professor: "Those fucking bastards."

Matthew agreed, but at the moment it was fruitless to waste the breath. His mind was feverishly working at a problem of which there seemed no solution: how to somehow get Hudson and Camilla out of the Scaramangas' clutches. Not only was his mind feverish, but the combination of the warm and humid night air, the escape and this continual racking of the brain had broken him out in a dripping sweat. How to save Hudson and Camilla from what was likely going to be a session of horrifying torture?

How?

Complicating the problem beyond its bounds were the facts that they were out here in these woods God only knew how far from the nearest village, and they had no idea where Hudson and Camilla were being taken. Matthew didn't know what had happened on the road back there, but evidently something had made the team of the Scaramangas' coach stumble and then the wagon's team had nearly crashed into the coach. Whatever had happened, were they still back there trying to get everything in order or had they moved on by now, which meant they'd given up searching in the dark? Would they remain there until morning and then start searching again? Matthew doubted it; they would probably cut their losses and consider that the young Englishman and the grandfather had no more value for them.

Anyway, he and Professor Fell were as good as lost.

But it was strange: for a while Matthew had had the feeling of being watched. It was not something he could say for sure, just a sensation that eyes were upon him. What? A deer? A fox? In any case, they couldn't stay here all night but where were they to go?

The professor had obviously come to the same opinion of their plight. He asked, "What now?"

"I have no idea."

"The problem-solver with no ideas? Dear boy, how can it be?"

Stop calling me dear boy, Matthew almost said in a little pique of frustrated anger…but he stilled the speech because he thought he heard the sudden *crunch* of a twig snapping. He immediately tensed. "Did you hear that?" he asked. The sound had seemed to come from the left, down in what appeared to be an area of even deeper darkness.

From that darkness issued a voice: "They've gone."

Instantly Matthew was on his feet. Fell struggled to stand, got his legs under himself and made it up the second time.

A figure came toward them. No…two figures. Moonlight illuminated long white hair.

Silva Archangelo, with Trovatello at his side, advanced forward. "Gone," the priest repeated. "Some spokes on one of their wheels cracked, but it seems not to have damaged their coach very badly. They got all the horses untangled, so…they're gone."

"My God!" Matthew's rush of nearly overwhelming relief almost put him on the ground again. "What are you two doing out here?"

"We were far ahead of them, but we saw the wagon and knew they must have you. Therefore I took it upon myself to construct a little impediment to their travel, hoping you might take advantage of it. I am thankful this road is not used very much this time of year, and no soldiers came along to move what I dragged over. Hudson and Camilla are still with them?"

"Yes."

Trovatello was pacing back and forth. He stopped, put his handless arms around the priest as if to pull him, and began to pace again.

"My friend has become highly agitated in a way I've never seen before," Archangelo said. "It happened right after we saw the black coach pass, and that strange rider who looked to be wearing a metal mask." At that, Trovatello approached the priest again and from the tongueless mouth issued harsh bleating sounds that made Matthew think urgency was involved. "Trovatello became this way in the tavern and pulled me out after the coach went past. His motions and attitude seemed to be vital that we get away. I think there's something important he wants to tell me. *Write* to me, I mean." To Trovatello he asked in Italian, "Something about the coach and rider?" With that, Trovatello struck his own chest with an arm and nodded vigorously.

"All right, my friend," the priest said soothingly. "We'll get to that." He turned his focus again to Matthew and Professor Fell. "Our horses are not far, but you'll have to walk. About a mile or so from here in a little clearing is a wagon that passed us on the road when we came up to the villa at Pappano. I recall there were two soldiers sitting up on the driver's bench. Those two men are lying on the ground with their throats cut. The horses are not in very good shape, but they've been grazing as best they could and I gave them water. If we start off now we might reach our cottage in Sante Vallone by morning." He spoke again to Trovatello, who once more nodded almost violently. A drift of clouds made the moonlight shine briefly upon the tormented man's face, and Matthew saw that his sunken eyes were wet with tears.

It was not an easy walk through the thick and rugged forest, with only the fickle moon to light the way. They reached the point where the priest's and Trovatello's horses were tied, Archangelo helped his friend up into the saddle and the back brace and then it was another long trek walking behind the horses to the clearing where the wagon stood. There lay the two Spanish soldiers, each with a gashed throat. Matthew figured the Scaramangas had no use for them since they didn't speak or understand Italian, and to prevent them from returning to the search party it was expedient to kill them. Either that, or they'd just wished to do it to keep up their sterling record of murders.

The wagon's team grumbled and balked when Matthew took the reins with Fell up beside him on the driver's bench. Of course they were sore, hungry and in need of care; who wasn't? The whip was nowhere in sight and likely lost and anyway Matthew wouldn't have used it unless absolutely necessary, yet an urging flick of the reins simply brought more grumbles, a few grudging paces forward and then a halt. It went on like this until Archangelo got off his own horse and walked to each member of the team, rubbing their noses and speaking to them quietly in the language they understood. Whatever he said, Matthew thought it must be from the mouth of God because after Archangelo finished his equestrian homily and remounted his steed the team started off—however slowly and with as little energy as if Matthew himself was yoked to the undercarriage—after another couple of shakes of the reins.

They reached the road and started south toward Sante Vallone, Archangelo's horse leading Trovatello's, Matthew as tense and disturbed as he'd ever been in his life, and the professor drowsing at his side. Soon Fell retreated to the back to stretch out for sleep, leaving Matthew alone with his thoughts of what might be done to Hudson and Camilla in the Scaramangas' torture chamber…wherever that was.

Around three o'clock Matthew stopped the procession to rouse Fell from his slumber and demand a change in wagon drivers. The professor protested that he'd never guided a horse team in his life, to which Matthew replied rather forcefully that it was time. Thus the professor took the reins as Matthew got some much-needed sleep in the back, and to Fell's credit the team at least did not meander off the road into the woods.

At first light there was very little first light. The sun was shielded by heavy gray clouds moving steadily from the south, and it seemed to Matthew that the entire world might be encased in gray gloom such as he felt. Just after seven o'clock by Matthew's reckoning the vineyard and village of Sante Vallone was sighted, and Archangelo led them down a narrow road past the small church to an equally small brown stone cottage where also stood a barn and corral for the horses. It appeared to Matthew even before Fell reined the team in—by now considering himself an expert driver though complaining about his sore and leather-blistered hands—that Trovatello was more greatly agitated than previously, thrashing his body against the backrest as a silent command for the priest to help him out of the saddle.

The team's horses were tended to first, unhitched from the wagon and led into the barn to be fed and watered along with the other two equines. Trovatello kept making agonized groaning noises, but the patch-eyed priest spoke softly to him, put a hand on his shoulder and was successful in calming him until the task with the animals was done.

The cabin was sparsely furnished, but cleanly kept and what furnishings existed were much used but also clean. The priest set about using his tinderbox to light several candles. Trovatello went directly to a chair and table upon which was placed a slanted book support holding an open Bible. Immediately he sat down in the chair, lifted a leg and began thumping his heel on the table.

"He's anxious to speak," said Archangelo. He'd brought in his saddlebag containing the quill and inkpot, and now he withdrew those and set them on the table, went to a shelf for a few sheets of paper, moved the Bible from its place and took off Trovatello's right boot. He brought two candles over, set a sheet of paper on the book support, dipped the quill in the ink-pot and put the quill between Trovatello's toes as he had before. Then, as Matthew and Professor Fell watched, the handless man angled his leg in a position only a trained contortionist could endure, and began to write.

Archangelo read the first sentence aloud: *"Mi ricordo."* And the translation given to the Englishmen: "I remember."

The writing scratched on.

Archangelo read by the candlelight: "When I saw the black coach and Lupo on his horse. It came back to me. The shock." There was a pause while the quill was redipped and returned to the writing foot. "The Family of the Scorpion. I betrayed them. They killed my wife and my children before my eyes. Then what was done to me." As he listened to this English being spoken, Trovatello made a choking noise and more tears glistened in his eyes but he seemed to catch himself from any further agony that would prevent his writing.

The quill was redipped.

"Mars and Venus Scaramanga. Grandmaster and Grandmistress. In the black coach."

Matthew said, "Ask him where they might have taken Hudson and Camilla."

The question was posed and the quill moved.

Archangelo said, "He writes that he's not certain but he's heard of an estate where the Scaramangas live. Just a moment, let me wet the quill again. All right, he says they might be taken there."

"Does he know where this is?"

"He says he does not, but he's heard from others it's not very far from Venice."

Matthew thought he could name someone who might know: the wine merchant Meneghetti. "Ask him what else he's heard about this place."

There was a pause while Trovatello wrote. After two dippings of the quill, the priest said, "He's heard the place is heavily guarded. Anyone who approaches the gate without a black key may be shot on sight."

"A black key?" Matthew asked. "Can he explain that?"

The question was asked, Trovatello wrote and Archangelo said, "The black key identifies a *tenente*." The priest looked over at the young man. "In your language that would be a lieutenant." He returned his attention to the paper. "It's awarded to someone of high standing. The leader of a team, or... wait, the quill's gone dry...someone who has already passed their security."

"Would a guard at the gate of this estate recognize *everyone* who has a black key? I mean, could someone with a black key get in even if the guard didn't recognize the face?"

"That he doesn't know," the priest said after the questions had been voiced and the answers quilled. "A moment…he's adding something." Archangelo translated: "A black key is impossible to get unless awarded by the Scaramangas or by another high-ranking lieutenant."

"Matthew?" Fell's tone was grave. "I don't like the direction in which you are thinking."

"What would you have me do? Turn my back on my best friend? Leave Hudson and Camilla to be tortured to death?"

"What I would have you do," the professor responded, "is admit that this is a problem you cannot solve. Listen to me Matthew, and I mean it! Hudson and Camilla may already be dead…or soon to be, and there's nothing you can do about it! What? Somehow—and I do mean *somehow*—find this place, if they're even there—and a black key—ha!—and go raging in like a lead-footed maniac? That would be your death, and what might that accomplish for your bride-to-be waiting in New York?"

It was a good question and it penetrated to Matthew's soul. What to do?

"You and I are incredibly lucky to get away from those people with our skins!" Fell went on. "Matthew, if Hudson Greathouse was standing before you he would say the same and you know he would. Let's get back on that ship to Alghero and out of here. Tell them the mirror couldn't be found. Tell them any damned thing, but Hudson and Camilla are lost. You have to accept it!"

What issued from Matthew's mouth next seemed to come of its own accord. "I have something to bargain with the Scaramangas. I believe I know where the mirror is."

The professor's face registered an expression of both anger and incredulity. "To hell with that damned thing! Forget it, Matthew! It's done!"

"No," Matthew said. "It is not." He turned toward the priest. "Tell me about Leviathan."

Now Archangelo's face became puzzled. *"What?"*

"The lighthouse. Tell me everything you know about it. I believe Valeriani hid the mirror there."

"Oh my God!" groaned the professor. "Are you catching items from the air now?"

"Tell me," Matthew repeated.

"Well, it's…" Archangelo paused to regard Trovatello, who sat staring numbly at the paper, his eyes glazed and his mouth sagging open. "Let me help him to bed first." He removed the man's other boot and gently pulled him up from the chair. Speaking quietly to him, the priest took a burning candle and guided his charge through a doorway back into another room.

In Archangelo's brief absence Professor Fell snorted and shook his head in dismay but made no other comment.

Archangelo returned without the candle but bearing a water pitcher. He said, "There's a well behind the church. I'll go fetch some water and we can have a drink, then I'll tell you what you're asking."

It was done, Archangelo poured water into clay cups for all of them, and he took the chair where Trovatello had been sitting. "Leviathan," he said. "You say you believe the cursed mirror is there?"

"I do."

"And *why* do you?" Fell demanded. "Of all places, why a lighthouse?"

"Some of the old Roman lighthouses used mirrors to reflect the signal fire at a greater distance. Other than that, you'll just have to trust my intuition."

"Pah!" Fell waved an indignant hand and turned away.

"It was called Leviathan when I was a boy," said the priest. "I think that name faded over time, but I remember."

Which was why it wasn't easily recognizable by the Scaramangas and others younger than Archangelo, Matthew thought. Surely at least one member of the Family of the Scorpion—what a name!—had passed the lighthouse on a ship, but the name Leviathan had been lost to the years.

"I don't know if it's in use anymore," Archangelo continued. "It was understandably very ancient when I was a cabin boy and much of it had already been damaged by storms, so...I don't know."

"Where is it?"

"On a small island of rock about a quarter mile off the fishing village of Chioggia, where the sea shallows. Chioggia would be thirty miles or so south of Venice."

"Insanity!" Fell spat. "I can't believe this!"

Matthew kept his attention riveted to the priest. "Why was it called Leviathan?"

"From what I could reason, it was called that because of how it was built. It's made of stone, of course, and it is constructed like the broad shoulders and head of a man, the head being the top of the tower and the stone 'shoulders' jutting out on either side."

The professor said with vehemence, "You have no certainty the mirror is there, you're simply grasping at—" He hesitated, searching for the proper term. Then: *"Seaweed."*

"I might be. Or I might be right. But as I say I have something to trade."

"Ridiculous! You're supposing that Valeriani took the mirror to this Chioggia, got a boat and sailed it out to this lighthouse?"

"Yes. Exactly."

"It could be done," Archangelo offered. "He could have hired a boat there or paid a fisherman to take him out."

"Well why didn't he just throw it in the ocean and be done with it?" Fell asked, still with considerable heat.

Matthew said, "You'll have to ask Valeriani. I suspect that the mirror is framed with wood and probably would float. If the lighthouse was abandoned and there were already mirrors in place to reflect the fire… who would look for it there, and even if they saw it they wouldn't know what it was."

"A fisherman who took him out would know!" the professor countered. "Oh, I can see it! 'Please sir, take myself and this strange mirror out to the lighthouse and I will leave it there but don't tell anyone!' What, then? Did Valeriani murder the fisherman?"

"He might have stolen a boat, taken it out at night and returned it," said Matthew. "That way, no one would know."

"And who might believe Valeriani had experience sailing a *boat?*"

"You will recall he took his alias from the name of his father's boat so he must've had some nautical experience. You can argue all you please, sir, and you can do what you wish…but I'm going to Venice to find the wine merchant Meneghetti."

"I will certainly do as I please and I will save my own neck by boarding that ship to Alghero! I will have a letter sent to Berry explaining your violent death, which should reach her sometime next year, and in Alghero I will tell the authorities all about this family of scorpions and that I am the *único superviviente*. Do you know what that means?"

Matthew was still not very proficient at Spanish, but he did know this. "Sole survivor."

And the professor's wide-eyed, crimp-mouthed response: *"¡Exactamente!"*

Matthew drank down his water. He walked to a small oval mirror on the wall and peered at the reflection of a dirty-faced young man with a beard growing out, his thatch of black hair a tangled mess and his cool gray eyes sunken in purple hollows. He might have already suffered tortures, but indeed he was currently tormented only in the mind. His gaze moved to a wooden crucifix mounted on the wall beside the mirror.

What else had Camilla said of Brazio Valeriani's words to Mars Scaramanga?

The mirror could not be broken by anything but—

"Do you have an iron crucifix?" he asked.

"Iron? No, only what you see," said the priest. "There's a larger Cross of God in the church, but also carved from dogwood."

Fell gave a harsh and ugly laugh. "What are you going to do, wave a cross at the Scaramangas and hope they fall down at your feet? They may fall down laughing before they stand up and skin you alive."

"Shut up," Matthew said quietly, and heard in his voice a tone he recognized from the voice of Julian Devane.

Something Julian—the self-proclaimed "bad man"—had said to him, many months ago after Julian had killed Lazarus Firebaugh and destroyed the book of drugging potions: *I hope some bad has rubbed off on you. You'll need it before it's over.*

And even staring at the crucifix there on the wall before him, Matthew decided he would kill Ottavio Meneghetti if he could not get the information of where Hudson and Camilla had been taken.

Not only that.

He would make it slow.

"Can I do anything more for you?" Archangelo asked. "I have some money in the jar on that shelf. It's not much, but you're welcome to it."

"I'll need some," Matthew admitted, "but I won't take it all." He turned from the mirror and the cross. "Is there a place I can bathe and shave? Also find at least a clean shirt?"

"There's a tub in the back room I can fill with water, and I have soap. I can find a shirt for you. Unfortunately neither Trovatello nor myself have any need of a razor for shaving."

"All right. Whatever you can do is fine enough."

"You're going after your friends, then?"

"I am."

"Insani—" Fell stopped speaking when he saw Matthew's eyes staring burning holes through him.

"And I can do no more for you?" Archangelo prompted.

"You and Trovatello have already done a great service. You saved our lives and gave us—me—a purpose. We'll be leaving after I clean myself up and I'll do it quickly, if you can get me the shirt. The professor has no need of anything but his hot air." They had eaten some dried beef and the dreaded dried sardines, some apples and figs from the remaining supply in the dead soldiers' wagon, and Matthew had need for a meal of hot food but he knew that time was very short. He approached the patch-eyed priest and put a firm hand on his shoulder. "You'll take good care of Trovatello."

"I have and I shall."

"Thank you for everything, and please offer your prayers. Professor, if you open that mouth as you're about to do I will knock your damned head off and I don't care how old you are." Then, once more to Archangelo: "I wish the best for both you and your companion." He smiled as much as the strain in his face would allow. "I'll never forget you."

"Nor I you, son," was the reply, and in the quiet of the cottage Matthew began to silently weep. He could not help it, for the stones of the fortress of hope he'd been building had suddenly cracked and the entire construction threatened to collapse. It was doubtful that Hudson and Camilla could be saved, he knew he might be going to his death and he would never see Berry again, never would there be a wedding, never a return to New York, never a happy life…

…never a life.

But he could not cut and run. Could *not*. His logic screamed to do so, to get aboard the ship for Alghero and tell them any lie about the mirror. Could he live with that and create a happy life for Berry?

No, he could not.

The die was cast. There was no retreat from what he knew he had to do.

The priest put his arms around Matthew as the young man wept, and as they stood together even the ex-emperor of crime lowered his head and turned away.

TWENTY-TWO

IT WAS GOOD THAT MATTHEW HAD GIVEN THE WAGON'S TEAM TIME TO rest, be fed and watered because for the remainder of the day he had to drive them hard, as well as himself. The gray, rain-swollen clouds were still thick overhead, the sun a weak candle. He kept to the driver's bench and had the professor do what he wished in the back because he trusted only himself to keep the team going at the pace he wanted, and though he felt a pang of regret for the strenuous toll being taken on the animals—and surely a shortening of their lives—he could not let them pause for further rest. They might drop dead by the time they reached the ferry at Mestre, but at least they *would* reach the ferry at Mestre before dark. He hoped.

Time was short. He felt it clawing at the back of his neck. Hudson and Camilla might already have been tortured to death, it was true. But not to at least *try* to find them? It was unthinkable.

It was late in the afternoon when the wagon passed through Mestre and arrived at the ferry docks. Across the slate-gray lagoon shone the golden lights of Venice. The water was choppy, the wind having strengthened from the south. A fee was paid, the wagon rolled over the ramp onto the sailing barge along with another open wagon hauling lumber. Two horseback riders joined for the trip across, and the ferry set off.

It was a rough trip and none of the horses appreciated the ferry's unpredictable undulations and the spray hitting them in their muzzles over the red-painted bow. When the ferry was being roped to the Venice pier, the thin, raw-boned captain who had a mass of curly gray hair and a gray beard down to his midsection approached the passengers with an announcement in Italian that Matthew tried to strain through his Latin knowledge. The best he got was that due to *il tempo*—a tempest? the weather?—*il traghetto*—and here there was a sign at the fee office so that meant the ferry itself—was *chiusura in un'ora*. One hour was what Matthew deciphered, and the answer to the Italian riddle was evidently that because of the worsening weather the ferry was shutting down in one hour.

With the professor seated beside him on the bench, Matthew set off through the narrow winding streets toward where he remembered Meneghetti's office building to be. The poor horses were almost at the end of their legs, and to go on much further there was going to have to be a change of transportation. For the moment he thought they could keep going but he was aware that overworking a horse past its point of fatigue could actually cause the animal to have a heart attack at any time, so this problem was an added pressure. In truth, he thought all four horses were nearly ready to drop.

Crossing many bridges and canals in this city of aquatic heritage, Matthew stopped the wagon in front of the two-storied wedding cake structure that bore the title of MENEGHETTI E ASSOCIATI on a brass plaque by the door. He ignored the angry shouts of carriage, coach and wagon drivers behind him, since the width of the wagon was taking up much of the street. They would have to go around, and to hell with them.

Professor Fell said, "This is where I leave you."

"Do as you please."

"Oh, I shall! And I shall think of you often as a young man who thought he was so smart and capable until the real world's evil extinguished his light. No need for demons from a mirror, Matthew...no need at all." Fell climbed down to the paving stones and Matthew did as well.

The heat of anger pulsed steadily in Matthew's face. He said, "You owe me."

"I owe *you?*"

"For what you put me through. The threats and intimidation...the atmosphere of terror...everything you did with those damned drugs to Berry and Hudson...that blood card...thinking I might have an assassin on me every time I left my house...around every corner and in the shadow of every door. Yes, you do owe me."

The professor came up close to Matthew, his amber gaze probing, his mouth curled in the slightest of cutting smiles. On his right cheek the injury of his knife wound had been cleaned by Archangelo and a small plaster bandage applied. "I've paid in full," he said. "I let you live."

And with that he turned and stalked away in what was the direction of the harbor.

Matthew stood alone.

He hesitated no longer. He went into the building, where in the marble-floored lobby the same attractive young girl sat at her desk applying a quill to one of a number of what might have been yellow invoices. She looked up quizzically from her work, put the quill in its holder and asked, *"Posso aiutarla, signore?"*

"English," Matthew said. "Wine. *Vino.*" But he was already passing her desk and opening the door that led to the flight of stairs. She stood up and made some exclamation of protest but by then the door had closed in her face and he was on his way up along the passage lined with hundreds of multicolored glazed clay tiles. Then through the next door into the red-carpeted hallway, straight to the door at the far end marked with the O. MENEGHETTI brass plaque, in through that door like a whirlwind and there sat the tanned, affluent-looking wine merchant in a beige suit trimmed in light blue, a white shirt and white cravat with a gold stickpin in the shape of a small wine bottle. Everything about the office was the same: the red and gold Oriental carpet, the huge oak desk, the bookcase behind him and on the desk a stack of papers topped by the brass monkey paperweight, the polished gold-toned inkwell and the stand of three quills, one of which was in his right hand as he'd been marking something on a thick sheaf of paper. Beside the desk stood the little table supporting six decanters with different shades of red and white wines and the four crystal glasses. The merchant in his high-backed black leather chair with the carved ram's heads on the ends of the armrests cried out, *"Cosa è questo?"* as the door slammed shut behind Matthew.

Meneghetti blinked in stupefied surprise, said, *"Che cosa vuoi—"* and then he seemed to draw back in his chair. The blue eyes in the well-fed face widened. "The English! You are—what are you doing here?"

"I've come for a visit." Matthew crossed the carpet to the desk's edge and Meneghetti rose to his feet. "Sit down," Matthew said, and the way he spoke it meant business…dangerous business if it was not obeyed.

Meneghetti sat. Was there suddenly a sheen of sweat on his forehead and glistening at the edges of the waxed mustache? "I'm to go home," he said and it almost carried a whine. "Home," he repeated. "I'm just to finish some signings here, it is so late in the day."

"Those can wait." The door suddenly opened and the frightened face of the office girl peered in. She asked Meneghetti a question and before he could reply Matthew said, "Send her away. We're just going to have a nice talk about the Scaramangas and the Family of the—"

"Stefania, io e gli inglesi stiamo solo parlando, puoi andare," Meneghetti said in a rush. The girl hesitated uncertainly, obviously trying to judge the scene, before she retreated and closed the door. Matthew had caught *inglesi*—English—and *parlando*—strained through Latin as "parlay" or talk.

He figured that if the mention of the Scaramangas or the Family of the Scorpion had gone much further poor Stefania would be dead by morning and he was sure good office girls were hard to find.

"My ears don't know what you're speaking," the man said.

There was definitely sweat on his face. "I haven't come to waste time with you," Matthew said through clenched teeth. "Mars and Venus took two of my friends. Where would they be taken?"

"*Signore, per favore.* I buy and sell wine. That is my life. I have a wife and two children. They are waiting for me at our home and I swear before God I have no idea of what you are saying."

"You'll tell me before I leave here, and if I have to I'll leave with your blood on my hands."

"*Signore*...Englishman...I am saying I do not know anything of—"

The door opened again.

Matthew turned to ward off whoever Stefania had sent upstairs to put the wild Englishman in chains.

Professor Fell came in, took a quick look around and before Matthew could say wink or blink the old man strode to the table of decanters, picked up one and hit Meneghetti in the side of the head with it. The heavy, thick-glassed decanter did not break, but the *thunk* of skull collision was impressive. The wine merchant gave a soft groan like yawning before taking a nice nap, his blue eyes in the tanned face rolled back, and he slumped down and slid off the chair as if his bottomside had been greased.

"You haven't gotten anything yet, have you?" Fell asked, all quiet innocence.

"No."

"Of course not. You came in here with your ass on your shoulders." He set the decanter down atop the desk. "That girl tried to stop me on the stairs."

"Did you kill her?"

"I kissed her."

"You *what?*"

"She's very pretty. I kissed her. I'm sure she doesn't know what to make of me, but I think I shocked her into at least two days of silence."

"You were going to the ship," Matthew reminded him.

"This fellow will be coming around as we stand speaking about motives and life philosophies. I'd rather spend the time we have to—" Fell didn't finish; he pushed the leather chair back, opened the desk's top drawer and began going through it. "Ah!" he said, holding up a silver letter opener that looked certainly sharp enough to cut through the usual wax seals. "And..." Next came up a small cowhide pouch that jingled and jangled when he shook it. This he tossed to Matthew, who took the opportunity to undo its drawstring and look upon the many gold coins within.

On the floor the wine merchant began to moan. A leg twitched and kicked against the carpet.

"Now…what is *this?*" From the very back of the drawer the professor withdrew a small, rectangular and beautiful tortoise-shell box with gold hinges. He opened its latch and gazed at the object inside that was set in its own bed of blue satin luxury.

Then he turned the box upside down and the black key clattered onto the oak desktop the same as any old harlot's hatpin pick to the nearest chest of booze.

"Latch the door," Fell said, and Matthew did.

The professor stood over the slowly awakening Meneghetti. He slapped the letter opener several times against his open palm, and looking down upon the wine merchant he said to Matthew, "Now you'll see how it's done."

Meneghetti sat up and rubbed his head with both hands. The bleary eyes took in the figure above him and he started speaking in Italian, his cadence sluggish and his brain obviously still fogged.

Fell said, "None of that. English only. Sit at your desk."

Did Meneghetti whimper as he struggled into the chair? Yes, he did, because he saw the black key before him on the desktop. As Matthew watched in what approached awe, the grandfather became once more what he had shrugged off like an old snake's skin.

Fell showed his teeth. The amber eyes blazed and even the bones of the face seemed to reshape into vicious angles. He somehow grew taller. He bent toward Meneghetti with a cold smile and in the chair Meneghetti recoiled.

The professor's voice was silk dipped in poison. "Which eye would you rather lose?"

"What? *What? Oh mio Dio, cosa—*"

"I said none of that," and with the cooly delivered statement he put the letter opener beside Meneghetti's right eye and jabbed it in. The eye bulged and Meneghetti gave a cry that sounded as if he were strangling on the very air.

"No crying out," Fell said. "No noise unless it's answering our questions. One loud noise and your eye goes. Where did the Scaramangas take our friends?"

"I can't…please…I can't—"

Fell stabbed him in the face just below the eye. The blood welled up like crimson wine.

"Please…I can't…they'll find me…kill me…kill everyone."

"You stupid fuck," said the professor. "I'll kill you *now.*"

"Please…who are you?"

Fell leaned in closer. Into Meneghetti's face the amber-eyed mulatto whispered, "I am your Death."

"Time," Matthew urged.

"This man is thinking someone will come to the door and save him but if anyone knocks at that door and he speaks one word I will put this…" Fell moved the sharp implement into Meneghetti's groin and pushed. A wheeze of pain mixed with terror followed. "I will ask again…one last time…where did the Scaramangas take our friends?"

"All right, all right!" the wine merchant blubbered with blood trickling down his face. "I tell! They have an estate…heavily guarded…around the coast, to the northeast…at Portegrandi. Go to Portegrandi. It is…it is past the hill of…seven trees. Past the hill of seven trees and you see it. Very big with red roofs."

"Thank you. And you will lead us exactly there, and if this estate is not at Portegrandi past the hill of seven trees that you've just conjured up…" Fell returned the blade to the corner of Meneghetti's right eye and applied pressure. Again he leaned forward and Matthew thought his entire face with its sharp jutting bones now looked like a cutting weapon. "You will eat your own eyes before you die. Stand up."

"Wait! No…wait…no…not Portegrandi. Mirano. Just beyond Mirano, two miles past the last villas. A road turns south." Meneghetti hesitated, perhaps realizing he had certainly put his feet and probably those of his loved ones in a grave. "They'll kill me," he pleaded.

"I understand you're good with a map," Fell said, as he ran the sharp tip across the bridge of the man's nose. "Draw one." He turned over one of the pieces of paper on the desk and pushed forward the quills. "Make it *accurate*, because you're going with us and if it's not exactly right I will delight in maiming you before you die. The map! *Ahora!*"

It was Spanish but it got the point across, especially since Fell put the blade's point against Meneghetti's forehead as he drew. When he was done he looked up, newly terrified at this action against his masters, and said in a choked voice, "Will you free me? When you get there?"

"Why should we keep you?"

"Oh, *signore!* Oh, all the saints bless you! I am needing the time to get my wife and children out of here! Oh, *grazie, grazie!*" He started trembling and choking again, his emotions overcoming him. He loosened his cravat and then his shirt. "I am having the trouble breathing," he managed to say.

"Stand up, then." Fell actually helped him to his feet and he slid the letter opener into his waistband. "We'll not harm you now, but you *are* going with us. Come on, get some air on the balcony."

Matthew saw what the professor did. Meneghetti did not. Matthew kept his mouth closed.

On the balcony over the stone-paved street, Meneghetti leaned against the railing and breathed in lungful after lungful. The professor looked up at the lowering sky, the light quickly fading. The wind had further strengthened. He figured they had less than half an hour to reach the ferry.

"I swear to you the map is true," the wine merchant said. "On my life and the lives of my children I swear it."

"Excelente," Fell replied, and then he hit Meneghetti in the back of the head with the brass monkey paperweight he'd picked up from the desk and held down at his side. Meneghetti gave a muffled grunt and looked at him in surprise, and then Fell hit him again on the left temple as hard as he could. Before Meneghetti's legs fully buckled, the professor took hold around his knees, heaved up with an effort that nearly cracked a grandfather's back, and sent him headfirst over the railing.

Someone screamed down below, someone else shouted, a horse neighed and those were the funereal musics for the broken-necked Ottavio Meneghetti.

"Upsadaisy," the professor said when he came back in. He threw the brass monkey aside. "Get the key and the map. We have to go *now*."

Matthew put the black key in his pocket, folded the map and squared that away as well. "Was that necessary?"

"No, but *he* liked it."

"He? Who?"

Fell's smile was a shade evil. "You know. *Him*." And it was true; the professor with his tigerish eyes and cutting-bone face had gone away once again and what remained—more or less, in Matthew's opinion—was the inquisitive collector of marine specimens from the mysterious briny deep.

Further urging was not needed. Matthew and Fell passed a young man in the corridor who immediately stepped aside. In the downstairs lobby three people were babbling to the office girl and gesturing wildly in the direction of the street, having had the body of Ottavio Meneghetti nearly land on their heads. She gave a cry and pointed to the young Englishman and the old grandfather, but they were already on their way out.

The scene on the street was from an Italian drama-comedy, a chaos of shouting people appearing about to fight each other as if a body falling from a balcony was a signal to rekindle the wars between the Capulets and Montagues, the wagon still clogging the way and the exhausted horses jumpy and snapping at a few brave souls who were trying to drag the vehicle onto a side street, other wagons and carts and coaches snarled in the tangle and tempers obviously far past the boiling point.

"Follow me," Fell said, and he started in the direction they'd come from the ferry. After a few fast paces, he stopped and nodded toward the street. "*That* one."

Matthew saw he was indicating a small brown coach with black trim, a two-horse team and a coachman up top with a peaked blue hat bearing a high white feather. The coach had slowed down to negotiate the traffic jam. By the oil lamp within could be seen an elderly gentleman and lady both craning their necks through the windows to observe the confusion.

"We're taking it," the professor announced. He drew the letter opener and held it like the most wicked knife any killer had ever wielded. At once he was pushing through the mass as the coach driver used his whip to spur the team onward. Before the vehicle could pick up any speed, Fell had opened one of the coach's doors and to the woman's scream lifted the blade and said, "Get out or you die," motioning at the same time with his other hand for them to leave through the opposite door.

In this case there was no language problem. They scrambled out, and to his gentlemanly credit the elderly swain helped his lady gracefully to the street.

Matthew meanwhile had climbed up the foot rungs to the driver, who summoned up some courage and struck out with his whip. It stung Matthew across the left shoulder, the pain giving him enough of Julian Devane's bad man to hit the driver in the mouth with an angered fist, pull the feathered hat down over his eyes and kick him flailing off his seat. Matthew caught the reins before they could slip down amid the horses. The professor climbed up beside him. Matthew gave the team a good slap of the reins and the coach surged forward past the blockage, with what sounded like every cursing voice in Venice shouting at their wheels.

They both realized they had little time to reach the ferry and many streets to negotiate here at the end of the working day. Matthew wished to ask Fell why he'd decided to return but for the present he had only to concentrate on driving the team and getting past other slower vehicles and the pedestrians who crossed the streets at all angles. On the way to the ferry an old woman who had to scurry out of the street in front of them threw a partly eaten apple that banged off the side of the coach next to the professor: a near miss and a new low.

When they reached the ferry's pier, Matthew was disheartened to see the ferry's lamps out about the bay's midpoint. Was it coming or going? Due to the rising wind the water had roughened into whitecaps and seafoam and it appeared the ferry was having a hard time of it, the sails alternately swelling and thrashing.

"It's coming in," Fell saw. "But whether it can make another trip, or not..."

"We'll find out." Matthew withdrew the pouch of Meneghetti's gold coins and sat waiting as the lamps and the vessel approached the pier.

Three horse riders and a wagon of haybales disembarked, all concerned looking dazed including the horses. Seeing Matthew and the professor on the coach, the long-bearded captain waved his arms and shouted against the wind, *"Niente! Niente!"* which decidedly meant *no*, as in no further crossings.

Did he change his mind when he saw the shine of the gold coin that Matthew was offering?

Niente.

It took two.

Then Matthew steered the understandably reluctant team onto the pitching ferry, the coach's wheels were lashed down to cleats nailed to the bulwarks on starboard and port, lines were cast off as they were the only fools on this last trip, the sails caught the muscular but mercurial wind, and Professor Fell hung onto the safety rail on his side of the driver's seat with a white-knuckled fist as spume broke over the bow, the craft yawed, rolled, pitched, heaved and surged. The horses struggled to keep their balance, and at the wheel the long-bearded captain who considered himself both a master of the waves and now richer than King Midas bellowed out some kind of Italian sea chantey that surely translated in any language to 'blow the man down'.

Matthew winnowed his hand into his pocket and gripped the black key.

Soon.

TWENTY-THREE

"THE COLONIES? I'VE HEARD MUCH ABOUT THEM. I'D CARE TO VISIT, but long sailing voyages are not my…what would you English say? Cup of tea?"

"I hate tea," Hudson said.

"It seems neither do you appreciate expensive *vino*." Mars Scaramanga nodded across the table at the still-full silver goblet that sat beside Hudson's dinner plate. "But you didn't answer my question, did you?"

The question had been, *What is your line of work*, the reply given, *I work in the colonies*. Hudson toyed with his fork on the platter of roasted pork, white beans and vinegared slaw. "I live by my wits," he said, anticipating a snide remark.

It was delivered. With a sidelong glance at his sister sitting on his side of the long dark walnut table, Mars said, "Oh dear, a life of abject poverty!"

Venus returned only a vapid smile, as her darkly penetrating gaze moved back and forth between the large-bodied Englishman and the svelte Spanish witch-hunter seated to his left. On the table amid the silver and gold platters of food burned two gold six-tapered candelabras, and above the table another chandelier of ten candles added further illumination. Standing at the wall behind the Englishman was Lorenzo with a knife at his belt on one side and a holstered pistol on the other. Behind the woman stood Pagani, identically armed, and at the dining room's polished oak door stood a third thick-chested bodyguard known as Greco, his arsenal being a sheathed rapier and a knife with a sawblade edge he had already displayed.

"I survive," Hudson answered, which caused Mars to lift his own goblet in a mock salute.

After the arduous journey Hudson and Camilla had been whisked out of the wagon, taken upstairs and pushed into a bedroom that was certainly a most luxurious prison cell with its overstuffed leather chairs and sofa, dark blue rug and blue-canopied bed big enough for four. Camilla's wrists had been untied, and so too had Hudson's which were bound by pieces of the previously cut cords. For him during the trip the cords had been knotted, reknotted and knotted again in a short rope around his neck connected to the cords binding his wrists so that he had to sit in an agonizingly uncomfortable bent-forward position. Plus his boots had been removed, a piece of burlap from one of the supply sacks was stuffed into his mouth and a final hard slap was Pagani's insult to his face.

Hudson quickly noted that unfortunately there was no window and no items that might be used in the beautiful bedroom to offer much resistance to a flintlock pistol. Three candles burned in a candelabra and there stood an oak chest of drawers—each drawer empty, he'd already discovered—and the drawers might be used as strikers but otherwise, no. There'd been a past instance in which Hudson had hammered a candle holder into a makeshift blade but that had been pot metal and this candelabra appeared to be sterling silver, so again...no. Before Lorenzo had turned the key in the lock, Mars in a black sleeping robe with red trim had looked in, his own face haggard from the trip, and said, "My sister and I are in need of rest, so pardon us for not showing further hospitality. That will come later when we get down to business. In the meantime, either Lorenzo, Bertanza, Pagani, Greco or Giaconi will always be on the other side of this door so mind your manners as good guests of the house."

"As a good host would you supply us some food and water?" Hudson had asked.

"Hm. Very well, I'll have a pigskin of water sent up. As for food, you'll dine with my sister and myself when we're ready."

Mars had withdrawn, the door was closed and locked, and Hudson was left wondering how a pigskin—actually a bladder used as a container for liquid since ancient times—could be used as a weapon and came up with nothing. He doubted that any bodyguard here could be slapped insensible with a pee sack, even heavy with water. They hadn't seen the wolfman since being taken out of the wagon, but he had to be prowling around here somewhere or it might be he was also getting his beauty rest.

"What do you think happened to Matthew and the professor?" Camilla had asked now that Hudson was able to speak.

"I hope they found someone on the road. Maybe they got to Sante Vallone. But really I hope they get back to that ship and out of here."

Hudson sat down on the bed. "Knowing Matthew as I do, though…it's hard to say."

"You care a great deal for your friend, don't you?"

"I do," he replied without hesitation. "We've been through a lot together…me nearly drowning in a well and him saving me…him getting me out of that drugged state at Fell's village…" He stopped, realizing that Camilla had no inkling of what he was talking about. "I'll tell you the whole story sometime."

"I don't think we have too much time." She sat on the bed next to him, and immediately he put an arm around her. She rested her head against his shoulder. Hudson thought that at this stage of their imperilment many other women would be trembling and weeping, but she was not. Her demeanor was of course downcast—as was his own—but her attitude was impressive in that she was not allowing herself to fall to pieces.

"I do know a good thing," Hudson said as he hugged her. "They haven't killed us yet. Oh…and another good thing. We're together."

She made a soft noise of agreement. He decided he should not be too very flippant or her shell might crack.

"We should get some sleep," he said.

"Ha," she answered.

"At least let's try. All right?"

"Yes." Her voice was soft but she was still hanging on. "Let's try."

And now, several hours after they'd held each other in the blue-canopied bed in the candlelit room and struggled for rest that evaded them, they sat side-by-side in the oak-panelled dining room with Mars and Venus across from them, the bodyguards present and armed for any disruption, the sound of the wind whipping and whirling around the house, and all hope as tenuous and perhaps as short-lived as the burning candles.

"So," Mars said as he took another bite of the roasted pork, "what would you ask of the mirror? That you be given riches? A crown and a kingdom?"

"A true wit?" Venus prodded. Hudson had noted she'd taken the chair on her brother's left, so their thatches of flaming red hair matched one to the other, and she no longer wore those hideous and demonic-looking silver rings.

Hudson took his time in answering. He started to reach for the wine goblet but hesitated because he feared it had been drugged. He'd advised Camilla in front of the Scaramangas not to drink for that very reason, though the water in the pig's bladder had seemed to be just water, no odor or tang of anything added. He said, "The mirror is a fantasy. If you believe in it, you both must be demented."

"Demented?" Mars smiled with his mouth only. "I take it then that you're such a sane man, and you *don't* believe?"

"Correct."

"Interesting." Mars put his fork down, his comments directed to his sister. "A sane man who travels halfway around the world in search of something he doesn't believe in. If I didn't believe there was some value in my chamberpot I wouldn't get out of bed and walk the five steps to use it. But here is this sane man at our table, sister. What do you think of that?"

"I think he's a liar."

Hudson said, "Whatever you believe you want out of this thing, you're not going to get it because it's not a doorway to the underworld. Even if you do find it, I doubt it'll give you any more than a hazy reflection."

"And the witch-hunter?" Mars's ebony gaze turned upon Camilla. "You also have come from your native country in pursuit of an illusion?"

"The Spanish government is curious about it," she answered with steadfast calm that may have been another illusion, but Hudson thought she was playing it well. "That doesn't mean it's real."

"Oh, my!" said Venus with a sharp little laugh. "A very fascinating book of the royalty of the underworld, a witch-hunter sent on a mission from Spain, Spanish soldiers, Englishmen…this broth does not make horse manure, does it, brother? It makes a most intriguing meal."

"Certainly so." In his crimson jacket and black breeches, his ruffled white shirt and what Hudson had noted was a fine pair of knee-high boots that appeared to be fashioned from some kind of reptilian hide, Mars Scaramanga might be a young count surrounded a bevy of servants and beautiful ladies instead of a rotunderie of killers, a cunning sister who seemed to have a strange red glint in those ebon eyes that might be the flicker of a torch on the walls of Bedlam, a silent executioner in a metal wolf's mask and a deadly cat that ate chopped-off fingers. He and Venus— her dressed in a purple-trimmed and high-necked light gray gown with a voluminous burst of purple lace at the collar—did possess the required royal villa. They also knew how to dress for dinner. Otherwise, for all their power and obvious intelligence, they were barking mad if they imagined this mirror would give them some gift that ordinary humankind could not grasp from the claw of a demon, nor would ordinary humankind wish to.

Hudson picked at his dinner. He had absolutely no appetite, though in the lowest dungeon of his soul he was well aware that this was likely their last meal. And what of it? The grave swallowed the hungry as completely as it did the satiated; the worst thought was that he and Camilla were destined to be the cat's feast.

"There's no use in torturing us," he said, to open a bad subject. "We don't know any more than you do."

Mars lifted a finger. "But you had opportunity to speak with Valeriani before we reached you. He might have said something of importance."

"He didn't."

"You tossed that off very easily. We'll get to that opportunity to stir your memory in a bit, but for now I'd like to hear about the colonies."

Hudson's first impulse was to tell the man to stick his ears up his ass, but then again…any delay of what might be the inevitable was the most appetizing plate upon this table, and though it likely *was* inevitable it would still give him time to think. So he began with a detailed description of New York, embellishing as much as could the mind of a man whose last book read concerned a tavern keeper's wanton daughter and a wandering preacher.

:*Venus*:.

Pretending to be interested in this mass of garbage the Englishman was spewing, Venus had heard her name spoken.

It had been a whisper, as if from the smoke that coiled off one of the candles. And it had been a strange voice—male and female commingled, it seemed—yet a voice she recognized because part of it was her own.

:*Venus*:.

And there again, still just the faintest whisper.

She realized the figure was standing to her right, behind her brother.

She turned her head…and there only a few inches behind Mars's chair stood the purple-robed, faceless entity Black had called Dominus. The dark hole where the face should have been was aimed at her.

:*Venus*:.

Did the phantasm speak, or was it her own phantasm she was hearing? Something real standing there…or something that had crawled from a crack in her mind?

"What are you looking at?" Mars suddenly asked her.

"*What?*"

He spoke in Italian: "I just asked that. You were staring as if you'd seen a ghost."

She answered in the native language, aware as she spoke that Dominus had neither moved nor evaporated into mist. "There are no ghosts here."

"Do you find our guests boring?"

"Yes."

"Then leave if you wish."

:*No*:, said the voice of Dominus, :*non te ne andrai*:.

No, you will not leave.

Venus had started to push her chair away from the table but now she hesitated.

Again in Italian, Dominus said, :*I have for you a message*:.

She looked away. Stared at her plate. The big Englishman was still talking, stalling for time though Mars was feeding him attention.

:A message:, Dominus repeated, and Venus felt herself flinch. Was this real, or was she falling into the abyss? She picked up her fork and turned it around and around in her hand as if it was a weapon either against her own mind or an invading specter.

"What's wrong with you?" Mars's voice came from a distant place.

"Nothing," she said, but she heard her own voice quaver.

"You're acting strangely. Can't wait to get these two into your chamber?"

"That's right."

"Patience, sister. My dinner isn't done and I enjoy a conversation that has nothing to do with the family."

"Suit yourself," she answered, and when she started to rise Dominus said, *:You are fated to fail:*.

She eased herself down again. Her heart was racing. Mars was once more listening to the prattling of that big bastard and the witch-hunter was staring at her oddly and Venus thought that if she had a real knife instead of this ham cutter she would slice the face off the bitch's skull.

:So sad:, the thing whispered. Her own voice? Yes, her own voice was in there but it was like hearing a mixture of a half-dozen voices—female and male—at once. She kept her head down, staring at her plate. When she picked up her silver goblet of wine in a hand that trembled she put it quickly aside again because in it she caught the reflection of the purple-robed figure standing behind her brother.

:So sad:, Dominus whispered, *:that you will die old and broken:*.

Stop, she commanded in her mind but Dominus was not silenced.

:Old beyond old:, the creature went on. *:All beauty extinguished. Your candle of life an ugly melted stub, and no one on this earth will mourn the wrinkled wreckage that lies in the coffin:*.

"Stop!" She had nearly shouted it, startling Mars so much he jumped in his chair.

"Christ, Venus!" he said, his face reddened. "If you don't like this, go to your room and feed your cat or something!"

Camilla quietly spoke. "Your sister is having a difficulty."

"You shut up! Bitch! Shut your fucking mouth!" It had come out in a rage of Italian, and now Mars turned his chair to regard Venus with a sharpened gaze.

"What's wrong with you? Are you having a fit?"

"No! It's just…we should get started! It's foolish sitting here talking!"

"Believe me, I understand your urgency." Mars gave her an infuriating half-smile. "But we will proceed on *my* time. Your toys can wait another ten minutes."

:Hear me, Venus. Listen closely:.

Her mouth worked but made no sound. She felt sweat on her cheeks and at the back of her neck.

:*The mirror is just a mirror. It is as the Englishman says…a fantasy that only the insane would grasp as truth*:.

"Lies," she said, and Mars just stared at her dumbfounded, as if he was looking at a stranger in the next chair.

:*There is no demon to grant your wish of eternal beauty. There never was*:.

"Lies," she repeated. And more forcefully: "You're a liar!"

"Who do you think you're talking to?" Mars demanded, with true anger rising in his voice.

:*Poor, poor Venus. So sad, so stupid to have put faith in the impossible*:.

She remembered what Black had said about Dominus…*a spirit to suit my needs*. And his final anguished cry on the rack: *Dominus, help me!*

But there had been no help from Dominus, and she understood why.

Because this spirit was born from a cauldron of lies, and it was the ultimate lie. It had entranced Black and turned on him when the time was deemed necessary, and now it was taunting her with this lie about the demonic mirror. Of course it was real. Of course a servant could be summoned to grant her everlasting beauty, and to Mars the physical safety from assassination that only the hordes of Lucifer could provide. She would not listen to this liar any longer, would not would not would not—

"It's for your *entertainment*, isn't it?" she said bitterly to the thing behind her brother.

"As a matter of fact, I do find conversation entertaining," Mars replied, his eyelids at half-mast. "I don't have such limited pleasures as yourself."

At that, Hudson gave Camilla a sidelong look, which she returned with equal sidelongity.

"Stupid!" she yowled into Mars's face. "I'm not talking to you!"

"Then don't talk to me! Are you going to pieces?"

Venus couldn't restrain a shudder, for she felt the thing watching her.

It spoke again, the eerie voice rising and falling in pitch. :*So sad, that poor Venus will end her life like this*:.

"Like what?" she asked.

And even as Mars answered, "Pieces…as in losing your senses!" she saw her hands changing as they gripped the edge of the table. In horror she saw the flesh wrinkling, becoming corrupted from the onslaught of years, saw the fingers thinning into claws, the dark spots of age blooming like black flowers in a diseased garden, and she caught her breath and dared not look at her reflection in the silver goblet because she feared she would see the unrecognizable and hideous face of Venus Scaramanga the old woman who had wished upon a useless mirror, had spent day after day and night after night expecting salvation from a spirit of the underworld, that she would be spared the most horrible thing in life…ugliness of the flesh.

:*Your future*:, Dominus said.

"*No!*" It had been nearly a shriek. "No no no!" She took her hands from the table and in one instant they were young and supple and unwrinkled again, and looking to her right the purple-robed entity was gone and there was simply her brother, staring at her with his mouth hanging open.

She felt sweat drying on her face. She curled her fingers once, twice, and a third time to make sure they were her own.

Mars cleared his throat. He patted his lips with his fine lace napkin, and to the unwilling guests he said, "My sister is obviously still overwrought from the rigors of our trip. Well, she must be satisfied and I am also eager to hear what you have to say after—"

"I told you we don't know anything," Hudson interrupted.

"What you have to say," Mars continued, "after my sister shows you her toys. Venus, are you up to this?"

"I am." She was inwardly quaking, but damned if she'd let Mars or the others see her as anything but in control.

"Pagani, go fetch Lupo," Mars instructed in Italian. "Tell him to go down to the…" *Chamber*, he was about to say, but he changed it to "… toyroom. Tell him to light the lamps, then you're excused for the night." Pagani left the room, Venus stood up and so did Mars. He spoke in English once again to those about to experience his sister's delights. "You will stand and you will offer no resistance. If you do, you will be cut enough to bleed but it will not be enough to delay the rest of our evening."

Hudson noted that the stocky dark-haired bodyguard Greco might not understand English but he understood the tone of voice enough to draw from the sheath at his right side the sawblade knife and pass it under his own throat in a slow slashing gesture, his other hand on the rapier's hilt on his left.

Hudson stood up, took Camilla's hand and helped her to her feet. Her green eyes were swimming but her mouth was a tight line and her expression was resolute. He smiled at her as best he could and said, "Stand back."

When she did he released her hand, lifted up his platter of food and flung it into Mars's face. Instantly Lorenzo drew his knife and took a forward pace, to be greeted by Hudson's fist crashing into his jaw and rocking him against the wall. Greco rushed around the table, his wicked rapier gleaming with candlelight as it slid from its sheath. Hudson grabbed Camilla, pushed her behind him, picked up a chair as Lorenzo came in again and swung it, catching Lorenzo on the left shoulder and knocking him aside with a *whuff* of pain. In the next instant the point of Greco's sword was under Hudson's chin and behind Hudson Camilla gasped as another blade stung the side of her neck.

It was only a ham cutter, but Venus reasoned it would do for the flesh of a bitch like this one. She took a handful of Camilla's hair and yanked her head back. Her grin at Hudson presented him with icy terror. "Don't you understand English?" she asked.

Greco's sword gave him a sharp jab on the collarbone. He dropped the chair.

Across the table, Mars was wiping the mess off his face and the front of his jacket with his napkin. He said, "Not unexpected, but irritating. Also useless." In Italian: "Take them out and down, and watch *him*. Venus, I'll change and join you."

Rubbing his shoulder, Lorenzo came up to Hudson, spat blood in his face and hit him hard in the ribs. Pain shot through Hudson and his knees wobbled, but with a supreme determination of willpower he remained standing and forced a laugh.

With Venus leading the way and followed by Lorenzo and Greco, they were taken at the point of sword and knife through the villa, out a back door and along a garden path to what appeared to be a caretaker's stone and red-roofed hut about forty feet behind the house. A dark oak, vault-like door was opened and before them, illuminated by lamps hanging on hooks from the yellow walls, was a stone staircase leading down. Lorenzo gave Hudson a push. They descended what Hudson judged to be twenty feet, into an arched-ceilinged, cavernous space that he thought extended for some distance under the villa. The glow of a multitude of oil lamps did nothing to cheer Hudson nor Camilla, for by their light could be seen a torturer's wealth of implements designed by hellish hands and minds.

Camilla caught her breath and her body stiffened as she recognized the Rack, the Knee Splitter, the Iron Spider, the Pear of Anguish, the Iron Maiden, the Spanish Donkey, a large vise to crush any portion of the body the torturer might choose, and other torments in waiting: all implements she recognized from the work of the Inquisition. Looking up she saw a pulley bolted to the ceiling with a rope hanging down: the Strappado, to which a body with hands and feet tied and laden with iron weights was hoisted and left to hang as the joints were slowly pulled apart. The weights themselves hung from wall hooks, and there upon the far wall was also hung a devil's arsenal of hooks, chains, knives of every length and description, saws, hammers and chisels to shatter the bones, files to grind the flesh to gory ribbons, and axes of several varying sizes all sharp-edged and brutal even in their solemnity against the wall. Standing beside this monstrous display was a true monster: the huge metal-masked Lupo, clad in a long black hooded cloak with scarlet trim. His black-gloved hands were folded before him as if reverential to this cathedral of evil.

Camilla reached for Hudson's hand and squeezed it. When Hudson responded by putting an arm around her, Venus gave a harsh laugh and said, "I think we have two lovers among us." She translated it for the amusement of the others and all echoed the laugh except for the ever-silent wolfman.

Hudson wondered if Lupo could speak, or if for lack of proper meat he'd cut his own tongue out and eaten it on a piece of bread smothered in tomato sauce.

The flippant thought evaporated as quickly as it had arrived. Was there anything he could do? *Anything?* Was it better to die fighting than to be tortured to death?

There was no way out of this for either one of them…unless he could get his hands on one of the weapons hanging on that—

Lorenzo gave him another shove and Greco's sword pricked his back. He was herded toward an ornate high-backed wooden chair that bore leather cuffs on the armrests and leather cuffs where his ankles would be when seated. An additional leather strap hung at the position of the neck. Carved into the chair were what appeared to be demonic faces straining upward from the very pit of Hades. There was no cushion—no comfort to be afforded in this chamber of the damned—and Hudson was appalled to see hundreds of holes in the chair's back and seat. A metal lever was set in the chair's right side. He figured that moving the lever would spring iron spikes up through the holes into the flesh.

He saw Lupo grasp Camilla's arm and pull her toward the rack while Venus stood to one side, watching through ebony eyes that glinted with evil expectation in the lamplight. Camilla's knees buckled, her face gone gray with fear. The wolfman roughly jerked her up once more. Her fear turned to anger, her teeth clenched and she hit out at the man's chest with flailing fists, only to be struck on the side of the head by black-gloved knuckles. This time she nearly fell but Lupo showed his strength by picking her bodily up and throwing her like a sack of trash onto the rack.

Again…was it better to die fighting than to be tortured to death?

He thought it was.

He suddenly tensed and smashed an elbow backward, aiming for Greco's face and at the same time trying to twist away from the rapier. His elbow caught Greco on the chest because the man had moved fast, but it was enough of a blow to send him reeling. Lorenzo's knife thrust at Hudson's side but he blocked the arm, struck out and got the man right in the mouth with a soul-satisfying *crunch*. Lorenzo lost the knife and it clattered to the floor.

"*Non ucciderlo!*" Venus shouted. *Don't kill him!*

At once Greco was coming at Hudson again, and though Venus's command was understood the rapier's point jabbed at his opponent like the head of a poisonous snake. As Hudson dodged aside he was tackled by the bloody-lipped Lorenzo and both of them crashed against the wall next to the torture chair. Hudson hammered at the man's head and shoulders, giving him blows that might've broken the bones of a lesser man. Lorenzo staggered back once more, and then from the corner of his eye he saw Greco's rapier coming...not the point, but the hilt and heavy decorative pommel swinging at him. It hit him in the forehead just above the right eye, and as he fell backward from the blow it caught him again nearly in the center of the forehead.

Darkness came up and swallowed him.

He awakened—possibly only a minute or so later—being pushed into the torture chair. He blinked, still dazed, and saw Lupo roping Camilla onto the rack, tying her at ankles and wrists with her arms splayed back over her head on the hard wooden platform. To add to this horror, Lupo gave the rack's tension wheel a single turn that brought from Camilla a gasp of pain.

Lorenzo stood spitting blood, two teeth, and muttering Italian curses. He retrieved his knife while Greco buckled around Hudson's right wrist the leather cuff on that side. Hudson shook his head back and forth to clear it, and for that effort Greco slapped him across the face.

"Wait!" Venus told them. Hudson was aware that someone else had come down the stairs and was speaking to the lady Scaramanga. Through the haze he made out that it was the old woman who'd appeared when they'd first arrived, had looked at the newcomers with disdain and then departed when Mars had spoken to her, probably giving her instructions to prepare the bedroom Hudson and Camilla had been locked into. The housekeeper? Yes.

Venus approached Hudson. Greco—who'd been standing at attention like a good soldier since Venus had given the initial command of *Aspettare*—retreated from her either in honest respect or abject fear.

"Can you hear me?" she asked. "No matter. We have two more visitors. The young Englishman and the old grandfather. Who would have believed such a thing?" She turned to survey Camilla stretched out and helpless. "You're so lovely in that position. I'm sure this man thinks so." In Italian she addressed the others. "My brother is calling for me. Hold everything until I return, it won't be long." She regarded Lorenzo who was leaning against the wall holding his mouth. His eyes were bloodshot and bleary and he appeared near passing out from the big Englishman's blows. "Are you all right?"

"I am, mistress." The voice was mangled.

"Can you continue?"

"I can."

"Come up with me and wash your mouth out. I'll send someone down in your place. Secure him, Greco." She stared at the big Englishman in the chair and made a decision. Her mouth crimped. "I give you permission to put the spikes in him." It was the woman she wished to slowly tear apart for her own pleasure, while the man held no interest for her but another sack of meat. She wanted to hear how a witch-hunter screamed.

"Yes, mistress," the other man said, but still he stood at attention until Venus, Lorenzo and the housekeeper started up the stairs.

Hudson's mind was reeling as well as his senses. Matthew and Professor Fell? *Here?*

His head was clearing but he kept it lowered as if he was still nearly insensible. The wolfman was standing about fifteen feet away beside the rack. Greco came back to the chair. He had put the sword aside, having to use two hands to buckle the restraint around Hudson's left wrist. Were they out the door yet? He couldn't wait any longer. He knew what he must do and he realized he would have three seconds at most. He gave a groaning noise to emphasize his helpless plight.

Greco started to fasten the buckle.

It had to be now.

TWENTY-FOUR

QUITE CERTAINLY IT WAS THE MOST EXPENSIVE OIL LAMP IN THE WORLD.

And probably the most valuable, because without its glow illuminating the map in the professor's hand the way could never have been followed in the dark. In Matthew's opinion it was worth many times more than the additional gold coin used to buy it from the ferry's master.

On the road past Milano that Meneghetti had drawn out, Matthew urged the team at a canter, the fastest speed he could coax out of them. The coach was buffeted by strong winds that swirled up dust as if ghosts had risen from their graves to observe their passage. The element of time pressed heavily upon Matthew but these horses belonging to the elderly couple had likely never been demanded to travel at such a speed for so many miles. Thus he might push them to a gallop for short intervals but he didn't want to wear them out as—hope within hope—he, the professor, Hudson and Camilla would need their energy for escape.

If they were still alive. And if he and Professor Fell would survive the next few hours.

If and if. Not a very good plan.

"I want to know," Matthew against the wind, "why you came back."

Fell was silent and Matthew thought he was not going to answer, but then the professor reached into a pocket and withdrew something gripped in his fist. He opened his palm and by the lamplight Matthew saw lying there a small dark gray crucifix a little over three inches in length, small and unadorned by any decoration.

"Iron," Fell said. "I realized why you'd asked the priest if he had one."

Matthew nodded. The professor had remembered Camilla's translation of what Brazio Valeriani had told the Scaramangas of an iron crucifix breaking the demonic mirror.

"Two shops away from Meneghetti's building was a store selling religious items," Fell continued. "I decided that perhaps I did owe you something."

"But you had no money. How did you get that?"

Fell shrugged. "I was in a hurry. I stole the smallest one I could grab." He returned it to his pocket. "Small, yes, but iron. I thought…if the mirror *is* found…then…we might wish to be armed."

"*We?*"

"As I say, I do owe you but not for the reasons you believe. I owe you for destroying everything I held of value."

"*What?*"

"Yes." Fell nodded. "But everything I held of value was poisoning me. I realized on Alghero, when I thought there was no more point in pursuing the mirror, that who I had become was dead to me. Or let us say, who I used to be. Oh, he's still lurking but I had put him away just as I put aside the idea—the wrong idea—of bringing Templeton back from the dead. It was a hard thing, to think back on what had been." He made a hesitation of studying the map once again before he went on. "I made an error in refusing to walk with my son that day, and I lost him…and on that day was the beginning of the loss of my wife, everything I had set out to be, and…all of it. I was enraged at the world, Matthew. It was never really about power, or wealth. It was about striking back. Can you understand that?"

"I can," Matthew said.

"Then that is what I owe you. I know things I have done or had done in my name can never be forgotten nor forgiven—like the murder of Richard Herrald, the creation of the White Velvet, other assassinations and intrigues—but the blood card with my fingerprint upon it said it all."

"What did it say?" Matthew prompted to the professor's pause.

"It said that in the end I will leave no mark upon this world but the memory of corruption, and what I *could* have been…the scholar, the man of letters and true worth, to discover things that would have brought real value and pleasure to my life…will never be. Am I sorry for myself? No. I am sorry for Professor Danton Idris Fell, a creature of shadow without substance." His head bowed toward the map. "I judge we have four miles to go."

It was a few minutes further before Fell spoke again.

"I want you to know that if this is indeed the viper's nest we think it to be, he will have to make another appearance. He will have to propose a bargain for two purposes…to get Hudson and Camilla out of there if they're still alive, and ourselves the same. I am going to presume that the Scaramangas have heard of him, since he had some dealings with the Italians over the years. Therefore, prepare yourself for his return."

"I think he already showed his hand on the balcony back there."

Fell laughed softly. "Oh," he said, "that was nothing."

Matthew replied, "I also have a bargain to make. Let us say, to pepper the soup. I'm going to tell them where I believe the mirror is."

"Of course. And they're going to demand that they're led to it *before* they release the others unless *his* bargain doesn't do the trick. That is why I have the crucifix in my pocket, just in case the mirror is not a fantasy. Be aware that this Leviathan might be your death and you have a lot to live for, Matthew. Your whole life ahead of you, and your sweetheart waiting."

Matthew felt a pang of the heart but he could not for the moment entertain failure or allow it to erode his resolve. He had come too far for that. "If you get out with Hudson and Camilla you should keep going straight to the ship."

"Oh, you're proposing now to save *my* life when I'm sure you wished me dead so many times? It is to laugh."

"Not wished *you* dead," said Matthew. *"Him."*

The horses cantered on and the still-rising wind whined along the coach on the road past Mirano. The last group of villas was passed, Matthew turned the team onto the map's road to the south, and upon it soon was sighted the roofs of an imposing villa with lamplights ashine and surrounded by a high wall of rough stones that appeared to be topped with broken glass. Matthew reined the horses in before a gate of black wrought iron. Just within the gate could be seen a stone guardhouse.

Matthew and the professor climbed down from the driver's perch and approached the gate, the black key in Matthew's hand. No one could be seen. Professor Fell reached out to touch the gate, and suddenly there were two men armed with flintlock pistols staring them in the face, both men dressed in black. A question was asked: *"Cosa vuoi?"* to which Matthew held up the black key and said, "English," and then motioning toward the professor, also "English."

Obviously the men were adept at their night vision, for one reached through the gate for the key and examined it. He spoke to the other, who went into the guardhouse and quickly returned with a small lamp burning low. This man held the light up to more closely inspect the key—looking for some evidence of forgery in size and shape that only an expert might note, Matthew thought. By the light's wash, Matthew did not recognize either of these men. How many guards there were on what appeared to be an imperial estate was anyone's guess, but at this point of entrance he didn't wish to run into Lorenzo, Pagani or least of all the wolfman.

The black key was handed back. The gate was unlocked but the pistols were still held ready. Behind Matthew and Fell the gate was relocked. One man made a motion for Matthew to lift his arms and then began searching his clothing, patting over the shirt and breeches. The pouch of gold coins was found, opened, laced up and given back with no apparent interest. When the professor was searched the letter opener was pulled from Fell's waistband and held to the light. Knowing how this would be done, the professor had taken the precaution of wiping any trace of blood off on the tail of his shirt. "Protection," Fell said, which brought no reaction but the blade was not returned. Then the small crucifix came out of the professor's pocket.

To the stony stare of his searcher, Fell put his hands together in an attitude of prayer and said, "Faith."

The man shrugged and returned it, and in this instance faith was rewarded. Fell put the item back into his pocket, the pistols were lowered and one of the men motioned the new arrivals up the long curving drive of white gravel to the villa beyond.

Nearing the house, Matthew noted that they were being shadowed by another man who was armed with both a blunderbuss and a rapier at his side. Again, it was no one he recognized. He thought that the Scaramangas might be powerful in their own orbit but evidently they were nearly imprisoned by it, and all this security must mean that several attempts had been made on their lives probably by other criminal organizations. What was the Shakespearean line? *Uneasy lies the head that wears a crown.* How true that seemed to be, and in this case the unease was that the head might be chopped off by any assailant who got onto this estate by day or night. But, judging from all these weapons on display, somehow getting onto this estate without a black key that passed inspection likely meant even worse than what the wolfman had done to Trovatello.

With that, Matthew had to silence his own thoughts.

They ascended six white stone steps to the front door, followed by their shadower. Reaching for the iron knocker, Matthew mused that twenty-four hours ago he would've considered himself insane to be standing here. He still considered himself insane, but it simply had to be done.

He knocked.

In a few seconds the door was opened by a short, slight grandmotherly woman wearing a pale violet caftan-like gown with a white collar and cuffs. She stood impassively staring at the visitors.

When Matthew didn't respond, the man with the blunderbuss behind them said, *"Signore, la sua chiave!"*

"English," Matthew said, confounded by this.

"He says to show your key," the woman answered, her English thickened by the Italian accent.

"Oh! Yes, of course!" He brought the key out again. "Matthew Corbett and Professor Fell to see the—"

But the woman was already motioning them in. They crossed the threshold and the door was closed. Into the marble-floored foyer came yet another man—this one hawk-nosed and his hair done up in a reddish-brown topknot—with a holstered pistol at his side. The woman said something to him, he nodded and went away, and she said, "Come along," to Matthew and the professor.

They were escorted through a number of large candlelit and elaborately decorated rooms to a windowed chamber with bookshelves, a gold-hued carpet on the tiled floor, and a sofa and chairs arranged around a small, square dark brown slab of a table.

"Wait," the woman said, and about four seconds after she'd left the room, Mars Scaramanga burst through another door followed by the topknot with his pistol in his hand. Scaramanga's shirttail was flagging and he had over one arm a gray jacket with a decorative blue paisley trim, as if he'd been interrupted in the process of dressing. He stopped just short of Matthew and the professor and gazed at them as if seeing some unbelievable wonder of wonders.

Then he pushed his shirttail in, took the pistol from the topknot, spoke quietly to the man and aimed the pistol between Matthew and Fell as the bodyguard quickly strode out of the room.

"You two," Mars said. He shook his head, his mouth crooked in a grin of amazement. "How did you ever find this place?"

"The better question would be, why are we here," Fell said.

"I can guess that. Some heroic idea of freeing your friends? They have just now descended to my sister's little playroom, which you will soon be seeing for yourselves."

"I don't think so." Fell sat down in one of the chairs. "Ah! Good to get a load off one's feet, isn't it?"

"Are you two totally mad? You had to know that once you stepped in here you would never leave. And how did you get in here without—"

A move to Matthew's pocket brought the pistol aimed at him. He showed the black key. "Meneghetti was very happy to give us this and draw a map as well."

"That fool will never see the sun rise."

"Too late," said Fell. "I already killed him."

The bodyguard with the topknot returned, spoke to Scaramanga and the pistol was given back to him. "My sister has to see this to believe it," Mars said. He turned a sharp glare on the professor. "What do you mean, *you* killed him?"

"Just as I said. He was a hardheaded son of a fuck but not hardheaded enough."

"Who the hell *are* you?"

"No one's grandfather," said the professor. "Sit down, Matthew, and make yourself comfortable."

"I say he stands."

"I say he sits." Fell's voice was a quiet hiss. "You have no idea who I am, do you?"

"Why should I, and why should I care?"

At that moment into the room came the old woman from the front door and behind her Venus Scaramanga and Lorenzo, who looked as if he had taken a beating under a pair of wild horses' hoofs. Matthew had the sense that he was seeing a display of Hudson's work.

"Ha!" Venus gave the exclamation not only as an expression of surprise but also one of triumph. "So you've come after your friends, yes? I can hardly believe my eyes aren't lying!" She spoke to the housekeeper in Italian: "Take Lorenzo to the kitchen and clean him up. Where is Pagani?" she asked the topknotted man.

"I think he's in his quarters eating his supper, mistress."

"Lorenzo, go take care of yourself. But first…" She took the knife from Lorenzo's sheath at his side, and then he staggered away beside the house-keeper. "Bertanza," she said to the other guard, "go down to the chamber and tell them I'll be along when I'm along." In English: "Mars, take his gun."

"We won't be needing guns, young lady," Fell said. "Tell me, why is it that sometimes such rich beauty as yours is accompanied by such dripping evil?"

"Take the gun," Venus repeated, and Mars did.

Bertanza the topknotted left the room. Matthew further dared the un-certain hospitality by easing himself into one of the other chairs.

"Shall I call for Champagne next?" Mars sneered. "Or do you wish us to leave so you might stretch out and take naps?"

"We want our friends freed," the professor answered.

"And I want the moon for a night light! Stupid old man!"

The professor leaned forward in his chair and Matthew saw Fell rising up in the hot amber eyes, a curl of the lips, a thrusting forward of the chin and some imperceptible and unmistakable show of adamant power.

"I am Professor Danton Idris Fell," were the next six words spoken. "Do you know that name?"

Mars shot a quick glance at Venus before he said, "You're a damned liar."

"You idiot! Dumb *fuck!* Why would an ordinary old man lie about that? Why would an ordinary old man even know the *name?*"

Now Mars and Venus exchanged more than a glance; it was a look as if they'd been mutually struck by a flying anvil.

"Prove you are who you say," challenged the sister.

"You've heard of White Velvet?"

Mars spoke up. "One of my men brought back some bottles from London as well as stories about the fabled professor. Gin is not in such favor here, though it was first created in Italy by monks. Still...yes, I've heard of it and tasted it." Matthew took note that the gun in his hand dropped a few inches. "A drugged elixir, yes? And very enjoyable to the senses, as I recall."

"It's all the rage in London. It could be all the rage in Venice, if you wished it."

"Why would I wish that?"

"Because it *is* a drug. Drinking a few bottles of it, one is—shall we say—entranced to drink more and more. It would become a most lucrative and demanding habit on the order of opium. If you were the sole supplier, you would have no need of dead fools like Meneghetti."

"Why don't I just create a drugged wine, then?"

Fell steepled his fingers together and smiled. "If you wish. I am willing to trade the formula for the two people you've taken down to 'the chamber'...and believe me, I have taken many to my own chamber so...I know how it's done."

Mars let go a breath. "*Oh mio Cristo!* You *are* him!"

The pistol dropped down to his side.

"One moment!" said Venus. "I don't care anything about White Velvets! To hell with that and this talk about fucking opium! You came here after the mirror, not to sell drugged liquor! So why should we let you or anyone else go to get it for yourselves?"

"If I may speak?" Matthew asked. He waited until their attention was focused on him. "I am also offering something in exchange. I believe I know where the mirror is."

There was a moment of silence before the woman spoke again. "*Believe?* What do you mean, *believe?* Do you know or not?"

"I'm not going to say I know with absolute certainty, but I know I can tell you where it *probably* is."

"Not good enough!"

"Would you release them if I told you?"

Mars said, "We would release them if you took us to the place and you were correct. Now where is it?"

The time had come. Matthew said, "It's in the lighthouse known as Leviathan, about a quarter of a mile off the coast of Chioggia."

"*Leviathan?* That name...written by the dead sorcerer's hand...but..." Mars frowned. "I've never heard of such a place!"

"Don't do many sea voyages, do you?" Fell prompted.

"Chioggia…is from here…I would say forty miles," Mars estimated. "*Leviathan*. That name." He turned to his sister with a growing air of excitement. "That *must* be it!" He seemed to catch himself and tamped his emotion down. "Go fetch Edetta," he instructed Venus, and she left the room without further comment.

They waited. Mars began to pace back and forth. In a few minutes Venus returned with the elderly housekeeper.

Mars spoke English to her for the benefit of his visitors. "Your husband was a captain of cargo ships, yes?"

"*Sí, padrone, il mio—*"

"English!" Mars interrupted.

"Yes, master. My Georgio—rest his soul—captained many ships."

"Have you ever heard of a lighthouse called Leviathan? Off the coast of Chioggia?"

She had to visibly put herself into past memories, her head bowed in thought and one hand up to her chin. It took her a moment to find what she was searching for. "Oh! The Chioggia lighthouse? Yes sir, I do recall my Georgio speaking of it. The light saved his ship more than once. But…it's not been called Leviathan since I was a young girl, sir. And I think it was nearly destroyed by the storms many years ago and left dark since then."

"Thank you." Was there a tremble in the master's voice? "You may go."

Edetta started to retreat but then paused. "The reason this stirs the memory, sir, is that on many nights such as this—with a storm coming in—I stayed awake and worried while my Georgio was at sea."

Mars raised an eyebrow. "A storm coming in?"

"Oh yes, sir. In the wind I hear it and in the bones I feel it. Yes, sir…a storm, and very bad." With that she gave a little respectful bow to both the Scaramangas and left the room.

"Leviathan!" Mars clasped his hands together. "That *must* be the place!"

"We don't know that until we see it," Venus cautioned. "And I say our guests in my chamber will stay exactly where they are until we have it in our hands."

"You have the proper information," Fell said. "There's no need to hold them."

No need? Venus thought. Little did this old fool know. He might be an important man in England but he was in Scorpion territory now, and her intention was to put them all to the pleasures of her toys when—if—that mirror was found. Even stepping foot into the toyroom had caused her heartbeat to quicken and her juices to flow. Why now would she surrender these flesh puppets when she had them all in her grip, and especially the two already in the chamber? And the last thing in the world her brother needed was more ways to dose himself with opium, no matter how lucrative this White Velvet might be.

She said, "We will make that decision." Mars caught her steely gaze and the implication in her tone of voice that was hidden from everyone but himself. He knew his sister's desires very well.

"We'll need our strongest horses," he told her. "If we leave within the hour we can reach Chioggia by dawn. There'll be fishermen's boats in the harbor, we can pay someone to take us out and back."

"With a storm coming?" Matthew asked. "Across a quarter mile of sea?"

"No matter. How is it you believe the mirror is there?"

"My profession is discovery."

"A simplistic answer. But who else knows about this?"

"Now…only myself, the professor, you and your sister."

"It *has* to be there," Mars repeated. "Leviathan. It has to be." To Venus he said, "Go find Edetta and tell her to have someone fetch Pagani here. I recall that Pagani used to be a sailor. We can use him, also…" He paused, considering the qualifications of his bodyguards. "Bracca. He's had sailing experience as well. We may have to take a boat across ourselves."

"Would that be wise?" Fell asked uneasily; he was already feeling the heave and lurch of rough waves.

"Any storm that's coming may have passed by the time we get there. If not we can wait it out on the shore." He turned his attention to Venus, who hadn't moved. "Did you hear what I said? Go find Edetta."

She had been staring at Matthew and running her fingers up and down the blade of the knife she'd taken from Lorenzo. He'd shifted several times in his chair, as if that might make a difference, but it had not. He thought it was the stare of a spider eyeing a fly trembling in her web.

"You go," she answered, her voice low and steady. "I want to take the handsome Englishman upstairs."

"This Englishman wants to stay exactly where he is," Matthew said.

Venus gave him a smile that other men might have thought incandescent though her ebony eyes had no part in it. "You're not afraid of me, are you?"

"Yes, I am."

"Nonsense! We're all *compatriots* here, are we not? I want to hear more about this mirror as I dress for the trip. I promise I won't hurt you." Her smile increased by several candlepower. "Why should I?"

Matthew looked to the professor for help but the old bastard just shrugged. It came to Matthew that alone with this deadly spider he might talk her into bringing Hudson and Camilla out of the torture chamber before they left for Chioggia. Doubtful, but it was worth a try. Still…this woman scared him as much as had Tyranthus Slaughter and the infamous sausage queen Lyra Sutch.

"Someone go with *someone!*" Mars said impatiently. "Venus, mind your manners!"

"Oh, I shall." She beckoned Matthew up from his chair.

"Will you come with us?" he asked the professor.

"I am so glad to be sitting on a soft seat I would have to be pried out of here." But he lifted his chin toward Venus and quietly said, "I would appreciate it if you would leave that knife on the table. And if my son comes to any harm in your presence, I will take it as a betrayal of compatriots."

At the same time Venus was thinking *And what will you do about it*, Matthew was thinking *Son?*

Had Professor Fell actually spoken that word?

"Leave the knife. I'm going to find Edetta," Mars announced, and he departed the room with the pistol still in hand.

The weapon went down on the table and with a mocking expression Venus held up her hands to show that she had no further blades hidden in any niche, crevice or cubicle. As Matthew followed Venus out, along a corridor and up a spiral staircase, he was reasoning that the Scaramangas did not know he wasn't of Fell's blood, and calling him "son" before them strengthened the shield of protection around him. So…all well and good, because this woman leading him up the stairs had fed Cardinal Black to her lynx and only the dead knew what else she was capable of.

Along another corridor at the top of the stairs Venus opened a door and the low, menacing scrowl that issued from a corner of the large black-and-red-decorated bedroom nearly caused Matthew to jump from his boots.

"Don't mind my Nyx," Venus said as she held the door open for his entrance. "She's missed me."

Against his better judgement and all senses at shrill alarm, Matthew walked into the room and Venus closed the door. He made sure she didn't lock it, which she did not. The bedroom had a massive red-canopied bed that was unmade, the sheets rumpled, and there upon the bed was *The Lesser Key of Solomon,* open to perhaps the woman's demon of choice.

"Bedtime reading?" He motioned toward the book.

"*Fascinating* reading. I presume you've read it?"

"I have no need to." Matthew caught sight of the lynx crouched in its corner, its yellow eyes glittering in the room's lamplight. "Is that thing allowed free reign in here?"

"You'll see she's wearing a collar and her leash is tied to the grip of my bath chamber's door. My sweet Nyx, were you hungry to see me?" she crooned to the beast.

Matthew did not like the use of the word *hungry*. He wanted to keep every item of furniture in the room—plush leather chairs, a dresser, a chair and small makeup table upon which was placed a royal battalion of little jars and vials along with a silver hairbrush and comb, a black chaise lounge, a full-length oval mirror on a stand that resembled cat's paws, a six-foot-tall crimson dressing screen decorated with intricate ornamentation, and the bed—between himself and that deadly creature.

"The mirror," she said. "The question that has been posed is: why would someone search for it if they didn't believe?"

"I was talked into this."

"All the way from England?"

"It's a long story."

"It's a long *distance*. Sit down, make yourself comfortable."

"In this room, impossible."

"Oh, you're the charming one! Pardon me." So saying, she began to unbutton her gown.

"You're pardoned, and I'm leaving." He made a move for the door.

"You *do* want your friends unharmed, do you not?"

He stopped with his hand reaching for the polished red grip. "What does that have to do with my leaving? We have an agreement."

"Your agreement is with my brother, and my brother is sometimes confused about what's best for the Family." She was in the process of removing her gown, finishing the work of unbuttoning many buttons. She turned her back toward him. "Unlace me."

"Tell someone else to do that."

"I'm asking *you*. Aren't you an English gentleman?"

Matthew thought this woman had about her an air of madness. What game was she playing? When he came toward her the lynx hissed and stood up, its body vibrating with murderous tension.

"Go on," she urged. "Unlace."

As Matthew did—his fingers fumbling in the attempt of his hands trying to avoid her skin—Venus was thinking that she would never allow this cur to violate her, as no man ever had or ever would, but being in the toyroom tonight she had been all ready—as the saying went—with nowhere to go. There was a slow boil in her blood. She felt in her brain and body the insistent ticking of self-desire. It had to be released, and soon. If there was no pleasure to be found in the toyroom tonight, it must be taken elsewhere.

She stepped out of her gown, turned and gave Matthew a show of her black bodice trimmed with red ruffles. More eyelets of red lace ran up the middle.

"Now this," she said.

"No." He drew back.

She shook her head as if in pity for a young fool, and when she walked behind the dressing screen she determined that when the mirror was found both he and the so-called professor would be killed on the spot, no matter what Mars had to say about it. In the cold center of her mind she had always known that her brother was weak, and though they were so tightly connected she thought at that moment she hated him too.

"May I leave?" Matthew asked, giving the lynx another distrustful glance.

She was silent. He could hear the sound of her silks coming off.

And then she came out from behind the screen, totally naked.

He went for the door and she stepped between him and the way out. In her right hand was a knife twice as long as the one she'd placed upon the table downstairs.

"I like that," she said, as she traced the blade's tip along the scar on Matthew's forehead made by the claw of the bear Jack One Eye years before. He dared not move, and as the blade continued on its journey he noted her nipples stiffening and sweat gleaming on her lower lip.

The blade played across the bridge of his nose.

Her voice was breathless, and nearly a plea. "Don't you find me a beautiful woman?"

As the knife flicked at the corners of his mouth as if to cut from it the response Venus desired, Matthew Corbett stared into the dead ebony eyes and said, "I find you the ugliest woman in the world."

The knife stopped moving.

With a chill of icy terror in her voice, Venus said, "Leave me alone."

"I certainly shall." Matthew stepped back and away from the blade… and then he noted that the naked woman's eyes did not follow him. Instead, they were widened and fixed upon something over his left shoulder.

He turned. Nothing there, but the lynx was making a God-awful hissing.

:*Venus:*, said the purple-robed figure a second time. It stood a few feet behind the young Englishman, and had seemingly walked through the wall of her bedroom. :*You cling to a lie:.*

"*You* lie!" Her face was strained, her mouth bitterly twisted. "You're the liar!"

Matthew backed away. She was still between him and the door. He changed his direction so again he kept a safe distance from the lynx even though it was leashed and tied. His heart was pounding, and he realized he was in the presence of the truly and possibly deadly deranged.

:*Poor sad Venus. I come to show you the future:.*

"You will show me nothing!"

:*Your beauty:,* Dominus went on, :*is even now fading. The young man has told you the truth. How terrible that you put such faith in a mirror that cannot be real:.*

"It *is* real! I'll have it! Get away from me!" She lifted the knife into a striking position.

Matthew held up his hands to ward off a blow, even as he knew the woman was not speaking to him but to some invisible entity that had entered the room.

Dominus?

Had Black's specter attached itself to her? That thing had only been a phantasm of his own corrupted mind!

Hadn't it been?

:*Dear Venus*:, the creature whispered, in a voice that seemed to whirl around the room in a maelstrom of a hundred voices that merged into one eerie intonation. :*Look upon your future*:.

She knew what her sin was: she had doubted the power of the enchanted mirror. It had been a small seed of doubt all along, and now on the verge of finding it she feared that in the tower of Leviathan there would be nothing but useless glass, and like useless glass she would crack to pieces in its presence.

Beauty, beauty…all for beauty.

:*Your future*:, said Dominus, :*without a mirror that cannot be*:.

With both rising dread and panic, she looked first upon her hands and saw the wrinkling begin. Saw the fingers thinning, no longer beautiful, and curling into aged claws. Upon the flesh bloomed the dark blotches of oncoming infirmity, and as she gazed with sheer horror on the future Dominus predicted the wrinkled old skin crawled up her arms and began to infect her shoulders, then across her chest in a flattening and coarsening of the breasts. She cried out, tears springing to her eyes…and then she dared to look into her own mirror.

What she saw there nearly appeared a corpse, the flesh shrunken in some places on her body and sagging in others, her breasts no longer her proud items but as flat as windless flags, her stomach a nightmare map of folds, her thighs blue-veined and shrivelled and between them the pubic hair thinned and gray.

And her face…the dried-up apparition of approaching death, her once raven-black hair a tattered white rag, her ebony eyes ringed with purple and sunken in the staring skull, and as she opened her mouth to cry out again the once fine white teeth were broken stubs like old rotten pieces of cork.

She released a shuddering breath. Across her hands the dark blotches grew, and in them death and decay and beauty forever lost, and with a cry of anguish she was determined in her fever of horror to cut them out and so began stabbing at the left with the knife in her right and as the blood flew up into her face and spattered into the air Matthew backed away until he met the wall.

The blade was gripped in her bloody left hand to attack the right, and cut and cut and cut and then it was not enough because the offensive hanging breasts must be slashed away, all this diseased flesh, all this tragedy, and as the knife worked and worked the blood ran down her body as if she had just stepped out from a bath in gore.

Still Matthew could not get past the madwoman flailing at herself with the knife. "Help!" he shouted. "Someone! Help!"

The knife stabbed and stabbed, and then when it fell to the wet red at her feet Venus Scaramanga staggered forward toward the creature she knew loved her more than any love in the world, and the bloody hands and trembling arms picked her Nyx off the floor.

Matthew heard the thing give what might've been a scream of blood lust, and then as the woman cradled it against her its fangs went for the dripping hands and fingers yet she did not release it, she held it tighter still and seemed oblivious to the pain as the creature further ripped with fangs and claws at her hands. She hugged it, crooning, and then it reached her face.

In her realm of ecstasy, in her world of self-pleasure and pain, Venus saw the purple-robed figure across the room, watching her.

She was very sure it thought her the most beautiful woman ever known.

And then it bowed its faceless hooded head, backed away, and vanished through the blood-spattered wall.

Only then did she realize where she was, and what was eating her alive.

And she screamed the scream of the damned.

As the door burst open and first Mars, then another of the bodyguards and Professor Fell rushed in, followed by Edetta, the lynx had already opened the woman's throat. Venus fell to her knees. The lynx kept tearing at her in a frenzy, whiplets of blood flying through the air, and with a cry of horror and rage Mars strode forward and brought the pistol up. Nyx whirled on him, hissing as if in protection of both its mistress and its meal and in its heightened state not being able to discern the difference.

Mars shot it through the head.

In the cloud of blue smoke the lynx's body slithered to the floor alongside Venus, who stared up at the ceiling with dead ebony eyes in a face no one could call beautiful.

"My God! My God!" Mars cried out. He knelt beside the body, touched the remains of a cheek, shook a blood-streaked arm as if trying to wake the departed…and then he stood up, strode to Matthew, lifted and cocked the pistol and pulled the trigger.

It was only a one-shot weapon. He drew his arm back to bash the young man's head in, and as Fell tried to dash forward the bodyguard Bracca—also armed with a pistol—caught him around the chest.

"What did you do to her?" Mars shouted, his eyes already red-rimmed and his face tight around the bones. "What did you *do?*"

"Nothing! I swear it!" Matthew's arm was up to shield his skull. "She took her clothes off, went crazy and started stabbing herself! Then she picked that thing up!"

"Stabbing herself? What do you—" His mouth wished to order Bracca to shoot this Englishman through the brain, but he realized there was no blood around the boy and his first glimpse of Venus had been her cradling the monster as it tore at her. *Went crazy*, the young man had said. *Took her clothes off and went crazy.*

He recalled the times he'd thought his sister was on the edge of losing her mind.

Now it appeared by all reason—whatever the hideous reason might be—that she had gone over.

He lowered his arm and turned again to face the body.

"My sister. Oh my God…my sister." Mars shivered as if struck by a hard, cold wind. His hand came up to touch the thatch of red hair on the left side of his head. What was he to do without his sister? They were inseparable…they were together in life…together…in the Family…they *were* the Family…what was he to do?

Tears were in his eyes. He felt weak and alone without her. He needed her strength, her very power of life to energize himself. How could he go on?

He knew what must be done.

The mirror.

At Leviathan.

He said, "I want to bring my sister back." To the professor: "Can it be done?"

Fell's face was grim. "If the mirror is what it's purported to be, yes."

"How?"

"I was going to summon a servant to bring my own son back from the dead. I had three to choose from, and I had chosen Asmoday."

Mars saw the book of demons open on the bed. He started to reach for it but stopped when he realized its pages and the surrounding sheets were spattered with his sister's blood.

"I have memorized the seal of Asmoday and the incantation," Fell said, speaking as if from the grave. "We'll need chalk to draw the seal."

"Chalk?" Mars was asking Edetta.

"Yes, sir. It's used in the laundry and to keep the silverware from tarnishing."

"Get some," he ordered, and she quickly left. "Pick that up, we're taking it," was the next command, for Bracca to retrieve the book.

And to Matthew and the professor, spoken with the urgency of torment: "We go *now.*"

TWENTY-FIVE

LEFT HAND, SINISTER.

It was what Hudson's old fencing master had told him. The left hand was the sinister side of the body and for most the weaker. So it was with Hudson.

But now, as Greco began to buckle the cuff on Hudson's left wrist to secure him to the spike chair, it had to be the sinister hand or nothing. And nothing meant death for both himself and Camilla tied to the rack, with the wolfman standing ready when that monster of a woman returned.

Three seconds. Do or die.

Do.

As Greco used both hands to grip the cuff and buckle, Hudson exploded out of his feigned insensibility.

He had mentally calculated the distance to the sawblade-edged knife in the sheath at Greco's right side. His left hand came out of the cuff before the buckle could be fastened. In a blur it grasped the knife's handle. In another blur it came out of the sheath and up across Greco's throat, and after the blood spewed forth and Greco staggered backward with both hands to the fatal wound everything became to Hudson a slow-motion battle for survival.

Even as Hudson began to frantically saw at the leather cuff binding his right arm to the chair, Lupo was at the wall of weapons. He pulled an axe from its hooks.

Camilla screamed a warning, able to lift her head enough to view the oncoming carnage.

As Lupo swung the axe, Hudson crashed the chair over on its left side and the axe blade tore a chunk from the ornate headrest that flew past Hudson's face. The knife was sawing at his right cuff, but had not yet penetrated enough to loosen the buckle's grip. Hudson heaved himself over so the chair was on his back as again the axe came down, thunking into the wood, and as Hudson feverishly worked the knife he prayed the wolfman would not trigger the lever that sprang the spikes.

He was aware that Lupo was bracing for a third axe strike, and with a cry of desperation and the strength of the doomed he tore the sawblade through the leather enough to pull free. As he thrust the chair off himself and rolled away from the wolfman's heavy boots he heard the axe hit the chair and then a clacking noise that said the spiked chair had now lived up to its name.

With the knife in his grip he got to his feet and jumped back as the axe swung inches past his chest. He realized Greco's sword was propped against the wall to his right, and it was going to have to be taken up and used with the sinister hand. Hudson saw the eyes in the holes of the metal mask make note of the sword. Instantly Lupo started to move to get between his quarry and the weapon, and Hudson had no choice but to throw the knife. It was batted away like an insignificant insect, but it gave Hudson time to get his stronger right hand on the sword, turn and face his opponent.

And then his hand and arm began to shake, the cold sweat burst out on Hudson's face and with an involuntary spasm his hand opened and the rapier clattered to the floor.

He could not hold a sword.

Did the monster behind the mask laugh? If so, it was a premature hilarity.

Hudson launched himself at Lupo's midsection with the velocity of a human cannonball. Before Lupo could get the axe lifted, Hudson crashed into him and though the brute was some sizes larger than the Englishman no one made of less than stone could've remained standing when hit by that kind of force. The wolfman flailed back and fell against some device that had spiked iron balls hanging from it on chains, and though he went down he still had control of the axe. Hudson was on his knees first, then on his feet, then at the wall of weapons, then lifting a second axe from its hooks...

...then turning on Lupo with the axe ready for battle and snarling, "Come on, wolfie!"

Lupo came on.

He charged forward with the axe at an overhead position but at the last second brought it swinging from Hudson's left. Hudson stood his ground, detected the feint before it swung and parried it, the impact of the two bladeheads throwing up blue sparks and nearly twisting Hudson in a half-circle. Then Hudson backed away with the axe up as a guard, knowing that being hit by a blow such as he'd just experienced was enough to almost cleave a man in two. Again the wolfman charged in and again the blades cracked together, the impact stunning Hudson's arms up to the shoulders. He realized he could not hold this beast at bay much longer without having his own axe torn from his hands.

Still backing away, he stumbled over the device that Lupo had knocked to the floor, and with that stumble came an expected axe swing that came close to taking the top of Hudson's head off if he hadn't ducked below it. His boot stepped on a chain with a spiked iron ball bolted to it. A deadly second's look told him the chain had come off a hook attached to the central part of the torture device.

Lupo rushed in again, axe uplifted. Hudson threw his end-over-end at the man's mask. The wolfman dodged down, the axe went over his head and crashed into something on the other side of the chamber, and by then Hudson had picked up the chain and was whirling the iron ball around and around over his head.

He let fly. The ball sailed true, the chain wrapped around the axe's shaft in the black-gloved hands, and before Lupo could tighten his grip Hudson wrenched the weapon away from him, scrabbled wildly at the handle before it flew past, nearly lost it, and with desperate fingers got firm hold of the thing. Then he began to stalk the wolfman, who retreated step by cautious step. In the holes of the mask the eyes blinked. Abruptly, Lupo turned away and ran to retrieve the axe Hudson had thrown.

Hudson made a decision.

He sprinted for the rack. From the corner of his eye he saw Lupo picking up the other axe. One blow from Hudson's own cleaved the rope that bound Camilla's arms to the rolling mechanism, the second parted the rope that stretched her legs, and though her wrists and ankles were still tied together by short lengths of rope she was at least freed from the rack's embrace.

Then he turned, and the wolfman was almost upon him.

The crack of the axeblades crashing together echoed through the chamber. The blow staggered Hudson and made his hands go dead. His own strike at Lupo's midsection was knocked aside with such force that the deadened hands lost their grip.

Hudson's axe whirled away.

Lupo lifted his weapon for a killing blow and Hudson threw himself at the man. He got hold of the arms, was shaken off, got hold again and Hudson hung on like a mad dog with teeth gripped on bloody meat. Suddenly the end of Lupo's axe handle came down on Hudson's left arm just above the elbow and the *crack* of a breaking bone told Hudson the battle was almost done. Pain shot through his arm and shoulder, a red haze rippled in his vision and he fell to the floor knowing the axe was coming next for his head.

What came next was Camilla Espaziel, leaping from the rack.

She landed on the wolfman's back. Before he could shake her off she had winnowed her hands under the cloak and under the mask, where the short length of rope that still connected them found Lupo's bull-thick neck. She curled her legs up to get her knees on either side of his spine and, sweat-faced and wild-haired, she wrenched back on his throat with every ounce of strength she could summon.

He thrashed and pitched, wildly swinging the axe again at Hudson who rolled out of the way holding his broken arm. As Camilla worked at strangling the beast he dropped the axe to grab at her hands with both of his, and Hudson knew that in another instant Lupo was going to throw himself backward to smash Camilla against the rack's edge, which he would've done if he was the wolfman.

Before Lupo could break Camilla's back in a violent reaction, Hudson picked up the axe and with his one arm swung the blade into the wolfman's right leg just above the knee. The blow didn't have all his power behind it but it was enough to sink into the flesh and around the blade the dark blue breeches turned darker and wet.

Lupo staggered, but he did not go down. Camilla kept up the pressure and Hudson wrenched the axe free for a second strike. A gagging noise came from behind the mask. Lupo made another effort to shake her off but was visibly weaker. Hudson chopped him in the other leg above the knee, yet still he did not fall.

Camilla felt the wolfman's hands on hers, trying to break the fingers. The length of rope was nearly buried in his throat and he made a strangled sound but her fingers were being pried loose by sheer animal strength. Hudson stood up with the axe in his hand. The chamber spun around him. He reared his arm back and struck the blade into the center of Lupo's chest. It sounded like hitting a tree trunk.

The wolfman shivered and gave a choked and guttural cry.

He did not fall.

Hudson hit him again. The chin of the masked face lifted up and Hudson could see the rope down so deep it was almost drawing blood.

He had to hit him in the chest with the axe a third time, as Camilla hung onto the man's back. Bone cracked. A mist of blood bloomed from the mask's mouth. When Hudson pulled the blade free, Lupo's damaged legs at last collapsed and he toppled forward onto the floor, where he began to crawl painfully with Camilla riding him.

Hudson thought he was going to have to chop this son of a bitch's head off to finish him. He saw the leather straps where the mask was buckled, the hair on the back of the head dark and close-cut. Camilla was exhausted from her effort and now she pulled her hands free and rolled herself off the man.

Hudson straddled Lupo's back and struck the axeblade down into the head.

After that, he moved no more.

Hudson found himself suddenly sitting on the floor beside the body, with Camilla on the other side. It would not have surprised him if the wolfman had suddenly sat up for a rematch, but with the axe fixed solidly in his brainpan he would be carrying a little extra weight.

He heard the vault door open up at the top of the stairs. Someone was coming down. Wearily, Hudson got up, put a boot against the back of the head, pulled the axe free with a wet *crunch*, and when a man with a topknot entered the chamber he was met with a greeting.

It only took a single swing for this one, as it caught him between the topknot and the eyebrows.

When the man lay on the floor, Hudson regarded him noting that the holster for his pistol was empty. Then Hudson had to turn away and violently throw up what little food was in his belly, because the battered and bone-broken warrior was sick of killing and this last one had been one too many.

Afterward, he walked to the wall of weapons and selected a small saw. With it he sat again on the floor beside Camilla. His focus was going in and out and his left arm was a cold throb of pain, but he had to hold on because at any moment someone else was bound to come down those stairs.

Could he kill anyone else?

He didn't know, and he didn't want to find out.

He used the saw to cut through Camilla's bindings. When she'd gotten them all off, Hudson said listlessly, "We have to get out of here."

"How?" she asked, her own voice a raspy whisper.

That he also did not know. He had to think. Problem-solving was Matthew's specialty, not his own, but when one's life—and the life one loved—was on the line, then…

The life one loved?

Where had that come from?

He had no time to probe his emotions. They were alive and he wanted to keep it that way.

He was looking at the corpse.

"We're going to walk out of here," he said. They had seen the gate and guardhouse from the back of the wagon when they'd been brought in. "Walk out through that gate like we own the place."

"What?"

"I'm not that man's size, but I might be big enough to fool someone at night. With the mask, the cloak and the gloves on…it could work. Who's going to try to stop *that* monster?"

"You might get out in that disguise, but they won't let *me* out. And what about Matthew and the professor? They're here, aren't they?"

"Yes. And what the hell are they *doing* here?"

"The same thing you would be doing here," she said. "Trying to save our lives is what I suspect."

He nodded. "Yes," he said again, because it was true. And another thing was true. "If you hadn't strangled that beast I'd be dead right now. Thank you."

"He was a large target," she replied. "I could hardly miss."

He wanted to hold her against himself with at least one working arm, but time was moving. Venus might return at any second. He said, "Help me get the gloves and the cloak off him." And added, "My left arm's broken, I can't use it."

When that was done, he asked Camilla to unbuckle the mask's straps. Then, as his curiosity was burning as much as his injured arm was paining him, he said, "Let's try to turn him over. I have to see his face."

It was an effort that further taxed both of them, but they got the corpse on its back. The metal mask's wolfish snout was somewhat dented by Lupo's fall but it would still do. Hudson lifted it off the face and looked down upon the dead man.

He was about forty or so, with brown staring eyes in a broad, square-jawed face. His dark hair was cut close to the scalp. There was a scar across his upper lip and leading up across a cheek. Ridges on the bridge of the nose attested to several breakages. Hudson looked at the bruise across the throat that was already blackening, and saw the additional scar where the man's throat had been slashed sometime in his history, likely damaging and perhaps severing the vocal cords. He mused that whoever had given this man the scars must've also been a monster.

He realized he was looking at the face of a soldier like himself, obedient to the call of battle.

And with that he regarded the wall of weapons, all the edged blades designed to maim and kill. They had been a great part of his life. What would his life be, without them? Because he was sick of war and death and killing, and at that moment all he wanted to be was with Camilla in whatever capacity she would have him.

Did he truly love her? He wasn't sure he knew what love was, but he felt close to her and comfortable in her presence, he wished to hold her and help her through the rest of her life as she would help him, and maybe that counted for much. True love? A mystery, just as was Camilla's belief that they had met and known each other in some distant age.

But this soldier who realized he sought the solace of peace more than anything in the world decided he would give love the opportunity to touch him, and perhaps that counted for all.

They had to get out of here. Camilla helped him with the gloves and the cloak. There was blood on the inside of the mask from Lupo's gory exhalation but it couldn't be helped. He decided against taking another weapon from the wall. She buckled the mask onto his head, and then they went up the stairs and cautiously out the door with the false wolfman leading the way.

What to do about Matthew and Professor Fell? He had an idea of how to get Camilla out through the gate, and himself as well, but how to get the others out?

They went along the windswept garden path but avoided the villa, going through the darkened area of ornamental shrubbery to the left of a driveway that continued back behind the house. Along the drive suddenly came a small brown coach with black trim pulled by two horses, the coachman unknown to Hudson. It rolled past them, heading away from the main road. As they moved carefully within sight of the gate and guardhouse, they saw the Scaramangas' large black lacquered coach teamed by four horses come along the drive from behind the villa. There were two men on the driver's seat, one of them Pagani and the second unknown. The coach halted in front of the villa's steps, and as Hudson and Camilla crouched down out of sight they saw Mars Scaramanga, Matthew and the professor come out of the house. Scaramanga was carrying a lamp, and he made a motion that looked as if he was telling the others to hurry. They all climbed into the coach, the vehicle set off along the drive, the gate was opened and the team was turned to the left in the direction of Mirano.

The gate was closed and locked again by two men at the guardhouse. They went inside and closed the door.

"All right," Hudson said, as quietly as possible behind the mask. "At least I know Matthew and Fell are out of there, thank God, and where they're going God only knows." Or the Devil, he thought. It didn't appear as if they were being forced into the coach. And where was the damned sister? He had no inclination to find out.

"Follow me," he told Camilla. "Right behind me. When I give you a signal, I want you to get into the trees and foliage as close as you can to that guardhouse and don't move until I motion for you again. All right?"

She nodded.

With his broken arm under the cloak, Hudson strode toward the guardhouse. He tried to stand as tall as possible and stretched his shoulders out as much as the insistent pain would allow. He knocked at the door and when it was opened the man who'd gotten up from their game of cards on a small table in the lamplight visibly recoiled. The other man of the duo, neither of whom Hudson recognized, also stood up as if he'd suddenly sat on a spiked chair.

The wolfman pointed to both of them and then to the villa.

Some question was posed in Italian by the first man. Hudson again pointed to the villa with a more urgent black gloved hand.

He was hoping these men had never gotten close enough to the fearsome Lupo to realize they were looking at a smaller representation. Not too much smaller, but still…the breath was held behind the mask.

The second man spoke to the first in Italian. Hudson saw they both wore pistols in holsters and there was a sword leaning against the wall beside the table.

The wolfman gave a grunt and another thrust of the hand that said in any language, *Move your asses.*

Would they think Venus, the housekeeper or one of the other guards had sent Lupo to summon them? The next few seconds would tell.

The first man looked at the false wolfman with true respect verging on trepidation. Then he gave a motion to the other to follow, and they started fast-walking up the drive to the house.

When the men had reached the front steps, Hudson lifted his right hand to signal Camilla. She came out of the foliage about ten feet from the guardhouse. By the time she'd gotten to Hudson he had thrown the heavy bolt that locked the gate, opened it and they were out.

They hurried on against the wind. Hudson expected someone to come chasing them at any minute but it didn't happen.

A good distance from the villa and into the night, Camilla stumbled and began to cry a little, but they were tears of relief and to be honest Hudson felt like crying himself.

They went off the road for a time to allow Camilla to unbuckle the mask's straps, and then he threw the mask into the weeds, put his arm around her and they walked on toward the distant lamps of Mirano.

Five

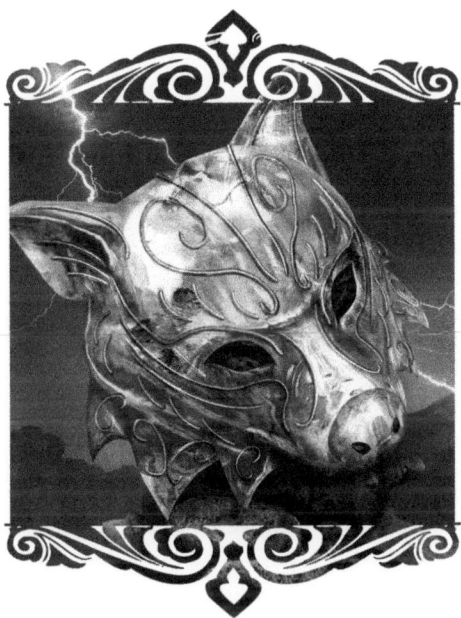

VENDEMMIA

TWENTY-SIX

MARS SCARAMANGA HAD BRACCA'S FLINTLOCK IN HAND WHEN HE knocked at the door of the third house. It was opened by a wizened, gray-bearded fisherman. The aged gent took one look at the man and the pistol and before Scaramanga could repeat his demand to be taken out to Leviathan he spat some Italian curse into the younger man's face, slammed the door and rebolted it.

Thus the Grandmaster of *Famiglia Dello Scorpione* stood amid the little stone cottages of the fishing village of Chioggia, a man thrice denied and even with a gun cursed and bereft of help.

He lifted his oil lamp and spun upon Pagani and Bracca. "You're taking us out!" he shouted in Italian against the wind. "Go on, find a boat!" The gun motioned them toward the wave-tossed beach twenty yards away, where the fishing skiffs were tied to cleats driven into huge logs on higher ground and even so were being battered by the encroaching sea.

Neither man moved, and Matthew saw in their expressions sheer terror.

Pagani spoke in a high, keening voice that echoed the wind off the bay, and Matthew could imagine what he was saying: *Please sir, don't make us do this, please sir, we beg you.*

"Go, I said!" Mars commanded.

And now the heavyset blonde-haired Bracca stepped forward, and he simply shook his head.

No.

Mars aimed the pistol at him.

Bracca shook his head again, another defiant *no*, and this time Pagani did the same.

Standing beside Professor Fell and both of them hard-pressed to maintain their balance against the wind, Matthew looked out upon the bay in the hazy gray gloom. Dawn was out there somewhere, but this day the sun was hidden in funeral shrouds and the churning whitecapped sea was a graveyard for fishermen and boats. Far in the distance, past the shouldered shape of Leviathan a quarter mile out, lightning stabbed triple forks into the waves and thunder rolled across the deep.

At this, Pagani and Bracca fled in the direction of the coach up on the road past the village. In their language Mars shouted, "Touch that coach and you're dead! Do you hear me? You're dead!" Whether they heard or not was an open question; they ran away between the cottages and were gone from sight.

The pistol's barrel went up under Matthew's chin. *"You!"* Mars seethed, his face a tormented rictus. "You're taking us out!"

"I can't sail a boat in this! The storm'll pass in a few hours! We can—"

"I'm not waiting a few hours! No!" The gun thrust harder against Matthew's flesh. "I said we go now!"

"We'll all drown!" the professor said. "For God's sake, be sensible!"

"Sensible," Mars sneered. "I want my sister back! I'm not waiting!"

"Listen to me!" Fell reached out, grasped Mars's gun hand and pulled it away from Matthew. In his other hand he held the book of demons. "I'm telling you that the mirror may be someone's fantasy! To try to go out in *this*, to find a mirror that may *not* be there, and may *not* have any power to do what you want...it's madness!"

"Then why did Valeriani even *want* to hide it?" Mars started to put the pistol back under Matthew's chin, but he dropped it to his side. "It's real. It *must* be real."

Matthew had had limited experience sailing a boat—his last was trying to escape Golgotha with Cardinal Black—but he thought that on a much calmer sea he could get them across without mishap. In this storm, though, and the greater storm that was yet to break...it seemed impossible. The skiff's sails might be torn to tatters before they got halfway out.

"A bargain," Mars said to both of them. "You get me out there...and whether the mirror is in that lighthouse or not...whether it's real or not... your friends go free without harm. I swear to that on my father's grave." The gun came up again, this time against Matthew's forehead. Mars cocked the trigger. "If you refuse to do this, I will kill you here and now and I will have Lupo tear your friends apart...slowly." His red-rimmed eyes were sunken in dark hollows and his mouth was slack. "You don't understand. I can't live without my sister. Not one day. Not *any* hours. What is your decision?"

Matthew thought the man was utterly crazed, and without his sister he seemed to realize he was a hollow shell. The weather was horrific but at least it wasn't pouring rain yet. Could he get a boat a quarter of a mile to the lighthouse? He'd noted that a newer lighthouse was built on a hilltop behind Chioggia, its signal now aflame behind a glass window, which meant that Leviathan had likely been abandoned for many years. Could he get them there without the boat capsizing? He was no expert sailor, that was the most certain thing. But he could handle the sail lines because they wouldn't be complicated in a fishing skiff. Still…a skiff out there in this blow?

What choice did he have?

"Professor, can you handle a rudder?" he asked.

"I think I can."

"Can you *swim?*"

"Like a flying fish," Fell replied.

"You may have to. Fly, I mean. All right," he said. "Let's find a boat that's not held together by old spit and seaweed."

Matthew imagined Brazio Valeriani doing exactly as they were, though the conditions for his trip had certainly been less life-threatening: finding a boat—him probably in the dead of night—and getting the mainmast up, sorting out the lines and untying the craft from its makeshift log anchor, except in their case the waves that came crashing in were up to their knees and strong enough to knock a horse down. Matthew had no idea what size the mirror would be, but evidently it could be handled aboard one of these boats and carried up to Leviathan's summit, and how tall the lighthouse was he couldn't yet tell.

Manhandling the thirteen-foot craft out into the bay was the first exercise in near-futility, and in this stormy soup Mars held the pistol inside his jacket—a sign that Matthew did not care for—to keep the powder as dry as possible. It occurred to Matthew that he might receive a bullet in the head before they returned, but then again Mars would need him to make sure they *did* return. In any case, Mars had the dubious comfort of a loaded pistol and that made him master of the moment though a gun would not save a drowning man.

They fought the waves to get off the rocky beach. Matthew got up in the boat and settled in the middle to man the double sails. Mars climbed up to the bow holding the lantern. The professor was drenched by the time he was helped into the stern yet he managed his grip on the book. Then Matthew said a silent prayer, began working the sails to catch any wind that wasn't viciously trying to slam them back where they came from, and in a tacking pattern the boat moved off with spume spraying over the bow and the waves pitching them up and down. Above Matthew the sails alternately were full enough to nearly tear the lines out of his hands and then as loose

and flapping as an old rotten shutter on a haunted house until at his shouted directions the professor could make a correction with the tiller.

Halfway there the boat was almost swamped and wind shrilled around
the mast. Where was the wayward son of an admiral and expert sailor Julian
Devane when he was needed? Here in this bucking bull of a boat Matthew
thought several times they were going over but the vessel righted itself on
the watery edge of disaster. Was a quarter of a mile ever such a distance in
human history? Matthew thought he heard the mainmast crack and he was
ready for the sails to collapse on their heads but maybe the old spit and
seaweed was strong enough after all.

Through the gloom and tumult came the shape of Leviathan, outlined
by a jagged streak of white-hot lightning.

He made out the jutting shoulders and a tower that was rounded like
a human head. Seventy feet high? At least that. Then he had to concentrate
again on maintaining the sails, aware that Leviathan itself was perched atop
what appeared a pile of dangerous rocks. Maybe thirty more yards through
this calamitous sea, and the boat scraped stone. Above them loomed the
lighthouse, which looked to Matthew to be itself a jumble of black rocks
eaten away by the storms of centuries.

Mars got out of the boat into a churn of knee-deep water and struggled
his way up onto what was more or less higher ground. He didn't help Fell
out or aid Matthew in hauling the boat into a firmer grip on Leviathan's
rugged island, but at least he held the lantern up, being at the moment a
human lighthouse.

They pushed against the wind that came around both sides of
Leviathan's squarish base, the sea spray hitting them like hailshot. A thick
door of ancient oak hung by one wooden hinge, and beyond was utter
darkness.

Did Mars's nerve falter? He held the lantern out to Matthew. His voice
was tight when he said, "You first."

Matthew took the lamp and entered.

Just within, stone steps worn by the ravages of time curved upward.
The interior smelled wet and musty: the aroma of centuries of the sea and
salt wind beating against the island and the walls. He started up, with Mars
just behind him and the professor following. Over the banshee whine of the
wind the sound of their footsteps echoed between the stones.

As he continued ascending, Matthew could hardly contain his curiosity
about what would be found in the tower. A question nettled him: if Brazio
had known an iron crucifix was the only item that could damage—or ultimately destroy—his father's mirror, why had he not used one himself on
the thing instead of bringing it here? He thought the answer might be in
Ciro's being compelled to repair the glass. Brazio might've feared just such a

compulsion, either attempting to repair it himself or taking it to an expert, and thus becoming an accomplice in his father's work. Matthew recalled what Black had told him in the house of Simon Lash, that the mirror had begun as plain glass but soon turned dark. Possibly when Ciro broke it, the mirror returned to plain glass? Then again turned dark when Senna Salastre's spell of enchantment took hold once more?

Therefore in its state of plain glass it could be taken to an expert and repaired without question, and this might've been what Brazio feared…that like his father he could not summon the strength to completely destroy the thing, even with the use of an iron crucifix much larger and heavier than the small item currently in the professor's breeches pocket.

Up and up Matthew continued, shining the lamp before him on the age-cracked steps. Thunder blasted outside with the vehemence of a hundred war cannons.

Black's voice, remembered through time: *Valeriani created a mirror that is not* simply *a mirror. It is a passageway. Can you imagine in your earthbound mind what planes of existence are connected by that passage?*

I don't wish to imagine, Matthew had said.

And Black's reply between his sharpened teeth: *A demonic being can be called to come through. A chosen one, of the caller's choosing. I understand that there is a time limit and a risk of injury, but—*

Good Christ, you are *mad, aren't you?* Matthew had interrupted.

But now, forty feet up, he had begun to sweat in the constricted humidity, the odor of salt leeched in the walls, the darkness above that the light was yet to pierce. He stopped. "Are you all right, professor?"

"Yes." Fell sounded a little strained from the ascent, but otherwise capable enough.

"Keep going!" Mars demanded.

Matthew continued but at a slower pace in respect for the professor's lung capacity, though obviously all those walks, hill climbs and outdoor activities on Alghero for three months had made a new man of him. Still, it was a laborious ascent dangerous at this height because there was no safety rail. Matthew thought that those Roman lighthouse keepers must've been of sturdy stock.

"Professor, watch your step," he cautioned, and received a grunt of acknowledgment.

Up and up.

Soon could be heard the louder shriek and moan of the wind. Were they climbing into the realm of spirits already rampant even on this side of the enchanted glass? They could feel the wind on their faces as it swirled into an opening above and whistled down the tower. Up and up, and then

Matthew reached the top and walked into a round, stone-floored chamber that must be the head of Leviathan.

Through a south-facing aperture six feet wide and the height of the dome the lightning streaked from turbulent sky to treacherous sea and the thunder crashed. In the tower's center was a recessed area—the firepit—where lay a mound of damp remnants and ashes of the last of Leviathan's signal flames. Above the pit the concave ceiling held a vent where the smoke escaped. Even after many years the odor of burned wood still lingered. Underfoot Matthew noted old bones matted with feathers: seagulls that had flown in and died here. Several of the carcasses were shrivelled and dried to resemble some of Professor Fell's bizarre marine specimens.

Matthew lifted the lantern to direct its light toward the opposite wall past the firepit.

And there were the mirrors.

They stood two to the left and three to the right. Four were rectangular plates of reflecting glass six feet tall, no frame around them, discolored and blotched by the elements. Two were cracked, one with a spiderweb cracking around a central point of impact where a gull might have struck it in flight.

The fifth mirror was the one.

There was no doubt of it.

Matthew realized he had caught his breath and heard the gasp, because here was what had bedeviled him since he'd discovered a copy of *The Lesser Key* at Simon Chapel's school for young criminals, funded by the professor. He hadn't known then how it really was a key to this thing, as Black had said a catalogue of demons…of servants to be called forth for a wish of power, wealth, beauty, or resurrection of the dead among other favors from the underworld.

But was it *really* so? The mirror crafted by Ciro Valeriani with the sorcerer's blessing of Senna Salastre was set in a plain oval wooden frame. Leaning against the wall facing the firepit like the others, it appeared to Matthew to be about five feet tall and a little less than two feet wide: a handful to get out here on a boat and up those many steps by one man alone yet it looked as thin as an English wafer. Matthew wanted to approach it but at the same time did *not* want to approach it, for he realized that though he had no belief in the object's ability to serve as a passageway between this earthly plain and the underworld, there was yet something about it that caused his boots to stick to the gull-stained floor and his blood to run cold.

Its surface—not totally black but rather the hue of dark coffee—did not reflect the light from the lantern in Matthew's hand.

It seemed to suck the light in, to fold it up as if in an ebon cloak. The rays of light from his lamp were simply extinguished when they touched the mirror's surface, and Matthew had never seen such a thing.

The rational explanation for this was—

He had none.

"Is that it?" Mars sounded near frenzied. "That's it, isn't it?" He turned upon the professor. "It's real! It *has* to be real!" He approached the mirror. Nothing could be seen in it but the opaque pall. He reached out to touch it, thought better of the action and drew his hand back. Instead, he gingerly tapped at the frame with the barrel of his pistol, which he'd moved from the protection of his jacket.

"What it is remains to be seen," Fell said, though Matthew could tell the professor was regarding the thing with a measure of the trepidation he also shared.

Lightning flashed closer to Leviathan, the thunder boomed and the wind through the aperture spun into the air the old ashes of the light-keeper's fire.

"What now?" Mars was asking both of them. "What's to happen?"

"Don't ask me," Matthew answered. "I want no part of this business."

Fell said in a voice of admirable calm, "As I understand, I am to draw the seal—the emblem—of Asmoday upon the floor in front of the mirror." He had the blood-stained book of demons in hand, and in the opposite pocket of his breeches from the crucifix was a piece of white chalk wrapped in a bit of oilskin paper provided by Edetta. Matthew thought Fell should take the crucifix out right now and attempt to smash the thing, but Mars's pistol had survived the watery ordeal and was there in his hand. He doubted Mars would shoot the professor, who though he had the book also had by the repetition of more than thirty times reading it a memorization of this entity that had first been planned to summon his son from the dead for a final farewell. It was his own head that would be threatened with a skull's divorce of the brains if that crucifix came out of the pocket.

"I know the necessary incantation," Fell went on. "What will happen after that, I have no idea."

"My sister. Will she…appear here…or where? Will she be sitting at her dresser at the house? Where?"

"You ask questions I can't answer. All I know is, the seal must be drawn and the incantation made. I am assuming that…*if* Asmoday appears…the request will have to be made clearly and quickly. Just the one request, and no more."

"But I'm taking the mirror with me when we leave. And *you*…you're going to be a permanent guest until I can learn these seals and incantations myself."

Fell just lowered his head into a shadow, and Matthew thought that meant the life of a New York problem-solver was worth as much as a dried sardine.

"Get to it!" Mars commanded, and this time he did motion with the gun.

"I will tell you before I begin that I had hoped to bring my son back from the dead…but not to *stay* on this side. It would've been only for a few minutes, then he would be gone forever. I understood that was the best I could hope for. To bring someone back to live again an entire *life*…it might seem…I have to say…both greedy and foolish, even to a demon from the world beyond."

"I don't care! And you don't know what's possible or not! My sister has to be returned to life…to me…to *our* world. I said, go on! Draw the seal!"

"Matthew," Fell said quietly, as the thunder blasted the heavens somewhere to the east, "will you bring the lantern over?"

Matthew did. Fell sat on the floor in front of the mirror with the chalk in hand. He kept the book open to a depiction of Asmoday's seal in case his memory had lapsed, and then he began to draw. Soon on the floor was what appeared to Matthew to be the squiggly lines and curlicues ending in arrowheads and anvil shapes within a circle inside another circle. In the space between the circles Fell began to write out the spelling of ASMODAY, each letter equidistant from one another. It seemed to Matthew that the first challenge of calling forth a demon was sitting on a stone floor drawing such a damned intricate thing. But Fell went at it with a careful hand, as gusts of wind blew in and circled round and round Leviathan's head as if scribing its own seal of sorcery.

"Hurry!" Mars demanded.

Fell stopped the work. "I will not. Don't you understand how *serious* this is? I planned for this moment—for myself—for *years*. If you want a positive result it has to be done correctly, otherwise…either nothing will happen, or…"

"Or what?" Mars prompted to the professor's pause.

"Or what might come through could kill us all."

The pistol, which had been held in a gesture of threat, dropped to Mars's side.

"Take your time, then," he said in a small and hollow voice.

"Thank you." Fell returned to the labor.

Matthew set the lantern down beside the seal-in-progress. He was impressed by the slender but wiry mulatto's formidable endurance, as old as he was, because the man had to be as bone-weary as himself. The rocking motion of the Scaramangas' coach had lulled Matthew into two hours of uneasy sleep complete with nightmare scenes of catlike demons ripping flesh and a shadow figure stabbing at itself with a shadow knife. He figured Fell must've gotten some sleep there in the coach as well, but he doubted that Mars had ever closed his eyes. The man's obsession with bringing his sister back from the land of the dead was as wildly lunatic as Venus's gory performance in her bedroom. These two were—or in the case of Venus, had been—the preeminent figures in the Family of the Scorpion? In his opinion they had been stung by their own choices, beliefs and directions in life, and for Venus it had been a slow poison finally made fatal.

For Mars…it was yet to be seen.

The chalk moved, and moved, and moved.

Lightning streaked, the thunder roared, the sea crashed on the rocks below and suddenly rain began to slam upon Leviathan, some of it blowing in to wet the floors and walls.

After a time Professor Fell sat back. He checked his work against the drawing in the book.

"I hope it's good enough," he said, which did not help ease Matthew's growing sensation of dread.

The professor reached up, grasped Matthew's hand and was helped to his feet. Matthew retrieved the lantern, and Mars came closer.

"Now," Fell told them, "I'll begin the incantation."

TWENTY-SEVEN

THE PROFESSOR STOOD BEFORE THE MIRROR AND SPOKE NOT IN THE shadowed tones of sorcery but simply in his regular conversational voice, quoting the incantation inscribed both in the book and in his memory.

"Hear me, Asmoday.

Hear me, bornless spirit.

Hear me, whom the winds fear.

Hear me, and make your powers subject unto me.

I invoke thee.

I invoke the terrible and invisible god, who dwellest in the void place of the spirit.

I invoke thee.

Thee I invoke, thy true name Asmoday, mighty and bornless one.

Hear me, and make your powers subject unto me.

Thee I invoke."

Then Fell was silent.

The mirror remained undisturbed, appearing to Matthew like a swamp pool all living creatures had abandoned.

"You haven't done something right!" Mars cried out. "The seal…the incantation…something was wrong!"

"It wasn't wrong," Fell said.

"Maybe you weren't loud enough!"

This caused the professor to curl a lip. "I don't think volume or lack of such is an issue here."

"Speak it again!" Now the pistol came up, aimed at Fell. "Go on!"

"You would kill me on the edge of discovery? Scaramanga, you're a damned fool."

"I'll kill *him*." The gun turned upon Matthew, just as Matthew knew it would.

Rain was pounding Leviathan's head and beginning to drip down between the stones. The next searing white flash of lightning and soul-jarring blast of thunder sounded close enough to have charred the boat and then shattered it to pieces.

"Speak it *again*," Mars said, the flintlock wavering ever so slightly in its aim upon the New York problem-solver who had never felt so far from home, Berry, and surviving the next few minutes. "This time, stand closer!" was Mars's next direction.

Fell obeyed. He spoke the incantation in exactly the same tone as before.

"Hear me, Asmoday.

Hear me, bornless spirit.

Hear me, whom the winds fear.

Hear me, and make your powers subject unto me.

I invoke thee.

I invoke the terrible and invisible god, who dwellest in the void place of the spirit.

I invoke thee.

Thee I invoke, thy true name Asmoday, mighty and bornless one.

Hear me, and make your powers subject unto me.

Thee I invoke."

Nothing happened. Matthew thought that either Asmoday was unimpressed with this attempt, or like the other demons of Hell the creature refused to leave its ruminations on how to conquer the realm of Heaven while reclining on a bed of lava in its chamber of ten thousand furnaces.

Nothing.

"It's not real," the professor said. He gave a short sharp laugh. "It *never* was real!"

"It is!" Mars shouted. "Speak it again! You're going to—"

"*Oh.*"

The sound—a muffled breath—had come from the throat of Matthew Corbett.

The lantern light was being sucked into the darkness of the mirror in a way that could not be explained nor even completely described, but Matthew had seen something move on the mirror's surface…or imagined he had. If the mirror was a swamp pool, an unseen thing had just barely caused the surface to tremble, as if a creature of large size was swimming underneath.

"It moved!" Mars came forward. "It moved, I saw it move!"

"No, it didn't!" Matthew protested. "There was nothing!"

But he knew he was lying, both to Mars and to himself.

"Speak it again!" Mars commanded. "Go on, speak it again!"

Professor Fell shook his head, because a disturbance on the surface of the mirror was like a swirl of oil and dirty water.

When he spoke, his voice was hushed as if he were witnessing the presentation of the most bizarre and fascinating organism ever to be revealed to a lowly marine biologist.

He said, "There's no need."

Was Matthew going mad, or did he see a shape forming in the miasma? Did the surface bulge as if something horribly powerful was about to burst free?

He could take no more of this. "Professor!" he shouted. "Break it!"

Fell just stared at the mirror, and Matthew realized with new horror that the man—the once-scientist who had dared to set a dream upon the Satanic—was wholly and completely transfixed.

"Break it!" Matthew shouted again, more urgently. "Professor! *Please!*"

The mirror's surface writhed like a nest of snakes. Whatever was coming out, it was going to be unstoppable unless—

"Oh my God," Fell suddenly said.

He reached into his pocket for the crucifix and in one continuous motion struck its shaft upon the surface. There was the sound of metal hitting glass, but the mirror did not break.

Fell quickly hit it second time, and as he reared his arm back to deliver a third blow, Mars Scaramanga cried out, "No!" and fired a shot that spun the professor around and sent the crucifix skidding across the stones past Matthew. Fell clutched at his side and collapsed to his knees; his face turned a sickly gray.

At once Matthew had dropped the lantern and was reaching for the crucifix. As he got hold of it Scaramanga was on top of him. The pistol's hot barrel hit him on the side of the head, stunning him. Another blow came down, striking his shoulder. Matthew hung onto the man's legs, trying to upend him. A third strike with the pistol caught Matthew across the back of the neck. And in this battle with the tumult of wind and rain sweeping in there was suddenly a sharp cracking noise and through a red-hazed vision Matthew saw the black glass veined with cracks, the fissures streaking across its surface in rapid succession. Scaramanga gave an anguished cry and, looking down at Matthew, lifted the pistol to smash the other's skull.

The crack-riddled mirror hit Mars Scaramanga. Behind it was Professor Danton Idris Fell, who propelled himself forward with the mirror as he had the table in Valeriani's kitchen: both as shield and battering ram. As the pair staggered across the stones toward Leviathan's aperture

Matthew had an instant to see a sight he would remember for the rest of his life and try mightily to forget.

From a dark slice of the mirror yet unbroken a claw the color of the swamp primeval came out and tore Scaramanga's face off before it withdrew in one beat of an evil heart. The muscles on the exposed skull jittered and twitched, the eyes bulging from crimson blood-cups...and then Scaramanga, the mirror and Professor Fell went over the edge.

The wind...shrieking. The sound of waves...crashing against rocks. That was all.

For a long time Matthew sat on the floor. His consciousness faded out and in again. He realized he had his arms around himself, and he was rocking back and forth as if he was one waking nightmare away from Bedlam.

"I'm all right," he heard himself say. Only the shrill of the wind replied. "I'm all right," he repeated, but it was a horrible moment because he wanted to laugh and cry together and he feared to do either, that he might never again stop.

"I'm all right," he said a third time.

And this time he knew he was.

How long was it before he crawled to the aperture and looked down? He would never know.

In the early gray light the storm was still raging. White-foamed waves streaked with green were crashing against the island's monstrous rocks seventy feet below. Of Scaramanga, the professor and the mirror there was no sign.

Dashed upon the rocks, the broken bodies swept away along with the broken mirror?

Likely so. He doubted anyone could survive that fall. Instant drowning would make certain of it.

He lay on his stomach looking over for a long time. His head, shoulder and back of the neck were a trio of throbbing pain.

Scaramanga, gone. The mirror, gone.

The professor, gone.

It seemed fitting to Matthew that the man who had wished to become a scholar of the sea's mysteries now had joined them.

He turned over on his back—another exercise in pain—and lying there staring up at the ceiling of Leviathan's dome he once more lost consciousness and drifted into what was thankfully a dreamless sleep.

When he awakened the light had changed to a paler gray and the wind and rain had lessened. Looking out upon the water he saw also that the waves though still whitecapped had settled down from their previous fury. The sun was a brighter spot in the gray and Matthew judged the time to be around eight.

Had he seen what he thought he'd seen or had it been a consequence of the blow to the head Scaramanga had given him? He felt the lump and touching it hurt like hell. He saw no trace on the stones of a bloody rag that would've been the remnant of a human face; there *were* streaks and splotches of blood, but Matthew reasoned they had issued from the professor's wounded side.

He crawled to the edge and peered out again, squinting in the stronger light. There was no trace either of the bodies, nor of the mirror. Silver shimmered on the waves, as the sun was trying to burn a hole through the clouds.

After a time in which he fought off another loss of consciousness, he crawled to where *The Lesser Key of Solomon* lay on the floor next to the chalk-drawn seal. It was of course a rare book, but there were probably many other copies in the world. What use was there to destroy this one?

But destroy it he did, by picking it up, getting laboriously to his feet and tearing out every page one-by-one. He let them fall to join the other victims. It took a while. When the pages were gone, he tore the dark brown, cracked binding in two and let those pieces drop as well.

Then the book of demons—at least this particular accursed copy—was gone.

He had dropped and broken the lantern and the oil had spilled out, the flame long extinguished. Though it was morning, darkness yet clung to Leviathan's staircase and he was going to have to make it down without a misstep sending him to his death. He gave himself some more time to gather his fortitude. Before he started the descent he rubbed the seal out with the toe of his boot, and then that too was gone. The last thing: he took the small crucifix with him.

He made his way carefully down the stairs, one at a time and his foot probing for the next. At last he reached the bottom without mishap and walking out into the warm, wet humidity and a lightly falling rain he saw that the boat was gone, likely wrenched from the rocks by the angry sea. In fact, he could make out the mainmast and sail floating maybe a hundred yards to the north.

A quarter of a mile to shore. Could he wait for a fisherman to hear his cries?

Matthew started working at the remaining hinge on Leviathan's old door. It was stubborn, but working steadily and with purpose he broke the hinge loose. Then with an effort born of necessity he lugged the door down past the rocks on the northern side of the island, waded into the water, put the door before him, climbed on top of it as best he could and began kicking toward the beach.

He abandoned the makeshift raft when he tested the depth for the fourth time and found rocks underfoot. Then he trudged up through the waves, past the other boats that were still moored there, stopped to empty the water from his boots, and walked through the village. Up on the road he could see the black lacquered coach and the horse team where it had been left. Pagani and Bracca were nowhere in sight.

Matthew dug into a pocket, felt the pouch of Meneghetti's gold coins and also the black key, which had remained in his possession after the chaos at the estate. In the other pocket he felt the crucifix, also a Leviathan survivor.

Hudson and Camilla. He was going to have to go back for them. Was it crazed? Yes, but it had to be done. He wasn't in fit fiddle to drive a team and the trip back would take all the daylight hours. He could sit down on the beach and wait until he felt nearly alive again, everything alert and his brain working properly, but he had to use what resources he could. If he passed out on the road, so be it. There was no other choice.

As he climbed up into the driver's seat and took the reins he could see from this slightly higher elevation over the village roofs to the bay. Moving sunlight shimmered silver on the water again, and Matthew could clearly make out the head and shoulders of Leviathan. It might stand for several more centuries, and no one who passed here would ever know what had happened up in that round dome. He hardly knew what had happened himself.

Professor Fell, gone to find his son...somewhere.

Mars Scaramanga, gone to find his sister...also somewhere, but Matthew was sure it would not be a place of beauty. If one really believed in the underworld, the Scaramangas would have century after century to discuss the vagaries of torture with the demonic kings, earls, counts and dukes. He was sure there would be ample opportunities for demonstration.

And the mirror?

Broken to pieces, the pieces now appearing simply as plain bits of glass from any regular mirror? If it had survived the rocks and later floated to shore or wound up in a fisherman's net, the backing Valeriani had designed to frame the item Senna Salastre created with unknown spells and sorceries might be used to hold a real mirror...this one gifted from a fisherman to his wife or daughter. This time a mirror to give human pleasure, not the inhuman kind.

Or bits of the frame might end up simply as firewood. Who could say?

As for the fragments of enchanted glass?

Unless the crabs, eels, shrimp, and—in Matthew's opinion—odious sardines could weave spells and recite aquatic incantations...the world was safe from any further incursion by denizens of the greater, darker deep.

At least, not from any mirror.

"Giddap," Matthew said, and though the team of the Scaramangas' best and strongest horses might not understand English they understood and obeyed the firm command of a young man on a mission.

TWENTY-EIGHT

IN THE BLUE TWILIGHT, MATTHEW HELD UP THE BLACK KEY.

Today there was only one man at the gate, and Matthew did not recognize him. The husky gent was armed with the usual pistol and sheathed sword.

A question was asked. Matthew didn't know what it was, but he said, "English for Edetta."

The man appeared puzzled about this and stood rubbing his bearded chin as he regarded the fine lacquered coach behind Matthew. Then he unlocked the gate and Matthew entered. The guard searched him for weapons, and the pouch and crucifix were found and returned.

He noted that no one shadowed him from the gate to the villa. On the front steps sat another bodyguard cleaning the barrel of his flintlock pistol, but the man hardly looked up at the visitor as Matthew approached. Matthew realized that there was definitely a sea change here, and his feeling was intensified when he started to use the door knocker and found the door about six inches ajar.

He entered the house, yet treading carefully and cautious of any movement to right or left in the rooms through which he passed. He saw no one.

Until he reached the sumptuous parlor toward the rear, where Edetta in a long lilac-hued caftan sat on the sofa before what Matthew considered an ugly, dark brown, square slab of a table. She was pouring herself a glass of white wine from a bottle that was already less than half full. As she noted his presence she raised the glass toward him and then had a sip.

When the wine had gone down she asked, "Is the master dead?"

"Yes."

"Did you kill him?"

"No."

"And Bracca and Pagani? Where are they?"

"I have no idea."

She took another small swallow. "You came back in the master's coach?"

"I did," Matthew said. "I want to take my friends out of here."

The white-haired, grandmotherly housekeeper showed a crooked smile. "They're gone. I'm told the big man killed Lupo. I never thought that was possible. You know, I never saw his face. They told me he was almost handsome."

Matthew was still fixed on the word *gone*. "You don't know where they are?"

"You don't know where Bracca and Pagani are, I don't know where the big man and the woman are." She closed one eye. "But know *this*…I do not really care."

"I can tell. What's happened around here?"

"Don't you understand? The mistress is dead, Lupo is dead, the master rode off in his coach in a frenzy and no one knew where he was going… now you say he's dead and you have the coach so it must be true. When the others hear that…well…they'll understand there's no one left to *guard*. Like myself. There's no one left for me to keep the house for. All this fine house. What will become of it?"

"Did you have a feeling that Mars was already dead?"

"He rarely leaves the estate. And only then for his gatherings with the others, which I understand—though I'm not supposed to—are held in an old monastery not far from here. The master never *ever* stays gone for more than a few hours. Never. When at daybreak he wasn't back…then at noon…now almost at *l'ora di cena*—supper time—I knew he was never coming back. Chiara the cook knew it too. Oh…everyone knew, but no one wanted to say it. So now the bodyguards have no bodies to guard, I have no one to keep the house for and Chiara has no one to eat her fine cooking…except myself, and she and I are going to finish off the choice *prosciutto crudo* which has been aged between the thighs of sixteen-year-old virgins and blessed by the Pope." She filled her wineglass again. "Not really, but it's very good."

Matthew was near exhaustion. He sank down in one of the chairs across the table from her and just remained staring at nothing.

Edetta said, "I saw and heard many things in this house. They tell me the worst was done down in that place where they took your friends. It was the sister's pleasure place. Yes, it's true." She nodded and drank again. "I knew the master was going to die, because he couldn't go on without his sister. It was a matter of time. A story to be written. A happy ending? For me, perhaps. I know where the master hid a great deal of money. I wasn't supposed to know, but no one hides things from a good housekeeper. So tonight Chiara is going to make supper for us and then I will give her some of the money. After that, I go to Rome to visit my daughter and her family. They think I housekeep for a noted physician. Then…I have always wanted a villa with a view of the sea. I will find a little town and I will find that villa and I will find that sea." She lifted the glass once more toward Matthew. "My happy ending," she said.

He roused himself from his lethargy. "The family. I don't mean yours, I mean the Family. What will happen?"

"Without a Scaramanga in charge, they'll fight each other. More things I'm not supposed to know, the old housekeeper who just creeps around dusting things and cleaning up messes. Well, there's a big mess coming. I think they'll fight each other into their graves."

"A pity," Matthew said.

At that instant a torrent of angry Italian hit him like a barrage of bricks. Twisting around, he saw that Lorenzo had entered the room and was stalking toward him. The bald bodyguard had a pistol holstered at his side, but he drew his knife and came on with his bruised and swollen face contorted by rage. The knife rose for a killing strike.

"No, Lorenzo," the old woman said, as easily as if speaking to a child displaying a bad temper tantrum. *"Lascia in pace il giovane."*

Leave the young man alone, was what Lorenzo heard. He answered in Italian: "Are you out of your mind? This bastard should die!"

"Settle yourself. The master is dead. He says he didn't kill him, and I believe it." She motioned for him to put the knife down. "It's over. Go to the kitchen and get yourself a bottle of wine."

"The master…*dead?*"

"Do not pretend you didn't already know he wasn't coming back. Everyone knows something happened to him. Well, he's dead. The story of a life begins and the story of a life ends. It's the way of things."

"I'll have my revenge on this son of a bitch!"

"No, you won't. There's no revenge to be had, so don't make a fool of yourself. The young man came to find his friends and I think he's half-mad himself, but it's admirable. Go on, get some wine and enjoy the peace and quiet instead of making such noise!"

"But…I—"

"*Go,*" she said more severely. "And if there are any furnishings you and the others want to fight over, you'd best get started."

Lorenzo paused. The knife came down. Matthew had understood none of this, but he saw only confusion on the face that Hudson had evidently done his damnedest to rearrange.

"What are we to *do?*" Lorenzo was nearly pleading for guidance.

"Live," she answered, and she put her feet up on the ugly square slab of a table. Matthew saw she was wearing pink silk slippers. "Go on, do what I'm telling you."

Lorenzo slowly put the knife back in its sheath. As if grudgingly accepting a scolding, he turned away and left the room without a backward glance.

"Thank you," Matthew said, understanding not the words but the actions and intent.

"What point is there in further bloodshed? None. As I told Lorenzo, it's over."

Matthew thought that if he continued to sit in this very comfortable chair he would then want to share supper with these people and wish to sleep tonight in one of their triple-wide beds. He stood up. "I have to find my friends, wherever they are."

"Understandable. I will inform you that I am also told the big man took Lupo's mask, cloak and gloves and walked out the front gate with the woman. He also killed Bertanza. The bodies weren't discovered until well after midnight. May I ask if the master met his death at the lighthouse? The one at Chioggia he was asking about?"

"He did."

"Leviathan," Edetta said. "What was there, he was so anxious to find?"

"He found it," was Matthew's answer.

She finished her glass of wine and poured in the last of the bottle. "You should go. Take the coach with my blessing. Just say my name if anyone objects, I'm everyone's *nonna* around here."

"Thanks again." Before departing the room he offered, "I hope you find your town, your villa and your sea."

She lifted her glass in a final toast. "Count on it," she said.

Matthew left the house and walked toward the gate. Night was coming on and the stars were beginning to shine. He was almost at the gate when he heard the noise of footsteps coming up fast behind him. A shrill alarm went off in his brain. He whirled around, his heart pounding, and saw Lorenzo taking aim at his head and cocking his pistol.

Lorenzo squeezed the trigger at a distance of less than five feet. There was no time for Matthew to save himself.

The hammer clicked home.

Nothing happened.

There was no resulting blast of powder and bullet.

Matthew realized the gun was not loaded.

Lorenzo gave an evil grin. He had a glass of wine in his other hand. In a harsh but not entirely inimical voice he said, *"Sii fortunato,"* after which he motioned for the lone man standing at the guardhouse to open the gate. Matthew went through and climbed up into the driver's seat of the Scaramangas' luxurious black coach. He shifted a bit to avoid the damp area that had suddenly spread at his crotch, urged the weary horses to make one more trip before they were fed, watered and tended to at a stable in Venice, and then he got the hell out of there.

On the road to the ferry at Mestre he twice nodded off to sleep. Both times he thought he was awakened by a nudge on the shoulder, but when he looked to the right to snap at Professor Fell next to him on the driver's seat he was alone. It was suddenly a very strange thing, not having Fell somewhere in his life, either as adversary or ally. He preferred the role of ally, but the price of it had been very high indeed.

Above, the stars had emerged in their dazzling glory. Matthew was elated to know that Hudson and Camilla had gotten out of the torture chamber and out of the house. If Hudson had killed the wolfman and a second bodyguard he must've not been too gravely subjected to Venus's toys, because he would've needed all his old strength and more to win a battle with that monster.

He knew what the *more* was in that thought. Her name was Camilla and she was Spanish. A witch-hunter? In title only, and that thrust upon her by dint of her family's reputation.

And here was a decision to be made. Camilla had undertaken this mission not only by order of the government, but to search for some answer to her question of the nature of evil: was it true that in this world demonic influence held sway, and her father Sebastian had recognized such in those he determined were witches and warlocks, or had Sebastian simply murdered those souls in need of his own justifications? She had wished, as she'd put it, to gaze into Hell…to find out if such a realm existed. Matthew thought she could talk a good game, as in her discussion of Satan tempting Jesus in the Bible, but in reality she herself was not wholly convinced.

He had the idea that Hudson and Camilla may have struck out from the Scaramangas' villa to their ship in the Venice harbor. It would be a ten or twelve mile walk to the ferry unless they'd managed to find a ride, and how they would get across without money was a problem but Hudson could figure things out. If they'd left the villa before midnight last night, and here it was approaching eight o'clock…where might they be?

Matthew was thinking in a circle, and the circle led back to what he was going to tell Camilla about the mirror. The whole event in Leviathan's head now seemed to him like a particularly bad dream. Witches? Ghosts? Demons? Rachel Howarth had been no witch. The "ghosts" that continually fought over coffee beans at Number Seven Stone Street might be attributed to the building itself settling, crunching and cracking as it did so.

But then again…there was the incident of the rich man who'd hired him in New York to delay a visit from what the man believed would be Death itself before he could make amends with his estranged daughter, and how—still shocking to Matthew—the daughter had turned out to be Death, herself having perished on the road to her father's house.

And…there was the night ride.

Matthew had tried his best to keep that at bay, but it was unexplainable. Two tribes of unearthly creatures locked in a perpetual war with Matthew cast into the middle and very nearly becoming—dare he ponder it—food for both?

Could he accept that he actually saw something come out of that mirror, and still consider himself a man of logical intellect? He'd wanted to tell himself that the blow from Scaramanga's gun had joggled his senses so much that what he thought he'd seen was all in his bruised head…and yet…

What should he tell Camilla?

He almost missed getting on the ferry, which was just throwing off its ropes at the pier. Going for a coin in the pouch—an exorbitant fee for a ferry crossing, but it secured his late place on the barge—he discovered the black key in his pocket. His was the last vehicle on, joining a horseback rider, a small carriage and a hay wagon. The ferry set off across a smooth bay toward the golden glow of Venice, and Matthew got down off the driver's seat both to stretch his legs and for another purpose. He walked to the starboard rail and without hesitation tossed the black key into the drink.

And that was that.

On his way back to the coach he passed the hay wagon and immediately stopped, because by the illumination of a lantern on one of the barge's lightpoles he made out two figures lying together, obviously asleep in the hay.

His heart leapt. He balled up his fist and knocked on the wagon's side, causing the old straw-hatted farmer up on the seat to turn around and fire some Italian lingo at him. Matthew ignored this objection and knocked again, harder.

Hudson opened a pair of bleary, bloodshot eyes and sat up with hay in his hair. He said, "What the *hell?*"

"Indeed," Matthew replied, with a great effort to keep his voice free from the overwhelming joy that soared his spirit. "You meet the strangest people on ferry boats."

"Matthew!" Hudson had shouted it, which caused Camilla to instantly sit up, wide-eyed and equally hay-haired. "Good God, boy! What happened to you?" Hudson looked past his friend. "Where's the professor?"

"What happened is a long story, and Professor Fell is no longer on this side of life. But I understand you had an interesting event with Lupo. How were you able to—oh, you're hurt!" He had seen that Hudson's left arm was splinted and wrapped with gauze down to the fingers to hold the support.

"Lupo," Hudson said. "And how did you know about that?"

"I had a conversation with the housekeeper."

"What?"

"We saw you and the professor leave in the coach," Camilla said.

"Yes, and there's the coach right over there." Hudson had just noted it, and he motioned with his good arm. "My God, Matthew! How did you get away?"

"And what happened to the Scaramangas?" was Camilla's next question.

Matthew said, "Since we'll be docking soon, I propose to buy us a proper meal and plenty to drink. In my case, *strong* drink. We should also buy some fresh new clothes, because I can tell you that mine smell to high heaven. Money is no object, courtesy of Ottavio Meneghetti."

"What?" Hudson asked again, obviously brain-blasted by all this.

"Meneghetti's dead. The professor killed him. To your question about the Scaramangas, I'll leave that to be discussed over a tavern's table. I want to know also how you two got here from the villa." A thought struck him, his curiosity once more at work. "Camilla...what does 'see fortunato' mean? Something to do with being fortunate?"

"A little more than that," she said. "It means 'Stay lucky'."

"Ah." Matthew nodded. It might not have been meant as a blessing from a criminal's bodyguard, but it was something to have inscribed on the wall at Number Seven Stone Street when he got back to New York. To a new life. To Berry. To...the future, which seemed now to him like a path of shining light.

He had to turn away from Hudson and Camilla for a minute because very suddenly he was weak in the knees and there were tears in his eyes.

Then came the question that he knew would be presented, sooner or later.

Camilla asked, "What of the mirror?"

TWENTY-NINE

MATTHEW SAID, "BY THAT WORD, WHAT ARCHANGELO HAD SAID, AND what Valeriani was *about* to say, I believed the mirror was hidden in the lighthouse." He paused to take another drink from his cup of excellent and strong apple cider. "So…after what happened to Venus, Mars demanded we take him there. To say the least, he was disturbed by her death and he believed the mirror could bring her back." Matthew shrugged. "It didn't work out that way."

"You're leaving out so much I want to pitch you into that fireplace," said Hudson. Not far from their table, a small and polite fire burned in a gray stone hearth decorated with carved lion's heads. They sat over dishes of roast beef, slices of ham, green beans, fried potatoes and creamed corn—a royal feast—in a tavern named *I Cantori Gioiosi,* translated by Camilla as The Joyful Singers. "You say both Scaramanga and the professor died at this lighthouse. How?" Hudson prodded. "And did you find the mirror or not?"

Matthew glanced quickly at Camilla, who sitting to the right of Hudson bore an expression of breathless anticipation.

"It was found," Matthew answered.

"And?"

Matthew addressed Camilla. "You were interested—if that's the correct word—in the nature of evil. What I understood you to be asking was: is there a realm apart from this earthly plain that influences humans to perform acts that *we* might consider evil, but would be considered by the participants to be…well, I suppose simply part of life. An *entertainment,* perhaps. I think you were asking if Hell exists. Yes?"

She nodded.

"And you wanted to know this, because you thought your father believed in the Devil's Hell, in witchcraft and sorcery, and that his rigid—and I assume righteous—belief drove him and his followers to the destruction of the Basque village you mentioned. So…if you could get a glimpse of Hell yourself, you would not hold Sebastian in such disgrace and shame as you've carried since you were old enough to understand. Is that correct?"

"It is."

"You have to know," Matthew continued, "that the nature of evil has been debated from the days of antiquity. It will be debated into the hundreds of years ahead, and there will never be a clear and certain answer to why humans—*us*—do such things. Is there a Satanic influence on the behavior and deeds of men? No one can say…and no one will ever be able to say…at least not on *this* side. It's been pointed out to you that even though your government calls you a 'witch-hunter', you're not that. You're not your father, nor do you have his motives. I would call you a 'truth-hunter'. From here, I think it's the finding of your own truth in life that matters the most."

Hudson had put his good arm around Camilla. His three cups of ale had put ruddy color in his cheeks. He said, "A fine speech, Junior Shakespeare. Did something come out of the mirror, or not?"

Matthew said, "It—"

"Stop," Camilla interrupted. She took a drink from her own cup of cider and for a moment she watched the small fire burn. "When I came to Alghero," she said softly, "I needed to know exactly what you've set forth. Would having visual, real evidence of Hell excuse my father for what was perhaps the execution of many innocents? Maybe there were some in that village who did serve Satanic forces, and my father wound up unknowingly being a part in their plan. Now…I don't need to excuse him. I need to *accept* him…who he was, what he did…the good and the bad…and I don't need evidence of Hell to do that. Can you understand?"

"I can," said Matthew, and he mused that by the hard-won release of a soul's personal torment, the singers in this tavern might well be angelic.

Hudson said, "All right, but what about Scaramanga and the professor? Both dead? Where's the mirror now? And what about the book?"

"Both dead. I would tell you that the professor saved my life…believe that, or not. As for the mirror…broken by *this*." He brought the small iron crucifix out of his pocket and set it on the table. "Then it went over the side onto the rocks and gone, along with the professor and Scaramanga. I took a little devilish delight in tearing the book apart and casting that to the waves as well."

"*Damn,*" was all Hudson could say to this. He'd already told Matthew their story, of how they'd walked for several miles away from the villa and thirsting for water had stopped at a farmhouse for a drink. The elderly man and woman there had gladly given them water and some chicken soup, allowed them to spend the night in their barn, and the next morning took them by horsecart to a Dr. Rovigo's house in Mirano where Hudson's broken arm was tended to. An exchange of a basket of fresh corncobs was made for the doctor's help, to which Hudson and Camilla were mightily grateful—as the two lovers travelling in Italy for both pleasure and business had been attacked by a band of a half dozen rowdies the night before, their money and carriage taken and their clothing dirtied in the ordeal, and both the farmer and the doctor considered it an absolute insult to the hospitality of Italy that such things could happen to foreign visitors.

"And what is your business, sir?" the doctor had inquired, speaking through Camilla and regarding the big, bruised man over the wire rims of his spectacles.

When Hudson's wits had faltered, Camilla had spoken up: "In England he's a professional fighter. A boxer, you see. We are here arranging to be part of an international match scheduled for Venice next spring."

"Oh ho!" said the doctor. "I would think your arm should be well healed before then, a large healthy specimen such as yourself. I shall plan to attend it! What is your professional fighting name, sir?"

From here on out—if he had his way—it would be what he told Rovigo: "The Peacemaker."

"Oh ho! I suppose when you give your opponent a slam down to the floor, you've made your peace, is that right?"

"Exactly."

"Lord save me from such a peace as in those fists!"

And so it went.

The Peacemaker and his lady were taken by Rovigo to a Mirano tavern and introduced to a throng of citizens there who became very excited and animated over this upcoming professional fighting match. This was the land of the gladiator, after all. Hudson's right bicep and fist had never been touched as much in his life. There was talk of bringing the mayor over for a glass of *vino* with these honored guests but fortunately for Hudson and Camilla the mayor was on business somewhere else and could not be located. Still, they were the feted honorees all day long and it went longer when some of the locals wished to hear about life in England.

Going back to Mestre, and the ferry to Venice? Oh, Peacemaker, our Sergio Bonacottacatero comes through with his haywagon every day in the cool of the evening, bound for such a ferry! We shall stand in the street to hail him and you and your lady shall ride with Sergio!

To be honest, both Hudson and Camilla had hated to leave the place.

"There's something else we need to discuss," Matthew ventured, after he'd taken another bite of the delicious roast beef. No dried sardines here, thank the fates! "What are we going to tell Santiago and de Castro?"

"Hm," was Hudson's response.

"We'll have to explain about Andrado and the soldiers," Camilla said.

"That's simple," Hudson replied. "We rode into a war. Andrado and the others were killed. My arm was broken when one of the Dutch soldiers hit me with a musket stock, and Black and the professor were killed in the same action…if you're sure Fell's dead."

"Shot, broken on the rocks in a seventy-foot fall, and drowned," Matthew said. "I believe his time has ended, and the strange thing is…I think I'm going to miss him. At least the man he had become, and that was for the better."

"I suppose every hero needs a formidable adversary. Don't fret, there are always more where he came from."

Matthew didn't respond to the comment. *Hero?* he thought. No…*survivor.* And he would wait to tell Hudson that he was pondering leaving the Herrald Agency after he and Berry were married. Would it be fair to her to go off on such dangerous jaunts as he'd experienced? He moved to another issue. "What about Valeriani and the mirror?"

It was Camilla who firmly said, "We found neither."

"They'll likely send someone else to search," was Hudson's next statement.

From Matthew came a shrug and: "Will it matter?"

"We'll probably be questioned individually." The Peacemaker speared a piece of ham on his fork. "We don't want anything to smell fishy."

Matthew nodded. He realized he himself smelled rather fishy from his trip back across the bay from Leviathan. They had left some baggage aboard the *Estrella*, but it would do to find a clothing shop and buy clean and fresh raiments. Thus their feast progressed, Matthew paid for the meal, and they set out to find a shop that had not yet closed for the evening.

Had a ship moored in a harbor ever looked so beautiful? None of the trio doubted such as they abandoned the Scaramangas' coach shy of the slips and approached the *Estrella* with packages in hand two hours after leaving the tavern. In truth, Matthew longed for sleep in even an uncomfortable belowdecks hammock but dreaded it too, because of what his nightmares might dredge up. He stayed awake in the hammock by lamplight far too long, even though Hudson was sleeping like a peacemaker who'd made his own peace not far away, and when he finally drifted to sleep he left the lamp burning.

His mind did present him with disturbing images of creatures beyond imagination and description churning within the dark glass like sickening ingredients in an unholy stew, but when he awakened and realized he was in the *Estrella*'s embrace he thought with immense gratitude, *I am safe.* And: *I have survived.*

His next thought, even more comforting, was: *Tomorrow morning when this ship leaves the harbor, every nautical mile will take me closer to Alghero. And after Alghero, a return to Italy by Spanish vessel, and then by Italian ship…to Berry.*

Every nautical mile, closer.

A final thought came before giving himself up to Somnus: *Stay lucky.*

He intended it.

He slept, and this time in the quiet sounds of a ship resting at harbor his only dream was of his bride-to-be, and the joy of crossing that great Atlantic from England to the port of New York.

Every nautical mile, closer.

Ten mornings and one thousand two hundred and sixty-one nautical miles after the *Estrella* cast off lines from Venice, Alghero's harbor bell began to toll as the ship was sighted coming in. It was a clear, sunny day with a hot blue sky, and up at the mainmast proudly flew the Spanish colors. On deck, Matthew, Hudson and Camilla stood watching the approach, which would be completed when the pilot boats rowed out to tow the *Estrella* to her berth.

Matthew hadn't bothered to shave during this journey, but he noted that Hudson had used a razor and kept himself clean every morning. Hudson had been taking long walks around the deck with Camilla at dusk and in the moonlight, either with his arm around her or holding her hand. It was clear the big gent was smitten by her, and she with him. One could simply tell by the way they looked at each other…also by the fact that Hudson had not slept in his hammock for several nights, and since Camilla had her own quarters…no one needed a problem-solver to solve what was obviously no problem for those two.

But all the good for it, Matthew thought as he watched them standing so close together they seemed already joined. He considered that Camilla had brought Hudson back from nearly the dead. And on this sea voyage Matthew noted that Hudson had brought Camilla back from her own torments, because he made her smile and laugh. He made those stunning green eyes sparkle. It was a wondrous thing to see, those two people who had only recently been so damaged now finding relief, respite and—yes— joy in each other.

The *Estrella* was towed in and the lines made fast. Matthew saw waiting at the pier Santiago's personal red coach with its elaborate gilt trimming and teamed by a pair of quite beautiful white horses, as the ship must've been recognized by the governor's ever-observant spyglass. Henri del Costa Santiago stood by the coach dressed in his indigo tunic and red sash adorned with the preponderance of shining medals. His shoulder-length curls of black hair were topped by an outlandishly large red tricorn decorated with a red and yellow cockade. Santiago appeared to be waiting patiently for the gangplank to be dropped, but then again his hands were on his hips and the toe of one of his boots was rapidly tapping the timbers.

The *Estrella*'s captain went across first, bowing to Santigo, speaking a few words and then returning to the ship to oversee some captainly duty or another. Matthew crossed the plank next followed by Hudson and then Camilla.

"I thank the stars you've returned safely!" Santiago said when all three were on Alghero earth. "But...where are the others? Andrado and his men?"

"Dead," Hudson answered. "The professor and Black too." He motioned to his splinted arm. "I almost paid with my life as well. You did realize we were going into an area of war."

"Yes, of course, but...well, you'll have to tell me the details later. For the moment, I am anxious to know if aboard the ship is a certain item we were expecting?"

"It is *not*," said Matthew. "We couldn't find it. Not that, nor Valeriani."

Santiago's mouth hung open. "*What?* All that way and all that expense, for nothing? I thought you said you knew where to search!"

"I did. But Valeriani was not a worker at a vineyard as I had anticipated. I have to say I was wrong about the whole thing."

"You English!" Santiago sneered. "Braggarts and impostors! *Señorita* Espaziel, make some sense of this for me!"

"Matthew is correct. We searched but we did not find. In my opinion, if there really is a mirror at all...the stories about it are fantasy. We found no evidence that anyone in the region we searched knew this man or had ever heard anything about such a mirror. It was simply a...as the English would say...wild crow chase."

"Goose," Hudson supplied.

"Wild goose chase," she amended to Santiago, who seemed to sputter without moving his lips.

"I can't believe this!" The governor plucked a blue handkerchief from inside his tunic, took off his immense tricorn and mopped the rising sweat from his forehead. "No result? *Nothing?* What am I to tell de Castro? And the authorities in the homeland? I say to you, *señorita*, that people in high places will be very disappointed in your failure to—"

"Just a minute." Hudson stepped forward, and Santiago—hardly recognizing the solid, sun-browned specimen who confronted him—stepped back, no matter that the brute only had one working arm. Matthew noted the coach's uniformed driver putting a hand on his sword. "Don't threaten her or anyone else. We did the job we were tasked. Andrado, his men, Professor Fell and Black died doing it, so get off your high horse."

"My high horse?" Santiago frowned, puzzled. "My horses are not so high."

"I'm saying, Camilla did what she was sent to do…participate in a search. She did her best. We all did, but it's over. There's no Valeriani, and we don't think there ever was a supposedly enchanted mirror."

Santiago's expression was cold. He held a hand out and snapped his fingers. "The book, *señorita!* I wish the book!"

Matthew quickly spoke up. "The book's gone."

"What? Zounds! *How?*"

Hudson pitched in, repeating what they'd rehearsed for this moment. "The Dutch found it when they ransacked our wagons. It was in a leather bag they took. Andrado was shot trying to get it back. He should be awarded a medal for his bravery, and it would be only fair if his wife was given some money to see her through."

"Yes, yes, yes!" Santiago waved an impatient hand. "And the other soldiers? They tried to fight too, didn't they?"

"They did. They were no match for cavalry swinging swords, and Black and the professor were killed the same way."

"Those Dutch monsters!" Santiago's eyes narrowed. "But how is it you *all* weren't murdered by the swine?"

Matthew said, "I would attribute that to staying lucky."

The governor gave a snort of derision. "Lucky is the English word meaning you fled for your lives and left my countrymen to die! Is that what happened, *señorita?*"

"Sir, these are honorable men but they are not soldiers of Spain. They performed the work you and the authorities in the homeland presented to them. There was no Valeriani and there was no mirror, and that is the end of it." Camilla's emphatic tone brought down the curtain of finality.

Santiago started to speak but seemed to think better of it. Nothing came out. He mopped his forehead again.

Matthew mused that it had been worth the couple of nights putting their stories together. Things might not completely dovetail, but how could the governor dispute what might have happened if there were no witnesses? Still, Matthew could tell that Santiago was both angered and a little suspicious, though he had no need to be. Why should they lie about anything…

though in actuality it had transpired that they were a very adept trio of fabricators, at least in this situation.

Whether it was wise at the moment or not, and perhaps it was because Santiago's attitude had gotten under his skin, Matthew said, "I hope you remember the agreement we made. Whether the mirror and Valeriani were found or not, I and every Englishman who wishes to leave this island will be given over to the Italians—with proper funding—to return to England. My part of that agreement has been completed. What say you?"

Santiago spent a moment looking at all three of them in turn as if trying to further judge the veracity of their remarks. Then he gazed with deadened eyes into Matthew's face, pursed his lips and said, "I have no memory of such an agreement."

THIRTY

ONE DAY AFTER THAT TREMENDOUS LIE AND INSULT TO HIS INTELLI-
gence, Matthew stood in what had been Professor Fell's chamber in the
prison. This morning when he'd gotten up from his cot he'd still been so
angry he'd thrown against the wall one of the finely painted clay cups afforded the Alghero guests by the ladies of the *Sociedad de Bienestar Madre de la
Misericordia*. If anything, Matthew's misery was acute. He left the broken
shards of the cup where they had scattered.

Damn the governor! he fumed. And speaking that lie with Camilla
standing right there! When Camilla had reminded the Spanish prig that
she'd been at the dining table and heard the agreement made, that donkey
had given a little smile under his pitiful mustache and said again he recalled
no such agreement and he was sure she had also not heard it.

Then he'd gotten in that fancy-ass coach of his, the driver had even
given a Spanish smirk, and he was off to gloat in his mansion.

But at least there would be no demonic mirror for the Spanish to play
with! One hope might be that his higher-ups in Spain would break Sir
Medals down to an infantry soldier and send him to fight in...say...the
worst place in the world, Prussia.

Damn the governor!

Why had he wandered here into the professor's quarters? He wasn't
sure. The place was as neatly organized as Fell had left it: the cot covered by
a spread in stripes of green and blue, the feather pillow encased in blue velvet, a chest of drawers, a small desk with a rattan chair before it and an easel
standing with a second rattan chair for the artist's comfort. On the easel was

the last work the professor was completing, a watercolor of a convoluted seashell being done in shades of sea greens, marine blues and browns.

Matthew sat down on the cot, which just by the touch he could tell was more comfortable than his own, due to the professor's advanced wealth in selling his artwork.

Would he ever get away from Alghero, off Sardinia, and someday back to New York? How long would Berry wait for him? How long *should* she wait? The answers to these eluded him; they were problems he could not solve, and thus he felt as helpless as at any point in his life.

Damn the governor.

It seemed to him that he was coming to the end of something. Everything he'd gone through—from his first experience at problem-solving with the late and sorely missed Magistrate Isaac Woodward in the fledgling town of Fount Royal to hear a witchcraft case, to his desire for revenge against the evil headmaster Eben Ausley, to the Queen of Bedlam and school for young criminals fronted by Simon Chapel and including the malignant Prussian swordsman Count Dahlgren, to the hunt for the cunning killer Tyranthus Slaughter and discovering Lyra Sutch's sausage specialty, to the task at Fell's Pendulum Island to uncover traitors and being set upon by the twin assassins Jack and Mack Thacker, to the River of Souls to catch a killer in the swamp and evade the eerie Soul Cryer, to England under the spell of Dahlgren and finding himself in Newgate Prison targeted by the golden-masked avenger Albion, to Samson Lash's mansion in partnership with the "bad man" Julian Devane to disrupt an auction attended by a host of murderers and find a corrupt doctor to free Berry and Hudson from a hideous mind-altering drug, to the strange, unearthly island of Golgotha where the memory was robbed and an unknown and unseen monster demanded human sacrifice as payment to prevent destruction by fire, to the lair of the deadly Scaramangas and the sorcerer's mirror in the lighthouse Leviathan—was now preface to where he sat in this chamber.

And it seemed to him also that he wasn't going anywhere anytime soon.

So many people came to mind, among them the robust and ribald Polly Blossom, the huge freed slave Zed who tried to swim home to Africa, the tormented Indian Walker In Two Worlds, the doomed mother and daughter Faith and Lark, the inventor and weapons genius Quisenhunt, the resolute and unstoppable young Tom Bond, Fancy the beautiful Indian also known as Pretty Girl Who Sits Alone, the brave Captain Jerrell Falco, the waspish Pandora Priskitt, the husky Magnus Muldoon who went from oafish lout to unforgettable hero, a girl named Quinn and the spirit of Daniel Tate, Rory Keen and the Black-Eyed Broodies, the enigmatic Lord Puffery, the soul-scarred Elizabeth Mulloy who wreaked terror in her identity of RakeHell Lizzie, Gideon Lancer the Sheriff of Whistler Green who'd turned a blind eye to a dead man's brain matter on the back of a coach, King Tabor the ruler of Golgotha who in truth wanted only the best for the lives of his subjects....

...and so many more, there in the pages of the book of his mind.

Coming to the end of something, he thought.

What? The end of hope, that he would ever see Berry again?

Damn the—

What is that? he wondered.

Over in the corner, amid a few pieces of artwork the professor had done and not yet sold or presented to anyone.

He had seen something that now caused him to stand, go to the corner and pick up a canvas about ten inches square.

It was a watercolor, of course. The professor's element. It was done in a myriad of soft greens and blues, and had in it as much of sky as of sea.

It was a painting of flying fish...a school of eight, rising up from a green-veined wave, shining in the sun, gliding toward a rocky Sardinian shore but destined to return to the home that had bred and sheltered them.

At the lower right corner was written in very small letters a name: *Danton.*

Looking at this art, it came to Matthew that if a fish had enough daring and strength to power itself into an uncertain world, and hopeful its endurance could take it back again where it truly thrived...then by God this puny human could find some of that for himself. It might take time but he would never give up the quest to return to Berry...never, even as he grew old and infirm and the young Matthew Corbett was no more.

Never.

He realized the picture had been signed not by the emperor of crime—ex or otherwise—but simply by the first name of a man of both art and science who had sought for a short time a life of peace. He took the picture out with him as a keepsake and an inspiration. Before he closed the door he said a silent final goodbye to the professor, who had become in the most unexpected way the best kind of friend...one who did not abandon.

He closed the door and went on.

When Matthew opened the door to his own quarters, the two uniformed Spanish soldiers who were sitting there—one in his single chair, one on his lumpy cot—immediately stood up.

"What is this?" he asked warily. They both wore rapiers at their sides.

One of them, the younger, surprised Matthew by saying in passable English, "You are wanted by the governor."

"What for?"

"Wanted by the governor," was repeated, the hook-nosed face all hard granite and no nonsense.

Matthew continued inside and leaned the picture against a wall. When he straightened up he put his hands on his hips in a gesture of defiance and said, "I don't wish to see the governor today."

If he expected the soldiers to bodily drag him from his chamber for some unknown offense, he was mistaken. The one who'd spoken shrugged and they started out the door.

"Wait," Matthew said, made curious by this reaction. Why had the soldiers come, if there was no pressing reason? "What does he want?"

The younger man said, "Chess."

So that was it. "You tell Santiago I have no desire to…" He hesitated. *"Play chess,"* he finished, in a quiet voice. His brain wheels were turning. "Very well, then. I'll go with you."

Perhaps today a fish might take flight?

He was escorted to the governor's coach, driven down the hill and through the sun-bleached town with its bustling morning activity. At the gated mansion he was again escorted—the soldiers on either side—up the staircase to Santiago's office, where the governor in a cream-colored suit with a darker yellow shirt and a rust-colored cravat sat behind his mile-long desk. Today he wore no hat, but he was smoking his clay pipe and the place was layered with blue smoke that wafted through the sunlight streaming from the large oval window.

As soon as he entered, Matthew said, "You want a game of chess? Certainly. But I want a condition."

Santiago wore an infuriatingly smug expression. "Condition away."

"One game. If you win, nothing changes. If I win, you keep that agreement you say you didn't make."

Did the man smack his lips? Maybe it was just getting a better grip on the pipe's bit.

"Do you agree to this?" Matthew asked.

"Let me think on this condition." He waved the soldiers out the door. "Thinking…thinking," he said. He puffed a gust of smoke that caught around Matthew's face and brought to him the aroma of burning leaves before it moved on. "All right. An excellent condition."

"Just a minute. I want you to write it out."

"Write out what?"

"Write out a document that states what I'm saying. I win this one game and you make good on the agreement you say you didn't make. I want you to sign it and put it in my hands."

"Oh, you don't trust me?"

Matthew did not have to force a laugh.

Santiago brought a piece of paper from a desk drawer. He dipped his quill in the silver inkpot. "You want it in Spanish or the dog's language?"

"I want it in good, solid, understandable English. Take your time." But so saying, Matthew held his hand out.

"*¡Misericordias arriba, Mateo!* Did you not use your chamberpot this morning? Are your insides aggrieved? I never saw you in such a state!"

"Just write it."

"I will offer two conditions to your condition. No time limit and I win in case of a stalemate. Is that agreeable?"

"Yes." He would like the stalemate win but it was probably no use and time-wasting to argue the point. In any case he had no leverage.

Santiago puffed more smoke and put the quill to its scratchy labor. After a few further dips in the ink, he brought out a wax seal and a red candle, which he put to flame with a silver tinderbox decorated with an engraving of a conquistador. Before he dripped red wax below his flowing and ridiculously ostentatious signature on the paper, he looked up quizzically and asked, "And what is my prize if *I* win? Please don't cling to the notion that having Englishmen in my jurisdiction is a pleasure to *me*. Look at yourself! Bearded like a beast, have not bathed since Jesus was a baby, and your manners are those of the primitive savage. If all Englishmen are like you, how can you not be at each other's throats day and night because of the revulsion? So what is my prize?"

Said grudgingly: "Name something."

"Hm...let me consider my own condition. Thinking...thinking...ah! Let us speak of chamberpots."

Matthew didn't like that direction of conversation, but he braced himself and said, "Go on."

"Exactly. I go *on* a chamberpot, which if I win this one game of chess you will clean every day for a period of—I'll be gracious—one month."

"That's disgusting!"

Santiago shrugged. "All conditions are not so tidy. Take it or go back to the prison, I'll have the coach brought around."

Matthew bit his lip. It would be a horror to have to perform that function. He recalled that the corrupt doctor Lazarus Firebaugh had made Julian Devane empty his chamberpot and had wound up nearly decapitated.

"While you're considering," said the governor as he placed the burning candle in a holder for later use and leaned back in his cowhide chair, "I will remind you that we've probably played thirty games. Somewhere in that number. How many do you recall winning?"

"More than a few."

"I'll remember for you: eleven. As I told you that day of your arrival and you learned to be the truth: I am a master at the game."

"Eleven wins isn't so terrible."

"I agree! Eleven wins against myself is very commendable, but nineteen or so losses not so very. I must say, though, that one reason I've appreciated your company is…you always go down fighting." He reached for the candle, dripped the wax and pressed the seal, after which he offered the paper to Matthew's hand. "Good, solid, understandable dog's language," he said.

Matthew read the agreement three times to make sure there were no holes in the loop. It set out everything he and the governor had settled on during the dinner at which Camilla had been a witness. He carefully folded the paper so as not to crack the seal and deposited it safely in a pocket.

Santiago stood up, blew smoke once more in the direction of Matthew's face, and with a dramatically sweeping gesture motioned toward the small table in the corner with two chairs facing each other over the now-familiar chessboard with black and white wooden pieces. Always Santiago chose the white so that he had the first move, but today he said, "I am feeling so generous today—and also so confident—that I shall allow you the white."

Matthew took his seat. Before Santiago sat down he rang a little bell on his desk and a female secretary came in—Jandra by name, Matthew knew. The governor asked for a bottle of Tempranillo to be opened and brought to the gaming table along with two cups.

"We wait," Santiago said before sitting down. When the wine came, the governor poured himself a glass and offered Matthew the same. The offer was politely refused, as Matthew had no intention of letting the strong Spanish-imported, garnet-hued wine take his head off whereas Santiago was accustomed to its kiss.

Thus with another blast of smoke delivered into Matthew's face from the wickedly used pipe, Santiago said, "Your first move…whenever you are ready."

Matthew began by moving his king's pawn ahead two squares. Without hesitation Santiago mirrored the move. The two pawns faced each other. Matthew brought out his king's knight, and again Santiago mirrored the move. A pawn advanced, and across the board another pawn entered the fray. In another few minutes Matthew took a pawn and Santiago returned the favor. Matthew was trying to take control of the board's center, but the governor created an effective block with a bishop and a knight. When Matthew captured a rook that had perhaps moved a few squares too recklessly—the governor's only fault being sometimes overly aggressive—Santiago took a sip of wine, sat back and studied the board for at least ten minutes.

So began perhaps the most challenging game of chess Matthew had ever played. Not only was the governor's skill far beyond Matthew's usual opponents at the Trot Then Gallop, the tobacco fumes served as both smoke screen upon the eyes and harsh assault upon the nostrils. Santiago slowed the game to a crawl, and when his queen vanquished Matthew's king's knight in what was an absolute blunder of a move on the young man's part, Matthew realized he'd best get his game in order or he was going to be elbow-deep in a chamberpot.

After the first hour of jousts, feints, near misses, attempted traps, squandered opportunities and chessboard assassinations neither side was closer to victory. Jandra peeked in, watched from the door for a while, and then quietly entered to observe the silent war. She was joined by the two soldiers who'd brought Matthew down from the prison, and soon after that two more men from the governor's office came in, one carrying official-looking papers that Santiago gave not a second's glance.

"I will have you in four moves," Santiago said, but it was wishful thinking because his aggression had led a bishop and his queen's knight into a trap Matthew had begun to set six moves before, and thus the knight went down, the bishop was yet threatened and Santiago's brash statement was meaningless.

Time was ally and enemy to both men. Santiago began spending ten to fifteen minutes deliberating each move as he relit his pipe and blew the fog of war across the battlefield. Through the haze Matthew could almost see the pieces fighting for their lives and the desires of their masters. When Matthew's queen's knight and queen's rook went down in the next few moves he felt the cold winds of defeat at the back of his neck while the hot winds of Santiago's pipe smoke throttled the front.

In the second hour of this battle of the Alghero titans, a rare blunder from Santiago put his queen in a precarious position. Two moves later, the lady of the black palace went down, and Matthew could nearly hear the governor give a mental curse.

But Matthew could not laugh too long, because Santiago's own maneuvering sent the problem-solver's queen to her doom, and the white king was being pushed into a corner by the governor's remaining bishop and rook.

Matthew was shocked when he pulled himself out of his concentration while Santiago huffed and puffed and deliberated how to blow Matthew's house down. He counted twelve onlookers in the room, some having brought in their own chairs. Matthew was aghast; was someone out there on the street selling tickets to this?

"Ah ha!" Santiago had nearly shouted it, to Matthew's fright. "Check!" And for the benefit of the audience: *"¡Comprobar!"*

Some actually dared to applaud, which infuriated Matthew, caused him to shovel more coals into the already fiercely burning furnace of his mind, he turned the check aside and two moves later said, "Check."

Woe to the warriors! Woe to the lords of battle! Back and forth still went the conflict, and in this exhausting fray Matthew deliberated that chess had never been a game for cowards or fools, yet it tested both bravery and foolishness in all.

And while Santiago had been looking one way, Matthew's focus had been turned upon another. Before the governor could react to carry out a quick murder, one of Matthew's three remaining pawns reached the ultimate rank of black-side squares, and Matthew said, "I promote that lowly individual to a queen," proving that small acorns might in time grow to mighty oaks, especially if in tandem with Matthew's last rook and coming at the black king with ferocious intent.

Matthew restrained himself from predicting how many moves to victory. There was no need. Short of a miracle, Santiago's king was to be trapped, and in this game miracles were very hard to come by.

At last, Matthew said, "Checkmate." And: "Would you translate that to the audience?"

The governor did not react with sour displeasure as Matthew had expected. Instead, he said to the gallery, *"¡Jaque mate!"* to a mixture of murmurings and applause. As the group began to depart, Santiago gave an honest smile and said, "A wonderful game! I shall remember it long after you've gone to England!"

"Thank you, sir. You put up an amazing fight."

"Indeed! And you do understand that I asked you to be brought here not only to play chess, but to inform you that I acted rashly and rudely yesterday morning. I have already put into motion orders to prepare for your leaving us...as well as the other English who wish to foolishly abandon this paradise. It will take a week or so. You'll be sent to Naples and depart for England from that harbor."

Matthew was stunned. "You mean...this game was—"

"Totally unnecessary and simply for my pleasure. I wished a challenging game and you delivered. Don't fret...if you lost I would expect you to clean my chamberpot for only three days before I told you the truth. So all is for the good, *sí?*"

"Sí," Matthew managed to say. He didn't know whether to be angry or relieved, but in truth he was simply joyful. "Thank you, sir! May I ask what caused the change of mind?"

"I was a bit aggravated that there was no result in finding either Valeriani or the mirror. In addition, a few days ago Isabelle purchased another diamond ring for her collection that I had wished she not buy, so that too was...as you English might say...under my skin. Also, my wife and I had supper last night with *señorita* Espaziel and—though of course nothing was said about this business to disturb Isabelle—it was pointed out to me quite clearly that you and *señor* Greathouse had done all you could in service to the Bourbon crown. Speaking of *señor* Greathouse, I barely recognized him at the harbor. What made such a difference?"

"A purpose," said Matthew, though he did not elaborate.

Santiago shrugged. "Well…about this mirror business…nothing ventured, nothing gained. And sometimes…only nothing."

"I will venture to say that no other house of state will be getting their hands on a mirror that doesn't exist."

"Precisely. And between you and me, this whole thing has been a ridiculous *fiasco*."

That word…the same in English as in the language of Spain, and equally understood.

Santiago stood up and so did Matthew. "I would task you to discover how many wish to leave here, and to have them come to my office and sign a register of release. As I say, orders have already been given and I expect you'll be departing within two weeks."

"Wonderful to hear. I appreciate the *señorita* vowing for us."

"Yes, she's quite fond of both of you, it seems." If he suspected more than fond of Hudson, he didn't reveal it. "By the way, she leaves for Spain in the morning. She'll be expected to report to her authorities, but I'm sure all will go well." He reached out and clapped Matthew on the shoulder. "Would you dine with Isabelle and myself one night before you go? I'm sure she'd like to hear what life is like in the kennel."

Matthew couldn't help but smile. "My pleasure."

"Excellent. But *por amor a Cristo*, please consider shaving and bathing. You are a handsome young man, you shouldn't hide your biscuits under a barrel."

"I'll tend to that."

The governor's coach was brought around for him and Matthew was taken up the hill toward the prison. As they ascended, Matthew saw ahead through his window a familiar figure putting flowers down upon a grave in the cemetery.

He slid open the partition that gave him access to the driver and said, "Stop, please." To the lack of response he corrected himself with some of the limited portion of Spanish he knew. *"Détente, por favor."*

The driver obeyed, Matthew got out and said, "I'll walk from here." The man seemed not to understand until Matthew waved an arm at him, and then he nodded and drove the coach away, to turn it around further up the grade.

Matthew walked through the cemetery. He reached the small, white-haired and white-bearded figure who knelt before the simple marker at the final resting place of Tabor King, and then he waited until Uriah Holloway had finished his devotion. Before he could speak the man, who'd been

Captain King's first mate on the ill-fated cargo vessel *Golgotha* and had been known in that capacity by the nickname of "Little Brother", spoke to him.

"*You,*" Holloway said, almost a sneer.

"Me. There's no reason for further antagonism."

"I heard you were gone."

"Gone to Italy, now returned."

Holloway stood up to his height of five feet three inches, if that. "Pardon me for not sending up a cheer."

"You might at that. I am told by the governor that within two weeks every Englishman who wishes to leave here will board a ship bound for Naples and from there back to England. I have his word on it." And in addition the signed paper in his pocket, though no longer needed. Still, Matthew had no intention of letting it out of his possession.

Holloway's scowling expression changed in an instant. He spoke the words quietly: "Back to England?"

"Correct. I assume you approve?"

The small man stared down upon the grave. His shadow lay across the flowers there. "Back to England," he repeated, but Matthew detected something strange in his tone. Was the man not gleeful with this news?

Holloway looked up toward the bright morning sun and then at Matthew. "I won't be going."

"What? I thought you'd be the first aboard the ship!"

"I might've been, a month ago. Now...no."

"Tell me what's made the difference!"

When Holloway actually allowed himself what might have been one small trace of a smile to match the small sun-darkened face, Matthew thought the world had tipped crazily on its axis.

"I'm going to be married in two weeks," Holloway said.

"Married?"

The smile vanished. "That's what I said, clean your ears out!"

"Please explain so I'll know I'm not either losing my mind, standing in a vision or drunk on the very air."

The smile returned, and this time Matthew might have described it with a word he'd never imagined using in regard to this feisty chip of old sea salt: dreamy.

"Madrona owns the flower shop on the Via Verdi...where I've been getting all the flowers for Tabor's grave. She speaks a little English...very little...but I'm teaching her. Oh, she's a fine lady, Matthew! And a looker, too! I mean, for our age. But a looker, I think! We took up together, and we've been having supper at her house and...you know, it happened fast, she and I. One day I hated this place, and then...seeing her smile every time I went to get the flowers, and hearing her voice...well, things go as they ought to."

"I'm sure they do," said Matthew, who still felt the world spinning around him.

"I know I've been harsh on you," Holloway went on. His tone toughened up again. "But I wouldn't change a thing I said and don't ask me to! You and me will never see eye to eye!"

Matthew thought that due to the height differences, it would be impossible anyway.

"My Maddie," Holloway said, drifting back into the dreamland where true love could touch even the most resistant heart. "We'll make us a great twosome, I know it. And I'm to work with her, with the flowers and all, and nobody this side of life can work harder than me. I'm going to make her a fine husband, Matthew, and I believe she'll make me a fine wife."

"I have no doubt of that," Matthew answered.

"So…no, I'm not going back to England. My home is here, with Maddie."

Matthew refrained from reminding Holloway that he would never have met his bride-to-be if they hadn't left the island of Golgotha, but what was the point? Sooner or later the little man would realize it on his own. "Uriah, I'm glad to hear this news and I hope you'll be very happy."

"Who wouldn't be, here with a woman you love in this paradise? Nasty, cold England?" He snorted. "Never heard of it!"

"One thing you can help me with, is spreading the news among others who wish to go back to—" Nasty, cold England? "Go back to their English homes," he said. "Would you help me in getting a list together?"

"I'll do it. I expect a few of the crew will go but not all. Like me, they're staying."

"Well, I'll speak to you later about it. Good day to you." Could he walk without falling to his face on this strange new earth? He started up the hill.

"Matthew?" Holloway called behind him. "My thanks!"

Evidently the realization was just beginning to dawn.

A few paces further on under the bright blue sky and Matthew thought: *Maddie?*

It was a little bit of England, brought here to stay on a sunny shore.

THIRTY-ONE

He knocked at the door of Hudson's quarters.

"Matthew!" the Great One said with a smile when he opened the door. "I was about to go find you. Come in!"

Inside the spartanly furnished cell, Matthew saw that Hudson had set a gray knapsack on his cot and some folded clothing lay beside it.

"Are you going somewhere?" Matthew asked.

"I am, and that's why I was coming to see you."

"Where are you off to? And I should let you know that before you start travelling around Sardinia, Santiago has renewed his agreement that every Englishman who wants to leave here will be returned to—" Matthew paused, because in his opinion Hudson wore a very strange expression, one he'd never seen before. What was it?

"I'm not going travelling around Sardinia," Hudson said. "I'm not going back to England, either. I'm going to Spain with Camilla."

"*Spain? Are you serious?*"

"I am." Hudson's big shoulders shrugged. "I've never been to Spain, but I do like the music. And I especially have feelings toward a certain lady of Spain."

"I see." Matthew realized how could he *not* see? Because that was the expression on his friend's face: the man was in love. Or simply in lust? He had to ask: "Do you love her?"

"Sit." Hudson motioned toward the single old wicker chair, also a presentment from the society of beneficent women.

Matthew took the chair and waited while Hudson seemed to compose himself for what he had to say.

"A good question," he began. "To be honest, I'm not sure what love *is*, or how it's supposed to feel. Yes, I've been married several times, but...this just seems different in a way I can't explain."

Matthew had to agree that whatever the feeling was, it suited Hudson well. The man was clean-shaven, his hair combed, he wore fresh clothing, had obviously bathed recently because he smelled of sandalwood soap and except for the left arm in the splint and the bandage wrapping appeared to be in the best physical condition of his life. His healthy weight had returned, he'd gotten plenty of sun and exercise on the deck of the *Estrella*, had even enjoyed some fishing with Camilla's help, and his entire attitude was one of positive energy.

In short...Hudson was happy.

"I'd like to find out if I love her...or not," he continued. "I know when I'm with her I feel...completed, in a way. Does that make sense?"

"If *you* believe so, yes."

"I like being with her, Matthew. No. I *love* being with her. And I have to say, it's a new experience for me and it's both exciting and a bit frightening. I don't think I've ever really opened myself up to anyone. With her...I want to."

Matthew thought himself a dunce. Santiago had said Camilla was leaving in the morning. Here Hudson was packing his clothes. But the idea that an Englishman—the sworn enemy of the Spanish and the same reversed—would by choice travel to Spain? No wonder it hadn't occurred to him! "An Englishman in Spain," he said. "Won't they run you up their flagpole as soon as you walk off the ship? In fact, won't they throw you over the side halfway there?"

"Camilla says she'll speak up for me, and I believe she does have some authority."

Matthew nearly choked. Hudson Greathouse, relying on the protection of a woman? A beautiful, highly capable woman, yes, but...again, the world was wobbling on its axis.

"And another thing," Hudson said, his voice taking on a more serious tone. "Camilla needs someone to help her get out of that country. As long as she's there, the people who've been pressuring her will see her not only as the witch-hunter's daughter, but the 'witch-hunter' to aid them in getting confessions from their political enemies. With this war going on between the Habsburgs and Bourbons with no end in sight, they'll expect her work to resume when she returns. She wants no part of it. So...she needs me, and I have to say...I need her, too."

"You can get her out, you think?"

"I'll give it my best." He proffered a sly smile. "But since I am unable to hold a sword again, and I don't choose to use a weapon, I will have to learn to use my wits. Become a problem-solver, like yourself. Sort of a...how should I put it? Someone who works in secret for the benefit of someone else?"

"Secret agent," Matthew supplied.

"Yes," Hudson agreed. "That."

"I am absolutely stunned," Matthew had to admit. "Not going back to England, but to *Spain*? If—when—you get Camilla out, where might you go?"

"Oh, I don't know. England, possibly. Switzerland could be a choice. Camilla tells me she's heard that in Switzerland they travel downhill in the snow on something they strap to their boots called 'skis'. She says they can get up to very fast speeds. Sounds like something I might like to try."

"Sounds like something that might break your other arm," Matthew said. "Plus both legs and your neck. Well, Switzerland could be nice but for God's sake don't go to Prussia."

Hudson laughed, and then in all seriousness he said, "We've done our part, haven't we?"

Matthew knew exactly what he meant. "We have."

"You know, it's strange...Camilla and myself, I mean. The way we feel about each other. Don't laugh, but she has this very unusual idea that we've known each other before, in some other time and life."

"What?"

"Yes, really. That we've known each other and we were fated to meet again. And I have to say...sometimes being with her...looking at her... listening to her and watching her listen to me...I can believe it."

"I've never believed in the supernatural and I won't at this point," said Matthew, whose lie was so large it was a boulder in his throat. He realized he had come a great distance from his adamance in Fount Royal that there was no such thing as witches or witchcraft...but then again, the stance suited the purpose that justice be served.

"I haven't asked because maybe I didn't want to know, but I have to: did anything come out of the mirror?" By Matthew's suddenly darkening countenance, Hudson decided, "No. Please keep that to yourself."

Matthew intended to. No one in this world would ever hear it.

Mars and Venus Scaramanga, dead. Professor Fell, the same. The mirror broken and gone. Cardinal Black, also broken and made into lynx food.

But one remained.

If the creature was real, and not a bizarre figment of Black's demented mind...

...what had become of Dominus?

"Camilla and I are leaving tomorrow morning at six o'clock," Hudson said, breaking Matthew's pattern of thought. "On the ship *Buenas Noticias*, if you can believe that. *Good Tidings*…as in tides of the sea. I'll be learning a lot of Spanish from here on out."

"It'll suit you just fine, I think."

"We'd like you to join us for supper tonight. The tavern of your choice. Is that agreeable?"

"Absolutely."

"Very good. Then we'll get a chance to tell Camilla what we've been through."

Matthew stood up, because it was time for him to move on. "I think we'd best not tell her *everything* we've been through."

"Don't worry," Hudson said. "We'll smooth out the rough spots."

Matthew had to hug his friend and Hudson returned the hug with one arm. Matthew realized that the man was still strong enough to break his ribs, God bless him.

The Great One had a little bit of dampness in his eyes.

He said, "You're not a moonbeam anymore, Matthew. You're a star."

Then he let Matthew go.

THIRTY-TWO

THROUGH A LOW-LYING CLOUD OF SNOW AND SLEET THE ENGLISH VES-
sel *Golden Comet* parted the chill Atlantic, its sails bloomed out to catch the
favorable wind, its prow set toward the harbor of New York, and a young
man aboard who stood upon the foredeck keeping expectant watch.

Matthew was bundled in a long dark green woolen coat, gray cap and
gloves. It was the morning of the sixteenth day of January, the year 1705. In
the galley last night Captain Dicksen Carr had informed him and the other
seven passengers that—by the calculations of map, currents and sextant—
land should be sighted near nine o'clock.

The time was three minutes after nine, according to the pocket watch
Matthew had bought during his few days in London. Maccabeus DeKay's
money pouch had been sorely depleted, but still had some life in it yet.
He wished for a spyglass, that he might with it try to pierce this morning's
gloom, but he had to put faith in the glass used up top where the lookout
chattered his teeth in the crow's nest.

On days like this—and there had been many during the three-month
winter crossing in a ship neither golden nor comet-quick—Matthew's mind
turned toward Alghero. He would envision himself walking in the warm
sunlight, the ocean breeze drifting past and with it the salt smell of the sea,
but always he would be walking hand-in-hand with Berry. It had been so
long. So many months, and such a journey. And now…when would the
lookout give his cry?

At the Boar's Head tavern on the last night before Hudson and Camilla
had departed, there'd been an excellent meal and much to drink. In truth,

they'd all gotten a bit tipsy, because when one had faced such death as they, some things needed to be remembered only in a haze. But Matthew and Hudson had reminisced about a number of events in their careers with the Herrald Agency that were suited for the lady's ears, and then Matthew had listened as the Great One and Miss Green Eyes—as Matthew thought of her as the ale sank to the roots of his brain—talked of their future together.

Wherever they might go in the world, it seemed to Matthew that it would be the right place. And watching them interact there was no doubt that Hudson Greathouse had taken the correct turn on the road of life. They teased each other in a gentle way, they touched with care and respect, and Matthew noted that each listened intently as the other spoke, which seemed to him a very high mark of a relationship. He doubted they would be joined at the hip, as in Matthew's view they both shared an air of independence, but he came away from the tavern thinking that great things were ahead for Greathouse and the lady Espaziel, and indeed the world awaited them.

He said his final goodbyes at the harbor the following morning. From the deck they waved, and then the big ox gave him a salute—the gesture of which Matthew understood originated from a knight lifting his visor to identify himself.

He returned it, from one knight to another.

Then he watched until the *Buenas Noticias* sailed out of sight, on a good tide.

The warmth of that morning was now a chilly memory. Matthew had his gloved hands in his pockets, where in one he felt the small crucifix he'd brought back from Italy. It seemed like a good idea to keep hold of something that could shatter the doorway to Hell.

And now the gate of Heaven opened.

From the crow's nest came the cry: *"Land ho!"*

He strained to see, but yet could not through the vaporous atmosphere. His heart was beating harder. Did he need another shave? He'd given himself one this morning when he'd awakened at three in anticipation of this being the day of days. No, he decided he was well-shaved. Some of the other passengers stood around him, also yearning for land underfoot, as some of this voyage had been of the rolling and heaving persuasion to accompany the rolling and heaving sea.

If Matthew had had his druthers he would've returned to New York when the blooms were out and the robins singing, to go along with the springtime in his blood. A winter wedding? Not what he'd hoped for, but then again there was beauty to be taken in the winter as well, and when one had such a beautiful bride in mind it was all magnificent summer.

There! The caliginosity for an instant had parted, bringing gasps of relief from the onlookers and revealing the shapes of tall-masted ships and structures beyond…then once again was closed by the weather's jester. By the brief reveal Matthew judged the harbor to be two miles distant…a mere inch compared to what he'd already travelled, but such an inch was never so long.

On sailed the *Golden Comet*, through mist and sleet and froth-topped waves.

Should he shave again? Hadn't he already decided that? He looked skyward as far as the murk would allow to see the gulls spinning round and round the topmast. And there he saw a quick glint of sun…and another… and another yet…and then to a cheer from the body of passengers the low gray ceiling gave way to tatters before the grace of Sol and the sun shone down on the panorama of New York.

Even at first appraisal Matthew could tell it was not the same town he'd left. North along Queen Street, past the Grigsby house and his own minuscule dairyhouse abode, six new houses stood and four more were in their skeletal state of framework construction. In fact, workmen were currently up on scaffolds hammering the points home. North along the Broad Way three new structures had gone up with three others in the process of being built, but these looked to be of commercial intent and one of the newer was—amazing!—framed to be four stories in height. Up on Golden Hill, two mansions were under construction. The harbor ahead was a veritable conglomeration of vessels large and small, itself a close-packed small town of ships. Smoke from house chimneys and industrial furnaces painted the air. He could see horses pulling carts and wagons along Queen Street and down along the town's curve where the structures—and their smoke—thickened. As he watched, he saw the teams of two wagons bang into each other and tangle up, one going south and one going north at perhaps a careless speed, and the traffic of horse riders, carts and other wagons was snarled on either side.

He smiled.

Home again. But to a different town, at that. What a difference time could make, and the industry of men always fascinated him. It appeared that while he'd been away New York was not only stretching its muscles toward the north, but that the southern and central portions of the town had *thickened*, in a way he could not fully explain.

He reasoned that within five years one was going to have to find a place in the country to enjoy peace and quiet away from the bustle and roar of business. Like in Brooklyn.

Matthew noted that in his time away New York had constructed its own Leviathan at the Great Dock. It was only a wooden framework with stairs, true, but it was at least seventy feet high. He could make out two men standing at its summit. The early sunlight glinted off what must be a spyglass on a tripod. One of the men held a pair of red signal flags waving them in some kind of pattern. In another moment Matthew figured out that there was a ship ahead of them being towed to a berth by the pilot boats, and this signal system—entirely new since Matthew had left town—was informing the *Golden Comet* that the vessel must dawdle until the pilot boats were free. So not only was New York quickly growing by leaps and bounds but the maritime traffic was such that one had to wait in line for harbor service.

Amazing.

At last the *Comet* was towed in without incident and its lines made fast. Captain Carr addressed the passengers to thank them on behalf of the company for their business, and Matthew was first down the gangplank like a shot, the large leather carryall he'd bought in London for his clothes, toiletries and Fell's flying fish artwork strapped to a shoulder.

No sooner was he on the dock—and struggling to find his landlegs as all ship's passengers had to do after a three-month voyage—when he heard the cry of "Matthew Corbett!"

From the usual chaos of fiddlers, dancers, food carts and hawkers of geegaws that no one had any use for but would buy just to get through the crush, a wagon had pulled up alongside the *Comet*. A number of men were waiting, likely for the ship's cargo to be unloaded.

"Matthew!" came the voice again. "Good God, where have you *been?*"

There in a buckskin jacket with a big grin on his face was the thickset John Five, whose curly blonde hair was topped with a coonskin cap. Long ago, John had been one of Matthew's companions in the orphanage taken over from the kindly headmaster Staunton by the vile Eben Ausley. Also, John had unknowingly been vital in helping him solve the problem of the Queen of Bedlam.

John clapped Matthew so hard on the back the problem-solver nearly went careening into the drink past a cart selling fried chicken gizzards. "Good *God!*" John repeated, his manner obviously become more boisterous since their last meeting. "How *are* you?"

"Fine," Matthew said when he'd regained his breath. "Better now, I mean…now that I'm back."

"Back from where? I haven't seen you in a twiddler's holiday!"

"I was working in Italy. And how are you?"

"Oh, I'm doin' great! That is to say…" His eyes darkened a few shades. "Master Ross passed away in the summer. His heart, the doctor said. But Master Ross must've had the feelin' his time was near because he wrote up some papers givin' me the blacksmith shop. We've got us some brand spankin' new forge equipment straight from London, just come over on your ship."

Oh, so *that's* why the *Comet* had the speed of a mudball! Matthew thought wryly, but he kept it to himself.

John's face suddenly brightened again. "I'm gonna have a baby!"

"Pardon?"

"I mean…Constance and me. Constance, mostly. I just helped. Lordy, I can't talk today!"

Matthew had to laugh. Constance was John's wife, the daughter of the Trinity Church minister William Wade though Reverend Wade had moved south and the last Matthew knew the church's minister was the six-foot-four-inch-tall, bespectacled and soft-spoken Bertram Fenclaren.

"Due in April," John said. "We're all a'bustle about it."

"I'm sure! Listen…so good to see you, but I have to go. Can we meet one night at Sally Almond's? My treat, and I'd love to see Constance."

"For certain, Matthew!" Again came the blacksmith's teeth-rattling bang on the back. "We'll carve that on our tree!"

Matthew headed off through the crowd, as several more vessels were unloading cargo, and the multitude of wagons and carts drawn up to carry the crates, boxes and bags made the place a mass of shouting and shoving, not to mention horses dropping their beans amid the ever-surging horde. He couldn't help but dread what this harbor would become in five years! Yes, hurray for progress but even Brooklyn might be too near for all this frenzied growth. Best set sights on the Bronx.

He hurried to his destination, along Queen Street to the Grigsby house. His breath in the cold morning air blossomed out before him like pale flowers. He did not pause at his own abode to unburden himself of the carryall, but strode directly to the door and knocked.

A sight for sore eyes! Marmaduke Grigsby opened the door, still in his red-striped nightshirt. Behind his spectacles on the moon-round face the large blue eyes nearly popped from their sockets, the heavy white brows twitched and jumped and the little tuft of white hair that remained on his scalp seemed to stand up like an exclamation mark.

The rotund and ungainly man was shocked to silence, which Matthew thought up until this moment would have been an impossibility.

"I'm back, thank God!" Matthew said. "Is Berry in?"

"I…um…*Matthew!*"

"I'm not a specter, Marmy!" He looked over one of the man's shoulders into the room, expecting Berry to come running forward. "Where is she?"

"Um…I just…well…"

"She's not home?"

Marmaduke got his tongue out of its knots. "Berry's gone to see Ashton!" he blurted out. "She's with—"

Oh my God! Matthew thought in a panic. The worst was true! He'd been away too long and that conniving McCaggers had conjured Berry away! Well, there was yet action to be taken! He threw the carryall into the room past Marmy, turned on his heel and fled in the direction of the yellow-stone, three-story City Hall on Wall Street.

"Matthew! Wait!" Grigsby called, but there was no waiting. The young man's boots grew wings. "Matthew! Matthew!" Someone called; it was Hiram Stokely the pottery maker, but Matthew had no time to hesitate so he waved and kept going through the bracing air. Then again: "Matthew! Hold up there!" It was Solomon Tully the sugar merchant but again time was precious. And a third: "Matthew Corbett! Lord have mercy!" Called by Madam Kenneday the baker pushing a wheelbarrow full of flour sacks. "No time, no time!" Matthew answered, and on he ran into the thickest of New York's hubbub, where it seemed all streets met and at the moment everyone in the town and all their wagons and horses were right there to impede his frantic progress.

Into the impressive front door of the imposing City Hall he flew—to collide with a smaller, slender figure who wore a nearly iridescent and eye-stabbing blue topcoat and an equally loud blue tricorn topped with a voluminous crimson red feather.

"Hold there! Watch where you're—*Corbett!*"

Matthew had run straight into the diminutive and in his opinion disgustingly disreputable High Constable Gardner Lillehorne, who he'd last seen on his way to Newgate Prison in London. What the *hell* was the man doing here? And most importantly, Lillehorne was standing between himself and Berry! Lillehorne's nostrils flared and his black-goateed chin jutted forward. "Am I going *mad?*" he demanded. "Are you an apparition? If so, you're the most solid spirit ever to assault a constable!"

Matthew started to go around him but Lillehorne's black-lacquered cane with its silver lion's head—somewhat tarnished, Matthew noted—might have been a lance planted in the center of his chest. "Explain yourself! Where did you come from?"

"England by way of Italy. Would you remove yourself, please? I have urgent business!"

"Urgent enough to knock an esteemed constable sprawling? You nearly disjointed me!"

Matthew realized he had twice said *constable*. Not *high constable?* When always he rubbed that in your face like hot peppers? "*High* constable, isn't it?"

"Laugh if you please! Go on, you young donkey! Give out your best *hee-haw!*"

Was there something of a choked sob in the man's voice? Though he had to get up those stairs to the third floor and McCaggers' eerie domain to rescue his love from the clutches of the ever-clutching city coroner, Matthew had to know: "What are you jabbering about?"

"I'm still important here, you can mark that!" The lion's head might have done the marking, in the three hard thumps it gave Matthew's chest. "Broken as I am, I still have influence enough to see you hung by your thumbs in the gaol!"

"Make some sense, Gardner! What's happened?"

"Dippen Nack, that's what's happened! Blast and damn the little fool!"

Matthew pushed the cane away and Lillehorne allowed it. The subject of Dippen Nack was a sore one to Matthew, since he'd witnessed the little boasting, billyclub-brandishing bully being torn to shreds by RakeHell Lizzie at the mansion of Samson Lash. But he had to ask, "What about Nack?"

"He disappeared when he was supposed to be on duty in London! In the section I had sent him to patrol! And just that night a high-ranking member of Parliament and his wife were out walking to their theater, to be set upon by three ruffians who beat the man senseless and stole not only the woman's jeweled necklace but her prized poodle named Snowdrop! So you know who they came after! Nack? Heaven forbid, he's still disappeared! Took up with other lazy unsavories of his breed and fled the city, most likely!" Lillehorne was almost spitting through his clenched teeth, his eyes wild with the fury of the powerless. "Oh yes, they came after *me!* Stripping me of my rank in that dingy little office and that bald-headed judge giving me the smelly eye! And what do you think *Princess* had to say about this? Plenty, I can tell you, and more thrown plates than words! I'm still at her mercy!"

Matthew had no doubt that being ousted from a position of social height and basically ordered out of England back to what she considered the dregs of humanity made Lillehorne's waspish wife want to sting everyone in sight.

"If Nack comes crawling back here," Lillehorne fumed, "I shall beat him to an inch of his life!"

Matthew said, "He probably won't come back." And by this time there wasn't an inch of him left to beat.

"I shall keep my eye out for him, though! And on *you* as well, Corbett! It was some strange business you got into with that fiend Albion!"

"Very strange," Matthew admitted. "Now…I regret your current position, sir, but I do have to go."

"Up to further intrigues, are you? Will you never learn to mind your own business?"

Matthew couldn't resist it: "Sir, my business *is* intrigues. Pardon me and good day." Before the dishonored scalawag could respond, Matthew was away from him and bounding up the stairs.

THIRTY-THREE

UP THE NARROW STAIRWAY ON THE THIRD FLOOR TO THE BUILDING'S attic and to McCaggers' door, and about to knock on it but thinking better and more urgently of his rescue mission Matthew opened it and crossed the threshold with neither permission nor apology.

He stood in the coroner's cathedral of bones. The strong winter light through the attic's windows fell upon what McCaggers called his "angels", the four human skeletons that hung from the overhead rafters. Adorning the walls of this macabre mansion were twenty or more skulls and wired-together assemblages of bony arms, legs, ribcages and hands that Matthew assumed McCaggers considered to be his collection of fine art. Animal skeletons, strange things that appeared to be combinations of animal and human bones that McCaggers had created with his use of wire, bottles and beakers of weirdly colored fluids, and a rack of deadly swords, axes, hatchets, hammers, and nail-studded clubs made this the zenith of places Matthew never wanted to set foot in and now that he was in wanted to get out as quickly as possible.

From the back of the chamber came a weak voice: "Berry?" And once more: "Berry?"

That bone-loving buffoon! Matthew wished to pause on his way following the voice to pick up a club and send the coroner to a coroner. He moved through this beautiful array and found McCaggers in his own little corner of the world where he'd put a desk, two chairs, a small brown rug—the color of grave dirt, Matthew thought—and a bed upon which the master of the realm now lay with the covers up to his neck. It had always intrigued Matthew that McCaggers got violently ill at the sight or smell of blood and decay, yet he chose to exist in this meticulously crafted vault of the dead.

"Well, well, well!" Matthew said. "What have we here?"

Ashton McCaggers was three years older than Matthew, had light brown hair receding from a high forehead and Matthew thought he might be called somewhat handsome, if one liked his look of being deathly pale. And he was well-named because right now he appeared nearly ash gray in color. As usual, he was two or three days away from a shave.

"Is that…?" He struggled to focus and reached for his spectacles on a little table next to his bed, where there also happened to be perched on a small stand what looked like a muskrat's skull. He got his glasses on. "*Matthew?* Oh Lord, it *is* you!"

"The one and only." Matthew had noted that in addition to McCaggers' sickly coloring, he sounded sick and wheezy. Probably ill from inhaling the dust of a thousand-year-old corpse that was stashed under the bed.

McCaggers tried to sit up and failed. "I'm sorry I can't be a better host, Matthew. So good to see you, but I am under the weather." So saying, he reached to his side for a bundle of cloths on the bed there and used one to blow his nose with explosive effect.

"What's wrong with you?"

"I have a drippy nose, a scratchy throat and I think a touch of fever. Also my right ankle has been severely sprained. Forgive me for not standing to greet you."

"Forgiven. I understood Berry was here."

"Oh, she was. She's such a friend, to visit me so early. She's gone to Sally Almond's to fetch me some chicken soup and a jug of my favorite ale that I can vow I so desperately need."

Such a friend, he'd said. Matthew approached the cot. "You're really feeling quite terrible?"

"Terrible with a capital T. And my ankle…oh, does it hurt!"

"How did it happen?"

McCaggers gave a great sigh and then he blew his nose again. "You do know, of course, that Berry likes to dance."

Matthew could see this coming. "You sprained your ankle dancing with her?"

"No. I sprained my ankle *going* to the dance with her. At the Dock House two nights ago. Then I awakened with this mortifying affliction yesterday morning. Berry has been so kind in bringing me food and keeping me company."

"I'm sure you've been enjoying her company many nights while I've been gone."

"Well...yes, but..." He straightened his spectacles because they'd gone crooked. "Oh my. Are you jealous? Of *me?*"

"I don't think it's been a secret that you've had designs on Berry."

"Designs? Well...possibly I did, for a while. But let me say...every time I tried to impress my designs I suffered a horrible accident. I almost went into poverty buying shoes after so many heels were broken walking with her, or I stepped into a hole, or tripped and fell into the mud, or... fell into something worse there on the street! I learned to leave my designs at home, I can tell you. Pardon me." He blew his nose again and wiped the thing with the cloth. Against his pallid complexion it was getting as red as a scarlet-lensed lantern. After a couple of sneezes he said, "Designs? If I had any further designs I'd be dead by now!"

Matthew had to look at the floor after this declaration.

"You know," McCaggers wheezed on, "I'm beginning to think...per-haps...that Berry is just a little bit bad luck for me. Do you believe such a thing is possible? Anyway, she loves you and she's told me so several—" He had to pause to release three sneezes in a row. "Several times," he finished.

"I love *her,*" Matthew said. "When I find her I'm going to ask her to marry me."

"Here?"

"Yes! Right—" Matthew stopped. Here? Ask Berry to marry him in this moldy boneyard? What a memory that would be, and not the kind of memory Matthew wished to make. "You say she's gone to Sally Almond's?"

"You only missed her by a few minutes. I must have my chicken soup and that apple ale I like so much!"

"All right, then." Matthew decided he could catch her at Sally Almond's tavern on Nassau Street. With brisk walking he could be there in about six minutes, depending on how crowded the street was. Best to propose mar-riage in a place of fine aromas than in this dusty dead man's parlor. "I'm off!" he told the sniffling wretch in the bed. "I hope you feel better soon!" He started for the way out, and glad to be going.

"Matthew?" McCaggers called, and the younger man paused. "Happy you're home. You've been missed."

Matthew thought Ashton really meant it. He appreciated the senti-ment, and it was worth a jug of Ashton's favorite ale to be sent up here soon. He gave the man a thumbs-up, went through the bizarre menagerie, out the door and down the stairs.

In the hallway as he was going for the next set of stairs in this build-ing that seemed made of staircases, he heard behind him. "Boy! Boy, come here!" And louder and more strident: "Boy! I said come here!"

What *now?* Matthew wondered, his brain in a tizzy. He stopped, looked back, and along was coming a thickly built man in a purple suit with a lighter purple paisley waistcoat, a white ruffled shirt and white stockings. He was wearing a towering, elaborately curled and powdered wig that fell heavily about the shoulders, and in one hand he held a sheaf of papers. As he reached Matthew he held the papers out and said, "Boy, I want these delivered to Magistrate—wait...who are you?" The bulbous eyes in the long-nosed and horsey face blinked. "You're not a messenger boy! Is that... Matthew Corbett?"

"It is." And Matthew knew who he was addressing, none other than the governor, Lord Cornbury, who today had obviously forsaken his usual costume of femininity and gone for the look of a hanging judge.

"I haven't seen you in quite some time! Where have you been keeping yourself?"

"I've been abroad, sir."

"Yes, so I have been. I mean to say, I just returned from England a few days ago."

"Good to see you again, sir. Pardon me if I—"

"Oh, the woe of it!" said Cornbury, clutching at Matthew's sleeve with his free hand to hold him in place. The horsey face had taken on the look of darkest despair. "One doesn't know when one is about to be stabbed in the back, does one?"

"One doesn't," Matthew agreed, eager to get to those stairs and down.

"Stabbed in the back most brutally!" Cornbury plowed on, though obviously through sorrowful ground. "And by my cousin, the Queen! It is most painful when family does the dirty deed, is it not?"

"I regret your difficulties, sir, but—"

"Difficulties?" Cornbury's hand tightened on the sleeve. "Difficulties? They are tragedies and I have no one in this world to rely on! Oh, I suppose you've heard the lies that are being spread about me! The whole town's heard it by now, and feasting on such nasty morsels! That Governor Cornbury has looted the treasury, that Governor Cornbury has spent a week of the most indescribable behavior in Philadelphia and thrown the town's money to prostitutes and Johnny Dandies, and—the most flagrant of horrid lies— that Governor Cornbury has been embezzling the town's funds since he took the oath of office! I suppose you've heard all that!"

"Only recently," said Matthew.

"I knew it! I knew it!" Cornbury did a little hip-hop of anxiety while still holding Matthew captive. "This talk will ruin me! And then I am summoned before my cousin, with all those rank enemies who've for years despised the very earth I walk upon yapping their lies in her ears and do you know what she says to me, her loyal cousin? She says 'we shall have to investigate these rumors'. It is an insult to my soul, Corbett! Therefore I refuse in the present and future to honor my cousin the Queen as I have done in the past! As for their investigations, I say *pah* on them! *Pah*, I say!"

"Well said, sir," said Matthew, pulling at his sleeve.

"Let me ask you, then." Cornbury's face drew closer, the eyes imploring. He whispered, "Do you know a good lawyer?"

"I shall turn over every stone in my search," said Matthew, just about to get his sleeve free.

"Ah! Thank you, young man! And if you can locate a suitable legal assistant by acting in my stead—quietly, of course, *very* quietly—I should reward you with a handsome bit of change. But you'll keep this to yourself, won't you?"

"Even myself won't know it."

"Perfect!" The hand at last released the sleeve. "Off with you then, I'm a busy man!"

"Thank you sir, and thank you for taking the time to speak to me."

"I have always been a man of the little people," said Cornbury, with a proud forward thrust of the double chins.

Matthew fled down the stairs for both life and sanity.

The Broad Way was jammed by a lumber wagon that had crashed over on its side, the horses loose from their traces and bucking in the midst of the shouting, confused throng. Matthew got through the mess to Nassau Street without being further accosted, and at Sally Almond's restaurant was told by Sally herself that Berry had gotten the chicken soup she'd requested but they were sold out of that particular apple ale, therefore Berry had been sent to the Trot Then Gallop for the popular drink.

"So good to have you back!" Sally said at the door, and again Matthew was off to his favorite tavern on Crown Street.

Would his legs hurry the pace? They could only run so fast. If he missed Berry at the Gallop, then maybe he could catch her again at McCaggers' attic but that was certainly a disagreeable place to propose marriage.

On he ran.

He burst through the door into the familiar and ever-comforting confines of the Trot Then Gallop. His first view of the place was of his friends Effrem Owles the tailor and Israel Brandier the silversmith sitting across a chessboard in front of the crackling fireplace. They looked at Matthew, recognized him and sat in surprise with their mouths open as Israel dropped to the floor the rook he'd just killed from Effrem's troops. Behind the bar the portly, gray-bearded Felix Sudbury let out a holler: *"Matthew Corbett!"*

And standing before the bar the young woman in a winter coat the color of summer wildflowers and a wide-brimmed hat the same turned toward the door.

It was a dream. It had to be a dream.

As he approached her in this place where everybody knew his name, Matthew saw her mouth open to speak it but he couldn't hear her for the blood roaring in his brain and in his near-frozen ears. Her clear blue eyes widened. In the candlelight her copious curls of red hair with coppery highlights shone with good health. She smiled. The gap between her front teeth was never more beautiful, nor were the freckles that were scattered across her cheeks and the bridge of her nose.

She dropped to the floor what she was holding in each hand.

A clay bowl of chicken soup secured with a covering of waxed paper. *Crash.*

A clay jug of very popular apple ale. *Smash.*

As Berry's eyes filled with tears she whispered two words he would remember to the last moment of his last day on this earth.

"My Matthew."

He couldn't move. His legs had betrayed him. But his mouth did not.

He spoke it as a hero should: with vibrancy, passion, and for all the world to hear.

"I love you so much. Will you marry me?"

Did she reply? Was he struck deaf? Did the ceiling just fall in upon his head? Because abruptly he was sitting sprawled in a chair and Effrem was putting a cup of liquor to his mouth and one sip of that could burn the winter's frost to summer's torch and what had she *said?*

"What?" he asked the spinning room. *"What?"*

Suddenly Berry's face was before him, the tears still in her eyes and streaking down through the freckles on her cheeks, and as she rested her head upon his shoulder he inhaled her divine aroma of cinnamon and also a touch of spiced apples—no, no, the apple scent must be from the broken jug in pieces on the floor but anyway she smelled so *nice*—she whispered in his ear what she had said before his ragdoll collapse.

"I love you so much. Yes!"

He kissed her. It was long and lingering, and it was also well-met.

Who began the applause? No matter, it spread and became a rousing cheer.

Matthew Corbett had come home.

"I want to hear everything," Berry said when Effrem had withdrawn and she was sitting at the table so close to him they were already welded, if not wedded.

No you don't, Matthew thought. He took another drink of the hot and delicious fire and said, "I—we—had a time of it. But I'm back, and that's all that matters."

"And of Hudson? Where is he? And Professor Fell?"

"You'll never believe it," he answered. An Englishman gone willingly to Spain? Good fortune to him, and Matthew hoped the Great One and his lady enjoyed learning to ski—who in the world thought of such a thing as that?—in Switzerland. He would tell Berry as much of it as he could, and maybe later in life—much later—he might tell her the whole of it, but then again...probably not. As for the professor...an ex-emperor of crime turned champion of virtue, even if he had to murder someone in cold blood to get there?

Equally unbelievable.

Was it wrong to keep what had happened in the lighthouse a secret from her? He might present the situation to the Reverend Fenclaren because he was unable to resolve it on his own. It was in its own way a problem of leviathan dimensions.

In time, after a few more kisses and the enjoyment of simply sitting before the fire in the company of Berry and his friends with nothing current to drive him into dangerous waters, Matthew decided he did need to stop by Number Seven Stone Street and see if either Katherine Herrald or Minx Cutter were there. He needed to give a report on Hudson's whereabouts. The poor sick and suffering Ashton McCaggers was not forgotten. Berry obtained a second jug of the ale and Matthew accompanied her to Sally Almond's for another bowl of soup. Then after promising that he, Berry and Marmaduke would come in the following evening for supper, Matthew walked his bride-to-be as far as the City Hall, they kissed and hugged again there in front of this monument to the reign of Queen Anne, the power of England and the beginning of a new era in the history of the world, and then he continued on his way to the office, striding on clouds instead of New York earth.

In the very familiar space at the top of the stairs he found Madam Herrald sitting at a desk going over some papers. A new development in her history: she was wearing spectacles. Instantly she stood up when he came in, herself fashionable as always in a royal blue gown with lighter blue ruffles at collar and cuffs and her long gray hair held back by several copper combs. She hugged him with what seemed to him nearly the strength of Hudson Greathouse. Her amazement at seeing him increased when he informed her of Hudson's decision. And increased again when told of Professor Fell's demise, but he explained that there was much more to the story and he would save it for a later report.

The ever-fighting ghosts of Number Seven Stone Street seemed to be pleased at his return, for there came the sound of a spectral punch followed by a half-heard grunt and then they paused their eternal fisticuffs to hear what he had to say.

Katherine also had something to say, "Matthew, I am so *greatly* glad you're here. Thank God for that! I want you to know I've been training a new recruit who's just arrived from England a few days ago. He's been a problem-solver on his own in London for a few years, and he seems very skilled. He may stay here, or he may report to the London firm. His choice. In any case, he's supposed to be here soon and I'm glad you're here to meet him. Minx hasn't met him yet either, and she's due here any minute."

"Excellent." Matthew decided it was time to tell. "I have asked Berry Grigsby to marry me and she has said yes. We've yet to make plans for the wedding but I intend it to be soon."

"That's wonderful news! I'm so happy for both of you!" Her ebullient expression then changed to one that showed a hint of dismay. "Let me ask…are you staying with the agency?"

"I don't know. It's dangerous work. Doubly dangerous for me now, without Hudson. I think it may depend on what Berry has to say."

"I understand, but what else would you do?"

Matthew shrugged. "I was once a law clerk. I suppose I could return to that profession and at least *attempt* to obtain a shingle."

"Let me rephrase my question: what would you *want* to do?"

"I'll give it some thought," he answered, though as he looked around the office that had brought him so much action, intrigue, adventure, and… yes…satisfaction he was hard-pressed to believe he'd be happy doing any-thing else.

They heard the door at the bottom of the stairs open and in another moment in came Minx Cutter, the blonde-haired princess of blades wear-ing a black leather jacket over a wine-red dress trimly cut and suitable for horseback riding. As Minx spoke to him with the same pleased amazement as had Katherine, Matthew noted that her black boots were tipped with studded metal…the better to kick the living hell out of someone if her knives didn't finish them off.

Katherine said, "Minx has just returned from a case involving a gang of horse thieves, a trained chimpanzee and a man with three arms."

"One of them was false," Minx added.

"I understand it was a hard-fought experience," said Katherine.

"Piece of cake," was the following reply.

Matthew didn't doubt that Minx Cutter's piece of cake was every man's worst chunk of tough cornbread.

Again there came the sound of the door opening and closing, then the noise of footsteps as someone climbed the stairs.

The man who entered was tall and slim, wearing a brown-checked woolen cap and a similar topcoat draped about his shoulders over a darker brown suit. Matthew judged his age to be around thirty. He was carrying a brown walking stick topped with what Matthew saw was the silver head of some breed of dog. A beagle, perhaps? The man had a long angular face, an equally long and slightly upturned nose, and as he approached the trio awaiting him he regarded them all with gray eyes and an expression that appeared to Matthew a shade haughty.

"Minx Cutter and Matthew Corbett," Katherine said, "meet Crofton Holmes."

Matthew shook the man's hand. A firm grip and dry palm. Minx just stared at the gent and the gent stared back before he gave his full attention to the older lady.

"Crofton is here to do some training under my auspices," Katherine continued. "I hoped you two might help us along."

"What should we do?" Minx asked. "Hold his hand in case he gets a little frightened?"

"Now, now! Let's play nice, children. Crofton has—"

"Miss," Holmes interrupted, his rather intense gaze fixed upon the blonde offender. "I don't believe your help will be needed, and I certainly did not ask for it."

"Good, because I don't give it out for free."

"Really? From the *looks* of you, I'd say I don't believe that—"

Statement, he was about to say, but the knife from the inside of Minx's leather jacket flashed out and the tip rested just beneath his pointed chin, encouraging a sudden silence.

"I'd watch your mouth, if I were—"

Then Minx stopped speaking, because under her chin was the tip of the long thin sword Holmes had quickly and expertly drawn from within the walking stick.

Matthew said, "In chess this is called a stalemate."

Katherine wore a faint smile. The children were getting to know each other in their own way. Slowly Minx lowered her knife and as Holmes lowered his blade Minx retreated a few steps. Matthew saw her regarding the man's sword with renewed interest.

"Shotley Bridge?" she asked.

"Hounslow," was answered.

"English bladesmiths," Katherine supplied to Matthew.

Minx narrowed her eyes. "Cut or thrust?"

"*Thrust*. Of course."

"*Cut*," she said, with a hint of vehemence.

Katherine said to Matthew, "Theories of—"

"Bladework, yes I know. Well, this is so far a lovely gathering."

"I am here for only a short time," said Holmes as he reseated his weapon into the cane. "I intend to return to England on a personal issue, and to be honest I'd hoped to ask one of the—" He paused in giving the evil eyeball to Minx before he continued. "One of the experts here for aid in this endeavor."

"What's the issue?" Matthew asked.

"A friend of mine was most brutally murdered. Another friend was mutilated and left for dead. His eyes were plucked out and his mouth slashed with a heavy blade. He never saw who attacked him. These gentlemen were both members of my social club, and I am attempting to discover the connection. I don't know if you've ever heard of Professor Fell?"

"In passing," said Matthew.

"Ah. Well it seems he's been missing for so long another figure has risen up from the bowels of the earth to take his place. I am told by an informant that my friends met violence at the hands of a vicious gang controlled by this figure, and that the action is basically an advertisement to other murderous criminals to join his pack. Again, why my social club has been the focus of this is a mystery I intend to solve."

"Do you know this mysterious figure's name?" Katherine asked.

"I have a name but it might not be more than an assumed alias. It is Doctor Sardonicus."

"And who's your informant?" Matthew prodded.

"A member of the royal family of Prussia, by the name of Count Karloff."

Matthew winced. "That doesn't sound very comforting."

"Sir," said Crofton Holmes, his eyelids at half-mast, "*comfort* is not our business."

Katherine cleared her throat as a way of clearing the atmosphere. "Minx, Matthew's going to be married soon. Isn't that grand?"

"I presume the lucky victim is Berry Grigsby?"

"I consider myself the lucky one, and if love can create a victim I gladly lie down upon its altar. I just saw her at—" Matthew stopped because Holmes had advanced upon him and seemed to be looking him up and down.

"A sophisticated young girl," the man said. "Curly red hair. Very healthy, and demonstrative in her emotions. Oh my…does she perhaps appreciate strong apple ale a bit too much?"

"*What?*"

"Also a fondness for…let me think…chicken soup?"

Matthew realized Holmes was able to detect these aromas from the spillage at the Trot Then Gallop. But the rest of it?

As if in reply to Matthew's unspoken questions, Holmes reached out and removed two long red curly hairs from the right shoulder of his topcoat. "She rested her head there," he said. "Demonstrative in her emotions. Sophisticated because I do catch an aroma of cinnamon that I believe may

be the lingering of a purchased scent. Does she indulge in the ale, sir? Oh…
wait, I'm a fool. A jug was dropped, was it not? There is a very small frag-
ment of dried clay adhering to your left boot."

When Holmes had given a self-satisfied smirk and stepped back, Minx
said, "*Anybody* could've told all that."

Speak for yourself, Matthew thought.

"The situation remains that Crofton is here for our help and we should
offer it to him with pleasure," Katherine said. "I believe then, Crofton, that
you've made the decision to join the London firm?"

"I have."

"Matthew, I know your wedding is at hand so I won't ask you. Minx,
would you have any interest in returning to England with this gentleman
on behalf of the New York firm and aiding him in this issue? I think your
skills might be of use."

"Pardon me," Crofton protested, "but I have not yet *formally* requested
aid. I certainly would think twice about travelling across the Atlantic with
this person and…" The nostrils of his long nose pinched. "Actually working
alongside such a creature!"

"Afraid I would show you up?" Minx countered.

"'Show you up'? Is that some kind of colonial language hitherto unknown by the human kind? What is the meaning, please?"

She dared to walk forward and get up right in his face.

"Humiliate the *fuck* out of you," she said.

Crofton gave a little stagger. Matthew saw his cheeks turn red.

The man recovered himself and managed a smile that was neither cold
nor mocking, but seemed in its own way genuine. "Miss," he said quietly,
"I would *pay* to see that."

Matthew thought it was time to get out before they started their blade
exercises right here and one or both of them joined the eternally battling
ghosts. If these two ever got together, it would be sheer luck. He said,
"Excuse me. Very pleased to meet you, Mr. Holmes, and I wish you great
success in your dealings with this Doctor Sardonicus. Minx…Katherine…
I'm going to my bride-to-be and luxuriate in her presence. If anyone wants
me, tell them to go home." He gave them all a little bow, but before he left
he glanced back and saw the princess of blades and the prince of insults
staring knives at each other.

"Hm!" said Minx.

And from Crofton Holmes, an even more indignant: "Hm!"

"Goodbye, Matthew," Katherine said, and then he was down the stairs
and gone.

THIRTY-FOUR

"I NOW PRONOUNCE YOU MAN AND WIFE," SAID THE REVEREND
Fenclaren. "Matthew, you may kiss the bride."

As if he needed any permission.

The wedding took place at Trinity Church at one o'clock on the sunny but chill afternoon of February seventeenth. Who wasn't there, in that
crowded house of God? Perhaps not Gardner Lillehorne, but even Lord
Cornbury had slipped in and sat at the back. No one seemed to recognize
him. But after Matthew had kissed Berry and she had kissed him back the
congregation of what seemed like hundreds broke the laws of propriety
when first someone—and Matthew thought it was Effrem Owles—began
applauding, and then someone—Felix Sudbury—picked it up and a third
and fourth someones—Hiram and Patience Stokely—carried it along and
by then it was a wave of noise that scared the pigeons up in the rafters to
flying around in dizzying circles.

With his arm around Berry, Matthew looked out upon all the won-
derfully smiling faces and noted at the back a few pews in front of Lord
Cornbury a man who had not removed his tricorn as the others had. This
older gentleman upon meeting Matthew's gaze now doffed the hat and with
a smile bowed his head slightly forward in a gesture that Matthew read as a
wish of good fortune.

And in the next blink of an eye, Magistrate Isaac Woodward was gone.

There would be a reception to follow at Sally Almond's that likely
might go on until the late hours. How all these people would fit into her

tavern was a problem even a problem-solver could not solve, but somehow Sally Almond would display her own powers of deduction.

Standing at the front of the church greeting the well-wishers, Matthew held Berry close. They had talked about many things…where they would live…children…his work.

"I'm conflicted about this," he'd said one night before the fire at Marmy's house. "I have enjoyed and do enjoy the work, but it seems unfair to you. I mean…you know it's sometimes—often—dangerous. My Lord, do you know! Yet…it gives me satisfaction. I wouldn't wish to go on any jaunts beyond the colonies. But…again…is it fair to you that I do *any* more work for the agency?"

"I don't know, either," she'd admitted. "Maybe in time. After all we've been through…right now I just can't say how I feel."

So they did have more discussion to be made on the issue.

As the throng began to thin out on their happy and boisterous way to Sally Almond's, Matthew and Berry were approached by the somewhat gangly Reverend Bertram Fenclaren.

"My congratulations to the both of you," said the reverend. "You make a wonderful couple."

"Thank you," Matthew replied. "It was a wonderful ceremony."

"Um…may I have just a quick word with you? And Berry too, of course. Shall we step back into the cloakroom? We can have a bit more privacy."

In the smaller room, Fenclaren seemed to be thinking over what he wished to say at some length, his brows knit together. At last he began: "Do you both know the widow Edwina Baffenthorpe? She owns one of the large mansions on Golden Hill. Her husband—a fine man very generous to the church—passed away in November."

"I've heard the name but I don't know her," said Berry. "Do you?"

"I don't," Matthew said.

"Evidently the widow Baffenthorpe knows of your reputation, Matthew, and she has asked me to present a request."

"What is it?"

"She believes…" Fenclaren hesitated, seemingly girding himself for further speech. "She believes her house has become haunted," he went on. "She tells me that at night she hears thumps and banging on the walls, the laughter of a little girl, and…I'm just telling you as she's told me…the sound of a large dog running back and forth in the corridor outside her bedroom. Also…another thing…in a bedroom further along the corridor her name has been scrawled on the wall along with a prediction of her death… the twenty-fourth of this month…and strange scratches and markings have been added to this particular wall almost nightly. She says...it's in red...and it might be blood."

"Fascinating!" Matthew had to admit. "What does she want with *me?*"

"She...wants you to spend a few nights in what she calls the haunted room, and...as she puts it...grab that ghost."

Both Matthew and Berry stood speechless.

"I will add," said the reverend, "that the widow Baffenthorpe promises a great deal of money for this service, that your bride is invited—if she should so dare—and you would have your privacy and the run of the house. In addition, I am to understand that the widow Baffenthorpe's cook is one of the best in the town. Anyway, I was asked to relay this request and I have, so I leave it up to you."

Matthew pondered it. In his opinion, whoever the "ghost" was, he or she wanted the widow Baffenthorpe to vacate the house for some reason. Hidden money? A valuable antique somewhere? Something her late husband had possessed that a nefarious villain wanted to get hold of? The "blood" might be some sort of chemical pigment, or if real then simply that of an animal. But the other points of the problem...the laughing little girl, the running dog, how the marks on the wall were appearing and of course the death threat were true challenges to be solved.

Yes, indeed...fascinating.

He looked to Berry. "What do you think?"

She didn't answer at once. It took her a while to reach the decision, but when she reached it she was positive of its direction.

"I think," said the love of Matthew's life, as a smile slowly crossed the beautiful freckled face and the blue eyes sparkled with her own budding thrill of adventure, "that it would be a wonderful place for a honeymoon."

And so it was.

EPILOGUE

Matthew Corbett walked through a cemetery.

It was well-tended, neat and orderly, but the stones had been allowed to remain as the earth had treated them…some slanting at various angles, and honestly none exactly straight.

It stood in the shadow of Trinity Church, at the western end of Wall Street where Wall met Broadway. On this warm midsummer morning he was looking for particular resting places. This cemetery, though set in such a city of movement and speed, seemed to him to have a quiet about it—a peace, maybe—that soothed the spirit. He thought it was a very good thing, that he'd come here to find it.

He stopped to regard one of the stones. It was old, and who could say how old? On it was the faintest impression of a cherub's face, with folded wings behind it. Time and weather had almost eradicated the image, as it had the names and dates and loving images of memory from most of these stones. But even so, Matthew felt in this quiet place the power of those who had come before, and gone on ahead.

There were so many. Who had these people been? he wondered. What had their lives been like? So many, and so many mysteries now hidden away. Whoever they'd been, they had carved this city out of the forested hills. They had put down the first wooden stakes of property, and nailed the first boards together that made a house. It must've been a tremendous undertaking and challenge, to build something out of nothing.

Nothing, that is, but a vision of what the future might become.

He walked on, and found a stone he was seeking.

On it, barely legible, was the engraving that read *Berry Grigsby Corbett, Loving Wife And Devoted Mother*, with dates of birth and passage that were truly almost wiped away.

And next to it was the stone that read *Matthew Corbett*, the rest of it gone to the ages.

His ancestor. To be more precise, his great-great-great…well, anyway, it was his grandfather from way back and he didn't know how many greats were between now and then.

In this July of the year 2052, the young Matthew Corbett had travelled by fast rail from his condo in Charleston, where he was a first-year lawyer in the firm Madison, Lopaka and Bodie on King Street. He needed some questions answered, and hoped he might find them here. What was he searching for, exactly?

A direction in life, he thought.

He was twenty-two years old, unmarried and otherwise unattached. He was tall and lean, with finely textured black hair cropped almost to the scalp as was the current fashion. His eyes were gray, flecked with dark blue, the colors of smoke at twilight. He had several small gold rings up the edge of his right ear, and under his light blue shirt the tattoo of an old sailing ship on his right shoulder simply because he liked the look of it. He wore a tobacco-hued jacket—or what used to be called "tobacco" since that was never used anymore—and well-worn-and-loved denim jeans.

He had found his way here after a visit to the Hall of Ancestry, but he was still lost.

Where to go from here? That was the question.

Matthew saw that to the left of Berry's resting place was the grave of the first son, Jordan, and the daughter Amelia. The second son, Eric, had moved to Virginia, where he'd become a lawyer and an administrative aide to Thomas Jefferson. Colonel Eric Corbett had been killed fighting for the young America at the battle of White Plains at the age of 64 in 1776, but he and his wife Julianna had had a son and two daughters and had seen the birth of eight grandchildren.

Thus the family of Corbetts over the years had moved across the new country, most of the men and several of the women entering the field of law in one aspect or another, and here stood Matthew, son of the Oregon lawyer Clint and the financial advisor Martina.

Where to go, from here?

He wished he could ask Matthew. What kind of man had he been? Someone who rode a desk, or…someone like the new Matthew wanted to be…a person with a sometimes burning and overactive curiosity, who longed for adventure and the ability and skill to right wrongs?

Was that asking too much, in this day and age? After all, he was poised to make a lot of money if he stayed with the firm, and of course the legal field existed to right wrongs, but it was obvious that his father had helped grease the wheels to get him a position at Madison, Lopaka and Bodie and he could not help but want something different. Something of his own. Was it disrespectful to turn his back on what he presently had? Was it stupid?

He'd had a talk one day with Chey Bodie that remained with him. *Are you happy here, sir?* he'd asked the elder gentleman. And a further question: *Have you done what you wanted with your life?*

Interesting questions, Bodie had replied as he sat at his desk before an oval window overlooking King Street. *I suppose…it all depends on the choices a person makes. I am happy, Matthew. I've worked long and hard to get where I am. It would be pretty foolish at my age to look back and wonder where else my life might've taken me. Still…sometimes when no one's watching I like to skip a stone across a pond, just to see how far it can go. Or I enjoy singing in the car, or lying in the grass at night trying to count the stars. I suppose I'm talking about the joy of doing the unexpected. Even the things you don't expect of yourself. That's maybe the crux of it. Is that helpful at all?*

Matthew thought it was, and thanked Chey Bodie for his advice. He believed he knew Mr. Bodie had seen the wanderlust in his eyes.

Now, here in the Trinity Church cemetery, Matthew bowed his head, said a quick prayer of respect, and bade farewell to the resting places of his ancestral family. Then he walked out of the cemetery to the curb on the street of this teeming, gigantic metropolis, pressed the comm microchip in his right palm and said, "E-Lyft."

It wasn't thirty seconds before a sleek, dark red craft settled to the curb. The door opened, Matthew slid into the back seat that came up around him to nestle him in padded comfort and the safety belt automatically clicked home. The driver's plastic partition soundlessly lowered. The man said, "You didn't say where you're going."

"I'm not sure yet." Back to the hotel? Or just drive so he could think?

"They're your credits, but I can't sit here too long."

"Are you a bionic?" Matthew asked.

He got a middle-finger answer.

"Okay. Let me think." Matthew got a glimpse of the man's ID pic, number and name on the small screen before him: John Huston, and the picture showed a rather rugged-looking and husky man in his mid-forties with a firm jaw, dark brown hair streaked with gray and deep-set eyes that said if you asked him again if he was a bionic you might wind up crumpled on the curb.

"Your credits," John Huston reminded him. "Ticking, ticking."

Matthew kept looking at the picture on the screen. "Do I know you?" he asked.

The man's eyes found his in the rearview mirror. "Never seen you before."

"You look familiar to me."

"Big city," Huston said. "Lots of faces." He gave a short laugh. "*Too many.*"

"Wait a minute," Matthew said. "Huston…Huston…I know that name from somewhere."

"Maybe you do."

"How can I?"

This time the man turned around so Matthew could see his full and to be honest dangerous-looking face. "I was an athlete," Huston said. "Used to be, I mean. Played two years of brassball and four years of hoverball, and I—"

"Bighouse!" Matthew said. "You're the one they call Bighouse!"

"'They'," the man answered with a little derision in it. "What do 'they' know?"

"No, I remember…I didn't watch all that reality show…it's too violent for my tastes…but you were in that show last season…the subway show."

"Right. The SBL. Five in, two out. Me and the transgender Marine."

Matthew had watched most of one episode of last season's Subterranean Battle League, where a five-member team chose their weapons and went down into what used to be the subways to make a journey from entrance to exit fighting the creatures and malignants that had taken root down there. The new drugs—particularly the A.I.-created dinosaur-human hybrid DNA that turned criminals into superhuman monsters—were truly turning the world into bedlam. The things down below were delighted to have fresh meat.

"I guess you've seen a lot," Matthew said.

"More than most." Bighouse cocked his head to one side. "Hold on. Maybe I *do* know you. You seem familiar to me, too…from somewhere… but I can't remember."

"Me neither. It's strange."

The man shrugged. "It's a strange world. The space pirates, the killer bionics, the virtual reality gangs. That weird multibillionaire nobody ever sees…you know, that guy who calls himself Sultan Gore…just announced some kind of new VR chamber you can buy that'll take you to any place in the past or future. I mean, virtually. Like a time machine, kind of. Know what he's calling it? Another weird thing: Dominus."

Matthew hadn't heard of this before, but the name Dominus stirred within him a strange a vague unease. He said, "The way people have gone mad for virtual reality, he'll make another billion dollars before the month is out."

"Don't need it, don't want it. When I was about your age back in 2032 I was happy to ride my motorcycle. A *real* motor, on *real* roads." He turned around, one hand on the control yoke. "What's your name?"

"Matthew Corbett."

"Okay, Matthew Corbett. Let's have a decision. Don't be like me, floating around from nowhere to nowhere. You go *somewhere*. Hear it?"

"I want adventure," Matthew suddenly blurted out. "I want…to know about things. To test my mind. Challenges. That's what I want." He decided to voice an idea he'd had for some time. "Maybe…a private investigator?"

"A detective? Do they still have those? Can't the Net do all that?"

"I'm sure there's still a need. I mean…people being people, no matter the times nor the tech…there's going to be a need to find out things even the Net doesn't know. Or what the Net knows but won't tell you."

"Hm," said Bighouse Huston, as if this made perfect sense. "Here you go." He had reached into the breast pocket of a short-sleeved bowling shirt printed with a palm tree design and brought out an old-fashioned business card, which he offered through the partition. "Adventure," he said. "I like that. Listen, Matthew Corbett, if you decide to get up and running, give me a shout. Maybe you could use a guy who made it through the subway alive?"

Matthew thought it was a real possibility. He took the card and noted the man's cell number and Net address.

Bighouse said, "Decision time, my friend. Where to?"

The man was right. It *was* time.

Two words came to Matthew. He didn't know where they might lead, but he had the feeling that this adventure—this new life—had only just begun.

"The future," he said.

Bighouse Huston seemed to understand what that meant, because without comment he put the controls into action.

The air car ascended to its computer-designated altitude.

And away it silently sped, on a shining path of light.

Robert McCammon

Robert McCammon
4/24/24

Milton Keynes UK
Ingram Content Group UK Ltd.
UKHW040634051224
3429UKWH00012B/35/J

9 781941 971406